PENGUIN BOOKS

The White Devil

Paul Hoffman is the author of three previous Thomas Cale novels, *The Left Hand of God*, *The Last Four Things* and *The Beating of His Wings*. He has written two stand-alone novels, *The Golden Age of Censorship*, a satirical comedy based on his experiences as a film censor and *The Wisdom of Crocodiles*, which predicted the collapse of the world financial system.

By the same author

The Wisdom of Crocodiles

The Golden Age of Censorship

The Left Hand of God

The Last Four Things

The Beating of His Wings

Scorn

The White Devil

PAUL HOFFMAN

PENGUIN BOOKS

PENGUIN BOOKS

UK | USA | Canada | Ireland | Australia
India | New Zealand | South Africa

Penguin Books is part of the Penguin Random House group of companies
whose addresses can be found at global.penguinrandomhouse.com

First published by Penguin Michael Joseph 2021
Published in Penguin Books 2022
001

p. 115, The Future Representatives of our Nation (February 24, 1877) courtesy of
California Historical Society CHS2013.1170)
p. 115, Lead paint advert from the Middlebury Register (October 04, 1918)
p. 165, Romanov family © Alamy
p. 255, Portrait in the wanted poster by permission of Nick Szczepanik

Printed and bound in Great Britain by Clays Ltd, Elcograf S.p.A.

The authorized representative in the EEA is Penguin Random House Ireland,
Morrison Chambers, 32 Nassau Street, Dublin D02 YH68

A CIP catalogue record for this book is available from the British Library

ISBN: 978-0-718-18557-2

www.greenpenguin.co.uk

Penguin Random House is committed to a sustainable future for our business, our readers and our planet. This book is made from Forest Stewardship Council® certified paper.

For my English teacher, the sculptor Faith Tolkien,
whose skill, extreme patience, and moral imagination
prevented me from becoming Thomas Cale.

'Paralell yuniverses in wich everi possibul variant of histori is beink plaid out at wunce may or may not eggsist; the kase is unprooved. We ar going to haf to liv with thaet uncertainti.'

– Heorge Ellias, *Scientifyk Amerikane*

Welcome those of you from the Old World, and welcome to the New.

In what way new, you ask? There must, you say, be men and women here in this freshly minted continent and they must, some of them, be high and low, and good and bad, as in all the very many kinds of world that have ever existed and which still exist on the great globe. The poor and the weak are here, of course, as are the rich and powerful. But in the United Estates of the Americas all men are equal except for those who are not; everyone has the same chance of being rich and poor except for those who don't. Everyone is free except for those who are not free; every man can look every other man in the eye, be he never so powerful – other than those who'd better not if they know what's good for them. In other places the common people do as they are told by men who have power by virtue of their talent for getting born in the right place to the right mother and father, or to claims of greater wisdom born of an education that made them fit to lead the herd. But in the United Estates any man, rich or poor, can rule over the great experiment in democracy if he can get the vote of his fellow countrymen.

A vote? Let me explain. In the United Estates' creation document it was written by the Founding Forebears that all those who could be called men were born equal, endowed by God with the right to choose their government by casting lots. A new chapter for mankind was being written. A new dawn was breaking. Laugh at the absurdity of the ignorant common man unleashed to rule not only himself but also his wiser and more thoughtful betters – and then allow this is a world that clearly deserved to be described as new, a world that is setting out on a great and terrifying experiment.

It is not, however, a world without its peculiar institutions.

[illegible] proper poem, Old Wind, [illegible]

[illegible] which [illegible] good and [illegible] the way [illegible]

[illegible]

PART I
Dallas

'Then the Lord said, *Where have you come from?* And Satan answered the Lord and said, *From going to and fro in the earth, and walking up and down in it.*'

It was just after midday and two men, one black, one white, were being taken through a courtyard to be hanged. As courtyards in prisons go it was large, and they had nearly a hundred yards to walk to reach the two separate scaffolds on which ropes, wet with rain from an earlier shower, dripped on to the trapdoors beneath.

Hands tied behind their backs, one five yards behind the other, the prisoners each had a guard on either side. Not to prevent escape, as such, but to control them in case the fear – which usually numbed the condemned – transformed into panic. They had approximately a hundred steps left to take in this life and a few more breaths than that. They had eaten the last meal, smiled for the last time; they would sleep no more: they would never wake up again. The black man was intensely alert. He looked at the warden's vegetable patch – Bibb lettuce, six purple tomato plants and three varieties of snap beans bursting with juiciness. Was he affronted by their insolence, knowing that the last thing he would taste now would be the taste of terror? Perhaps he saw nothing at all. The white man following behind seemed not calm but indifferent. He blinked only occasionally. Then he tripped – just a little – and recovered quickly.

'Mind yure step, Bechette,' said one of the guards. 'We gotta deliver you to the rope all crackerjack.'

The white prisoner turned his head slightly to one side and spoke for the first time that morning.

'My name isn't Bechette, I didn't have anything to do with this murder, I wasn't in the country when it happened.'

The older guard had heard many protestations of innocence – a few (a very few) turned out later to be true. Sometimes these performances were pretty convincing, but after so many years he thought he now could tell innocence from desperation. Of course, by the time he was involved in taking these men to the gallows it made no difference what he believed. But Bechette's tone was one which he couldn't place. Such a detached observation made no sense on such a terrible morning.

Halfway now. From one of the few windows overlooking the execution site a convict started to sing, a good voice but almost as high-pitched as that of a young girl.

Suummetiiimes I feeeeel like a feather in the air
Suummetyeeyeimes I feeeeela like a feeeather in the aaaair

The voice dropped a surprisingly long way: *Lord, Lord, I know my time ain't long.*

Someone shouted:

'Shut yure pie-hole!'

But the voice sang on as the walk continued.

Suummetiiimes I feeeeel like a muuutherless child
Suummetyeeyeimes I feeeeela like a muuuuuuuutherless child.

Bechette appeared not to hear the music at all. Despite, or perhaps because of the mournful beauty of the song, the black prisoner seemed only more agitated. But then he did something odd: he stepped aside to avoid treading in a puddle. At this a look of anguish crossed the face of his fellow prisoner, as if the simple act of a man wanting to avoid getting his feet wet had broken through the mask. He started to slow and the guards next to him tensed, moving closer to grab his arms.

'Easy now, Bechette. Let's do this quick, eh?'

Soon the first prisoner was at the foot of the first scaffold stairs. His guards were surprised to see the Hangman coming down the steps from the second scaffold with a deeply concerned look on his face. This was an agitated man, which in turn worried the guards, who looked to do this work in as routine a fashion as possible. But the Hangman ignored them and walked straight to the second set of guards as they headed for the second gallows.

'Mr Bechette, is it?'

An ecstasy of hope from the bound man. Reprieve! Reprieve!

'I must apologize to you, sir . . .' *No apologies. No reprieve begins with an apology!* '. . . but the inclement weather has caused the trapdoor on the white scaffold to jam. I'm afraid you must hang on the black scaffold. I regret this, but there's nothing that can be done. But be assured, Mr Bechette, that you will not hang using a Negro rope or a Negro hood. You have my word as a gentleman.'

Honour satisfied, he turned and walked over to the black scaffold and started up the steps, calling out behind him, 'Bring up the coloured prisoner in twenty seconds.'

'Feel right sorry for you, Bechette,' said the young guard. 'Shit, bein' innocent an' all, looks like if you didn't have bad luck you wouldn't have no kinda luck at all.' It was his first hanging and he was anxious to show that he wasn't bothered.

'Now you shut *yure* pie-hole,' said the older guard. 'And keep it shut.' He turned to the second prisoner. 'Just wait here, Chief.'

. . . like mah soul is on fiiire . . .

By now the black prisoner was taking his last step on to the scaffold proper. His legs gave way, but the guards, experienced men, held him firm and eased him forward on to the trapdoor.

'Please don't let me fall.'

'We won't. It'll be all right,' said the older guard.

The Hangman, still not entirely over his exasperation at the morning's impropriety, looked impatiently at the condemned man. 'I can't hang you, Cuffy, if 'n' you won't stand on your own two feet. Think of the trouble you're causing. We all have our job to do – mine's to hang you, yours to get hanged.'

. . . I'm heeeeaven bound . . .

Perhaps shocked at being spoken to in such an odd way on such an occasion, the prisoner straightened his legs and took the weight of his body. The older guard put his hands into the small of his back and gave him a gentle shove to position him on the badly drawn white circle that marked the centre of the trapdoor. The executioner stepped forward and reached up to the noose. Bechette watched, unmoved, as the black man lowered his head, a reflex, to make it easier for the noose to drop into place. His breaths came in quick gasps now, shallow and rasping.

'Don' hang me. I can't die. I'm not ready to die. I don' wanna die.'

The hood went over his head and muffled his words.

. . . Haaave no freeends . . .

At the signal the two guards quickly moved back from the condemned man. The Hangman stepped off the trapdoor and over to the lever. The condemned man called out what sounded like 'Clover', the executioner pulled the lever, the trapdoor opened and the prisoner fell like a stone for just under six feet – then in a snap of an instant stopped dead, the top of his head projecting just above the gallows floor.

Then there was only silence as the man shivered slightly, as if in a cold wind. And that was that.

Bechette now had fewer than five steps to take in this world – yet his expression was set like a stone. The two guards barely had to touch the unresisting prisoner for him to be on to the trapdoor and the faded white circle at its centre. The Hangman stepped forward with the noose and went to place it around Bechette's neck. At the last, Bechette shied away like a horse refusing to be haltered.

'Sir, this is no way to behave. Let us be dignified at such a time.' Again the Hangman tried to loop the rope around Bechette's neck and again Bechette twisted his head away. The Hangman signalled to the guards, who moved in and tried to hold him still. Bechette bucked and strained, groaning with the irrepressible frenzy for life.

Appalled, the Hangman stood back from the struggle, 'You are only making things worse for yourself.' An arguable claim, no doubt, but true or not it had no effect on Bechette. 'Grab him, for God's sake!' cried out the older guard to the Hangman. 'Grab him!' His attempt to do so instantly failed as Bechette wildly threw him off. But the effort unbalanced Bechette and he staggered back into the appalled Hangman.

Barely sane, Bechette thought he was being attacked by the Hangman and, without looking, turned and shoulder-charged him with all the power that might be expected of a man trying to escape the embrace of Hell itself. The Hangman crashed into the wooden rail, hitting it with the great force of his excessive weight.

This caused the nails that held it in place to give way almost completely. On tiptoe, he waved his hands like some fleshy windmill, straining to keep his balance – but the nails renounced their twenty-year grip of the wood and with a great tearing sound launched the Hangman into the void. Half a dozen jailers scrambled on to the gallows and hauled Bechette to the floor, pinning him there.

Bound arm and knee, Bechette was taken back to his cell and heaved inside. It was just a little more than nine minutes since he'd left. For a few minutes, his body vibrated with the terror of this experience. And then he fell asleep.

I

Despite the depth of his sleep, there was no rest for Bechette. He was woken by a presence in the cell, but when he tried to stand he was painfully jerked back by a chain looped around his waist.

'Sorry about that. I thought it best to be cautious.' The speaker was dressed in an immaculate white suit – silk and cashmere. His face was at once amused and friendly. 'Quite the helter-skelter, this business, Mr . . . ?' The man paused, watchful. Nothing. 'Only I know it's not Bechette . . . which, of course, is what you've been claiming all along.' The prisoner gave away nothing; he did not flinch or seem relieved – which might be considered odd under the circumstances. 'You see, all the fuss you caused up on the scaffold inspired the Federals to look into your case a little more carefully. I'm ashamed to say it didn't need to be all that much more carefully. It only took a few hours to establish your innocence of the murder they' – he gave a little grimace of contrition – '*we* . . . were going to hang you for.'

'Apology accepted. I'll be on my way.'

'Unfortunately, there's the matter of our late Hangman, Mr' – he paused – 'someone or other.'

'He's dead?'

'I'm afraid so.'

A beat.

'It was self-defence.'

'I'm very much inclined to agree,' said the man in white. 'But it's tricky.'

'No, it isn't.'

'I can see why you might think so. From your prospective, it was self-defence.'

'Fuck my *per*spective . . . it *was* self-defence.'

'And yet Mr . . . whatever his name . . . was not in any sense attacking you. He was a legally convened officer of the court carrying out his duty. A Hangman at the command of a properly constituted court of law is not committing an act of violence of the kind that can be legally defended against.'

Another pause.

'Who *are* you?'

'Louis Van Owen, fourth governor of the great estate of Texas. At your service.' A smile of a rather strange sort. 'Possibly.'

'If you're the governor, that means you can pardon me.'

'I can.'

'And will you?'

'Try to understand my position. Feelings are running high concerning poor . . . Mr Selo, that was the Hangman's name. The prison guards are unhappy at any suggestion that someone who kills an estate official in the act of carrying out their sworn duty should go unpunished. My position is . . . complicated.'

The prisoner stared back and took his time.

'So what can I do for you?' he said at last.

'I had a feeling you'd understand.' Governor Van Owen laughed, a pleasant sound. 'First of all, we need to be honest with one another. Unusually honest. This business is really all very extraordinary – so many unlikely chances all coming together at just the right moment. What are the odds? You condemned to death for a crime you didn't commit. Me not taking the slightest interest in just another hanging. I hadn't even heard of you until yesterday. Then the stunning drama on the scaffold – what a predicament! And lo and behold, not only do I now know who you are not, I miraculously discover who you *are*. What a run of bad luck you've had . . . quite the Calamity Jane.' He laughed, as if encouraging the man in front of him to enjoy the joke. 'How interesting life is!' He waited and so very much enjoyed the moment. 'Isn't that so, Mr Thomas Cale?'

Thomas Cale [pron: ka.lɛ]

From the Vikipedia Albionis

Thomas Cale (b.769?; Modern Era b.1923?), also known as Vinegar Tom and the Sea-Green Undefeatable, has become the measure against which military leaders compare themselves, and military academies throughout the world teach his tactics.

Cale was raised by the military wing of the Redeemers at the Sanctuary, a training seminary for an extremist religious sect that believed they were called by God to destroy sinful humanity. Redeemer Altine Bosco (later Pope Bosco IV 782–784; ME 1937–9) believed Cale to be the promised Left Hand of God who would lead this apocalyptic slaughter. At the age of fifteen [citation needed] Cale escaped from the Redeemers and went to Memphis, where he was taken under the wing of the controversial politician and philosopher IdrisPukke. Eventually he became bodyguard to Arbell Materazzi – a largely ceremonial role. There were rumours of a sexual relationship between them, but the historian Aleixo de Menezes has shown conclusively that this is rooted in Redeemer *verum falsum* or 'false truth'. Cale was recaptured by a Redeemer Army after they defeated the Materazzi at the Battle of Solsbury. Rehabilitated by Bosco, Cale led the Redeemer Seventh Army against the Laconics at Golan and inflicted the first recorded defeat upon them [citation needed], revealing himself, despite his age, to be a shrewd, ambitious and skilled military strategist.

Escaping for a second time to Switzerland, and reunited with IdrisPukke, he swiftly added political skills to his military talents. Nevertheless, his attempts to obtain a military position with the Axis powers, consisting of the Swiss, the Hanse and the Northern Hegemon, were a failure, largely because of his rivalry with the much better connected Conn Materazzi [citation needed]. After the near-annihilation of the Swiss at the hands of the Redeemers at the Battle of Bex he persuaded the now panic-stricken Axis to allow him to create a new peasant army. Using a range of groundbreaking tactics and technological advances, he brought about the collapse of the Redeemer armies in less than eighteen months, resulting in a notorious mass suicide at their military stronghold, the Sanctuary.

Subsequently, Cale disappeared for nearly two years, amid unsubstantiated claims of a mental breakdown. He re-emerged in 789 (ME 1942) leading the enslaved Helots in their insurrection against the notoriously brutal Laconics. Whether Cale was responsible for the massacre of the entire population of Laconia that ended the campaign or was simply unable to control the Helots is a matter of fierce debate. When the Axis powers moved against him in 783 (ME 1945) he spent the next ten years gradually taking control of the Four Quarters. In territories conquered by Cale he introduced complete reform of the legal systems, establishing elected juries and habeas corpus, free education and basic health services for the poor, property rights for married women and a civil service based on merit by means of anonymous exams. During this period he also invented the roundabout [citation needed].

He emancipated the Jews in ME 1949, despite widespread and violent opposition that led to the anti-Hebraic uprising the following year, which he ruthlessly suppressed at the cost of some 20,000 lives among the anti-Semites [citation needed]. Eighteen months later he faced a Jewish and Eslamic uprising when he banned genital mutilation of both female and male babies. His suppression of the riots that followed was equally ferocious.

However, disaster struck when he became involved in the Boll Shevik Revolution of ME 1955 and was ousted from power in the Four Quarters. He managed to bring victory to the Boll Sheviks but was arrested by Stalovek, later to become notorious as 'the greatest mass murderer' in history. He was taken to the Special Object 110 prison in Vidnoye [citation needed], and various sources claim he was either executed there or that he escaped. Believing Cale still to be alive, the International Court of Rights at the Hanse has issued a warrant for his arrest on charges of Crimes against the Humanity committed during the anti-Hebraic insurgency, the White Terror, the Ten Years War and the Boll Shevik Revolution.

See Also

- Materazzi Empire, Collapse of
- Redeemers, Atrocities of, Theology of, Collapse of
- Boll Shevik Revolution (disambiguation)
- Conn Materazzi, Execution of

2

If the collective memory of every tyrant who ever lived was lost from the history of mankind, their vices could be restored in every detail by a study of the life of Thomas Cale.

– Sir Water Radleigh

All things taken into consideration, Thomas Cale was very possibly the least worst tyrant who ever lived.

– Joennifer Harlow

Those of you unfamiliar with the name Thomas Cale – if there can be any – will wonder why this was such an extraordinary thing for the man in white to say to the wretch sitting in front of him in a Texas condemned cell. Consider if he had used the name Napoléyon, or Jehngis Cahn or Moa Tse Dung. It was the same. It was so preposterous that the man who was not Bechette snorted spontaneously as if physically unable to contain his contempt.

'Are you off your head?'

Van Owen was not at all offended.

'I hope not, for your sake. If you're not the great man, then your usefulness to the only person who can save your life is not worth a bowl of homeopathic soup made from the shadow of a pigeon that has died of starvation.' A pause. 'Well?'

The man who was not Bechette seemed to relax a touch, as if there was a certain pleasure to be had from what he was about to say.

'Whose throat do I have to cut?'

Van Owen smiled, pleased with himself.

'I'm so glad we don't have to plod, Mr Cale.'

'How do you know I'm not lying to save my skin?'

'The great unwashed, Mr Cale, may not recognize greatness in a man, a noble bearing, that ineradicable power of command . . .' He laughed, again a pleasant sound. 'I'm afraid I knew it was you as soon as I looked through the opening in the cell door. I saw you eight years ago in Riga when I was part of the team from the United Estates negotiating a trade deal with the Hanse to stop them blocking our exports of chicken wings.' He smiled at Cale as if he'd uncovered a treasure long searched for. 'Why don't we get you out of here, Mr Cale? That will instantly make the world seem like a brighter place.'

Two hours later Cale was heading towards what his dubious saviour called the Casa Amarillo, a few hours from the estate capital. 'It's a simple place, the yellow house – but all the better for it.' Then, with a touch of mockery, 'Just the right kind of spot to refresh one's ragged soul.'

For the first hour of the journey Cale stared out miserably enough over the cotton fields of the Dallas Blacklands, full of former slaves scouting for pests: bollworm, flea hoppers, cut worm and spider mites. But then the cotton gave way to a long stretch of something like the uncut meadows of Vallambrosa he used to love and he stopped brooding and seemed to Van Owen almost bewitched by the rolling expanse of grasses and wild flowers.

'Tell me their names,' said Cale, like a man who expected to be obeyed. Van Owen was more curious than irritated by his tone. Odd that such a giant of power and destruction, this Khan of the Four Quarters, should be so moved by a wilderness of flowers.

'That,' he said, pointing, 'is what we call in Dallas . . . purple paintbrush . . . beautyberry – the one that looks like purple holly. That's . . . uh . . . firewheel, I think.'

'What about that one there?' said Cale, indicating a flower that looked like a flat-topped black bulrush, with bright orange petals hanging down below. Van Owen shifted awkwardly.

'Not . . . quite sure.'

Cale stared. Van Owen gave in.

'The locals call it Jezebel-in-a-skirt.'

'What's a Jezebel?'

'A black woman. A sort of –' He interrupted himself. 'That's brown-eyed Susan . . . and . . . uh . . .' A bird, startled by the passing of the carriage, exploded out of its hiding-place in a pocket of brushwood and shot away in a thrumming of wings and a two-tone whistle.

'Gentleman Bob!' called out a delighted Van Owen, and stuck his head out of the carriage window to watch the bird dip and whistle its way over the prairie. He pulled his head back in to discover a slight smile from Cale, the first time he'd seen any sign of happiness on the lined face. 'Gentleman Bob,' repeated Van Owen. 'Bobwhite quail. Hunted them all the time as a boy. There used to be so many you could throw a stick at them and get your dinner. Prairie used to cover everything. Now there are more cotton rats than quail.'

'You're the governor – why don't you do something about it?'

Van Owen shrugged. 'Ain't no money in Texas bluebonnet and scarlet sage.'

3

Besides exhaustion after a dreadful war with Spain, the reason that the South gave in to the demands of the North to free the slaves was that when it came to cotton, slaves were already becoming more trouble than they were worth. It took one slave ten hours to pick the seeds out of one pound of cotton lint so that something useful could be spun with it. Slaves could barely pay for themselves against the cost of buying, feeding, watering and putting a roof over their heads. However, a face-saving minor clause in the Slave Emancipation Act provided that with enough congressmen in support (an impossibly large number, it was thought) a petition could go to the Supreme Court to decide if any such vote was permitted by the Constitution. American slavery was to go the way of the serf and the eunuch.

And then forty years later some guiltless devil invented the cotton engine. A cotton engine could process ten thousand pounds of cotton in a single day and free up ten thousand Negroes to plant and tend and pick the white stuff and turn cotton from a waste of money to a means of printing it.

– Jubal Cartagena, *The Devil's Engine: Technology, Politics and the Re-emergence of Slavery* (Harvard Press)

'*The cup that cheers but not inebriates*?' said Van Owen.

Cale looked at him.

'Tea, my dear fellow. Or something stronger?'

Cale very much wanted something stronger but knew to keep clear of drink when so much was at stake.

'Tea is fine.'

Not for the first time in his life, Cale was struck by how many different worlds, the beautiful and the ugly, the pleasant and the disgusting, the scintillating and the dull, whirled about each other cheek by jowl. Yesterday he was waiting to have his neck wrung at the end of a rope, today he was about to have a nice cup of tea.

'So . . . what do you want from me?'

Van Owen looked benevolently at Cale.

'Oh, don't ask what you can do for me, Mr Cale, rather let's consider what I can do for you.'

'All right, what can you do for me?'

'In this part of the world, I can easily pass for a sophisticated man. But the truth is I believe a considerable number of things that a truly cultured person of the Old World would consider trite. For example . . . that there is always someone worse off than you. In my hick sort of a way, I've always found that to be a comforting banality. Take you, Mr Cale . . . You could easily be saying to yourself that nothing could be worse than that hideous experience of standing on the gallows yesterday. But that really isn't so. The Janes, for example, are prepared to pay $150,000 for the pleasure of, according to their ambassador, wrapping you in a blanket soaked in pitch and setting fire to you like a match. As for what the Applewhites intend to do to you, it makes me feel ill just thinking about the first hour of your execution, let alone the twelve hours following. When the Federals arrested you for something that, for once, you hadn't actually done, you were skulking in a woodshed paying $100 a day for one plate of bog potatoes. You're not just running at a slight discount, Mr Cale, you're all washed up and rotting on the beach. There's nowhere to run for the Left Hand of God.'

Van Owen beamed at Cale again. '"Where Thomas Cale goes, a funeral surely follows," isn't that what they say? So very many funerals, Thomas – not that I believe more than half the dreadful things they say about you.'

'What do you want?'

'Look, Mr Cale, I am about to tell you something that puts everything – my reputation, wealth, life itself, all of it – into your hands. You'll understand why I hesitate.'

Here was a man fully aware that he was standing at an exact point in his life where everything that came next would be utterly different from what went before. There's a reason why few of us can point to such a moment in our own lives – these moments burn. We're right to dread them the way a wild animal dreads fire.

'I want you to kill the Chancellor of the United Estates.'

It would be reasonable to expect that Cale's life – a life of pain, murder, madness, the rise and fall of empires, the death of kings, the theft of kingdoms, the birth of tyrannies – that all this would have made him immune to shock. Cale did not reply. I do not say he was astonished, amazed, aghast or stupefied because these words are not up to the task.

'John of Boston?'

'You know of another Chancellor?'

'*Why?*'

He was not in fact asking for an explanation of Van Owen's reason, let's be clear; he was expressing in a single word what a mystery it was to contemplate the assassination of not just a man of great power but the most adored; the handsomest, cleverest, most charming, most convincing, most able: John of Boston was the receptacle of all hopes, ambitions and desires for a New World of freedom, prosperity and justice, and from all kinds: the young, the old, the disaffected, the deprived, the progressive rich, the enslaved, the cynical, the pessimistic, the lost, the meek, the sick. He was the world's hero. What possible benefit could there be worth the risk? It was to throw yourself off a cliff in the hope that decisiveness and daring might oblige your body to sprout wings.

'My reasons are my own.'

'If you want me to kill him, I think I have to insist.'

'Really? Do you think I'd have asked such a thing if I thought you had even the slightest excuse to say no? I could ask you to climb Mount Sionai to kill God Himself and you'd not be in a position to refuse. I offer a way out: the remote Bermudas, warm and like paradise, they long for you.'

Another pause and a smile.

'Besides, there is every chance – *every* chance – you'll not be his executioner at all. You don't think I was just hoping you'd turn up? You're a coincidence – a very fortunate one. I've been planning this for many months. There is someone who is ready, as we speak, to fire the first shot. Only if he fails – and I have every expectation he will not – would you need to strike. You are an insurance policy on which I expect never to make a claim. It was his life or the life of John of Boston. Faced with that choice, there was, of course, no real choice at all.'

'You're right,' said Cale. 'I'm sorry to say it doesn't matter why.'

4

The New-York Times.

Given that three of the five judges on the Supreme Court are owners of large cotton plantations, we await with no little trepidation the judgement on the Constitutional legality of holding a vote in Congress to re-enslave the black persons of this country. Who knows what evil to this Union may result if they choose to open this Pandora's box of wickedness?

Virginian Extra.

Many in the North are well-meaning, decent people, but their newspapers and populist politicians have provided no news, but only lies and misinformation. They spread perverted portraitures of Southern slavery, contemptible caricatures of Southern society, and cast harrowing calumnies upon the Southern character. It is to repair these lies and educate the misinformed in the North that this divisive issue has gone to that hallowed institution, the Supreme Court.

The next day Van Owen returned to Casa Amarillo with something long and thin wrapped in a blanket.

'It's a Carcano, double shot,' said Van Owen.

Cale picked up the weapon and gave it the kind of cool appraising once-over of someone at least knowledgeable in such devices, something he certainly wasn't. This was an oddity, given his role in bringing the first of such weapons to the battlefield twenty years before. But those were rudimentary one-shot devices useful only against massed ranks because they were so cumbersome to load and so inaccurate. The Carcano was not designed for anything so crude as killing human beings but only to hunt game, and then only by the fabulously wealthy. A Carcano cost the same as a small house in the fashionable part of a minor capital city.

'It won't be a problem,' said Cale.

Later that afternoon he was taken near to the site in Dallas by Van Owen. He was given a key and instructions. Walking about two hundred yards, he came to a bushy copse behind which was a wooden compound in which tools were stored for use in the municipal park just back from the road along which John of Boston would be passing. It had been built there at Van Owen's instructions and the paperwork lost so that no one in the Parks Department even knew it was there. It gave Cale excellent cover and a resting point for the Carcano which would make an accurate shot more likely.

He left the compound and spent twenty minutes wandering up and down the road along which John of Boston would approach, using his heel to cut a divot in the grass beside the road to mark the fifty yards from the compound.

Back at the Yellow House, Van Owen was less talkative than usual. Then:

'Tonight, I'll bring our' – his humour now a little weary – 'our third *musketeer* to meet you. He'll stay here until John of Boston arrives.' He made as if to continue, then stopped. But he could not keep quiet. 'This isn't just a murder, Mr Cale. John of Boston is moving too fast – far too fast – in the matter of the rights of the Negro. The South won't have it. He'll pitch this country into a civil war that will burn this great United Estates to the ground. I tried, God knows I did, to get him to compromise. This is one man's death against the death of hundreds of thousands. Against the death of an entire nation. And the Negroes will come out of it as bad as ever they were. Or worse.

Cale looked as if he were about to say something considered.

'I don't care.'

Sighing, Van Owen chewed the tiniest morsel of cake in the distracted way you might expect of a man about to kill a king.

'Before I forget – what name do you want to be known by?'

'Savio,' said Cale.

'Does Mr Savio have a first name?'

'Dominic.'

Dominic Savio was a pasty-faced stool pigeon from his days in the Sanctuary. Hopefully, he was long dead, but if by chance he was still alive the thought that he might end up hanging from a scaffold without his genitals for a crime committed by Cale was a pleasing possibility.

'His name's Oswald Hidell.' Nothing more. Then: 'That's his real name.'

'Not very wise.'

'It's of central importance to Oswald that his act is done in his own name.'

'He wants to be famous for this? What an extremely bad idea – for the two of us, I mean.'

'Normally, discretion in an assassin would, I agree, be the very least of the qualities one would demand.

'But Oswald needs this act to be his and his alone. He wants to live in history, and at his trial he wants the chance – the only chance he'll ever have – to address the world to explain his reasons for such a terrible act.'

'He sounds like the last person you should be using. More to the point, he sounds like the last person I want my life to depend on.'

'I understand. But consider my choices: people ready to kill for money or other rewards tend, by definition, not to follow a code of honour. No offence.'

'None taken.'

'Anyone truly competent and professional enough to understate the task would be foolish to do so. Wouldn't you agree?'

'Most definitely.'

'Well, that was my dilemma. To ask . . . ah . . . *qualified* people would be to invite certain refusal while handing over the power of life and death to the kind of people who would certainly use it against me if it suited them. So I waited for a suitable, as it were, professional candidate to present himself – but oddly enough he never did. Until I came across Oswald Hidell.'

Van Owen took another nibble at his cake. 'Oswald's name came up nearly a year ago during an investigation by the Federals into the attempted assassination of General Nixon.' Van Owen paused for a reaction.

'Never heard of him.'

'Nixon was retired – a crackpot who saw conspiracies

every-where – usually ones organized by spook-loving Northern elites designed to destroy the virility of the South.'

'By virility, I take it you mean slave ownership.'

Van Owen smiled. 'It could certainly bear that interpretation, yes.'

'Just a minute . . . you said *attempted* assassination.'

'Yes,' said Van Owen. 'Oswald missed.'

'Please go on,' said Cale. 'I can feel the noose tightening around my neck with every word.'

Van Owen seemed oddly relaxed. 'I doubt anything as merciful as a rope would be involved. Yes, Oswald missed and, yes, that might seem to be a significant flaw in view of the importance he has for both of us. But there are . . . *mitigating* circumstances.'

'Such as?'

'An inadequate weapon, for one thing. Oswald is a good marksman – believe me, I've watched him shoot. But he only had access to a poor-quality hunting rifle – and it was a very difficult shot, nearly a hundred and twenty yards, at night, and in bad weather.'

Although not much of a shot himself, Cale knew good marksmen who would not have even considered making an attempt under such circumstances.

'And the other thing you were talking about?'

'Just bad luck. Very bad luck.'

This struck home more for Cale than it would for others: he very much believed in luck, particularly the bad kind.

'Explain.'

'Simple enough, really. Nixon dropped his head just as he fired.'

'Says Oswald.'

'Yes, he did say that – but so did Nixon. He confirmed that if he hadn't dipped his head to blow on an inkblot, the bullet would have left his brains all over the wall. All things considered, it was a damned good shot. There was no time for a second.'

'Why wasn't this Oswald put on trial if he tried to kill someone important?'

'He was handed over to an associate who knew I had an interest in persons of a particular kind – though not, of course, why. At any rate, at first I thought Oswald was just a crackpot with a grudge.' He looked at Cale. 'Let me be clear: he *is* a crackpot with a grudge, but he's also more than that.'

'I don't know whether to be worried that you're a bit of a bishop yourself,' said Cale.

'Bishop?'

'Bats in your belfry.'

'The thought has crossed my mind that I'm insane. But I'm persuaded after much careful consideration that this is not the case. I know that I'm doing a terrible thing, but I also know very clearly why I'm doing it.'

'And Oswald?'

'His motives, on the other hand, are . . . a mixture of vanity and, surprisingly enough, genuine insight.'

'You'll understand, Governor, that all this requires an enormous amount of trust on my part.'

'It does, doesn't it? But it seems to me, on reflection, that your great experience of the wayward human mind could be invaluable in keeping him stable – something we both want . . . or should I say *need* . . . very much indeed, if we are to survive.'

Cale thought about all this for a minute or two. 'Why did he want to kill Nixon?'

'Nixon? The General argued that freeing the blacks was a shameful injustice – like most Southerners, he thought freedom for slaves was an attack on his freedom to own them.'

'The contradiction didn't occur to him?'

'Do contradictions occur to anyone when their deepest interests are threatened? In my experience, people are a very emotional sort of animal. Even if they're very clever, they use their cleverness to justify their desires rather than to guide them.' Van Owen seemed happy to be conspiring with someone he regarded as an equally gifted student of human moves. 'And not that many people are particularly clever, are they?'

'But you're an exception?'

Van Owen smiled.

'Something I don't understand,' continued Cale.

'Yes?'

'Why did Oswald want to kill Nixon for trying to stop the blacks getting legal rights but now wants to kill John of Boston for trying to give them the same rights?'

'I'll bring him tomorrow and you can ask him yourself. But be careful. Question him gently, by all means, but don't pin him down too much when he contradicts himself. Admire what you can admire, and tell him so – and if you can't find anything, pretend. From time to time, between all the half-baked opinions – and my God, he's a pedant – there's an intelligence in there, real insight. But he's all over the place, and he's getting worse. That's why I decided to bring him here to you. No balanced man is going to kill a king, not like John of Boston, but you've got to keep him level enough to go through with it.'

'But not enough to make him have second thoughts.'

'Second thoughts would be bad for both of us – but especially for you. Then it'd be Thomas Cale having to pull the trigger.'

A letter from prosecuting counsel of the Hanse International Criminal Court to the Lawyers of Thomas Cale (appointed in his absence) from the records of a case of alleged Crimes against the Humanity committed in the context of armed conflict by said Thomas Cale since ME 1942 (when the Maastricht Statute entered into force).

FILED
Plurus Superior Court
Brumaire 33
Clerk of the Court

THE INTERNATIONAL CRIMINAL COURT OF THE HANSE 12TH
Thermidor ME 1956

Pre-Trial Chamber II

1. Judge Antoine Kes-Mbe Mindola, Presiding Judge
2. Judge Tomoko Arkane
3. Judge Rosario Salvat Aitalan

BLANDINO & SMI STATUTORY DEFENCE ADVOCATES

My Dear Bolly

You have asked us to discover to you Thomas Cale's verbatim record of his early life. We do not believe that article 7 requires this of us. However, in a spirit of cooperation prior to his trial in his absence, we are prepared to provide this document in exchange for dinner at Quaglino's – it goes without saying, but I'll say it anyway, at your expense.

The following brief account was written by Thomas Cale at the age of 15 or 16 (his exact age is unknown) although we can't make the dates agree very precisely with other biographical dates we have. It was confiscated from the files of Sister Althea Wray, the Somatist founder of the 'talking therapy' for the insane, under whose care he was committed for six months. There is plausible evidence that he faked the allegedly severe nervous breakdown for which she was treating him in order to ensure better handling during a period of incarceration for unspecified crimes. Sorry to disappoint you if you were hoping for something that will help in Cale's defence – as usual, it's the familiar attempt to put himself in the best possible light, by claiming that the accusations against him are either lies put about by his enemies, or the vulgar exaggerations of popular myth, according to which he is 'held to be guilty of every crime ever committed, from the theft of chickens from a henhouse in Lower Arsewipe to the murder of the two princes in the tower', or that responsibility for the crimes rests with someone else entirely.

I can also confirm that we have no substantive knowledge of Thomas Cale's current whereabouts, despite your (rather hurtful, if I may say so) claims to the contrary. We've heard a rumour that in his attempt to get away from the very long arm of Stalovek (look what happened to Trotskii), he fled to the United Estates. Guilty as he may be of the many charges this office is bringing against him, there's absolutely bugger all evidence to support this claim. As a final gesture of goodwill – and in return for a bottle of Château Tropcher when we have dinner at Quag's (the '42, not the '51) – we have just had a more or less credible sighting of Cale nine months ago in Argentiner. On the other hand, we have also just received a not completely dismissible claim that he died fourteen months ago in the Comoros. As always, and in every respect, Cale remains a slippery bugger of matchless talent.

TRANSCRIPT OF THOMAS CALE'S OWN ACCOUNT OF HIS EARLY LIFE. *Circa* summer 783 or ME 2019

My parents sold me as an ickle boy to the Redeemers for sixpence. In the Sanctuary I was chosen out by Redeemer Bosco (later Pope Bosco) for special training. This meant even more beatings than usual, being taught to read (usually a sin), beatings, special access to the library of banned books, beatings, endless practice in war strategy with a room full of wooden models, more beatings, an extra three hours a day of fight training, more beatings. When I was fourteen or fifteen I caught that mad bastard Picarbo, the Lord of Discipline, cutting up a girl. I'd never seen a girl before. I had the sense to leave before he noticed I was there – but sadly for me I got an unaccustomed attack of pity and made the first really stupid decision of my life: I came back and killed him. One girl was dead, but there was another. Cut a long story short – I got her and Vague Henri and that bugger Kleist out of the Sanctuary and we made it to Memphis, all rich fuckers, uber criminales like Kitty the Hare, and everything for sale (and everyone). If you was a buyer, it was heaven. If you was the bought, hell. But after the Sanctuary – for me it was bliss.

Still, I tried to keep on the low-down in Memphis but got into a fight with rich kid Conn Materazzi and fucked him and his friends up pretty bad. Went to prison but was sprung by Chancellor Vipond and his dodgy half-brother IdrisPukke, who both realized the Redeemers were the coming threat and wanted to pay me to rat them up – which I would have been happy to do for nothing. Vipond squared the fight with Conn's uncle, Duke Materazzi. I got a sweet deal for me and Vague Henri and even that bastard Kleist. Then things went bendy. Vipond got wind of the Redeemers wanting the Duke's daughter,

Arbell Materazzi, dead on account of her being the prophesied 'Whore of Babylon'. Now I had entry to the library of banned books, and I never came across any Whore of Babylon or heard Bosco mention anything about her. But Vipond and her daddy were real spooked so I kept my gob shut. So now me and Vague Henri and Kleist were made bodyguards to Arbell – or God's gift to mankind, as she and everyone else saw it.

Even after I saved her life she still looked at me like I was something the cat dragged in – she thought I was just a killer. Completely true as this is, I'm not all bad when you get to know me.

But then she did get to know me. Then she couldn't get enough of me. And I believed it all – which just goes to show that you can be a very bad boy and still know fuck all about what's really going on. Still, in those days I thought women were a kind of angel. First time I saw Arbell naked it would have been no surprise if she'd had wings. I thought I'd gone to Heaven. And I did, in a way.

Still, I should've realized that Bosco was up to something with all that claptrap about Arbell being the Whore of Babylon (she was a lot more treacherous than any whore I ever came across). So then it all played out exactly as Bosco had planned – or even better. He gets control of the Materazzi empire and Arbell sells me to him in exchange for the life of her father and family. Now you may think you understand that she was in a difficult position – but I believed in her. She sold me to Bosco so that he could make an example of me by burning me alive in Peter's Square in the Sanctuary and take an entire day doing it. Think about that when you feel sorry for her. Think about the fact that I saved her life twice. Think about the fact that I proved that her deaf-and-dumb brother all of Memphis laughed at because he was the family idiot was really as smart as a whip. Think about the fact that I saved that dritsek of a husband of hers and nearly lost my life doing it.

But then it turns out that Bosco didn't give a damn about me killing Picarbo. I was the one he wanted. And why did he go to the trouble and the risk of bringing down the most powerful war engine of the previous two hundred years? He told me, he told me with tears in his eyes, and all the while begging my forgiveness for all the pain he'd inflicted on me my whole life, that I wasn't a person at all – I, me, Thomas Cale was the wrath and disappointment of God made flesh. God was so angry at the failure of Humanity to be worthy of the gift of His only son who they'd hanged (very slowly) for offering mankind the gift of Salavation that He was finally going to solve the problem of His greatest mistake. All the beatings and training were for one thing: yours truly, the wrath of God, was supposed to wipe every last human being off the face of the earth, after which I would ascend into Heaven to be reunited with the rest of my godly self.

I knew Bosco was an evil bastard but I didn't know he was completely fucking crazy. It took me six months to escape but I did it in the end and made my way to Spanish Leeds. So now you know.

Allegedly, after writing this, he left Sister Wray, for reasons that are unclear, and returned to Switzerland. After the Redeemers annihilated the Swiss army at Bex under the command of Conn Materazzi, Cale began his extraordinary climb to absolute military control of the armies opposing them (you have to hand it to him – history has seen nothing like it since Joanne of Arc).

I should also tell you that the Materazzi government-in-exile have written to us demanding that we include a charge of conspiracy and murder against Cale concerning the execution of Conn Materazzi. If you have any evidence concerning Cale's lack of involvement in Conn

Materazzi's execution, I'd be very happy to make this go away – God knows the list of indictments is too fucking long as it is.

See you at Quag's. The week of the 32nd is good for me.
Best to Debo.
Piggers

5

After waking, Cale made himself three very strong cups of coffee and looked around the room for a distraction. All he could find was a copy of the *Navalon News*, subscription $2 per year. There was no doubting that it was a local paper in that the front page was confined to what the readers regarded as of significance in the world: themselves. There was a paragraph presenting a petition to the Estate senate requesting that the name of Zaragoza province be formally changed to Willie County. There was a plea to avoid beating small children. Oddest of all to Cale was a report about a riot in Man Hattan caused by a row between patriotic working-class supporters of Mark Tweain, a native composer of low comic operas about murderers, juvenile delinquents and absurd adventures in time, and the upper-class Hispanophile admirers of the grand opera of the Old World with its kings and gods and high tragedy.

The Tweainians had turned up at the hoity-toity Ópera Bourbon and started throwing an assortment of objects at the singers during a production of Hidalgo's *Eumenides*. These objects ranged from rotten eggs to dead cats to bottles filled with a liquid made from dog-shit. The panicked authorities had called out the militia and twenty people had died in the street violence that followed. Cale was used to irrational acts of human cruelty, but to kill another human being over an *opera*?

Not having been there for above two weeks before his arrest, he was beginning to think that the United Estates was a strange sort of place. Given his experience of strangeness, this was a remarkable thought.

'I want to give the people of the United Estates something to think about.'

Oswald Hidell was, thought Cale, somewhere in his mid-twenties, although he looked like a twelve-year-old whose body had grown to the size of a man but not developed any of the other signs of maturity. The tone of his announcement – for it was surely that – was self-aware, amused, but contradicted by the look in his eyes, which were suspicious and truculent: here was someone familiar with being dismissed. 'And I don't need someone to back me up.'

Cale smiled. Fifteen years in which he'd had to do as much politics as killing had schooled him well enough to disarm the rude and hostile.

'That's what both of us are very much hoping,' said Cale pleasantly. 'Mr Van Owen has told me of your skills as a marksman. They're very much better than mine.'

Van Owen looked at Cale, somewhat surprised.

'Then why do I need you?' said Oswald.

'Plan B is never better than Plan A, or it'd be Plan A. But it's best to have one all the same.'

A chilly silence from Oswald. He looked at Van Owen.

'I want it understood that, even if for some reason of bad luck I miss and you're able to succeed,' he said, the last with his voice dripping in doubtfulness, 'then credit for firing that fatal shot still comes to me.'

Van Owen's eyes relaxed very slightly.

'I know I can speak for both myself and Mr Savio that unloading full responsibility for John of Boston's death on to you is all that either of us dream of.'

Even Oswald had to smile at Van Owen's honesty. '*Can* he speak for you, Mr Savio?'

'Indeed he can, Mr Oswald. You can just call me Savio.'

'Savio,' said Oswald, as if weighing the man with the sound of his name.

'I'll show you to your room.'

'I won't share.'

'Of course not.'

With that, and another doubtful look at Cale, he allowed himself to be ushered out of the room.

*

Besides a grunt of acknowledgement at breakfast in the kitchen next morning, Oswald barely looked up. Then:

'You a good shot?'

'Fair,' said Cale. 'Not more.'

'Well, we'll see 'bout that later.' Another few minutes of brooding, followed by: 'Van Owen said you were in Rus a while. How come?'

'I was working as a bodyguard for a delegate from the Hanse. He was negotiating various trade deals, so we moved about a lot.' Over the years, Cale had needed to work on a great many lies in general and cover stories in particular. The best lies involved keeping as close to the truth as possible so that you were not caught out in the small ways. The bodyguard story was one of his best, in his opinion, because it gave him such a convincing way of explaining how he had moved among the great and good of the Boll Shevik Revolution (that is to say, the deranged and the murderous) without claiming any great status for himself of a kind that might arouse suspicion.

'A bodyguard?'

'Yes.'

Later, Oswald seemed restless and Cale suggested they play chess. At first, he rudely declined then changed his mind.

The game lasted an hour. By the time it became clear to Oswald that he was going to win, Cale watched him inflate like a balloon – but a balloon trying not to burst under the influence of the excess air generated by his triumph. Oswald was aware in some way that his reaction was too strong and that he must keep a grip on himself. He managed this by going back to his days in Rus and offering Cale the benefit of his insights. These pearls – Oswald clearly regarded them as such – were an odd mixture of him whining about not being given an important position in the government (he'd been given a job cleaning fish in a factory) and good sense:

'There's no system that can be entirely new. That's where the Boll Sheviks went astray. They wanted to invent the wheel their own way. Even if it was square. You have to create a society that has the best of both worlds.'

*

Late that afternoon Van Owen arrived with a second Carcano and some pistols. He took them through the woods to a clearing about twenty minutes from the house.

'I can't say you won't be disturbed, but they're familiar with guns around here. Just be friendly and let Oswald do the talking. They'll remember your foreign accent,' he said, looking at Cale.

Van Owen left them to it, and they spent twenty minutes checking the Carcanos, assembling and reassembling them. Then Oswald walked down to a tree about a hundred yards away and nailed a circle of material to the trunk about the size of a human head then a rectangle the size of the trunk of a man's body just below.

'I'll be taking my shot from between fifty and seventy yards at most,' said Cale. When he came back, Oswald looked at him a little too dismissively.

'We used to say in the Marines: train hard, fight easy.'

Cocky little shit, thought Cale.

'Go ahead,' Oswald went on.

'You're the main man – don't you want to go first?'

'I'm not the one who needs to practise.'

Having torn the paper off the cartridge with his teeth, Cale poured the powder and the minié round into the muzzle, drew out the ram and in one graceful movement rammed powder and ball to the barrel breech and replaced the ramrod with great speed and deftness. Raising the weapon, he pulled back the lock, dropped the percussion cap in place, cocked, aimed, breathed in and then out slowly. He fired. And missed.

Oswald looked on thoughtfully. 'Pity you can't shoot as well as you can load.'

As it turned out, Oswald was a good teacher: clear, patient and knowledgeable. He wasn't to know that Cale had been taught by the best marksmen money could buy and even then had not improved by much. Half an hour of practice got him back to the level of his previous mediocrity. Another thirty minutes and the quality of the Carcano helped to make him a little better than that.

That evening, flushed with success at having so comprehensively demonstrated his superiority in marksmanship over Cale, Oswald was in a good mood and had decided to give the taken-down-a-peg-or-two interloper the benefit of his philosophy of life. As he talked, it became clearer that for Oswald the essential problem with both the United Estates and the Boll Shevism of the Rus was that neither world could meet all his needs. To him it seemed obvious that if the impulses of a small but defined group of people – the wealthy, the powerful of whatever stripe, presumably via a brick wall and a firing squad – were checked, then the natural state of things would reassert itself: decency, cooperation, a talent for partnership between people of every colour. Once there was justice and tolerance and a fair distribution of money, everything would be all right. Other than the firing squad, much of what he had to say would have had a great many perfectly nice people shaking their heads in agreement.

Cale had, of course, been one of the victimized and poor but had also been one of the rich and powerful. And what was so wrong, after all, with peace between men and women? What was the problem with wanting love, understanding, tolerance and justice for all? Cale examined his conscience to try to work out whether his frustration at listening to all these admirable ambitions was merely down to the fact that he had come to like money and power and didn't much like having lost them.

As Oswald talked on, moments of insight following on flights of the fanciful or the foolish, it became clear that he imagined for himself an important but entirely vague role in the New World: his part in bringing it about would be recognized by him becoming a very important person without any obligation to improve the standards of education, say, or the quality of steel, or the management of the health of the citizens. His skills would be well paid and much admired. He seemed sure that without taking responsibility for anything in particular he would be able to exercise a huge influence over the course of future events. At one point, smiling as if he knew something Cale could not possibly know, he went to his bedroom and came back with a book whose title he was careful to keep hidden.

'Listen to this,' he said with a cat-got-the-cream grin. '*In whatever arena of life one may meet the challenge of courage, whatever may be the sacrifices he faces if he follows his conscience – the loss of his friends, his fortune, his contentment*' – Oswald paused then emphasized the conclusion of the sentence – '*even the esteem of his fellow men – each man must decide for himself the course he will follow.*' He looked up with a sort of wildly excited, knowing triumph. Then he began to read again.

'*A man does what he must – in spite of personal consequences, in spite of dangers and pressures – and in his ability to do so against conventional measures of virtue or goodness is the basis of all human morality. For true courage, a man must look into his soul.*'

He shut the book and placed it with great ceremony on the table. 'Do you know who wrote that?'

Fortunately, Cale did not, so he was not subject to any foolish temptation to upstage what was coming. 'No idea,' he said.

'These lines,' said Oswald softly, 'were written by John of Boston.'

When Cale emerged from his room later, he could see Oswald was ready to go out.

'A walk?'

'I'm going into Navalon.'

'Is that wise?'

'Van Owen doesn't own me, and you certainly don't.'

Tricky, this.

'Of course not. But given how close we are . . .' He let this hang, vague but clear.

'What?' said Oswald, exasperated. 'Do you think people can read my mind? *He looks like the kind of person who might kill a bigshot.* You don't know Dallas, Savio, but I do.' He laughed. 'These people are as nosy as hell. They know we're here – hiding just makes us look odder.'

He wasn't going to be argued with.

'Mind if I come?'

He could see that Oswald wanted to refuse, and also that he was wondering if it was wise to be so hostile.

'Suit yourself.'

It was a two-mile walk, and most of it was in silence. When they got into the centre of Navalon, Oswald turned to him.

'See you at the post house in an hour,' he said, and walked off.

Cale watched him go, but in a few seconds a middle-aged man with a soapy smile emerged from a shop two doors down holding a tray with glasses filled with red wine and slices of oranges and decorated with a large sprig of green leaves.

'Mint sangria, sir? A real taste of the old South.'

Much as he wanted to avoid a sales jabber, the little tears of water on the glasses spoke of the temptations of ice. He took the offered glass and tasted. Cold bliss!

The salesman watched as if nothing in life could ever give him so much pleasure as the sharing of the cooling scarlet beverage being enjoyed by the suspicious man on the boardwalk. But he welcomed suspicion – misgivings were the rocks upon which he had constructed ten thousand deals.

Next to the glasses on the tray was an immaculately folded napkin of white linen, starched and pure. The salesman waited until Cale had drunk half the glass then drew back the napkin to reveal a set of teeth.

'Remarkable. No?' he said, as if there could be no denying this was a long-lost work by the hand of Michel Angelo. 'These, sir, are an example of the finest dentures available anywhere in the world. Notice I do not say "false" teeth, because there is nothing false about them. Here is no enamelled wood, no walrus, no ivory. These are real human teeth from the battlefields of the Old World. These are from Switzerland itself, where the young men who sacrificed themselves so nobly against the false religion of the wicked Redeemers were brought up on a diet rich in milk, cream and yojurt.'

'Yoghurt,' said Cale malevolently. 'The "g" is hard.' Why so aggravated about such a trivial mistake? Because it was certain, if the claim by the salesman was actually true, that the late owners of the teeth had been men who'd died under Cale's command. The only exception would be if they had come from the disastrous Battle at Bex. That would be worse: at Bex, Cale had been obliged to burn the bridge over the River Glane in order to stop the Redeemers from following the fleeing Swiss soldiers and slaughtering every one of them. Unfortunately, this had involved stranding two thousand men on the opposite bank where they were murdered, and not quickly, by the frustrated

Redeemers. It was at Bex that the Redeemers broke with the universal practice of hanging anyone caught stealing teeth on the battlefield with the dual aim of helping to fund their war against the human race and sending a warning to any soldier who opposed them.

'Now I can see you asking how I could possibly know these teeth are of the Caucasian purity I claim they are. This is, you're thinking, a salesman's folderol. I understand that . . . indeed, I couldn't agree more that there are lies – damned lies – and the braggard docio of advertising. But I give you the word of a man whose word is his bond that none of the teeth in these prosthetic dentaduras is of coloured origin. Our teeth are free of even the slightest trace of the descendants of Ethiopia.'

'You're right,' said Cale. What he was right about was unclear to the salesman.

'I'm sorry . . .'

'You're right that I'm asking how you could possibly know.'

The salesman was relieved – he had sensed some awkwardness about the response of the man, but now all was clear.

'I have been a purveyor of diamonds, sir, in my time, and may I say a skilled one . . . but not even the most skilled appraiser of gems requires the eye that's needed to gauge a tooth that's free of the taint of negrura. Of course, even the slow-witted could tell the tooth of a field Negro with a few months of careful tuition. But what about your demi-meamelouc? How many Southerners could tell someone who is one-thirty-secondth black if they were standing in front of them with a magnifying glass? Precious few. Now consider what it would take to appraise the tooth of such a person on its own, sin otra pista, and see the black shadow suffused within. It took me ten years of relentless study to spot the dim and distant frailty in the molar of a passé blanc.'

'Passé blanc?'

'One who passes as white – the child of a demi-meamelouc and a white man. One sixty-fourth black. Not even such a dilution is allowed. At the Diesdedos Emporium we know your mouth is a sacred place.'

*

It took Cale about ten minutes to pick up Oswald and watch what he was up to. Nothing interesting; he mostly confined himself to looking in shop windows. Oswald was so wrapped up in his own world it was easy to keep an eye on him and take in the town of Navalon as well. According to the Welcome sign, Navalon had a population of 3,221 and was HOME OF THE BIGGEST ROSE BUSH IN THE WORLD! It was, rose bush aside, pretty much like a dozen other small Southern towns he had wandered through before his arrest for murder. Main Street was wide but made of dirt. Wagons of various kinds were parked carelessly, following only the rule that there should be space in the middle of the street just wide enough for a single wagon to pass. There were ruts big enough to rival El Gran Cañón. Side by side, there were the usual boarded wooden stores (GUITIEREZ CHINA, GLASS & QUEENSWARE) and a few small workshops (TEXAS CIGAR MANUFACTORY). Others were mysterious: COONEY – GROCERY-CUM-FANDANGO PARLOUR. Less mysterious but odd was a wide building with a long sign stretching above which stated AUCTION. But most of the writing on the sign had been painted out, leaving a long, white, empty space. Beneath it was a gathering of seven or eight men sitting and standing about in the way of such groups he'd seen in small towns everywhere from Batoor to Bumfuck. Ranging from their twenties to late forties, they appeared to have nothing to do but be idle, yet they stared out at the world as if they saw exactly what it was and weren't impressed. In this American incarnation they all wore hats; black bowlers for the elder; straw boaters for the young. The majority had their hands in their pockets and they glanced at the passing Cale in a style which spoke clearly: *I discard you*, they said. Hips were worn swaggeringly to one side. An older man was boasting to a younger:

'"Lieutenant," I say to him, "yure a damn son of a bitch and you can suck my ass."'

As he moved up the street and turned towards the post office, Cale looked back at them. Now, with the light striking the mostly blank sign at an oblique angle, he could just read the words that had been carelessly painted out: it had once read: AUCTION & NEGRO SALES.

Cale was waiting in the post house when Oswald turned up. As soon as he entered, he took a letter out of his inside pocket and joined the queue to buy a stamp. There were four women in front of him, all black.

Cale moved away to an assistant on the far side of the post house watching over a counter of mixed goods from tins of tobacco to boxes of buttons. There were also surprising numbers of news-sheets from all over the Estates, not just the South: the *Weekly Register of Baltimoare*, the *Green Bay Advocate*, the *Washingtone Herald*. There was even a news-sheet in Prussian, *Der Lutheraner*, for the thousands of Antagonists who had fled to Spanish America to escape the persecution of the Redeemers.

'How can I help you, sir?'

'Do you have a news-sheet from around the town of Malfi?'

'The *Malfi Palladium*? Not in stock, sir. But we can order it in two days.'

Behind Cale, the postmaster looked up from his ledger and noticed Oswald at the back of the queue. He stopped serving the middle-aged coloured woman at the counter.

'Sir!' he called out to Oswald. 'You can come to the front here.'

'There's a line,' said Oswald.

'These ladies won't mind.'

It was hard, thought Cale, to know what the ladies were thinking – on all of them, a look without expression settled over their features, as if they had not heard the exchange and took no view even if they had. He'd seen that expression before, indeed had offered it to the world on many occasions in his childhood. *I am not here. This is not happening.*

'But *I* mind,' said Oswald.

As for the postmaster, there was a definite look on his face: resentment and anxiety.

'It's our policy, sir, no exceptions.'

'There are now,' said Oswald.

The coloured women still remained without expression – no sign that this was a hero standing up for them. There were two white men who'd been chatting at the far side of the office. From amiable Southerners renowned for their hospitality to watchful hostiles took only a moment. Cale wondered what he would do if they moved to the door or intervened. Probably nothing. This was unfamiliar territory for him. Fortunately, it was unfamiliar for the man behind the counter. He was a postmaster by temperament as well as profession – he didn't want any trouble. He started serving the woman in front of him again. The woman waited. *I am not here. This is not happening.* And the two white men stared at Oswald as if imagining slowly peeling his skin with a butter knife.

Outside, after an excruciating five minutes, Oswald made no reference to what had happened.

That evening, Van Owen arrived and at dinner Oswald said and ate little. Claiming he was tired, he left before the cake Van Owen had brought.

'All the more for us,' said Van Owen cheerfully. 'So, Mr Savio, what breed of cat is Mr Oswald, do you think?'

'His hair is falling out.'

Van Owen sighed. 'Will he make it?'

'Hard to say. But John of Boston had better hurry up if he wants to be killed.'

Cale told him about the events at the post office. A glum smile from Van Owen.

'Oswald's gotten in trouble about the coloured thing before,' he said. 'He was in court a year or so back and he sat in the section reserved for blacks and wouldn't move. Saintly, no?' Cale looked at him. 'The thing is . . . you know why he was in court in the first place?' He paused for effect. 'He'd been arrested for beating his wife. Not for the first time, either.'

'People are strange.'

'Aren't they, though?' A beat. 'Your old dad say that?'

'My father sold me to the Redeemers for sixpence when I could barely talk.'

Cale told him about the false teeth.

'The coloured problem. It's very complicated.'

'Funny how often that word comes up when people want to justify something ugly.'

'Very well, then, let's call it what it is: it is ugly. If I could get rid of the Southern taste for humiliating the dark peoples, I'd do so. But I can't. A hundred years won't eradicate that . . . unpleasantness in the Southern character.'

'Then why not leave them to it?'

'And go where? You're a man of experience. Tell me the peoples who don't have a taste for unpleasantness – the country where decency rules. Can you?'

'Not so much.'

'As a general rule, the Southerner really is what they claim to be: gracious, considerate, hospitable to strangers in a way I've never seen anywhere else on this earth. A truly honourable people.'

'Except when it comes to Negroes.'

'Exactly so.'

Neither of them said anything for a while. Then:

'Why do you want to kill John of Boston?' asked Cale.

'I thought you didn't want to know.'

'On reflection, it doesn't seem quite right to kill a man without a reason.'

'I thought your reason was that you wanted to save your own neck.'

A pause while Cale considered this.

'Still,' he said at last.

Van Owen grimaced. 'The South wants to march backward; John of Boston wants to march forward. If the Supreme Court gives the go-ahead and a bill to re-enslave the Negroes gets to Congress, John of Boston won't let it happen and he won't let the South secede, either. The result will be a war that will fill El Gran Cañón with blood and, in my opinion, end with the South in ruins. I need time to persuade the South to see that they could preserve most of what it used to have if it would only be happy with waged slavery rather than the real kind. But with a re-enslavement bill coming through Congress, they won't listen to me. So I've got one option left. If John of Boston dies, the game shuts down and we go back to the start and see if I can find an ugly compromise that no one is happy with – just happy enough to avoid a bloodbath.'

'But kill him – someone else carries on.'

'But we have a Constitution like no other, Mr Cale. It has rules which allow all kinds of men to have power: hero-worshipped goody-goodies with a will of iron like John of Boston, but also spineless time-servers like Deputy Chancellor Lincoln, who the law states must succeed until the next election in three years. A spineless time-server is all that stands between this country and ruin for everyone – blacks, too. And it just so happens that spineless time-servers are just up my street.' Van Owen finished the last of his cake without his usual relish. 'It's confirmed. Our Chancellor will be here in four days.'

So the long hours to the visit by John of Boston passed with Cale watching Oswald as if he were a volcano that might erupt at any time. Then it was the early evening of the night before. Van Owen turned up, pale and nervous.

'The thing to remember, Thomas,' IdrisPukke had said, for reasons Cale had forgotten because as a sixteen-year-old he'd not really been listening, 'is that people in their thousands secretly suspect themselves of a great significance not supported by the evidence of anything they've ever done or even tried to do. With better luck, with the right chance, they know they could have been contenders in life – the successful businessman, the great composer, the person of substance; millions feel that life has robbed them of their consequence. But fortunately, for the rest of us, something in them has the sense only to dream and not to act. To simmer but not boil.'

Oswald's simmer did not make him fractious or tense but came across as nervous excitement, an opera singer about to take the stage in his long-awaited leading role.

'There's something I want you to understand,' said Oswald. Cale considered his thoughts about the bliss of ignorance but said nothing. 'Do you know what I think of John of Boston?'

It was true that Cale had considered asking in more detail what it was about the great man that made Oswald determined that he should die, when John had worked hard enough and with some considerable risk to advance the rights of the coloureds that Oswald so passionately believed in. So why kill him, of all people? But it was just one contradiction among so many that Cale thought existed in Oswald's brain; it must jostle for position along with all the others.

'You need to understand I'm not some murderer with a grudge. I understand this is a terrible act. John of Boston is a good man. I believe that. I don't deny his courage in standing up for the poor and the risks involved in doing so.'

Cale wanted to ask the obvious question.

'I know what you're thinking,' said Oswald, a tiny gleam of triumph in his eyes. But he was right. 'Why will I kill him tomorrow? He's so clever – wise, even – so able to persuade and bring people along with him against their will, so good at pulling things together that don't belong and making the stitches hold. Such a great man that he's going to make the United Estates work. He'll find a middle way through all this injustice and poison. He'll find a way to sweeten the bitterness so that it will carry on. But the United Estates will still be cruel and unjust – but better by just enough so that it carries on, forever exploiting the poor and favouring the rich. "Let justice reign even though the Heavens fall."'

'What's the good of a just and equal wasteland?'

'You been talking to Van Owen.' Cale was surprised.

'You think I don't know why Van Owen wants John of Boston dead?'

'So why are you helping him?'

'It doesn't matter to me what his motives are. He thinks he's using me, but it's the other way round. If I don't stop John, he'll go on compromising with the oppression of the black peoples of this country. The blacks will be free in name only: the Federals will still kill them with impunity, the rich will still pay them a pittance, their children will die fettered by disease instead of chains. They will have no vote.'

'Van Owen says that John of Boston won't let the South secede at any price?'

Oswald smirked. 'Van Owen is wrong. Boston doesn't understand Southerners. Like all your liberal reformer gooners, he thinks that, because he's in the right, he just needs to be firm with these deplorable persons – they're not going to fight a war that'll destroy them over a bunch of darkies. But he'll think again and back down when he sees they mean it. I'm the only person who understands that a war that brings the South to its knees is the only thing that'll work.'

With any luck, thought Cale, *I'll be long gone before either of these mad bastards find out who's right. Probably neither of them.*

'History and fate will bring John of Boston to me tomorrow, and Van Owen is just a part of fate doing its job – and so are you.'

And then a moment as if Cale were looking into a deep and muddy lake and in the darkness there was the swift brief flash of a fin – 'People talk,' said Oswald. 'But I act. That's the difference between me and everyone else.'

6

Although it had rained all night, by late morning it had turned into a beautiful sunny Dallas day and the crowds, excited to see John of Boston and his exquisite wife, were flowing excitable as any babbling brook towards the best places in Dallas to see the gorgeous pair. John of Boston, actor handsome, professor smart, the older brother, wise father, golden son; and then his consort: superb, blooming. Their charism lit up the crowds.

Walking together for about fifty yards, Cale and Oswald, a pike and a perch haunting that happy stream of people, were carrying their carpet bags as inconspicuously as possible along a road full of families and workers chatting excitedly and waving a hundred variations of the brand-new flag of the United Estates – bars of red and white and a circle of stars for each of one of the members of the union that sung out loud against the antiquated domains of the Old World of the Four Quarters. Here, as long as you were over twenty-five, were not a woman or black, your voice was as good as anyone's voice. This was the greatest country in the world and the greatest time to be a part of the commonwealth of ordinary men.

But it wasn't just the happy, happy crowds bustling to get the best view of the enchanting Presidential couple, and Cale and Oswald slouching towards their crime, who'd come to Dallas that day. Earlier that morning, three old women, sisters, had appeared in the city seething with something that would have seemed to any passing Texican like excitement. But it was much older in its origin than excitement and very much more horrible. *If* that Texican could have seen them, that is.

Let me explain.

Consider the poisonous things that are at the very edge of sight: the flea, a hemlock seed, the fang of a spider. These are giants compared to the three sisters. Incomprehensibly old, they are smaller by far than the eye could ever see. This trio of itsy-bitsy hags have haunted the world since there was such a thing to speak of, sometimes tormenting one person sometimes an entire people, but always fastening on those approaching a moment when everything afterwards will be utterly changed from what it was before.

Meet the three Fates, also known as the Kindly Ones: Enid, Doris, Glad. Enid spins the thread of life, Doris reels it out, and Glad (or Gladys) chooses the moment when it should be cut. To them, human existence is a pantomime arranged for their amusement and delight, a slapstick ballet or bladder-leaking cabaret choreographed in blood and improvised with pain. Have you heard laughter in the dark? Have you ever had the sense that someone is watching you? Now you know why.

They had been looking forward to this day in Dallas for centuries. This was not just a momentous death, a weighty death, it would be a death at the hands of someone who'd always been a favourite of theirs. Even though Thomas Cale didn't have the slightest notion of their existence, his genius for the kinds of calamity that thrilled them so deeply had given him a special place in their hearts. Not that they had any, of course. Today was a treat to be savoured.

And why 'Kindly'? Because in a pointless attempt at buttering up this eternal triangle of malevolent crones the view emerged that by referring to them in appreciative tones they might be flattered into going away and getting their pleasures somewhere else. Others, who understood them better, called them the Tiny Ones.

Cale and Oswald also divided and headed for their assigned places – Oswald to a tower used for storing grain where he'd been employed for several months. Cale turned out of the self-sifting flow of happy gawpers and climbed up a bank of steps to the path next to the park, where there was hardly anyone. Even with the Carcano dismantled in two inside the carpet bag, he felt as if a sign were hovering overhead pointing out his bad intent. He tried not to walk too quickly as he moved on another thirty yards, and then looked back – not suspiciously, not that, but as if you had suddenly heard a surprising noise and were naturally just curious where it had come from. He turned into the bushes that hid the false tool shed.

He couldn't find the key. Yes, he could. He opened the lock and it clicked open as smoothly as if it, too, were implicated in the plot and wanted to speed him on his way to kill a great man, a superior man, a man who might transform the ugliness of the world, and to do this dreadful thing solely in order to save his own skin. But then it was his skin, after all, that was the skin involved. Thomas Cale had done terrible things, and he had done good things. You could argue that possibly millions were alive because of him, and you could also argue that millions were dead on his account. He had tried to run away from the world on a number of occasions – and was trying to do so again – but the world always came after him.

'Whatever is unacknowledged in your character happens to you as fate,' IdrisPukke had said to him one day when, again, he was not really listening. He was beginning to grasp what he might have been driving at.

Dropping the carpet bag, he stepped up on to the crate and slowly eased his head above the fence. Then, the first snag of the day. The divots he'd scored in the grass at the eighty- and fifty-yard marks were now obliterated by the muddy footsteps of people who had taken a short cut to the top of the plaza that edged the road. It was not a major problem, but it was a reminder of the power of small events to kill you.

In an assassination, the murderer suffers agonies, while his victim approaches unconcerned. To kill a man is an extraordinary thing – imagine standing on the edge of some terrible cliff and staring down a thousand feet at the sea below bursting on to the broken rocks – the horror and the dread and yet the joy that you might leap in a moment and fall in a terrible ecstasy. Then stepping back, feeling your heart beating with unfathomable bliss that you have come this close to the very edge of life. That's something of what it's like for the sensitive assassin.

But for Cale it was different. Born with a genius for violence both personal and on the battlefield, killing was simply a task which had become necessary because, since he was a small boy, people had always been trying to kill him first. He was sick to the back teeth of violence, and had been for as long as he could remember – but strangely enough, this weariness had no effect on the numbers of the dead who always followed, just like in the proverb, in his wake.

So, he waited, standing on the wooden crate holding the just-assembled Carcano cradled in his arms. He tried to think no thoughts, feel no feelings, instead to be purely watchful, intensely staring at the road leading into the plaza from which John of Boston would emerge. But he was no longer the icy boy he used to be, schooled by hunger, pain and cold to squat inside his head, immune to the outside world. He was distracted now by everything going on around him – the women in particular: the happy crowds were bursting with well-off women of fashion wearing hats and blouses, and skirts stained with the lurid colours of the latest dyes made from tar of coal. Each one of them seemed to blaze at him like a garish beacon, warning him of the unnatural danger to come, screaming mauveine at him, gaudy fuchsine, livid safranine and induline, blindingly deviant colours never before seen in the world.

But no sign of the beautiful pair. A minute. Two minutes. Ten. Cale felt he was lying in a coffin underground, fighting to stop the terrible panic surging in his chest. A woman's blazing coquelicot percher blew off in the wind. A burst of laughter from the crowd. Then, an urgent ripple of excitement. The dark blue-black carriage of John of Boston pulled slowly into the plaza, the man himself in sober grey, his wife in an outrageous pink and with a tiny hat on top of that unfathomably queenly head. From the head of a statue dedicated to the spirit of liberty, the three sisters watched the spectacle unfold with a relish that can come only from the approaching climax of a long-anticipated treat.

Now the practised instincts of Cale's past emerged and the crowd receded, as if a thick transparent curtain had been pulled to separate them from him and the deed to come. The sound dimmed; it felt like his ears had been stuffed with wool, his breathing rasped. The carriage moved along the top of the square then slowly turned. As it did so, a small girl in white ran up to the carriage and held up a bunch of snow-on-the-mountain. The carriage stopped at the sweet command of the Leading Lady and she took the flowers with a laugh of delight. They moved on. In the carriage behind came the guards, with others running alongside, scanning the mass of enchanted people. Still it came on, picking up speed a little, not too much.

Now the Carcano came down, resting on the wooden fence but supported by a sock overstuffed with sand. Cale took aim, running the routine not just in his head but whispering to himself. *Breathe, breathe out, completely empty the lungs. Bad. Try again. Breathe.* Slowly, he brought himself down. *Bring the sights together, focus on John of Boston's chest then concentrate back on the sights, pull the Carcano on to the shoulder, twist in the hands as if wringing a towel. And, as always, at the point of no return, time slows, the breath stops, and the heart. Hard eyes on the sight and the chest. Hold. Wait. Hold.*

Then John of Boston flinches, anguish on his face, a grimace as if at distasteful news; his hands clench. A distant bang. He raises his fists, coughs then slumps forward into his wife's chest. Startled, she bends over and looks into his face like an anxious mother at her suddenly afflicted child. Her arm reaches around his shoulders. Above the grain silo a startled flock of pigeons takes the air. The little girl still running alongside the carriage hears the shot, stops and looks around, uneasy, as if an unfamiliar voice had called out her name.

Cale aiming. *Is he dead? Shoot or not shoot? Don't shoot. Wait.* Then John of Boston's hands move to his throat. *Damn! Not dead. Not dead. Shoot. Shoot or die.*

Cale snatches at the trigger as John of Boston's wife opens her mouth to scream. Black-hole screaming. He shoots. The scream passes over his head.

The bullet miraculously passes through the tiny space between the flesh of man and wife. Missed.

But the carriage has stopped. *Reload! Reload! A chance of life.* A rapture of scrabbling at the cartridge powder, bullet, rod and breech. *Too slow! Too slow!* The carriage is moving on and away. He throws the ramrod to the ground and raises the gun a second time but, oiled by sweat, the weapon slips as he raises it – but is instantly caught and raised again. *Aim.* Shaking like a drunk, he takes a lead once more.

Don't snatch. Don't snatch. The carriage picks up speed. 'AWAY! AWAY!' shout the guards.

And then the shot.

But not from Cale.

In slow time, one of the guards, holding a pistol in his hand, jumps on to the carriage step and in his panic slips and falls, fetching his head a dreadful crack on the sharp edge of the carriage door. He falls heavily on to the road, and the pistol goes off as Oswald fires a second shot from the silo. But it's the bullet from the guard's pistol that hits John of Boston in the head, causing it to explode in a fine mist of blood and bits of brain and bone. A large flap of his skull hangs down, attached by hair and skin.

With the utter relaxation of the dead, he lolls back in his seat, his buttocks slipping forward, his body sliding downwards to the floor.

Amazed, mouth open, out of the corner of his eye Cale notices a man kneeling on the grass, distraught, punching the ground three times with his fists.

Can't watch. Down from the step, Cale gasps as icy water fills him from inside out. Another place of never going back.

He tries to break down the Carcano – a rapture of blundering. Hands shaking, the coin doesn't fit. *Fucker! Fit! Fit! Full of shame, the coin has swollen so that it cannot be used.* Using his left hand to steady his right, he guides the coin into the slotted screw and turns. It won't budge. *How?* Then it gives. *Calm. Calm. Breathe.* He turns the Carcano over and loosens the second screw. Then he folds it in an awkward V and stuffs it into the carpet bag.

The key, I've lost the key. No, there's the key. He drops the bag and, again holding his right hand in his left, aims it at the lock. *Slow down, slow down.* It turns. Still shaking, he eases open the door. Now he becomes aware once more of the outside world: shouts, other screams, footsteps running past. He opens the door a little more and eases himself out into the shrubs. He listens. Looks from side to side. Nobody near. He reaches back into the enclosure and picks up the bag.

Shit!

He'd forgotten the sock filled with sand. He rushes back to the steps, grabs the sock and, going back to the bag, opens it and shoves it in with horribly quivering hands, checks the path outside, returns, picks up the bag, slowly steps through the shrubs and starts to walk towards Main Street, calmly, even though at his back the whole time he can hear the hounds of Heaven snarling at his heels.

7

Cale endlessly presents himself as the military genius who arrives as all is about to be lost and manages to sort out the mess. Most often, he either exaggerates the mess or it's a mess he caused in the first place. He was a scrambler who never had a plan, strategic or tactical, that did not break down or change out of necessity in the field, with the result that he repeatedly plunged his armies into uncertain, seemingly desperate situations, only to emerge victorious in a series of glorious muddles.

– Loraine Cornwall, *Blundering to Victory: A Reassessment of the Military Skills of Thomas Cale Cornwall Loraine (Pingüino)*

So far from being exaggerated, Cale's claims to greatness as a military leader have yet to be properly understood. His creation of an army of Swiss peasants able to take on and defeat the Redeemers, one of the most formidable armies of modern times, is alone sufficient to place him among the very best. He did not beat the peasants' ploughshares into swords – which they had no idea how to use – but made it possible for them to adapt their ploughs as weapons. The same applied to everything they had been proficient at using since they were children: wheat flails modified with nails became arms of deadly force. What had once been a hayfork became the feared *muongmazler* (monk killer). The very wagons they used to carry wheat and horse manure, and which they knew how to handle like prodigies in mud or snow, became moving fortresses, adapted to become near-impenetrable.

– E. F. Halstein, 'Patterns of Change and Continuity in Quarterine Warfare', *Journal of Military History* (Brumaire ME 1958)

Cale was sitting on a grubby-looking bed in a grubby-looking room where, if you were unwise enough to walk across the floor in bare feet, each step would feel as if someone had left a thin smear of jam over the floorboards. He was staring at the opposite wall and had been doing so for the last hour as the light outside faded to evening. He blinked from time to time but otherwise did not move.

There was a soft knock at the door. Instantly, he was up and had grabbed a pistol from either side of his bed. He pushed himself into the wall on the left side of the door.

'Yes?'

'It yure packidge, suh.'

It was the bellboy – no way of knowing if there were people behind him. It was more dangerous to act strangely.

'Just a second.' He put the pistols on a table and covered them with his jacket, handles pointing towards the door.

He opened the door, smiling pleasantly and trying to look as if he'd just woken up. A quick look confirmed the bellboy was on his own. He gestured him to come into the room. Inside, the bellboy took out a small packet. Cale reached out to take it, but the bellboy held it back out of reach.

'Sorry, suh, cost more'n I thought.'

'How much more?'

'Thirty dollar.'

What was the point in arguing? Cale took out his purse and counted out the money. The bellboy handed over the packet.

'I want you to bring my meals up here.'

The bellboy smiled. 'Suh, this ain't really that kinda hotel.'

'A two-dollar tip in it for you.'

'Each time, suh?'

'Yes.'

'An' a dollar for the cook.'

'Why?'

'He gotta put it on a tray.'

'For a dollar?'

'No, suh. The dollar ain't for putting it on a tray, the dollar's for him to keep his mouth shut.'

'Let's make it another dollar – for you to make sure both of you keep your mouths shut.'

'Our lips are tight, suh. Even tighter for another dollar.' The bellboy smiled again, playfully mischievous.

This time Cale did respond. 'You've had all you're going to get from me. Disappoint me, and you'll be smiling on the other side of your face. Do you know me?'

The look of friendly devilment faded from the bellboy's expression. The performance vanished with it.

'I understand you very well, suh.'

'Good. I want dinner in two hours.' The bellboy nodded and Cale opened the door to let him out.

Five minutes later, Cale was lighting a pipe of the bellboy's overpriced Mexican black and taking deep breaths. Five minutes after that, he was back on the bed, the long-anticipated numbness soaking his heart in a couple of hours' worth of carelessness.

It had been a while since he could afford to buy the drugs that had been such a help in causing his fall, if not from grace, then from power and wealth. The poverty resulting from being on the run from almost everyone had wonderfully improved his health.

It was two hours before Cale began to emerge from sleep and it was to the sound of heavy knocking on his door. Befuddled by drugs, Cale knew he couldn't defend himself so he just opened the door. It was the bellboy with a tray of scrambled eggs and polenta. Cale paid him and ordered more junk.

'Did you hear?' said the bellboy, obviously distressed. 'The sons of bitches killed John of Boston.'

Cale, eyes drooping, looked at him. 'Who did it? Do they know?'

'Sons of bitches,' said the bellboy.

Cale smoked another pipe, leaving the eggs and polenta to congeal by the bed. Van Owen had argued, and he should know, thought Cale, that the best way to avoid capture was to remain in Dallas. After a few days he would encourage the notion that the killers must have fled. In three, four days at the most, someone would come for Cale at the boarding house, take him out of Dallas and begin the long journey to warm obscurity in the Bermudas. Was Cale convinced by this? Hardly at all, but what he believed didn't really make much difference. On the other hand, Oswald was clearly determined to claim sole credit for killing John of Boston. If he was caught, could he be relied on?

And Van Owen? He most certainly didn't trust the governor, but there was something unusual about him, of a kind he'd come across a few times in his life: ruthless and ambitious men who possessed an idiosyncratic sense of obligation which they took seriously as long as their most pressing concerns were not under threat. All Cale could do was wait and see and act and try to survive. What were his chances of being alive by the end of the week? *As weak as a homeopathic soup made from the shadow of a pigeon that had died of starvation.*

The great pleasure of opium was that it enabled him to think about the Sanctuary and the one thing about the place he'd loved, although he'd only realized that he loved Vague Henri long after he was dead. He fell not into a sleep but a kind of trance of black smoke, muttering with laughter and memories. He was back with Vague Henri a few days after Cale had broken him out of one of Kitty the Hare's prison cells. The pair of them were sitting on a bench in the Promenade des Bastions in Spanish Leeds listening to a brass band playing 'I've Got a Lovely Bunch of Coconuts'. They were eating cream horns and watching ranks of pretty girls, happy as starlings, walking up and down the esplanade and showing off their loveliness. Cale was having to feed bits of the cake to Vague Henri because the recently late Kitty had smashed the fingers of both his hands.

'What do you like best?' Cale had asked. 'Girls or cake?'

Vague Henri had thought about this for a moment.

'I prefer . . .' he'd said at last. 'I prefer girls and cake together.'

8

When he'd finished killing John of Boston, Oswald hid the Carcano behind several sacks of wheat and made his way down the six flights of the grain silo stairs to the exit, where he was immediately challenged by a Federal alerted by several members of the public who'd heard the shots and seen a man at the sixth-storey window. But before Oswald could say anything his supervisor came into the room and told the Federal he worked at the silo and could not be involved. Who, after all, would plausibly believe that a mildly difficult but reliable employee they'd known for a year had just murdered one of history's great men? The Federal, deciding he'd arrived too quickly for the assassin to leave, was reassured by the supervisor's certainty and was anxious to clear the grain silo of those who had good reason to be there, and so he quickly shooed Oswald outside but told him to stay put for later questions.

Oswald interpreted this sensible move by the Federal as yet more evidence of his complete superiority over the Dallas police force, which had inflated in him after their failure to arrest him following his failed assassination of General Nixon. The Nixon suspect had been described as leaving on a horse, when in fact Oswald had been walking; and as being black-haired and over six feet tall, when he had pale brown hair and was a mere five feet eight. They'd also determined that the slug that missed the General was from a pistol.

All doubt and failure, all dread of insignificance had left him: the sacrifice of John of Boston had transformed him in a moment from a squirt into something imperishable; his soul began to magnify and swell, inciting him into Elm Street, urging him past the Thanksgiving Tower and blessing him along Pacific Avenue towards the boarding house rented for him by the governor where he was to wait for further instructions.

But the Tiny Ones now turned their attention from cutting the string of John of Boston's life to the man who had prompted them to get out the scissors. Five minutes after Oswald had floated away, lush with prestige, the Federal realized that the man he had told to stay outside was gone and that in some regards he fitted the description of the murderer he'd just been given by a fellow officer, based on reports by witnesses who had seen the shot from the silo window. Blessed with intelligence and an instinct for the shape of things, and inspired to act decisively, he ran to the mounted constables who had gathered in the Plaza in force and, taking his courage in his hands, identified Oswald with more certainty than he had any right to hold. The Captain of Horse, given confidence by the confidence of the Federal, ordered the dozen men to spread out in the direction another of the silo workers had seen him take. The city was already packed with Federals for the visit of John of Boston, and details of Oswald's appearance had spread a half a mile in front of him by the time he walked into the last street but one before the refuge he would never reach.

His height and slightness of build made Oswald easy to spot along a sparsely populated street. Only a few minutes before, a young Federal had been given his description. The sighting, almost immediately, of someone who matched the report, left the young and inexperienced Federal slightly unsure – it was too much of a coincidence and he allowed Oswald to pass and move on before he began to follow.

'Sir, could you wait up a minute?'

Oswald kept walking.

'Sir, I'm talking to you.'

Oswald stopped and half turned to the Federal, an affected look of puzzlement on his face. He smiled. 'Sorry, Officer. I didn't realize you were speaking to me.'

'Just a few questions, sir.'

'Sure.'

'Have you been anywhere near the grain silo on Elm Street?'

'Me? No. I just came out to buy some smokes. Something wrong?'

'Your address, sir.'

Oswald turned away and gestured. 'Boarding house on Ten Street.'

He started to move off, as if the conversation was over.

'Sir, I haven't finished talking to . . .'

With that, Oswald turned, taking the small double-barrel vest pistol from his pocket. He pointed it at the Federal, who raised his arms, mouth opening in alarm.

Oswald cocked the gun slowly and fired, hitting him in the chest. The officer fell to the pavement. Oswald stared at him for a moment and, seeing that he was badly wounded, turned and headed back in the direction he had been going before he was stopped. But then he turned again, aiming at the officer groaning in pain and trying to get up. With great composure, he cocked the weapon a second time, walked back about twenty feet towards the wounded man and pulled the trigger. It clicked but did not fire. The Federal tried to get to his feet, as if standing might save him. Oswald cocked the gun again, took aim and shot him through the head.

Five minutes later, having decided the boarding house was too close to the murder of the Federal, Oswald was on his way back into town when he turned the corner of Chula Vista and walked into a group of six policemen. He was immediately arrested.

9

In time, history will reveal that Thomas Cale's greatest and most enduring legacy was his work behind the scenes at the Versailles Conference. The agreement that he fashioned there has, perhaps, saved the lives of millions.

– Johan Lessing, *Versailles and Its Legacy* (Oxenford, ME 1994)

Nothing could more powerfully underscore Cale's failure to be anything more than an unusually bloody mixture of gangster and warlord than his inept handling of the negotiations at the Versailles Conference. His failure may have cost the lives of millions.

– Grace Dooley, *This Violent Peace: Legislative Failure after ME 1945* (Princestown, ME, 1997)

Lying on a filthy bed, snoring in the middle of some murky pipe dream, Thomas Cale visited the friends and lovers of the past: Vague Henri, Artemesia, both vanished and gone; and always, too, the old beasts: Bosco, Kitty the Hare, Stalovek.

And sooner or later, always the ghost of Arbell Materazzi passing by in his nightmares, staring at him full of indifference and contempt, passionately kissing another man, who was always different but always as beautiful as a young god. The jealousy burning under his skin, not into his heart but into his bowels, making him sweat, making him paler than dry grass, feeling as if his death was very near.

But that druggy afternoon, she saved his life. In time, you'll come to have some appreciation – or perhaps not – of why her appearance in his dreams created in him such rage that she woke him up.

A contributory factor, it should be said, was that the bellboy had increased his profits by cutting the bhang with cornflour. Otherwise, notwithstanding the enraging presence of Arbell in his dreams, Cale might have slept right through up until the moment the men who had come to kill him cut his throat.

At any rate, and whatever the multiplication of causes, he woke, bad-tempered and with an ugly taste in his mouth. Slowly, he sat up, stared balefully at yet another plate of scrambled eggs and polenta spiced with a congealed dollop of tomato paste and swallowed a cup of water to get the horrible taste of bad dreams and stale opium out of his mouth. His nightmares seemed to have leaked into the very air of the room.

His bladder was full enough that it hurt (perhaps this had helped to wake him up as well), and he went into the sectioned-off bog to take a leak. The boarding house must have seen very much better days sixty or seventy years ago. The bog was big enough for a bath, long gone, and once had a window above head height almost the length of the wall. To save on expensive glass it had been blocked off, and all that remained was an opening barely the size of a man's head, so there was hardly light enough to see where to piddle.

There was some pleasure in the relief of pain. He came back into the bedroom and its rancid air, went over to the window, opened it up on to a small balcony and clapped-out fire escape – also a sign of better days.

The room was at the back of the boarding house and overlooked an alley leading from the rear entrance. Just after he opened the window a man entered the alley, looked around for a moment and moved into a doorway. He took out a pistol, checked it and, satisfied, drew as far back into the shadow of the doorway as possible.

Cale ran to the table in the centre of the room and pulled out the two guns, the Fanshawes, given him by Van Owen. He opened the door, woodpecker fast, a quick look down the hall. No one. Holding a gun in each hand, he walked to the top of the stairs and looked down. He waited. Nothing. Decide: go back and try to make it down the fire escape, where his chances in the open were poor, or stay here unknown, where his killers were restricted in their movements and didn't know he was aware of them. A flight below, a cautious moving head appeared, paused then moved upward, tilting up as it did so.

But Cale had pulled back. He moved on again. A second man following, and a third. The third man saw Cale as he pecked his head over the bannister to take another look, shouted out a warning and fired upwards twice.

Decide: stay and fight on the stairs, where he had two single shots against three men, all with double-shot pistols? Or run. He turned and sprinted back to his room and locked the door, immediately blowing out the two oil lamps.

On the stairs, the men waited for a reload then warily moved up. It took them a full minute to reach the top floor. The corridor would only take two abreast. The two shortest men, crouching slightly with pistols pointed, moved on, with the third man behind them, big as well as tall, also pointing. Cautiously, they made their way to Cale's door. They whispered together about what to do next.

'Hey, chappie,' said the leader through the door. 'We just want to talk. We've got a job for you.'

No answer.

'Come on, chappie. We promise no harm. Just a chat.'

He did not expect to be believed – the tone mocked the soon-to-be dead.

The speaker gestured to the big man. He moved in front of the door and prepared to shoulder his way in. There was a loud bang from inside.

The big man stepped back, startled. The other two, alarmed, looked at each other, puzzled as to what to do next. A beat. The man to the right of the door, obviously in charge, gestured urgently to the big man to break it down. Rocking on his heels, he burst into life and hit the door with a loud thud, burst through and collapsed on the floor with a crash.

Instantly, pistols pointing, the other two came in behind him, professional in their caution, each scouring one side of the room, confident in the other to protect them on their blind side.

There was no one. Fearful, they double-checked, stepping through the room as cautious as you like. The window was slightly ajar. The leader walked over to it, considering the possibility that Cale was on the fire escape. Opening it, he called out.

'Peyton!'

'Yo!'

'See in'thang?'

'Nothing here, boss.'

Both men were now looking at the only place that Cale could be – the bog with its absent door.

They moved towards it as if walking barefoot over broken glass, the room lightly tainted with the smoking wicks of the two recently extinguished lamps. They came slowly to the empty doorframe. A pause. The second man took a deep breath, then, with great speed, ducked his head in and out of the door. Even in the dark his boss could see the wide eyes. Another pause. This time, gun through the door first, he put his head around the frame and kept it there, pistol aimed at the far corner.

'OK, boss.'

The other men, leery like, approached around his shoulder. Both waited, sizing things up, guns still pointing; then, guarded but relaxing, they walked into the jakes.

Cale was sitting on the floor against the far wall with his legs splayed out in front of him, the feet fallen to one side, ungainly. His right hand was holding the handle of a single-shot pistol and the barrel was shoved deep into his mouth. The wall and the left side of his head were covered in blood, skull and brains and, even in the deep gloom, they could see red dripping down one side of his face.

Involuntarily, their shoulders dropped and they began to breathe more easily. The boss nodded to his second to check the body out. Still careful, he moved over to the dead man and bent down to search his jacket for proof of who he was. To do so he had to squat in a narrow space between the jakes itself and Cale's dead body, and over-balanced.

As he did so, the dead man came to life, pulled the pistol out of his mouth and shot him through the chest. Dead pretty much instantaneously, he fell forward on to Cale, who used him as a shield as he raised his hidden left hand holding his second pistol and fired at the boss, too astonished to have moved. Not even Cale could miss from seven feet away and he hit him in the stomach. Screaming, the boss collapsed to the floor.

Cale was expecting the big man to come through the door now, and this was where Cale's lucky streak that day seemed certain to come to an end. He pushed the man still on top of him away and went to grab his only chance of dealing with the third man: this victim's loaded pistol. In death, a spasm had locked his grip on the handle and Cale had to scrabble at it desperately to free it. One second, two, three. The big man would be through the door and catch him defenceless. Four. Five.

But nothing.

Cale freed the pistol at last and stood up, holding the gun at the door. A few years ago, before the scag had drained his strength, he could have held the body in front of him as a shield. Not now. On the floor the wounded boss was groaning in agony.

'Uhh, uhh, uhh, uhh, uhh, uhh, uhh.' Cale stood on his hand and the gun slipped from his grasp. Pick it up or not? He did so and stepped over the groaning man. Then come out firing or take a look?

A swift look, then in and straight back out again. The big man, and he really was big – six foot six and twenty-five stone – stood quite still, staring at the door. At his feet a puddle of urine was forming.

Cale wondered whether to question him. No murderer so low in the pecking order would know anything. Cale shot him in the chest and he collapsed as if a stone axe had delivered the blow.

Cale walked to the window and eased it aside, staring down at the doorway in which the fourth man had hidden himself.

'Peyton!'

No reply.

'Peyton! I'm talking to you. One of your friends is still alive. Answer me, or I'll blow his head off.'

A pause. Then:

'What do you want?'

'I want you to deliver a message to the governor.'

'I don't know what the fuck you're talking about.'

'Tell him I'll be seeing him. You can do that, can't you, Peyton?'

Peyton was thinking. 'Sure. I'll tell him.'

'Off you go, then.'

Peyton didn't move.

'If you don't leave, Peyton, I'm gonna shoot your friend, and then I'm coming for you.'

Peyton made a run for it, charging like the clappers down the alley. Cale fired. And missed. He fired the second pistol. That missed too.

Peyton, unharmed, was gone.

Cale was not disappointed. It would have been a difficult shot even for someone who was any good. It didn't signify much. He could be out of the boarding house in two minutes. In fact, it took a little longer. He was calm enough, practised enough, to search the three men – the boss had died while he was trying to shoot Peyton. The search didn't reveal much, or indeed anything, but it gave him nearly $200 and a (fairly good) watch inscribed *To my loving husband, Monroe. When you see this, pray think of me.*

Before he left he went back into the jakes and washed off the congealed scrambled eggs and polenta stained with tomato paste he'd used to create the impression of blood and brains. For a few moments he considered the three dead bodies: people see what they expect to see.

10

To his surprise, the Federals did not ask Oswald Hidell anything about the assassination of John of Boston. This made Oswald uneasy that, for some reason, impossible to imagine, they had not made the obvious and vital connection. In fact, the Federals were still gathering evidence about Boston's death and were expecting a bigger picture of his assassination to emerge. It seemed to them impossible that a lone gunman could have been responsible: there must be second and third gunmen and a conspiracy. There be cabals and plotters behind the death of such a great person. For now, they decided to concentrate on the death of their colleague on Ten Street.

'Why did you kill Peace Officer Tippett?'

'A Federal got killed?'

Oswald asked this question with a little smirk on him that made the officer want to smash his face in.

'You know a Federal was shot because you shot him.'

'I haven't done anything to be ashamed of.'

'We have seven witnesses who saw you shoot Peace Officer Tippett.'

'I believe,' said Oswald, 'it is standard operating procedure to provide a suspect with a lawyer and to advise him of his rights. This is the United Estates, am I correct? The rule of law – heard of it?'

'You were seen shooting Peace Officer Tippett.'

'That, of course, is deliberately provocative. I was going about my lawful business and I was arrested. That's all I have to say because that's all there is to say. Except that I shall be taking the Federals to the court for brutality.'

But the Federal could see that, far from being indignant or frightened, the man in front of him wasn't sweating at all – he was calmer than all the people around him. He gave the impression that he knew he was smarter than everyone else and that he was going to play the present moment for all it was worth.

An hour later and with no further news of other gunmen, they decided to begin questioning Oswald about the death of the First Man. They brought in the gun found at the grain silo and placed it on the table.

'You killed John of Boston.'

'You seem to be much better informed than I.'

And so it went on. Inside, the place was packed with Federals and watchmen of various kinds. Outside, a large crowd had formed, but no one was clear if they were angry, in mourning or just nosy.

'We need to take him to the county jail. Clear out anyone you can't personally vouch for and let's be gettin' this thing over with.'

Half an hour later, handcuffed and with two Federals holding him by the arms, six or seven of them marched Oswald to the basement, where a black prison cab was waiting to take him away. Even if the officers had done as they were told and removed anyone they didn't know, the basement was still full of hacks. There were five newspapers in Dallas alone and already three had arrived from out of state in the six hours since John of Boston had been proclaimed dead. As they waited to go into the basement, one of the Federals holding Oswald taunted him.

'If anyone out there tries to shoot you, I hope they're as good a shot as you are, buster.'

Oswald was untouched. 'Don't be so melodramatic. No one's goin' to shoot me because they all want to know if I did it and why I did it.'

'I thought you were innocent.'

'I've done nothing to be ashamed of.'

'So you keep sayin'.'

'We're going!' called out the Federal in the lead, and the line moved into the basement. Shouts as Oswald arrived with a holding Federal on either side.

'Did you kill John of Boston?'

'BACK UP! BACK UP!'

'Did you shoot him?'

'Clear a way! There! Damn you!'

'Did you shoot John of Boston?'

'I've done nothing, nothing to be ashamed of.' A look of exasperated and innocent patience.

'Did you shoot . . .'

The Federal holding Oswald by his right elbow saw a man stepping towards them out of the rows of shouting hacks. He was holding a pistol that hung down flat to his left leg.

The Federal jerked back on Oswald's arm, trying to protect him by putting him behind his body, but in the tight space and with Oswald's left arm held by the other Federal, all he succeeded in doing was to turn the prisoner's body into the approaching man so that he presented a bigger target. Oswald, seeing in that second what was happening, tried to draw his hands in front of his body to protect himself. As he raised the pistol, the man yelled, 'You killed my man, you hound!' and fired. There was a loud bang and Oswald's face puckered into a wince of terrible pain.

'Ooooohwwwww.' He fell backwards, pulling the two Federals on top of him. 'Aaah.'

'He's been shot!'

'He's been shot!'

The cry went around the basement like a peal of cracked bells.

'Hidell's been shot!'

FILED
Plurus Superior Court
Brumaire 33
Clerk of the Court

THE INTERNATIONAL CRIMINAL COURT OF THE HANSE

From the records of a case of alleged war crimes and crimes against humanity committed in the context of armed conflict by Thomas Cale between ME 1942 and ME 1956 (when the Maastricht Statute entered into force).

BLANDINO & SMI STATUTORY DEFENCE ADVOCATES

Dear Piggers

Thanks for your letter of the 34th instant.

Delusional as always, your confidence in the case against Thomas Cale is based on a mixture of bias, fairy tale and the malice of his enemies. Every time we examine the actual details of the claims made against him what emerges, at the very least, is far more complex than the pantomime villain of popular legend. In many cases he turns out to be, if not necessarily the hero of the situation (not even his admirers – and there are more of them than you imply – would accuse him of heroism), then barely connected with atrocities for which he is widely held to be the chief perpetrator. The massacre of seven thousand officers of the Hanse Expeditionary Force in the Karakan forest was not only not supervised by Cale, there is now unambiguous documentary evidence of his being two thousand miles away in Moscow at that time. The formal evidence will be supplied to you in due course, but I'd just like to take this opportunity to spill the wind out of your sails. Let me repeat, this is an increasing pattern with regard to the allegations against my client.

In the matter of the alleged conspiracy against Conn Materazzi outlined by the Materazzi government-in-exile, I've been taking evidence from Albert Kleist, a close associate of Cale's from as far back as his days in the Sanctuary. He claims that while Cale couldn't abide the late Conn, he had an attack of conscience and decided against perjuring himself at Conn's trial for dereliction over the defeat at Bex (as he'd been bribed to do, according to Kleist). During the trial Cale even went as far as defending Conn's decisions during the battle. But he quickly realized Conn was beyond help and that he was just damaging his own chances of advancement. After such an enormous disaster, there had to be a sacrifice. Accuse Cale of hard-boiled pragmatism by all means, but not of murder. Up to a point, I'd say he behaved pretty well.

As for him laughing at Conn Materazzi's execution, my witness says Cale was on top of the bell tower of Carfax – too far up for anyone to see what he was doing. The claim of conspiracy from the MGE is a horse that won't run, so you can drop it with a clear conscience – if you have one, that is.

Would the 38th do for Quag's?

Love to Decca

Yours

Bolly

11

Whatever doesn't kill you makes you stronger. It was a phrase that had always irked Cale. For one thing, it was an expression enthusiastically touted mostly by people who hadn't endured much suffering of any sort, let alone the kind that kills. For another, his considerable experience of deadly anguish had led him to the conclusion that while surviving the adversity that came close to destroying you certainly would toughen you up, it would also injure you in some correspondingly unpleasant manner. Broken bones that hadn't put you in the grave mended, wounds from injuries that hadn't killed you healed – but they left you with chronic pain and joints that ached when the weather was bad, or for no reason at all. So late at night, unable to sleep, lying next to some weary tart or one-night-stand, he would try to modify the saying so that it chimed more closely with real experience – something he set great store by, especially his own. So far, he had come up with: *Whatever doesn't kill you makes you strong in some ways but weaker in others.* While it was not as dapper as the original, he felt it more than made up for this by being factually accurate. Mostly, people regarded facts as awkward, plain at best and frequently horrible; and if not horrible, then grotesque; and if not grotesque, then revolting; and if not revolting, then unspeakable. 'People are atephiles, Thomas,' IdrisPukke used to say. He would then pause. 'What is the origin of the word "atephile", young man?' Cale would sigh with boredom and intone, 'Ate is the goddess of illusion; *philautia* is the ancient Greek word for "self-love" and "vanity". An atephile is someone who is infatuated with their own ideas and ignores anything that contradicts them. When it comes to the comforting legend over the ugly fact, atephiles must have the legend.'

'Go on.'

Another sigh from Cale.

'"Atephobia" is from the ancient Greek *phobos*, "to run away from". An atephobe is someone who fears living in a state of delusion.'

'And . . . ?'

Another sigh.

'All people who are to be taken seriously must cultivate atephobia. Atephobes are very rare and should be listened to above all others.'

It may come as no surprise to you that both these words had been invented by Idrispukke and that he spent much of his adult life attempting to promote their widespread usage. It may also come as no surprise to you that this attempt was a complete failure.

Cale's situation, looking at it neither optimistically nor gloomily, was hopeless. He had money and a head start, although having a head start implied a direction towards a possible place of safety, and there wasn't one. As a result, it was hard to know whether the news he discovered soon after escaping the boarding house really made things much worse. As he walked down the street he saw a newspaper stand on the opposite side and a group of people buying in a kind of frenzy. As one of them left, broadsheets in hand, he could see the oversize headline on the front page of the *Dallas Sun*.

GOT YA!
JOHN OF BOSTON'S SLAYER CUT DOWN

He joined the pack of buyers, bought a sheet and, head down, headed for a Hobo Highboy, a benevolence shop that sold clapped-out clothes to the indigent.

It was not a part of Dallas where it was difficult to find a dark alley to hide. He made a shutter behind some offal bins whose smell would drive most living creatures away, loaded the pair of double shots, took out his knife then changed into the clothes he'd just bought from the thrift shop.

Truisms usually get that way by being true, and when Cale woke just before dawn he felt all too deeply the dark and miserable nature of his situation. Clearly, Van Owen had always intended to have him killed and, thinking objectively, this was a reasonable strategy, as long as you weren't Thomas Cale. It was not clear to Cale, however, what action to take. Going back on the run was not an attractive proposition, given that now he'd have an estate governor after his blood (not forgetting the very large number of others who wanted him captured or dead – though these were in no way mutually exclusive). And if Oswald talked, then he'd have the Federals following close behind. And it was this that decided him. He could see only one way ahead, and it was depressingly difficult and dangerous.

The fifteen- (or fourteen-) year-old who had escaped the horrors of the Sanctuary and made it to success as the bodyguard of the beautiful and powerful Arbell Materazzi – that gorgeous, treacherous bitch – would have been better equipped to be here now than his certainly wiser, kinder, infinitely more rounded but worn-out and drug-addicted present incarnation. But then again, he was not the boy he used to be.

Pulling his newly acquired and grubby cap low down on his head, he made his way out into the street and bought coffee and a slice in the nearby market and read through that day's broadsheet, which had more news, none of it useful, on Oswald's shooting and on the announcement that John of Boston was to be replaced by Abrahan Lincoln. It was traditional among the cynical to ask of any murder: who benefitted? Mr Abrahan Lincoln, clearly. But except in passing there was no significant mention of Governor Van Owen besides recording the expected platitudes on the late Chancellor '. . . *great man . . . we had our differences . . . national tragedy . . . no stone unturned . . .*'

Cale walked on, ruminating on a question, both on his own behalf and, more pleasantly, on behalf of Louis Van Owen, that used to be asked every night by a redeemer before the boys in the Sanctuary escaped into sleep: *What if you should die tonight?*

The walls around his recent employer's estate had once been intimidating but had been modified to suit a place which was now more of a big house than a fortress. The changes had been done well if your judgement was based on principles of elegance, but badly if you consider the purpose of walls to keep people with evil thoughts on their mind on the outside. I could tell you of the derring-do of Cale's act of breaking and entering, the swashbuckling, the climbing and guard-dodging, the narrow escapes and cunning ingenuity but, being wise, you know the sort of thing. Let's say that half an hour brought him to the door of Louis Van Owen's apartment.

He listened at the door. Nothing. He turned the ornate handle, whose every cog and spring screeched out a warning, as if personally affronted at Cale's illegal entry. He kept going – too late now. He pushed gently and the hinges squeaked their alarm. He slipped in and drew his pistol and a knife. He was in a spacious hall of what was clearly a large apartment within the mansion. In the days not so long ago, when Cale occupied such places, he didn't just lock his bedroom door but every door on the way to the bedroom, and made sure that there were two lines of guards: one inside, one outside. He was surprised Van Owen was so careless with his own safety. It implied he was unused to evildoing. If he were, he would have realized that what you could do to others, others could do to you.

He approached the door into what would be the living room. It was ajar – mentally, Cale shook his head. He listened for a moment and, very slowly, as if he were no more than the wind, pushed the door wider. He listened again. Nothing. Then another of those woodpecker darts of the head. No one there. Then another, longer look. Light in the room came from a log fire in an enormous, absurdly elaborate fireplace big enough to hold a town meeting or roast an elephant. He moved into the room, over-decorated in the way of the rooms of the wealthy from Memphis to Timbuctoo: stuffed with things meant to reassure the owner of his own good taste, despite the fact that, mostly, the artefacts had been chosen by someone else. He could now hear something, alarming because he could not place the sound – a muffled slapping, a pause, then another, and every now and then a murmur he could also not place. It was coming from behind one of the doors at the far end of the room. Again he moved forward, following his knife and pistol, all the time, the odd combination of sounds continuing with the same rhythm. At the door he stopped to listen: the same disconcertingly unfamiliar noises. The muffled thud now had an edge he also couldn't place. He tried the handle. It was a much more delicate affair than the one into the apartment and moved soundlessly.

'Bollocks!'

This was shouted, of course, only in his mind. The door was locked. But this was an elegant construction in a pretentious apartment and not really built to keep out an assault by your determined type of desperado. Restrained violence would do it. He placed his shoulder a foot from the door, snapped the handle downwards and shoved hard. It gave way more easily than he expected and he was inside the room without having made too much of a racket. Three remarkably odd things presented themselves to him.

The first was Governor Van Owen. He was strapped, hands and feet, to a large wooden frame on castors and dressed as a milkmaid, the dress tucked up around his waist. Around his knees were a pair of white bloomers. His buttocks were a livid red, almost approaching the vermilion bottom of a mandrill Cale had once observed in Memphis Zoo as a boy. The cause of the blushing rump dotted with spots of blood and the odd slappy sound was a broad leather paddle studded with small metal pins. The strap was held in the immaculately manicured hand of the second odd sight: a woman, blonde hair piled high and arranged in plaits that only some hair sculptor of unusual genius could have created. She was wearing a fabulous red dress of silk, decorated with semi-precious stones and enough on its own to astonish at any imperial ball. But what made it odd as opposed to astonishing was that the front of the dress was not. That is to say, the front of the dress did not exist.

The work of a dressmaker of both great technical skill and great filthiness of mind, it had been designed to allow her breasts to be revealed in all their natural peaks and curves and counterpoints of pink, rosy and pale, and the nipples, with the benefit of rouge, were an enticing cherry red.

Though beautiful, she was not young, but the skill of the tailor in drawing a transparent sash across the swell of her rounded tum did not try to disguise her little pot but by cradling and lightly veiling her tummy only made her seem more shapely. Below this sash the garment split again but slashed to meet when she was still, so only in moving would she reveal what Van Owen called her rosebud underneath, dusted as it was with powdery talcum mixed with cochineal.

But neither the bound man in a dress nor the lascivious costume of the woman with the paddle was what most astonished Cale: it was that Cale and the woman had met before.

This was a great many startling things to take in at one time, but being recognized was a matter of life and (a very unpleasant) death.

The woman was Dorothy Rothschild, known as much for her astuteness as for being El Grande Horizontal – a term which in no way implied disapproval, except, of course, from the usual list of mugwumps and finger-waggers.

She gave absolutely no sign of recognizing Cale. This was not necessarily reassuring. Cale knew very well that Dorothy was the kind of woman who would tell Death himself when he came for her that she was far too busy to see him now and that he should write to her secretary for an appointment. While she might have been pretending not to know him, and doing so remarkably well, she was not entirely able to hide her fear. He gestured her over to the frame that held the tightly restrained Van Owen. While realizing something alarming had happened, he was facing towards the wall and could see nothing of the action.

'What's going on? Dorothy? What's going on?'

Cale signalled Dorothy to turn the frame around. As she did so he put the unpleasant business of murdering the innocent aside in order to enjoy the moment of revelation. He was not disappointed. The mixture of astonishment and horror that passed over Governor Van Owen's face was exquisitely yummy.

But he brought himself quickly under control: in seconds, the smooth, ironic, subtle look of cool and effortless command returned. Cale was impressed.

'Ah, Mr Savio,' said Van Owen amicably, as if he were not strapped hand and wrist to a wooden frame, dressed in a milkmaid's outfit and with a pair of bloomers around his knees. 'You have me at a disadvantage.'

Whatever style was, thought Cale, this was it. Not to be outdone, Cale acted as if there was nothing at all to be remarked upon about the situation.

'Sorry I didn't let you know I'd be dropping in. There wasn't time to get to the post office.'

They looked only at each other's faces, Cale, in particular, refusing to take in the unsettling apparition before him. It was not that he was a prude, but what man wants to be presented so graphically with the strange desires of another man? Dorothy Rothschild was old and wise enough to stay completely still.

'I know what you're thinking,' said Van Owen.

'I very considerably doubt that,' said Cale. 'But before we go on I think it would be in the interests of your friend if she were not involved.'

'I'll be going then,' said Dorothy.

'Afraid not,' said Cale.

'Are you going to kill him?' she asked, pretty calmly, considering.

'He certainly deserves it.'

'Are you going to kill me?' A certain catch in her throat beneath the apparent composure.

'Why would I do that?'

'You look,' she said, 'like a very killing gentleman.'

'You shouldn't judge a book by its cover.'

'But people usually do,' she said. 'So I'd say there was something in it.'

'I grant you that – and also that my appearance here, armed to the teeth, well . . . it's reasonable to be concerned. But what can I say to reassure you? Except that while I have killed frequently, it is only rarely that I've done so with pleasure.' He looked her over (her face, that is; this was no time for gawping, however tempting), hoping very much to find a reason not to kill her. But it was hard to do so. The words of IdrisPukke came back to him, as they always did in such circumstances, where the law of survival met the appeal of kindness. *Always resist your first impulses, Thomas, they are often generous.*

IdrisPukke would, of course, have been appalled that Cale was even considering killing an innocent woman. But then *his* life was not the one at risk. If Dorothy realized he was Thomas Cale, she was a terrifying threat. If he killed Van Owen, she was a terrifying threat. On the first count, he was reassured. He was beginning to doubt whether even such a talented dissembler as Dorothy could hide recognizing him so completely. Her conversation would, surely, have given her away just a fraction. He could read a lie as easily as if it were a book for slow children. It was no accident he'd managed to stay alive so very long.

She did not know him. And this complete and absolute certainty began a process which was to have the most terrible consequences. Inside him, a scintilla of a spark landed upon the parched dead leaves buried deep in one of the dry sumps of his heart.

'As you can see,' he said to Dorothy, in his most matter-of-fact I'm-being-straight-with-you-so-you-can-trust-my-blunt-manner-of-speaking style, 'I'm the kind of person' – he gestured to her with a smile – 'the kind of killing gentleman who can get to anyone. This means I can certainly get to you if you speak about what you've seen here tonight. Do you give me your word?'

'Yes.'

'Very well. I'm going to put you in that cupboard and lock the door and you are going to say nothing when you're let out. Is that clear?'

'Yes.'

'And do you understand the consequences of breaking your promise to me?'

'Yes.'

'Then we have an agreement.' He gestured her towards the large and heavy tallboy in the corner of the room. She looked at Van Owen.

'I'm asking you not to kill him.'

'It speaks well of you, being under such peril yourself, that you'll stand up for another. Let me tell you, frankly, I admire it. But he's a dead man. And my advice to you is not to say another word in case you talk yourself into the ground along with him.'

Silently, she made her way over to the tallboy and stepped up into its cavernous space. Cale closed it behind her and locked the door. He walked back to Van Owen.

'Now, what were you saying?'

'I realize,' said Van Owen, 'that I'm not in your best books.' The attempt at humour was undermined by a failed attempt to swallow as he spoke. 'But I'm asking you not to hurt her. She's a very sensible woman – indeed, astonishingly wise. She won't say anything.'

'Goodness,' said Cale. 'We're all being so self-sacrificing, we three. I wonder if I should let her out, cut you down and we all hold hands and sing a nice hymn – how about "He That is Low Need Fear No Fall"? You know, something uplifting before the unpleasantness to follow.'

'I didn't have anything to do with killing Oswald.'

'Your point being that it follows you didn't try to have me killed either.'

Van Owen looked, thought Cale, sincerely astonished at this. 'I don't know anything about this. I swear it.'

The control had almost completely deserted Van Owen now. *Could this be true?* thought Cale. *But not a chance.*

'Tell me what happened,' said a desperate Van Owen. 'A few minutes more won't hurt. You'll believe me if I tell you there's an absolute pain-of-death order not to come in here at night.'

'Keep your voice down. Neither of us wants your guest in the cupboard earwigging on any of this.' Cale, not in any way looking to be convinced of the ridiculous notion that Oswald's murder and the attempt on his own life were coincidences, was prepared to listen for two reasons: first, that he was curious to hear what on earth Van Owen was going to say to save himself, and second, because a dangerous voice was whispering mad words into his ear.

The human soul is not a single entity; it is best regarded as a family, happy or unhappy, as the case may be. The husband and wife in this ghostly inner household may be a loving couple or they may not have spoken to each other for years. The children may be handsome and beautiful or dwarfish and ill-tempered; they may love and obey their parents or barely tolerate them. Unlike a family of flesh and blood, however, these spirit people can never leave. This inability of the soul to abandon bits of itself is the source of all the trouble in the world. The dwarf brother and the sister queen, the bored husband and the disappointed wife, the idiot cousin and the lunatic son are yoked for ever until they part at death. And right up until the last moment every one of them, no matter how ugly, no matter how despised by the others, no matter if they have been shunned to the attic or the basement, damp and unvisited, all of them are waiting for the chance to have their say.

It was one of these basement-dwelling spirit goblins that was murmuring in Cale's inner ear and had been doing so from the moment it realized that Dorothy Rothschild did not know him from Adam. The last time they had met was in a vast ballroom in Spanish Leeds where Cale, still only fifteen or so, had been guest of honour for some empire-saving victory over someone or other. Eye-poppingly gorgeous twenty years ago, she was both the most famous courtesan in the Four Quarters and its most accomplished informant. But Dorothy had not recognized him. She had seen him every other day for months when he had been the observed of all observers, the bright hope of the age, hated and feared and relied on in equal measure. But the woman who never missed anything had not recognized him. In the soul-prison that held one of his maddest dwarfs, the lock turned and let this inner hobgoblin loose to whisper a lunatic and abscessed song that in a moment had taken the reins of his sanity and would not be denied.

'Go on,' said Cale to Van Owen.

'Cut me down, if you wouldn't mind.'

A pause.

'Why not?'

The truth was that looking at the governor with his bloomers around his knees was putting him off. He'd had enough of Van Owen's inner world. Dorothy must be very agreeable to put up with this and still be ready to speak up for him.

He cut Van Owen down and watched, admiring his composure, as he walked without rushing across the room and put on a magnificent dressing gown. In a moment he was transformed back into the governor who had so skilfully arranged the death of John of Boston and set in train the vanishing of the perpetrators of that dreadful act.

Cale looked him over, smiling. 'Truly, Satan, thou art a dunce, and cannot tell the garment from the man.'

'Sexual desire,' replied Van Owen, 'is a terrifying leveller.'

'A bit like death,' said Cale. 'Sorry to disappoint you. But then you recently tried to have me killed.'

'I did not.'

'You can say it, but it's hard to believe. I'm sure you understand.'

'I do. Of course it looks bad. All I can say is that it wasn't me.'

'It's just a coincidence?'

'I seem to remember you saying life is full of them. And there's a long queue of people who want you dead, you have to admit that.'

'I accept it's possible,' said Cale reasonably, 'though unlikely. But this isn't a court of law, I can't be balancing the evidence here, just the probabilities – and it's the probabilities that are going to kill you.'

'Kill me and there's no haven in the Bermudas.'

'It was a golden dream, but now I'm awake. I think I'll be more secure sorting things out myself than giving myself up to your tender mercies.'

'What can I do to persuade you?'

'Nothing.'

Cale could see the cold settling around the heart of the man opposite. It takes a while, at least a few seconds in his experience, for the really terrible things in life to become actually touchable, for understanding to make its presence felt on the pulse. He let the blood beating in Van Owen's veins become thready with the inevitability of eternal extinction. 'Unless.'

With these two syllables the exhausted lungs of despair burst with the fresh air of invigorating hope. Cale let Van Owen gasp and heave on the shore of deliverance for a moment.

'These are my conditions. Try and negotiate with me and I'll kill you just out of irritation. Understand? You will deposit $50,000 in an account I've set up at the Wells Bank. You will provide me with all the necessary documents to support the identity of the name of that account. You will sign a letter confessing to conspiracy in the murder of John of Boston. You will provide me with all assistance whenever I should require it, and swiftly. And finally' – and this was where the great insanity that had always stalked through the life of Thomas Cale made its latest entry – 'you'll find a place for me at Malfi.'

The first demand was outrageous. The second banal. The third terrifying. But the fourth was incomprehensible.

'I don't understand,' said Van Owen. 'Malfi is in the middle of the Estate. Why would you want to go there?'

'Curiosity killed the cat,' said Cale. 'I do, and that's all there is to it. I don't want anything important, as in a job I mean, but I may come back to you on that from time to time.'

'But if there are other people trying to kill you – and there are – why don't you want to get out of the country?'

'If they followed me here, as you claim, they can follow me there. But as long as I'm here with my little piece of paper guaranteeing your peace of mind as long as I'm still alive, it seems to me that I'm better off where someone really powerful and deeply motivated concerning my welfare can keep an eye on me.'

These were, in fact, pretty good reasons. It was just that they had absolutely nothing to do with why he had decided to stay, a decision born of Dorothy Rothschild's complete inability to recognize him.

'About the signed paper,' said Van Owen. 'What if something happens to you and it's nothing to do with me?'

'You're fucked.'

12

In their search to discover whether or not Thomas Cale was the Left Hand of God (an incarnation of the deity created to destroy sinful mankind), at the age of sixteen months the Redeemers isolated him in a stone cell. The same conditions were applied to a dozen other children of a similar age who had also been recently taken from their mothers. No one in authority talked to them for six months. Food was delivered through a small opening in the cell door. One hour a week, the children were released into a common area and allowed to meet. Within a month, the children stopped playing together or talking to one another. Two of the children starved themselves to death by refusing to eat. On their release, the surviving children continued to show signs ranging from general sadness to terrible anguish. Three recovered adequately enough to be reinstated into Redeemer life. Thomas Cale seemed not to have been affected, except that he developed a habit of avoiding the company of others. The fate of the other children is not recorded.

–Sister Althea Wray, *The Well of Despair: Soul Murder in the Very Young*

Proceedings of the Society of Somatists (Ventose, ME 1948)

Sister Althea Wray [pron: rei]

From the Vikipedia Albionis **Philosophy of**

A somatist or mind doctor, Sister Wray angered many mind-therapeutists by warning of the dangers of kindness and compassion when treating patients. All too easily, she claimed, mind therapy became for the patient 'a crutch made out of pity'. But it was also a snare for the doctor in that it fed their need to be admired by the patient for their healing wisdom while at the same time feeding their purses for months and even years. Wray claimed to have solved this problem by always carrying a ventriloquist's dummy with her that was often harsh and critical of the patient while Wray was (largely) gentle and kind. In this way, the patient could be both cared for and wisely prepared for the pain of becoming healthy. No physical therapeutist, said Wray, could return a patient's badly broken leg to full function without causing sometimes severe pain, 'and the human body is the best picture of the human soul'.

Anna Freud (founder of Freudunism) described Wray's practices as a 'sadistic' attack on patients and a 'slander' on mind therapeutists.

'Come in,' said Sister Wray. It was a soft and attractive welcome. The servant opened the door and stood back from Cale, ushering the boy forward. 'I'll be back in an hour exactly,' he said, and pulled the door shut.

There were two large windows to the boy's right which flooded the room with light and, at the far side, sitting by the fire in a high-backed chair that looked comfortable enough to live in, was a woman. Even sitting down, Cale could see she was more than six feet tall, notably taller than Cale himself. Sister Wray was covered from head to foot in what looked like black cotton. Even her eyes were covered with a thin strip of material in which there were numerous small holes to allow her to see. Strange as all this was, there was something much stranger: in her right hand and resting on her lap was some sort of doll. Had one of the children in Memphis been holding it, he would not have noticed – the Materazzi girls often had dolls that were spectacularly splendid to behold, with madly expensive costumes for every kind of occasion from a marriage to tea with the duke. This doll was rather larger, with clothes of grey and white and a simply drawn face without any expression at all.

'Come and sit down.' Again the pleasant voice, warm and good-humoured. 'Can I call you Thomas?'

'No.'

There was a slight nod, but who could know of what kind? The head of the doll, however, moved slowly to look in his direction.

'Please sit.' But the voice was still all warmth and friendliness, completely discounting his appalling rudeness. He sat down, the doll still watching and – though how, he thought, could it be so? – taking a pretty dim view of what she was looking at.

'I'm Sister Wray. And this,' she said, moving her covered head slightly to look at the puppet on her lap, 'is Poll.'

Cale stared balefully at Poll and Poll stared balefully back. 'What shall we call you, young man?'

'Everybody calls me sir.'

'That seems a little formal. Can we agree on Cale?'

'Suit yourself.'

'What a horrible little boy.'

It was not especially difficult to surprise Cale, no more than most people, but it was no easy thing to make him show it. It was not the sentiment that widened his eyes – he had, after all, been called a lot worse – but the fact it was the puppet who said it. The mouth didn't move, because it wasn't made to, but the voice most definitely came from the puppet and not Sister Wray.

'Be quiet, Poll,' she said, and turned slightly to face Cale. 'You mustn't pay any attention to her. I'm afraid I've indulged her and, like many spoilt children, she has rather too much to say for herself.'

'What am I here for?'

'You've been very ill. I read the report prepared by the assessor when you arrived.'

'The killy-cornered half-wit that got me locked up with all the headbangers?'

'She does seem to have got the wrong end of the stick.'

'Well, I'm sure she's been punished. No? What a surprise.'

'We all make mistakes.'

'Where I come from, when you make a mistake something bad happens – usually involving a lot of screaming.'

'I'm sorry.'

'What's there for you to be sorry about? Were you responsible?'

'No.'

'So, what are you going to do to make me all right again?'

'Talk.'

'Is that it?'

'No. We'll talk, and then I'll be better able to decide what medicines to prescribe, if that seems called for.'

'Can't we drop the talk and just get to the medicine?'

'I'm afraid not. Talk first, medicine after. How are you today?'

He held up his hand with the missing finger. 'It's acting up.'

'Often?'

'Once a week, perhaps.'

She looked at her notes. 'And your head and shoulder?'

'They do their best to fill in when my hand isn't hurting.'

'You should have had a surgeon look at you. There was a request, but it seems to have gone missing. I'll sort out something for the pain.'

For half an hour she asked questions about his past, from time to time interrupted by Poll. When Cale, with some relish, told her he had been bought for sixpence Poll had called out, 'Too much.' But mostly the questions were simple and the answers grim, though she didn't dwell on any of them, and soon they were discussing the events of the night Gromek was killed and Kevin Meatyard escaped. When he'd finished she wrote for some time on the several small sheets of paper resting on her left knee as Poll leaned over them and tried to read, and was pushed repeatedly out of the way like a naughty but much loved dog.

'Why,' asked Cale, as Sister Wray took a couple of silent minutes to finish writing and Poll took to staring at him malevolently, although he also knew this could not be so, 'why don't you treat the nutters in the ward? Not enough money?'

Sister Wray's head moved upright, away from her work. 'The people in that ward are there because their madness is of a particular kind. People are sick in the head in as many ways as they're sick in the body. You wouldn't try to talk a broken leg into healing and some breaks in the mind are almost the same. I can't do anything for them.'

'But you can do something for me?'

'I don't know. That's what I'm trying to find out.'

'If you'd let her, you naughty boy.'

'Be quiet, Poll.'

'But it's right.' An unattractive little smirk from Cale. 'I *am* a naughty boy.'

'So I understand.'

'I've done terrible things.'

'Yes.'

There was a silence.

'What happens if the people paying for me stop?'

'Then your treatment will stop as well.'

'Not very nice.'

'I don't understand.'

'Just stopping – when I'm still sick.'

'Like everyone else, I must eat and have somewhere to live. I'm not part of the order that runs the Priory. They'll keep you in a charity ward, but if I stop paying my way, they'll turf me out.'

'Yes,' said Poll. 'We haven't had Redeemers to look after us all our lives.'

This time Poll went uncorrected.

'What if I don't like you?' said Cale. He had wanted to come up with a stinging reply to Poll but couldn't think of one.

'What,' said Sister Wray, 'if I don't like *you*?'

'Can you do that?'

'Not like you? You seem very determined that I don't.'

'I mean decide not to treat me if you don't like me.'

'Does that worry you?'

'I've got a lot of things to worry about in my life – not being liked by you isn't one of them.'

Sister Wray laughed at this – a pleasant, bell-like sound.

'You like answering back,' she said. 'And I'm afraid it's a weakness of mine as well.'

'You have weaknesses?'

'Of course.'

'Then how can you help me?'

'You've met a lot of people without weaknesses?'

'Not so many. But I'm unlucky that way. Vague Henri told me I shouldn't judge people by the fact that I've been unfortunate enough to come across so many shit-bags.'

'Perhaps it's not just luck.' Her tone was cooler now.

'What's your drift?'

'Perhaps it's not just a matter of chance, the dreadful people and the dreadful things that have happened to you.'

'You still haven't said what you mean.'

'Because I don't know what I mean.'

'She means you're a horrible little shit who stirs up trouble wherever he goes.' Yet again, Poll went uncorrected and Sister Wray changed the subject.

'Is Vague Henri a friend of yours?'

'You don't have friends in the Sanctuary, just people who share the same fate.' This was not entirely true but, for some reason, he wanted to appal her.

PART II
Malfi

'To Carthage then I came, where a cauldron of unholy loves sang all about mine ears.'

– *Confessions*, Augustine of Hippo

13

In the Four Quarters of the globe what person of taste reads a book from the United Estates or goes to see one of their execrable pantoperas? Who looks at an American picture or statue? What does the world yet owe to American physicians or surgeons? What new substances have the chemists of the United Estates discovered? The only thing of note about them is their vile hippocrisy in claiming to be the land of the free while also asserting that millions of the dark races of Africa are fit only to be owned like cattle.

– Dr Sydney Smith-Johnson, in *The Edinburgh Review*

Malfi! Legendary place it was – Xanadu, the Camelot, the White City, Babylon, Zion and Westernesse all rolled up into one extraordinary place. Here the greatest scientists of the age found money as well as refuge, musicians thrived, writers blossomed, philosophers ate at the best tables. Malfi was the fountain and the origin of the American naissance that would light the time to come. And all of it because of one woman. The owner of Malfi was, in all but name, a queen. But this is too infinitely small a title to describe the magnanimity of that elevated mind and soul: she was the Empress of the new Enlightenment itself. She is introduced here with so many striking designates, though she was known to Thomas Cale by only two: Arbell Materazzi.

Cale stood in front of these gates, having slouched towards Malfi possessed by as many emotions as might be found in a Vikipedia of the passions. Now, in the middle of his life, Cale found himself in a dark wood: the few paths lead nowhere, the light is thick and deceptive, the guides absent or unreliable, no ball of thread to give him clues. Intelligence or courage is of little value here; only the instincts (intense, treacherous) drive him through this terrible wilderness, fleeing from his old self, ignorant of a new. To Malfi and Arbell Materazzi Thomas Cale has come. What does he expect to find here? An explanation? A plea for forgiveness? A scream of terror? But what if, what if . . . at the moment of the great reveal, he is welcomed with every wronged lover's dread – the traitor who laid waste their very soul looks at them and says: S*orry, do I know you?*

Cale was not the only person coming to Malfi full of hope and fear. A couple of dozen arrived every day, looking to get their foot in the door, wet their beaks, elbow their way into a share of what was on offer at this most golden of troughs: Malfi! Land of opportunity for anyone, regardless, who wanted to make something more of themselves. The now-forgotten philosopher Willam Slief, perhaps fearing that if he were understood people might not be so impressed by his intelligence, was notorious for his obscurity of language and verbose turn of phrase. But there is one observation he made that may even be profound. (Poets may regard the metaphor he coined to describe human existence as somewhat laboured or clumsy (impedimental, peccant, coucicouci) but, happily, no one reads poets or listens to what they have to say any more.) Slief's one contribution to human understanding seems (possibly) to be this.

*All human life is like a windmill that works only because of a paradox. One part of it is fixed in the ground and must not move. The other, the sails of the windmill, are ever moving in response to a wind that is, over the course of a day, a month, a year, ever changing from gentle to ferocious. A windmill is always fixed, always moving – and in this tension and this tension alone lies its nature. Our human nature is the same, he (*probably*) argued. To claim that human nature is fixed is wrong. To claim that it is always changing is wrong. It is, like the windmill, to be defined by the relationship between the always fixed and the constantly shifting.*

One of these metaphors was making his way along the last half-mile towards Malfi. He was a black man in his early twenties, one Ray Jackson. His fixed human nature lay in the fact that he was a young man going out into the world to find out who he was and what could be done with that world to make him happy, in just the way that young men have always done and must always do. So what was the new force in the affairs of men that blew him here? More of that later – except to say that this wind brought with it the three hideous sisters (menacious, ferine, rod-in-the-pickle) skipping along behind him.

The Philadelphia Inquirer.

THE NATION CONTINUES TO MOURN
JOHN OF BOSTON!

Chicago Tribune.

ANTI-SOUTHERN RIOTS!!

Charleston Daily Courier.

BOSTON'S DEATH A BLOW TO
NORTHERN ANTI-SLAVERS

The New-York Times.

A SECOND ASSASSIN???
SOUTHERN SLAVERS BLAMED!!!!

Daily National Intelligencer.

CONSPIRACY RUMOURED!!!!

SOUTH REJECTS CLAIMS AS 'VILE'!!!!!

14

It had been a month since the death of John of Boston – and Oswald – and there were as many theories about the pair as there were bubbles at a children's party, and about as substantial: the murderer acted on his own; the murderer was only the tip of a conspiracy involving almost everyone. So desperate was the government under its reviled new Chancellor that it did what all governments do when faced with confusion and a lack of answers: a commission to look into who was responsible was set up under the chairmanship of the highly respected judge Vivian Phinersee (highly respected by the government because he could be relied on not to report for years and to come up with a finding that caused as little in the way of controversy as possible).

Given that, sooner or later, the name of Thomas Cale would come up as being involved in anything monstrous, it was surprising there was not even the slightest mention of his name in regard to the death of John of Boston. After all, he'd been denounced without the slightest evidence for ordering the death of Trotskii, the treacherous attack on Pearl Haven – a day that still lives long in infamy – the building of the Iron Wall, the destruction of the Iron Wall, instigating the General Strike, starting the Great Depression, initiating the Hungarian Revolt, ordering the invasion to bring the Hungarian Revolt to an end, starting both the Great Leap Forward and being sole architect of the Great Leap Back and, most notoriously, organizing the collapse of the great banking houses in the crash of 08.

But about the death of John of Boston, no one breathed a word in relation to Thomas Cale. If this gave him solace, it was unjustified.

Should Thomas Cale have known that the world was not going to forget about him?

Yes.

Should he have kept on running from the many and hideous deaths on the hunt for him?

Yes.

Did it make any sense to try to hide in a place where people of every kind from every one of the places where Thomas Cale had left his mark for good or ill came to share in the golden world of Malfi?

No, it did not.

Why was he here, then?

Being wise, you don't need me to tell you. But let me try. History, we all know, is unreliable, defective, false. Arbell Van Owen (née Materazzi) of Malfi was a power in the United Estates because of her widowed wealth, but when Cale had first met her she was young and a beauty, already a byword for loveliness, intelligence and grace. 'You are not a person,' Bosco had once told Cale. 'I have scoured out everything human in you to make you what you were really born to become: anger made flesh.' What could such a creature do on seeing an Arbell Materazzi for the first time but fall? (plummet? collapse? plunge?)

Of course, many little boys with unattractive faces or unattractive temperaments fall head over heels in love with the prettiest girl in school and, when they are ignored, or taken up for a while and *then* ignored, do not go on to be responsible for the death of millions and the collapse of empires. But then, who can say how many tragedies, the little and the large, have played out, are being played out, and will always be played out because of a beautiful little girl or boy laughing at an ugly little boy or girl?

They first met when Arbell was only seventeen; Cale was two or three years younger (nobody was sure). She was spoilt and self-obsessed in the way that beautiful girls and boys are prone to be. I ask of you, the plain and the badly off, to be reasonable: how can they be anything else?

For a while she smothers him in love and passion, then turns aside. Why? Why does anyone turn aside in such a way? Two things could be said. One, that something deep inside her feared the power of his soul to burn her up. Two, he had a habit, long since unlearned, of eating with his mouth open and slurping his soup.

How are the gifted young supposed to act but careless and uncomprehending of the harm they do? How are the young like Thomas Cale supposed to feel in turn? For the Tiny Ones, gourmets of human suffering, such youthful treacheries are like blood in water for the shark. And this particular blood had a taste for them as delightful as one of those wines that connoisseurs are ready to lay down to ripen for half a lifetime before the ecstatic opening.

For Cale, in loving Arbell, came to feel something he had never guessed existed: joy.

You should know then how he lost it and how that loss brought him so unwisely to the gates of Malfi. Forgive me, Reader, if I return again to the moment of her betrayal of the young boy. Nothing can be understood if this is not understood – whether you think he was betrayed or not.

After the defeat of the Materazzi at the Battle of Solsbury, Bosco had immediately seated the young and terrified Arbell in a basement in Memphis in an attempt to persuade her to help him capture Thomas Cale.

'What I require, madam, is that you write a letter to Cale that you will give, as it were, secretly to one of his friends. In this letter you will ask him to meet you outside the walls at such and such a time. I'll be there, and with such numbers that he must surrender.'

'You'll burn him alive,' said Arbell.

'I will not,' said Bosco, raising his voice. 'Whatever you think you feel for him, you cannot understand what he is. Try to save him, which you can never do, and all you will achieve is the destruction of your father and the condemnation of your people.'

'I can't,' said Arbell.

Bosco sighed sympathetically. 'The choice you have to make now is a kind no one would envy. Whatever you do will seem wrong to you. You must either destroy a father you love, or a single man you also love.' Arbell stared at Bosco as if transfixed. 'But though this choice is harsh, it is not so harsh as you fear. I will find him sooner or later in any case. You must believe me when I say' – and he tried to be especially unconvincing; he wanted her to work for her betrayal – 'our reputation for cruelty is one put about by our enemies.' He sat back and sighed again.

'Tell me, young lady, for all your love for this young man, a love I can see now is certainly genuine' – he paused to let her swallow this sugary poison – 'haven't you felt something about him, something' – he searched for the right word – 'fatal.'

'You made him like that with your malice.'

'Not so,' replied Bosco reasonably, as if he understood the accusation. 'The first moment I saw him when he was very young there was something shocking about him. It took me a long time to put my finger on what it was because it simply didn't make sense. It was dread. I dreaded this little boy. Certainly it was necessary to mould and discipline what was already there, but no human being could make Cale what he is. I am not so boastful. I was merely an agent of the Lord to incline his nature for our common good and in His service. But you have seen this in him and it frightens you – as well it might. The kindnesses in him that you have sometimes seen are like the wings of the ostrich – they beat but will not fly. Leave him to us and save your father, your friends and yourself.'

Arbell started to speak, but Bosco held up his hand to silence her. 'I've nothing more to say. Consider it, and make your decision. I will send the details of the time and place when we will meet Cale. You will either write the letter or you will not.'

Two Redeemers who had been standing by the door moved forward and gestured for her to leave. As she went through the door Bosco called out to her, as if reluctantly sympathetic to her plight. 'Forget that you owe Thomas Cale your life. Do the right thing, my dear.' The door closed and Bosco said softly to himself: 'For the lips that to him now are as luscious as honeycomb, shall be to him shortly as bitter as wormwood, and as sharp as a two-edged sword.'

He walked over to a thickly curtained partition and pulled it to one side. Cale, gagged and bound to a chair, stared at him with an expression you might describe as malevolent, except there is no word in any language, dead or living, to describe what was in Cale's heart. The guard removed his gag.

'She won't give me up,' said Cale. 'She knows I'll find a way to save her and her father, because I always find a way.'

Bosco smiled agreeably. 'Well, you certainly are a most formidable young man, so perhaps you will. But will you want to when she hands you over to me?'

'She won't.'

'Why don't we wait for her reply and see.'

They did not have to wait long, less than half an hour. Bosco read the letter without expression. He handed it over to Cale. Can the heart swallow a stone? Had you been there, you would have seen it.

But pity poor Arbell the terrible pangs of private desire and public obligation, the dreadful and impossible betrayal involved in either choice. But it was worse than it seemed because in her heart of hearts (and the yet more secret one that lay within that heart) she had already decided to betray Thomas Cale. Thrilling though he was to her, it was the same strangeness that aroused her that also aroused distaste for him. He was so violent, so angry, so deathly. Bosco had seen right through her to the other side. How, given who she was, could she be other than refined and delicate? And, make no mistake, this refinement and delicacy was what Cale adored; but Cale had been *beaten* into shape, hammered in dreadful fires of unimaginable fear and pain. How could she be with him for long? A secret part of Arbell had been searching for some time for a way to leave her lover, unawares, it is only fair to record. And so as Cale waited for her to save him as he had twice done so for her, she had already chosen.

No doubt, being wise, you understand the terrible nature of her choice. But do you understand his coruscating rage? Ask yourself what it would be like to be exchanged in such a deal by the woman who had given you the gift of joy and had now cheated you not just of life – bad enough, that – but of any hope of joy ever again. Never. Never. Never. Never.

Mulling over all this (brooding? moiling? agonizing?), Cale waited at the gates of Malfi for ten minutes before a wagon arrived to take him to his destination. The coachman was clearly besotted by Malfi and delighted in intimidating his invariably overwhelmed passengers with facts about the place – it had seven hundred rooms and two thousand windows and could house five thousand people, which, of course, did not include people who were not exactly people: butlers, servants, black servants, gardeners, black gardeners, and so on. Two towns (one for whites, one for spooks) hidden behind the hill took care of them. Malfi was a small city in one building. It was surrounded by three thousand acres of lawns, artificial forests, thirty fountains, a mile-long canal with gondoliers, a labyrinth the size of a small town, grottoes, galleries, ponds and sculptures and an orangery that held a thousand trees. Was Cale impressed? Indeed he was. It's true that all this excess made him laugh as well, but even this high priest of the unmoved was bemused by the unrelenting opulence of the place. It also pleased him that it enabled him to feel deeper contempt, if such a thing were possible, for Arbell Materazzi. What a vulgar little thing she'd become if this was all she could do with her money.

Cale rolled up to a guard station almost a mile from the palace itself and was dropped off with his coffer at the door.

'In there,' said the coachman, irrelevantly and with a wink. He cracked his whip and was off.

Cale walked through the door. Almost immediately, a large butterball of a man rushed out of an anteroom and into the hall.

'Yeah?'

'I'm Dominic Savio.'

Cale could see the name ring something in his fat brain.

'The new deputy?'

'You have an office for me?'

'Yes, suh.' He reached under the desk, lifted up a heavy flap of wood and pointed the way into the back of the building.

Settled into the disappointingly small and uncomfortable office – disappointing because it didn't look like much account was paid to the Chief Deputy of Outer Wall Security – he ordered a cup of tea.

'Wud yew like a Ring Ding with that, suh?' Cale stared at him. 'A cake, suh. Kissed with apricots.'

Cale decided that accepting a cake kissed with apricots looked weak.

'Just bring the tea.'

Outside in the corridor, the constable spoke softly to himself.

'Who'd he bum to get a job like this?'

Now Cale was here, he was not so sure Arbell would fail to recognize him, even though he'd grown a beard and let his hair grow halfway down his back. She had been besotted with him once; and surely every woman (however treacherous) would sense the presence of the person who had been inside her for the first time – something in his eyes, his voice. This was, of course, the part of him that loved her still whining in his ear. On the other hand, he was eight inches taller than the last time she saw him; two stone heavier; his voice was deeper by far, and hoarse, and quieter. His eyes had seen things that would have leached the colour from a stone. And above all: people see what they expect to see and nothing else. The greatest troubler of the age, a Napoléyon, a Cesur, and probably dead in any case, was not going to turn up in Texas after twenty years having taken the job of managing a bunch of fat and useless nightwatchmen.

An hour later, in his rooms, he stared out of the window and smoked his way through several pipes of Fermented Perique Mixture 79 – the best Dallas had to offer. It tasted like rotting leather and burnt hair. He scanned the great façade of Malfi and its thousand glowing windows and wondered which of them was hers.

FILED
Plurus Superior Court
Brumaire 33
Clerk of the Court

THE INTERNATIONAL CRIMINAL COURT OF THE HANSE

35th Brume ME 1956

BLANDINO & SMI STATUTORY DEFENCE ADVOCATES

Dear Bolly

I haven't told you this, so burn the letter and don't tell anyone, not even Debbo. At last we've a confirmed sighting of Cale in the United Estates. Excitement all round here – particularly as we've now got the only accurate portrait of him (apparently, he was obsessed with not having his picture drawn – bugger knew he'd be on the run someday, I suppose). It was provided by Riba Wiitenberg (and yes, I'm talking about the wife of presidential hopeful Arthur). It's a wonderfully treacherous story. Cale saved her life when he was a boy, and they'd stayed close and he'd let her draw him, for some reason. Now she wants to do her civic duty, but in return, we tell no one, not even her husband – except we're to give him a big slice of the credit if we bring Cale in. Talk about the slimy pole. Poor old Tom.

Things look pretty good around co-operation in the Estates. Lincoln is wetting himself for a good deal with the Hanse over cotton tariffs so he can get those frightful Southerners off his neck. He's promising to do everything except take it up the arse to keep us sweet. And even that's negotiable. So – looks like we might get to take on my career-making (and your career-ending) trial, after all.

Piggers

PS Burn the fucker now.

15

Inky-Winky Panda
Inky-Winky Cat
Inky-Winky Crocodile
Snakefish, earwig, rat

– Professor Lamont Draft, *Can You See What It is Yet? Children's Games in the Gilded Age of the United Estates* (Altavista, ME 1985)

It was Saturday in the governor's mansion in Dallas and all was noise and mayhem from the horde of children who'd massed to celebrate the birthday of the youngest of the Van Owen clan, Aris (named after his Uncle Aristotle in the (vain) hope the child would be included in his will). This was the first celebration of any kind held in the governor's mansion in the weeks following the death of John of Boston. Given that he had been slaughtered in Dallas, that the mass rioting in at least a dozen cities had only recently died down, and that the huge attendance at mass vigils had begun to thin, it was only now that Nick Van Owen felt the world was ready to accept that life, however sadly, must go on. A children's party in which everyone in Dallas who was anybody was invited was a particularly excellent way to stifle criticism that it was too soon after the national tragedy to rejoice about anything. Only a mugwump of the first order would deny a child a party on their birthday.

The tables in the Founder's Room whimpered under the weight of Coco puddings, syllabubs and Hungry Ghost pies. At once the door burst open and Aris Van Owen shouted out, 'Uncle Nick! Uncle Nick! Come and play Inky-Winky with us!'

Nick, brother to Louis, swept down the room as the attending adults also turned to watch his theatrical entrance.

'What's all this noise, you clangorous children? What's the cause of all this giddy turbulence?'

'Is that my present, Uncle Nick?'

'This?' replied Nick, looking at the brightly wrapped box he was carrying as if astonished to see it under his arm. 'Oh no. This is a drainpipe I bought to replace one I broke earlier.'

'*No, it isn't!*' screamed the children together.

Nick shrugged.

'Look for yourselves if you care to, but expect to be disappointed – unless you happen to be devotees of drainpipes.'

He handed the package over and Aris fell on it – a starving man presented with a roast chicken. He carried it over to the presents table with the other children shouting: '*Open it! Aris, open it!*'

A woman kissed Nick on the cheek.

'I knew I could rely on you Nick – always late,' said his sister.

His apology was interrupted by the roars of appreciation from the table. Aris was holding up an impressive child-sized reproduction of the helmet of Achilles, Greek heroes then being all the rage in Dallas. The obvious cost of the helmet soothed his sister's irritation.

'*Thank you*, Ummclafank.' Aris's gratitude became muffled as he placed the helmet over his head.

'How fitting,' whispered Louis. 'The biggest asshole in Greek history.'

Nick laughed. They were interrupted by the helmeted Aris.

'Come and play Inky-Winky with us, Uncle Nick,' he repeated, grabbing his hand and leading him over to the games table.

Spread out on it was a large piece of paper covered in an inkblot which stained almost the entire sheet.

'What is this Inky-Winky that you speak of?' asked Nick, though everyone in the South had played the game time out of mind.

'Well, you see, Uncle Nick,' explained the small boy carefully, 'in secret, someone draws an animal in lots of splodgy ink, and then you fold the paper down the middle and squash it together to make a blot, and then you have to guess what the animal is. You get two guesses, Uncle Nick, and if you get one wrong, we all shout "Inky-Winky!"'

'And if I get one right, which I'm bound to do?'

'We all shout "Hurrah!"'

'All right, children, start practising your acclamations!' The children were both appalled and impressed by his terrible confidence.

Nick looked at the ink blot intently. Then he closed his eyes and opened them wide with an expression of absolute certainty. 'It's a tasselled wobbegong.'

'Inky-Winky!' screeched the delighted children. Nick looked crestfallen at his defeat. The children were triumphant at having got one over on the adult world. Nick sighed and closed his eyes again. And again he opened them with the look of a man who has found gold.

'I have it! I have it!' declared Nick to the saucer-eyed children. 'It's . . .' He paused to prolong the delicious torment. 'It's a pink Argentinian fairy armadillo!'

A roar from the ecstatic children. Huge laughter from the adults.

'Inky-Winky! Inky-Winky! Inky-Winky! It's a pig! It's a pig! It's a picture of a pig!'

Nick groaned with disappointment and put his head in his hands and seemed to weep. But the children had no compassion for their defeated enemy. They squealed and laughed like the drain that Nick claimed he'd brought for Aris's present.

'I need to talk to you,' muttered Louis to his brother. Nick looked up, still distraught, and looked at the children accusingly.

'I think you're all ganging up on me to make me look like a ninnyhammer. But I have no time to get to the bottom of this grotesque prestidigitation because I must go and talk with Aris's wicked Uncle Louis.'

'Read this shit, have you?' said Nick, staring out of the window of his brother's office and waving a piece of paper at him between thumb and forefinger, as if to avoid more contaminating contact than was absolutely necessary.

'What is it?'

'Listen to this – it's by that rabble-rousing coon Luther. *I have a dream that one day the estate of Texas, whose leader's lips are presently dripping with the malignity of re-enslavement, will one day be transformed into a place where black boys and black girls will be able to join hands with white boys and white girls and walk together as sisters and brothers.*

'What about that for sentimental camelshit? What I say to that' – he smiled to acknowledge that what he was about to say was something his brother would regard as a dreary commonplace, banged his fist on the table like any common demagogue and put on a ridiculous Southern accent – 'is re-enslaveeery neeow, re-enslavereeey tomorrahhh, re-enslaveery fo' evuh!'

With a barely audible sigh, Louis Van Owen put down the pen with which he had been writing a review of the first opera written by one of his countrymen, Mark Tweain, *The Girl of the United Estates*, which had premiered the previous night at the Dallas Opera House.

'You're a caution, Nick,' said Louis to his brother, 'but you and your friends are going to have to realize that you can't be always eating the niggers for breakfast, dinner and tea. The winds of change are blowing over this continent, and if you don't bend, you're going to break – and the South along with you. Or do you want a civil war?'

'If that's what's needed. The South is built on slavery. No slavery, no South.'

'Goddammit, Nick, you've got to give up something.' He looked directly at his brother. 'I mean it. Do things my way and we can preserve most of what you want.'

'Even the dumbest Neeegro,' said Nick, mockingly stretching the word, 'knows shit with the bag open, Louis. You can't just change a name and think everyone'll be fooled.'

'Wrong again, Nick. Perception is everything.' He thought better of this. 'All right, it's not everything. But it's eight points out of ten.'

'John of Boston saw through it.'

'And look what happened to him.'

'Luck,' sniffed Nick. 'You can't depend on someone just turning up and blowing the head off your enemy every time they look like they've got you by los testiculos.

'Every great enterprise needs a touch of good fortune.' Had he been there, Cale would have admired the fact that Louis van Owen looked as innocent as Mary, with or without her lamb.

'Besides, looks like Lincoln has more backbone than you thought.'

Louis Van Owen smiled. 'The solution to every problem is another problem. We'll see whether we can loosen up his spine in due course. I mean it, Nick. I'm relying on you to bring the more hot-headed gentlemen of the South with me on this. They trust you because you're as free with your gums about a glorious war for freedom as they are. But let me make it as plain as . . . yes . . . shit with the bag open. You want Malfi back in one piece, you'll do it my way. You want it back razed to the ground, you'll go to war. Simple as that. Do we understand each other?'

At first Nick Van Owen scowled like a teenage boy, but then the most lovely and charming smile crossed his face.

'Always, dear brother.' But then his mood changed again, and just as quickly. 'I hope the soul of our miserable cunt of a brother is now burning in Heaven for leaving Malfi to that bitch and that precious little sodomite son of hers.'

'Denmark? A sodomite? That's not at all what I hear. Rather the opposite, but if you know something solid, that could be useful.'

Nick's face contorted with the effort of climbing down. 'I didn't mean he was an *actual* sodomite – but he *is* a stuck-up little prick who's going to inherit what belongs to us.'

'Unfortunately, being a stuck-up little prick isn't a crime.'

Louis allowed him to calm down. After a brief struggle, Nick laughed.

'I suppose not. I had stuck-up-little-prick tendencies myself when I was Denmark's age.'

'Are you going back to Malfi tonight?' asked Louis, hoping to move the conversation towards something less likely to vibrate his brother.

'Yes.' He changed tack again. 'Little bird tells me that frigid bitch Arbell has been talking with Martin Luther.'

'It's in hand,' replied Louis, turning back to his review in the hope that his brother would drop the subject.

'Is it true?'

A pause.

'Yes.'

'She has no right, Louis – no right at all – to use our money to support that goddamn darkie shit-stirrer.'

'Unfortunately, the courts think it's her money, Nick.'

'We should expose that nigger-loving bitch for what she is.'

'We don't have any proof, Nick. Besides, believing in the rights of the dark peoples isn't actually a crime.'

'It will be.'

'Only if you defeat the North in a civil war. I'll give you odds of a hundred to one and think my money as safe as houses.'

'You, a coward, brother?'

'Yes, I am, if it makes you any happier.'

Nick stared at his brother. His face was unreadable. 'I'm sorry I said that, Louis.'

'We need her money: first, because it's ours; second, to stop her spending it supporting the North. Two birds, one stone. If it comes to war – and I have every intention of making damn sure it doesn't, we'll need Malfi money to save Malfi and to save the South. We put in our fortune, then others will follow. Only that kind of money will buy us the men and guns to give us any chance. That's why you have to stall the hotheads, Nick, no matter you're a hothead yourself.' A beat. 'Are you with me, brother?'

'You're the only man I know can go into a hole behind a weasel and come out in front – so I guess I am.'

'Other than to get her declared insane, the only way to have the will annulled is if we can bring up Arbell on a morals charge. But the courts aren't going to hand us Malfi without something pretty goddamn solid and a pretty solid couple of witnesses to back it up. Be patient and leave it to me. I have someone in mind with most of the talents required.'

'Most?'

'Nobody's perfect, Nick, don't you know that?'

'We should use Saul Gaines.'

'Her steward?'

'Yes.' Nick's expression was defiant.

'Her *black* steward?'

'Yes.' Still defiant.

'Well, well – aren't you a mass of contradictions?'

'He's well fitted for the job.'

'I don't doubt his abilities or his intelligence. But he's black, Nick. How do you think that'll go down in the Supreme Court when we attempt to have Arbell declared morally delinquent?'

'He's the black golden boy, isn't he? He's published a book, talks like a gentleman, educated at Vorday. Besides, he's smart – we can come up with white witnesses once he's winkled out what she's up to. We don't need a witness for now, we need an informer. He's the man.'

'No.'

'Yes.'

'He's too trustworthy. Though I'm pleased to see you recognize he's a remarkable person.'

This was said in a provocative way – and Nick was not a difficult man to provoke.

'For a spook.'

'He's a remarkable person by any standards, Nick. Do you really think that if you'd been born in some rancid little shack in Shittsville Alabamy, you'd have made it as far as Gaines?'

'Then why don't you marry him to your daughter?'

'Now you're being tiresome. I told you, Gaines is far too straight to work for us. He won't slide. What he will do, in my considered and almost certainly correct opinion, is go straight from your efforts to suborn him and head directly for Arbell, who'll see faster than grass through a goose what you and me are up to. I have someone better fitted for the job. So leave it with me.'

'Who?'

'You're not going to let me finish this, are you?' said Louis, putting down his pen.

'Who?'

With a long sigh Louis leaned back in his chair. 'Once upon a time, Nick –'

'Before you get going,' interrupted Nick, 'a thought strikes . . .

Nobody likes a Mormon. There's a universal excitement to be had over an anti-Mormon crusade. Those God-bothering anti-slavers in the North think the Mormons are a bunch of dangerous heretics. We could raise a storm against those polygamous sons-of-bitches that'd blot out the piping clamour against the restoration . . . that could, y'know, unite the country. What do y'think, Louis?'

At the same time as Louis was about to give his not very encouraging answer, some 1,500 miles away in New York City's Grande Central Station a young gurrier with a bucket of paste and a sheaf of papers was slapping up the first sheet of a wanted poster issued by the International Court of the Hanse. There was a drawing of the man, accused of Crimes against the Humanity, along with the offer of a reward for his capture: $50,000. Inevitably, the poster was hardly on the wall when a crowd gathered to gawp at such a staggering sum, all memorizing the face in sweet hope of a huge reward for doing nothing at all except keeping their eyes peeled. By the next day, a thousand of these posters were up in the City. By the end of the month there would be no town in the United Estates that did not have a portrait of Thomas Cale offering to make its inhabitants rich beyond imagining.

The Dallas Herald.

Last night at the Dallas Opera House Mark Tweain's *The Girl of the United Estates* showed our great country the way forward not just in music but in our approach to our manifest destiny in the world. Why is there any need for us to copy slavishly the traditions of the Old World with its operatic forms strangled in the dead hand of the classical past and as artificial as a papier-mâché rose? Tweain gives us an art that is more direct, more forceful, more up-to-the-minute in every way. Polly Perkins is a type of modern woman you could meet on any New York street, sassy and confident, and centuries away from the parking and barking eighteen-stone sopranos of Old World opera, fifty years of age and pretending to be woodland nymphs or the goddess Venus. I suggest we stop calling our new works opera at all to show that we are ready to break with the past. Let us call it musical pantomime or Pantopera and let us acknowledge that Tweain has shown us a new way of understanding the modern world in a form that combines all forms – his work is realistic, comic, absurd, serious, tragic, vulgar, high and low. In other words, it presents life in a form that accurately reflects human existence in a way that no other art form has done before. Let it be *the* Estates art form from now on! As we have shown the world the way ahead with our votocracy despite the Old World's cries of horror, let us do the same in our art.

Governor Louis Van Owen

THE FUTURE REPRESENTATIVES OF OUR NATION.

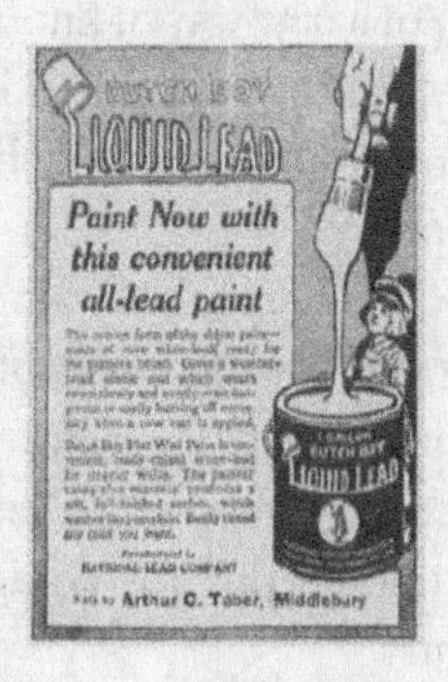

16

She was as beyootiful as a butterfly and as prowd as a queen
Was pretty little Polly Perkins of Chikasaw Green.

– *The Girl of the United Estates*, Mark Tweain

Cariola was sitting in the big chair in Denmark's room, one leg tucked underneath her and the other swinging carelessly just above the floor. The chair was so called not because it was particularly large but because it had once dwarfed the five-year-old Denmark, for whom it was set aside by Aristotle Van Owen. Much spoilt by his stepfather, it came with a silver bell to ring whenever he wanted something. Needless to say, it did not stop tinkling with his demand for biscuits or lemonade or anything else he thought he could get away with, until his mother removed the clapper. She constantly told her servants not to spoil her son, but he was a great favourite and they found his constant demands hilarious, rather than irritating, as they ought to have done.

'Well, *cher*,' said Cariola as Denmark tried and failed repeatedly to get the hang of a new way of knotting a tie he'd read about in the *New York Gazette*, 'I hope you're making sure none of the klè poupe get their nails into your pretty little hide.'

'Clay poopay?'

'Blonde dollies, cher.' All rich white girls, even if they had hair as black as a raven's wing, were blonde dollies to Cariola, pale and insipid husband-hunters beneath contempt. All except Arbell.

'Girls don't like me,' said Denmark. 'My nose is too big . . . and there are rumours that my equipment is so enormous I might do them an injury.'

'Oh no, *cher.* Send these ignorant bimbows to me and I'll put them right. I've seen how piti your kok is. Nothing to be afraid of in the slightest.'

'The last time you saw my kok, Cariola, was when I was eight years old. I can assure you that in the intervening period matters have improved frighteningly.' She laughed like a little silver bell herself. 'Did you want something, or are you just slacking off your duties, as usual? I suppose you must have some, though I've never been sure what it is you actually do all day.'

'Mwen? I am your manman's eyes and ears in this place, ti gason.'

'Tee gasson?'

'Little boy.'

Denmark looked at her and smiled. 'Perhaps, Cariola,' he said cheerfully, 'you'd like to practise being somewhere else.'

She stood up, somehow making it clear that deciding to leave was entirely a matter for her.

'Your manman says you must write to Senor Gray to accept his invitation – and also to remind you to be on time for dinner tonight with that malpwop, Van Owen.'

A few minutes later she was making her way through the corridor next to the great ballroom and saw Nick Van Owen heading towards her, proof, thought Cariola, if any were needed, that all that was required to call up the Devil was to say his name. She began to sashshay in such a way as, she hoped, clearly expressed her irritation that he should dare to walk down a corridor where she was going about her business.

'Well,' said Nick, 'it's the lovely Cariola. You really do get more beautiful every time I see you.'

The Hunterian word, long forgotten, for a speaking look was an eeliad. But no eeliad ever given spoke more clearly than the one thrown by the young woman in reply to Nick's gallantry. By moving to one side of the corridor he had forced her to turn sideways in order to pass, but as she did so he moved again, blocking her way completely.

She stopped still and waited. It is a pity the Hunterians did not have a word for a way of speaking by standing still.

Nick sighed, perhaps genuinely trying not to offend her further. When he spoke again the tone of waggish seduction had vanished entirely.

'I'm sorry if . . . I am clumsy. But I would . . . Cariola' – he said her name with a rather touching regretful gentleness – 'like to know you better. Or for you to know me better. I am not my reputation.' He spoke as if her greater understanding of the real Nick Van Owen truly did mean something to him. Her shoulders moved as if to suggest a softening, then slowly she looked up at him with another look that spoke of there being, perhaps, possibly, might be, a fraction of a quintilla of a change in her coldness towards him. 'Come to dinner with me tomorrow. In my apartments.' A gasp from Cariola. 'Don't be alarmed. I promise there will be a chaperone. Bring anyone.'

She raised her eyes to his, it had to be admitted, very handsome face. Her look spoke of wariness still, even suspicion, but also of a slight, an imperceptibly slight, easing of her implacability towards him. How to speak without giving away too much this tiny change of heart. But she spoke more softly to him than at any time before and halfway through allowed the tiny tip of her tongue to rest for a moment on the soft pink of her upper lip. '*Je préfèrerais,*' she said in her lowest voice, heavy with promise, '*avaler une tête de sèpan a sonèt d'abord tout en nourrissant un bébé à un makak affamé que de toucher un cheveu de votre tête de tout tripay.*' Which is to say*: I'd rather swallow a rattlesnake head first while feeding a baby to a hungry ape than touch one hair of your shitty head.* She smiled as only Cariola could smile when she chose to. 'I must go, monsieur, Madame expects me back immediately. I'll send you a message.'

He stood back to allow her to pass. She moved on, watched by Nick with an almost unrecognizable tenderness as she passed out of sight. His expression changed, but it would be hard to describe in what way.

For three days Cale was left to wander around Malfi asking a few questions – not many – and letting the men he was now in charge of talk while he considered what shape things were in. In the light of his experience of transforming entire nations, it was not the hardest of tasks. Then, on a particularly beautiful summer morning, a black servant arrived with a letter summoning Cale to 'The House', as everyone called the city-sized palace. Inside was a sealed envelope that he was instructed not to open but to present at the guardhouse. He was puzzled by this, as his careful inspection of the grounds near the house didn't contain such a structure, nor would a guardhouse seem to have much purpose, given the ease of entry over the decorative walls that surrounded the palace.

As he came close he could still not make out anything like a guard block – until he was almost on top of the apparently ornamental walls: the defences were almost entirely hidden. What appeared to be low walls topped by filigree iron railings were just the top of a trench extending, he presumed, all around the palace. An alley led straight down, preventing more than one person at a time from passing through, and descended some thirty feet into a wide, waterless moat with a narrow staircase rising up to a bunker halfway up the trench. Along its length there were about twenty murder holes in the wall to allow constant fire to rain down as far as the next block, some fifty yards down the channel, where he could see another guard block also peppered with murder holes. As a solution to keeping the palace safe he had never seen something so elegant and yet so brutal. He climbed the stairs and arrived at a kind of kiosk.

'Name,' said the man.

'Savio.'

'Billet.'

Cale passed over the sealed envelope. In ten minutes he was in a tastefully decorated room with many books on its high walls and a large polished desk behind which sat a slim and very simply dressed older man wearing glasses and writing in an enormous ledger. Forgetting himself – the lordly habits of years as A Great Man were not easily forgotten – Cale went to sit in the single chair in front of the desk.

'I didn't ask you to sit down,' said the man behind the desk. Cale stopped, cursing himself for allowing the possibility of such mortification. A minute-long wait as the man wrote in his ledger. 'Now you can sit,' he said.

Cale did as he was told. The man looked him over as if utterly bored by the task.

'Why're you here, Savio?'

'To take up my duties running the security for the outer walls.'

'But why you? Who are you to take up an office of such mighty responsibility?'

'I was under the impression that Governor Van Owen sent you my references and that he'd had the information personally verified.'

'True. But how did he do that, Mr Savio, personally verify 'em? Because while the claims made here speak highly of yure experience, they speak of occurrences very far from here and in situations where even I'd be hard put to dig up sure validation. Looks pretty scaly to me.'

This was a fair point, thought Cale. The history of Dominic Savio was not so much a lie as a very watered-down version of the truth. Savio claimed to have been a superintendent of the defences at the siege of Germantown, whose fortifications Cale had actually designed and built. Savio claimed to be experienced, but not so much that it would be odd that he'd applied for such a lowly post as the one at Malfi. And so it was for the rest of the history – little enough compared to his great works but still true, in a manner of speaking.

'Given that all your experience took place so far away and in bloody circumstances, how could the governor be so certain a' you?'

'You'll have to ask him.'

Being a little affronted seemed to be the right thing to do. A truthful person would be indignant at having his truthfulness impugned – although having his truthfulness impugned did not bother Cale in the slightest. The man looked at him.

'What's your verdic' about the guard you've taken over?'

His judgement, one that could have been made by a five-year-old starved of air at birth, was that it was a collection of fat, useless, idle incompetents.

'Only been here a few days. In my experience, first appearances can be deceiving. Don't you agree?' The man did not respond. 'Ask me in a week and I'll give you chapter and verse.'

'A week, Savio? If I see you again in two months, you can consider yourself mighty privileged.' He sat back as if to defy an answer out of Cale.

'I see that I required both an invitation and a pass to come into the palace grounds.'

'Yeah?'

'Will this always be the case?'

'T'will.'

'If you don't mind me being blunt, given that I'm head of external security, I find that a strange state of affairs.'

'Do you?' Again the man just stared at him. 'Goodbye, *Mr* Savio.'

The man went back to his ledger. Cale stood up and made to leave. The guard with the silk jacket and the snake eyes had already opened the door.

Outside, he was subject to the same routine – another guard walked silently in front, leaving Cale to follow – but this time the guard turned to the left. However Cale was going to be shown out, it was not through the same gate.

They moved along an assortment of paths, left and right, occasionally seeing in the distance some well-dressed toffs, a few gardeners, and so on. He was being taken further away from the house and deeper into the gardens, where there were no more reassuring sightings of people. This was all wrong, but Cale had no choice but to keep following. Now they had arrived at a deserted criss-cross of paths with walls to one side and a thick hedge in front. Halfway in, the guard stopped and turned, drawing a knife as he did so.

This was odd, thought Cale – not the drawing of the knife but that there was only one person doing it. But then another guard appeared from behind a bush on one side of the green and another from a second bush. Looking over his shoulder, two more showed themselves behind him.

Listening carefully for the sound of the men behind, Cale turned to face the guard he'd been following.

'Tell's who yew are,' said the guard.

'I've already told your man in the office.'

'He din't believe you.'

'It's the only answer I've got.'

'For yure sake, friend, I hope that's not true, 'cause I've been told to get a better one, and I'm a biddable sorta feller.'

Cale was considering his options, short and long term. This might seem oddly cool-headed, given the apparent peril of his situation, but he was good at peril, hazard being his thing, as it were.

Perhaps they were just going to beat him up in order to get the truth out of him. Or perhaps not. He could, of course, fight it out – the odds were bad, but they'd not be expecting someone with his talent for savagery. But he was doubtful he could bring it off – he was not in good condition. He was not – and it was a joke he often told himself – he was not the boy he used to be.

'So,' said the guard, 'gonna sing or not? Me? I'd druther yew didn't. Don't like yure face.'

'That's a pity,' said Cale, 'because I like yours. Not everyone can wear their eyes too close together, but I think on you it looks quite fetching.'

'I don' care one pinch of owl dung, what yew think, yew . . .'

Before he could finish, Cale started running, watched by the guards, bemused by the sight of a man pointlessly heading straight for a seven-foot-high and densely packed hedge and diving into it as confidently as if he were plunging into a deep pool. His momentum carried him halfway through the thick greenery before the matted branches stopped him dead. The guards watching what they had thought was a pointless attempt to escape suddenly realized that he was almost through to the other side.

Cale had been lucky – the main stems of the bush which formed the hedge were thick as a small trunk and planted close together. If he'd struck one of them at high speed, he wouldn't have had to worry about a beating. No one was going to be able to follow him quickly without taking the same risk. As he got to his feet on the other side he heard the mildly satisfying curses of the men he'd escaped.

'There's a way in up there!' he heard one of them shout.

About four feet in front of Cale was another thick, tall hedge. He was in a maze. He groaned in frustration as about thirty yards to the left down the corridor of leaves he saw the guards enter. No time to plan, he raced off in the opposite direction and further into his trap. He pushed his hand into the hedge to find a way out. But inside the hedges here there was a strong wooden trellis to prevent happy maze-goers from cheating – something that wasn't necessary on the outermost wall of the maze. Swearing at his luck, he started running again, trying to remember anything he knew about mazes – something about always turning left, or was it right? Bollocks. He ran on, turning and twisting whenever a gap opened, listening to the shouts and commands of his pursuers. But now the shouts calmed and receded and Cale stopped to gather his thoughts. They realized they didn't need to rush, as long as they covered his retreat to the exit. He moved on, hammers in his brain, but almost immediately came to what looked like a dead end. As he stewed over the unpleasantness that would surely come he saw there was another cleverly disguised turning in the hedge. Slowly, he peeped around the corner and took in the extraordinary sight ahead of him. At the centre of the maze was a bench, and on that bench were two people dressed in clothes of great elegance. A woman, perhaps in her early forties, was sitting with her legs up on the bench with her fabulously embroidered skirt pulled up to her waist. Kneeling on the ground and fully dressed was a younger woman, twenty perhaps, holding her legs apart and lazily and lasciviously licking and kissing between the older woman's thighs. From time to time she stopped and gazed up into the eyes of her lover and a look passed between them that Cale had never seen before and never would again: a glance of joyful devilment on the one hand and fearful bliss on the other at the delinquency of what was happening between them.

'What are you doing to me?' the older woman said, as if the existence of such pleasure were beyond comprehension. 'What are you doing to me?'

The girl on her knees laughed with pure delight. Then she drew her head back, eyes always on her lover, and Cale gulped at the split second of blonde hair, pink lips and shimmering red. Then the girl buried her head in between her lover's legs and a shudder and groan of delight ran through the older woman.

Cale stepped forward. 'Excuse me.'

The older woman jumped and squealed as if brimstone had been poured on her head, her expression changing in an instant from bliss to terror. The young woman on her knees, however, simply stood up and stared at Cale coldly, as if he had burst into a room unannounced.

'What do you think you're doing?' she demanded.

Cale – aware that there was little time – was undiplomatic. 'I could ask you the same thing.'

The older woman shook and started to cry.

'It's all right, Sophie,' said the girl.

'I'd say we need each other's help,' said Cale, 'so listen and make your mind up quickly. There are a collection of very bad men about to enter here who intend to do me harm. In return for my absolute silence, I want you to refuse to leave here without me. Do we agree?'

A pause. The girl turned to the older woman, who was now whimpering in terror. 'Do be quiet, Sophie.' Then back to Cale. 'Come here and sit between us.'

In a few seconds the three of them were arranged along the bench, Cale and the girl giving the impression that there was nothing odd about a long-haired, bearded desperado sitting between two gorgeously dressed aristocrats, as if the only trouble they had was how long it would take for the cucumber sandwiches to arrive.

'Will you shut up!' said the girl as the older woman struggled to bring her sobs under control. Immediately, two of the guards, knives drawn, ran into the enclosure and stopped dead at the startling sight in front of them. They said nothing. An impatient voice called out from behind the hedge.

'Well?'

'It's, ah. It's all right, suh. You kin come in.'

The guard who'd threatened Cale cautiously emerged from behind the hedge.

'What do you want?' said the girl irritably.

'We've, ah . . . come to arrest that man.'

'No, you haven't, he's with me. He's been here for hours. You must be looking for someone else.'

'We need to take that man with us.'

'Do you know who I am?' said the girl.

It had been Cale's experience in the past that whenever anyone said this it was always a sign of desperation and never produced any useful effect. But not this time.

'Um . . . yes, Miss Hetty Summerstone.'

'And do you know who this is?' she said, nodding towards the pale-faced older woman.

He winced. 'The wife of the Ambassador for the Hanse.'

'Your name?'

A reluctant pause. Then:

'Strobe.'

'One of Moseby's people?'

'Yes, madam.'

'I'll be having a word with him.' She stood up, Cale and the recovering older woman with her. 'Now, we're leaving.'

Sour but apparently powerless, Strobe stood aside, and the unlikely trio walked out of the centre of the maze, leaving the bad-tempered but impotent guards behind.

'Do you know the way out?' asked Cale, smiling.

Hetty turned to him as they walked on and smiled (more devilment). 'This place is practically my second home.'

They did not talk again until they emerged from the maze ten minutes later.

'We're going this way,' said Hetty, making it clear that he should go anywhere else but with them.

'I'm afraid I'm going to ask you to escort me out of the palace grounds, if you don't mind.'

'I *do* mind.'

'I'm afraid I'll have to ask you anyway.'

'Make him promise to say nothing, Hetty,' said the terrified woman. For the first time, Cale looked at her directly.

'I don't know anything. I know how to keep my mouth shut and I know how to be grateful. Just pop me outside and it'll be as if I never existed.'

In twenty minutes, accompanied by Hetty, Cale was driving in a rather splendid coach straight across the great bridge that led over the tunnel defences and in a further five was dropped off at his quarters. As he got down he turned back towards his saviour.

'You were pretty cool back there, if you don't mind me saying.'

'I *do* mind.'

Cale laughed out loud and turned to leave.

'What's your name?' she called out, and when he turned back this time she was smiling.

'Dominic Savio. If you ever need help.'

'How on earth could you help me?'

'Didn't your mother tell you not to judge a book by its cover?'

'I believe she did on one occasion say something banal of that nature.'

He laughed again and walked on.

Later that evening, mulling over the events of the day, Cale was hard pressed to come to a conclusion about what they meant. The whole business seemed heavy-handed, given that his significance in the scheme of things at Malfi hardly seemed important enough for what might have been very nasty indeed. Would Governor Van Owen have taken the risk of having him killed when Cale had made, in his own mind, a convincing claim to have arranged to have the details of his involvement in the death of John of Boston delivered to a dozen news-sheets if anything happened to him. As it happened, Cale had made no such plan. He didn't need to – he just had to persuade Van Owen that he'd done so. On the other hand, the attack might have been nothing more than a personal grudge. What if the man he'd replaced had been a friend of the guard who'd attacked him – Strobe? His boss, Moseby, might have known nothing about it. It could all be a whirlwind in an eggcup. So reacting in the wrong way, or reacting at all, could bring disaster. How many times in great matters and trivial had he seen how much of life was floundering in the dark with only hindsight making any decision you might make or not make either evidence of unmitigated brilliance or total incompetence. History was written by people who believed in reason as the greatest player in human affairs, when Cale knew, with his weary familiarity with failure and success, that intelligence and foresight (qualities he flattered himself he possessed in unusual abundance) were just two of the players, and often pretty minor ones – spear carriers and amiable types who got stabbed late in the second act – in the great bedlam and muddle of human life. If mankind's existence were a play, it would be condemned as one from the imagination of a useless hack – the opening conventional, the progress either unbelievably dull or crudely melodramatic, the characters inconsistent or hysterical, the climax mangled, the ending lame and the meaning of the whole either trite or completely incomprehensible. Nevertheless, it was a play he'd like to see on the stage.

At any rate, he made a decision and wrote to Van Owen, laying out the events of the day – not including the encounter with the extraordinary Hetty Summerstone – and asking for his response. Then it was off to Dallas by first post. This was a surprisingly swift business because Malfi was the playground of the rich and the powerful where a great deal of not at all playful business was transacted. The postal service was marvellous. Despite Dallas being fifty miles away, Cale had his answer by the end of the day. Van Owen instructed him to stay out of sight and well guarded and that the matter would be quickly dealt with. Was he reassured by Van Owen's reassurances? Probably.

The next day, early, Moseby, alone, arrived at the guardhouse and asked for Savio. He was shown into the poky office, where Cale was talking to his second-in-command, lately arrived back from the riots in Chelsea. Cale sent him away, amused that he was astonished to see the Head of Security here in person.

Moseby was an odd mixture of the ingratiating and the hostile. Clearly, someone had stood heavily on his tail and he was alarmed – but he was also resentful at having to apologize to someone he regarded as utterly inferior.

'I want to be clear I knew nothing about that nonsense yesterday.'

Cale said nothing, just looked at him pleasantly, forcing him to continue without the benefit of a clue as to whether he'd cooperate.

'It seems that idiot Strobe was a friend of Aldana, the man you replaced, and decided he was important enough to take exception to the decision of his betters.'

Cale nodded, giving away nothing and enjoying himself hugely. It was always a pleasure to watch the self-important eat a weasel.

'His pay has been docked – a month's salary. And he's been demoted.'

Cale kept nodding and then breathed in. 'I'm sure Strobe thinks better of his failure to give me a good thrashing. But let's not get things out of proportion. I'd rather you didn't demote him.'

'That's a matter for me,' said Moseby, with considerable irritation.

'Still, I'd rather you didn't.'

Cale watched the last of the weasel going down.

'Very well.'

'And I was wondering whether you'd had a chance to reconsider – you know, about giving me a personal pass to the palace. I really do think it would be of real benefit to the overall security of the place – and I'm sure we both want that.'

It wasn't just that Cale disliked Moseby and wanted to make him suffer – though it was a welcome addition – he wanted to see how much extra weight he could rely on. The last bit of the tail of the weasel scratched its way down.

'I'll have it sent to you later today.'

With that, he stood up and left. Sensitive to the pain of others, Cale enjoyed listening to Moseby grinding his teeth all the way back to the palace.

You may have been wondering why Cale was so generous to Strobe, given that, at the very least, he'd intended to give Cale a hefty beating. It certainly had nothing to do with the Hanged Redeemer's advice to repay a blow to your left cheek by offering your right. As a boy, he'd been enraged at the idea that he should forgive the Redeemers for what they'd done to him, but now he saw it as, used with discretion, a subtle insight: the problem with revenge at a practical level was that its satisfactions usually came at the cost of escalating a conflict in an ever-increasing level of tit-for-tat acts of usually murderous retaliation. As a result, when he was master of great matters, he tried usually to do a bit of cheek-turning where it was possible, but when it was not possible made sure that whoever he retaliated against was left in no position to get their own back. He'd modified the Hanged Redeemer's advice to: *If a man strikes you on the left cheek, either, very occasionally, pretend it hasn't happened or utterly annihilate him from the face of the earth.* A number of religious persons had pointed out to him that his 'adjustment' demonstrated a shameful failure to understand the profound nature of what it was the Hanged Redeemer had been attempting to teach. Cale regarded his own solution as the more insightful.

But on this occasion the Hanged Redeemer's contribution was shown to be right. The permanent pass Moseby had promised was delivered later that day not by a messenger but by Strobe himself. His demeanour when he arrived was completely different from the hostility of their last meeting.

'Wanted to hand this to you m'self,' he said.

'I see.'

'To thank you for stoppin' Moseby from reducin' me. He was real mad when Van Owen gave him a feesting last night . . . I mean, real mad with me.'

'Governor Van Owen came to see him personally?'

'Not the gov'ner, his brother, Nick. Old Aristotle Van Owen left him a big 'partment at the other end of the house in his will to make up fer leaving everything to the wife. He's here six months outa the year. Only the Duchess has greater heft in Malfi.'

'The Duchess?'

'That's what everyone calls her. 'Cos she used to be a princess, you know.'

'So why don't they call her Princess?'

'Could do, I s'pose. People take the fact that in the United Estates we have rule for the people by the people pretty serious. They don't like the idea of nobs ruling over them. When the Nish ruled here . . . bastards –'

'Nish?'

'Y'know . . . Spa*nish.* When the Nish ruled here it was Infantas and Marquesses and all that camel-shit. Calling her the Duchess, it's a sort of joke.'

'Affectionate, or something else?'

'People – white people – think she's too easy on the spooks by a long way. She was pushing her luck hard when she decided to pay them same wages as us – but then she sorta changed her mind, in a manner of speakin'.'

'How?'

'She raised black wages but gave the whites more as well. There would ha' been really bad trouble if she hadn't backed down – that kinda thing may go up North, but it don't go down here. I guess she learned somethin' there. She still gives spooks jobs that should be ours. The Steward of Malfi is a real big man, runs the whole place day to day – he's a black fella.'

'So, she's not popular?'

Strobe sniffed meaningfully. 'Can't say that, rilly. No gainsayin' she's black-eyed with raven tresses just like you read about in novels, but she's got a reputation fer bein' kinda cold and stony. You gotta hand it to her, though, she's spread the wealth about in the way her husband never did, nor any of the Van Owen family – built new houses for everyone who works on the estate, schools for the kids – blacks, too – but she realized it had to be segregated. So she's well liked enough. But, like I said, cold. So that's why they call her the Duchess.'

'Chief Moseby tell you himself – that I stopped your demotion?'

Strobe laughed. 'Did he hell. I knew he was real angry at me 'cos Van Owen pissed in his ear. He tried some woggle about speaking up fer me – but I'm too old a girl not to know cowshit from wild honey when I hear it. I knew it must ha' been you.'

Or, thought Cale, *he got the word from his deputy listening at the door.*

So Cale poured him a drink and they chatted away happily for a couple of hours, in which, in exchange for some excellent whisky, he learned a very great deal and found himself a new friend. Events that yesterday had looked fatal – Van Owen trying to have him killed and powerful enemies out to step on his windpipe – today were happily explained and everything was super-dooper. No news, IdrisPukke used to say, was ever as good or as bad as it first seemed.

For today, black clouds had turned to balmy sun and he decided to enjoy it before turning his attention to his next problem, whatever that might happen to be.

17

Mon afternoon, Memphis

Sweetheart Tom

Both of us must be clever, be careful. Don't let anyone ever find out about us. You won't believe the hell that will follow. I feel bad about lying – unsafe and on edge. But I feel utterly totally completely wonderful when you are holding me,

I long for you
I worship you
I'm insane for you
Arbell

– Jenufer Smythe, *The Letters of Arbell Materazzi to Thomas Cale: Fact or Forgery?* (Atlantic)

Night in a room full of seventy boys is a noisy business for the first hour after the lights have been extinguished: snores, the restless groan of so many badly made beds on which the would-be sleepers moved about to shed the skin of the horrible day, the occasional laugh from those who had made it into the land of Nod, in which happier times existed, the more frequent gasps and moans as the dreamers fled somewhere just as bad as their waking life. But slowly, a calm of sorts descends. This was the best time of day for the eight-year-old Thomas Cale, the best moment of life itself in the house of desolation. With the blanket pulled over his eyes and wool stopping his ears, he could imagine he was on his own in a world where being alone was a terrible sin. In the absolute dark he could be almost anywhere, away from Redeemers, away from boys, away for the moment from the constant threat of pain, away from ideas of sin, just away. That night was particularly special in that he'd stolen two tack biscuits, hard as the hob of Hell, from Dominic Savio, who'd been given them for squealing on another boy. Now he was away from hunger, too. Then he began to sense something moving. It was not something in the dormitory but from deep inside, a vague sensation in the stomach, growing and growing, expanding and rushing, so intense, so wonderful and glorious and beautiful, until it filled him up from top to toe, filled every cell in his heart and feet and brain so wonderfully and utterly and completely full of joy.

Rosewood was the township where the blacks who served Malfi the house lived. A fair number also worked for the vulgar newly rich types who lived in nearby Nemesis, attracted there by proximity to the glamour of the court of Arbell Van Owen. In Harrison, the settlements for the white lower orders, Rosewood was known as Muntown. The pastor in Rosewood was the Reverend Joseph Hanson, and it was his habit to say goodbye to his congregation of a Sunday after the service. This Sunday was no different, except that he caught blown-by-the-wind and dragged-by-the-Tiny-Ones Ray Jackson on his way out, clearly trying not to be cornered by his new pastor. But Joseph was too artful to be dodged.

'You're new to Malfi, son.'

'Yes, sir.'

'Not just passing through, though, you've been here more than a fortnight.'

Ray was apparently somewhat put out that Hanson knew even that much.

'I came to Malfi looking for work at the big house. Heard there were great opportunities for a coloured man here.'

'Can be,' said Hanson. 'Any luck?'

'No, sir. I . . . I have to see a person about a job, Pastor. I'm glad to have met you.'

Before Hanson could speak, he'd turned his back and was walking away as fast as possible without actually breaking into a run.

*

There was no sane reason why Cale was hanging around Malfi instead of getting safely fat in the remote Bermudas, but love, as you almost certainly know from personal experience, makes people crazy, particularly the thwarted, betrayed kind. What did he think he was doing here? He did not think, of course. Instead, he kept himself busy. How many wonderful things – pyramids, canals, empires – have been created by people trying to avoid dealing with what's really eating them? Cale avoided the volcano moiling under him by working hard on the immediate task of bringing the security of the outer grounds of Malfi up to standard. It was interesting enough work, without being particularly demanding. The system had fallen so far into disrepair and general incompetence that major and satisfying improvements were easily possible. He rearranged rosters, began proper training and introduced rigorous physical exercise to bring the flabby and lazy guards up to scratch. He was very much harder on himself in this regard. He was in the worst physical condition of his life. But it was vanity that drove him more than pragmatism. If he was to meet Arbell he was determind to be as close to the God he was once claimed to be by the mad Pope Bosco. The neglected outer walls were repaired or improved, the decayed signalling systems rebuilt. After the horrors of the last year, it was a pleasure to drift. It's extraordinary what can be ignored if you have something to do and a nice place to do it in. He didn't even think about the fact that it couldn't last.

Once Cale had been with the great statesman IdrisPukke when some diplomat from the Hanse had asked him what was the most important thing to understand in politics.

'Events, my dear fellow,' IdrisPukke had said. 'Events.'

He suspected at the time that IdrisPukke was just being deliberately enigmatic, as usual trying to strengthen his reputation for an almost supernatural insight into the way the world really worked – certainly neither Cale nor the diplomat knew what he really meant, though both pretended they did. But it stuck in his mind and, thinking it over through the years, he decided there was something simple and straightforward at the heart of it. The world was full of people with ideas about how the world should be organized in line with their own beliefs and interests, well intentioned or evil, as the case may be. But almost nothing ever worked out the way it was intended or expected to. IdrisPukke was right – events changed everything. The Brews had a saying: *If you want to make God laugh, tell him your plans.* Well, *events* were God's little jokes on mankind. *Events* were what were real in life, and very little else. Of course, if you're a nobody living in the arsehole of nowhere with a population of like-minded dullards, events may be few and far between. But this was Malfi, and in its multiform gyrations of pitch and toss an *event* of some kind was bound to happen. A wind was moving through the balmy doldrums.

One bright morning the house of Malfi woke to terrible screams and cries of 'Murder! Murder! Murder most foul!'

Within minutes, Jefferson Moseby, Head of Security at Malfi, was shown through a crowd of the hysterical and panicked into a bedroom in one of the most exclusive corridors in the house.

'Get these goddam people out of here!' he shouted to his men, who took more than five minutes to sweep up and shovel out the assortment of gawping nobs (*Do you know who I am? Unhand me, sir. I want your name immediately*) who'd gathered to witness the horrible sight of Almand Lord lying on his bed with his throat cut. Lord was a wealthy, ruthless, notoriously promiscuous Southern businessman whose philosophical system could best be summed up as a determination to hate his neighbour but to love his neighbour's wife.

He was not the first murder victim at Malfi by any means, but he was certainly the most important. As Moseby stared down at the corpse – eyes wide in a fixed horror and pain and what seemed like gallons of blood everywhere – he cursed his luck: *if I didn't have bad luck*, he complained to his wife, *I wouldn't have any luck at all.* An objective person might have pointed out that his growing misfortunes had more to do with the fact that his many sins were coming back to haunt him and retribution was long overdue. Luck had hardly anything to do with it at all. And now this. They'd be looking for someone to blame, and who better, he thought, full of self-pity, than Jefferson Monroe Moseby.

'What have you got?' he said to Strobe, who had been the first guard on the spot.

'He was seen with a woman 'bout eleven o'clock las' night.'

'Identified?'

'Still lookin'.'

'I doubt a woman did this. He's a big fellow.'

'I'm rememberin' he fought a couple a' duels. At least I think I heard that. Revenge?'

'Well, check on it.'

'And the window was open and it was chilly last night.'

Moseby walked over to the window and looked down. The ancient ivy and the numerous crenellations would have made it possible for someone to climb up.

'Send someone down there to keep people away. I'll check it myself later.'

'He was a real ladies' man, they tell me. That's what the duels were 'bout.'

That was all he needed. He'd let an important guest be murdered, and maybe he'd have to arrest someone important too. Worse and worse.

They both stared glumly at the dead man for some time, until another of the guards came up to them.

'One of the guests, she tol' me he was on trial for murder las' year in Odessa. He was acquitted.'

'Obviously – he wouldn't be here if he hadn't been acquitted, would he?'

'Jus' saying, boss.'

'If it was revenge, it could be for that.'

'Doubt it, boss.'

'Why do you doubt it, Lyman?'

''Cos it was for killing a nigger. Shot him down for organizin' the other kneesgrows to asks for better pay.'

'An organizer, you say?'

Lyman checked his notes. 'Yeah. The Coloured League.'

'Never heard of them.'

'They a league fer coloured folks.'

Moseby was suddenly inspired: this might not be a catastrophe, it might be an opportunity for salvation. He realized that what he needed to get out from under the iniquities (bribery, fraud, the odd murder) about to find him out was a crisis – a crisis that only he, Jefferson Moseby, could identify and then solve. If it was the wrong solution, what did that matter? Find the murderer and do it quick and all might be overlooked. He turned to Lyman.

'That person who tol' you 'bout the trial, I want to see 'em in my office in twenty minutes.'

18

Three days later, in a dark room in the basement of the main guard-house of Malfi, Moseby was examining a black man sitting at a desk with his hands tied behind his back. He did not look well.

'Now, son,' said Moseby, placing a carpenter's mole wrench on the table. 'I've been real patient with you. But I'm feeling a bit dainty this mornin', so you better get a wiggle on. Until now, we've gone easy on you because we don't take to torture in this country, but there are people next door who would like to pull your fingernails out – but despite your crimes, all I've done is inhibitin' yure sleep and some water-dippin'. I know you murdered Mr Lord because your accomplices, they've told me everything. They put all the blame on you. I know you're the leader of the local chapter of the Dus'Men. I know it all.'

'It's not true,' gasped the prisoner. 'I don' know nothing 'bout this man . . . never heard of the Dusk Men.'

'*Dust*, not Dusk. You know that. You think that I'm stupid, don't you, son?'

'No, suh.'

Moseby pointed at the mole wrench, on which he'd daubed a plentiful covering of red cochineal paste.

'You're forcing me to send in those persons next door. And I don't want to. But, let's be clear, son, either your signature is going to be on that confession or your nuts are going into that wrench.'

A week later, after three shots of Rock whisky, Strobe was beginning to talk to his new friend Savio about the murder of Almand Lord and the alarming conspiracy uncovered by Jefferson Moseby, which had, in a few days, shocked the entire country.

'So you beat it out of him?' said Cale.

Strobe laughed. 'Never touched the feechee son of a bitch. Torture's 'gainst the constitution.'

'So he just stuck his neck in a noose because you asked him to?'

'We gave him some encouragement.'

'Really?'

'Kept him awake, walked him around the room for twelve hours at a stretch and dunked his head in a barrel a' water.'

'Certainly sounds encouraging.'

Strobe considered carefully. 'Got to hand it to the kneesgrow, we had to go the extra mile to fear him up.'

'I don't understand.'

'Moseby – he daubed some red painty stuff on a wrench and threatened to rip his bollocks off. That did the trick.'

'So why did he kill Almand Lord?'

'Lord beat some agitating coon to death for stirring up his workers – only he did it in broad daylight in front of fifty witnesses.'

'But he got off?'

''Course he got off. The only thing 'markable about his gettin' off was it ever went to trial in the firs' place.'

'So it was revenge?'

'No, no, no,' said Strobe as Cale refilled his glass. 'It was a' scuse. It got the 'Dessa niggers real angry, so the Dus' Men took advantage to get recruiting your coloured malcontents to start a race mut'ny.'

'Dust Men? Doesn't sound very frightening.'

'Dus' Men because they're gonner turn their oppressors – that's you and me – gonner turn us to dust.'

'What do you know about them?'

'Dus' Men? Nothing. They're a secret 'sciety, gonner threaten our very 'xistence – a 'xistencious threat. They're everywhere.'

'How do you know?'

'Stands to reason. The shades hates us. This is big stuff, Savio. Nick and the governor are comin' tomorrow. I'm tellin' you, we broke this whole thing wide open. Turns out they wanna kill Denmark on account of him bein' your all-white golden boy. Send a message.'

'I suppose,' said Cale after a moment, 'there's a way in which you *can* be all white and golden at the same time. A pretty useful-type confession, that.'

Strobe looked at him and leaned forward, as if concerned there might be eavesdroppers about.

'You heard Govna Van Owen's due this afternoon?'

A pause. Then:

'How often does he come?' Cale asked.

'Reg'lar. Thuh road from Dallas to Malfi's 'bout fifty mile and it's about the straightest, bestest, fastest road in thuh United Estates, on account of that how Governor Van Owen got the citizens to pay for it to be that way. Got a waystation for fresh horses and everythin'. Can be here in two hours if'n he likes to.'

It was late evening of the next day when Cale was summoned up to the house and quickly shown inside through the side entrance of what amounted to a lodge inserted in the main building. He was kept waiting long enough for it to get on his nerves but was finally taken to an elegant room, in the centre of which was a large desk that had carvings on it of gods and monsters so ornate and so strange it looked as if it had taken a talented lunatic a lifetime to carve.

'I see you're admiring the escritoire,' said Louis Van Owen. 'Deranged, isn't it?'

'Specially made for you, was it?'

'But I'm glad to see you're in such good spirits. Enjoying the place?'

'It's all right. It isn't a good idea, meeting like this.'

Van Owen ignored him. 'How much do you know about the murder of Almand Lord?'

'Just the gossip.'

'Which is?'

'That some coloured gang of politicals killed him in revenge for getting away with murdering some Chartist work reformer.'

'And what do you think yourself?'

'Don't think much at all – don't know anything about it.'

'Except?'

'Except they must be exceptionally skilled to get into Malfi, murder someone and then get out again without a trace.'

'I see. I'm not really knowledgeable about such things, but I know you have some skill in breaking and entering. Could you do it?'

'I wouldn't try unless I had to.'

'Because?'

'Very little chance of success.'

Van Owen grimaced.

'This political gang, the Dust Men, must be remarkably dangerous people if they succeeded where a man of your skills fears to tread.'

'Very remarkable.'

'A very considerable threat to the Union, people like that.'

'Absolutely.'

'If there were enough of them, a threat to our very existence, an existential threat, wouldn't you say?' Van Owen smiled. 'Well, they would be if they weren't a collection of coots, loons and asswipes. They've attacked the odd postman in the street with a blunt axe, but a Dust Man getting into Malfi is about as likely as one of them sprouting wings.'

'The existence, real or not, of a gang of daring and well-organized Negro evildoers with a careful plan for overthrowing the Estates would be pretty useful for a man like you.'

'Taking the high moral ground, Mr Cale? I must say I hadn't pegged you as a hypocrite. As for the Dust Men – if daring Negro evildoers with a cunning plan don't exist, it's merely good sense to invent them. People believe what they want to believe. Yes?'

'So if it wasn't flying Negroes, who was it?'

'Almand was a notorious adulterer as well as a mean bastard. He forgot he was in Malfi and not in that shithole Odessa, where he could kill a man in broad daylight just for asking for better wages. It appears he thought that he could get away with seducing the wife of an ambassador to a country where even looking at a married woman in the wrong way counts as a dishonour so great you have to ritually disembowel yourself unless you slaughter the man who's offended you.'

'So you've come to bring the real murderer to justice?'

'I most certainly have not. The death of John of Boston hasn't had quite the effect I'd been hoping for. It turns out his successor has decided to act like the leader of a great nation and not like the time-serving coffin salesman we all took him to be. It seems he's determined to keep the Federals in the South and put a stop to my efforts to prevent the United Estates from tearing itself apart.'

'I can see that would be disappointing, given you went to so much trouble.'

'Very droll,' said Van Owen, and sighed. 'Ah well – the iron law of unintended consequences.'

'*Whether we fall by ambition, blood, or lust*,' intoned Cale, smiling, '*like diamonds we are cut by our own dust*.'

Van Owen laughed. 'One of yours? Sounds like the kind of poetry you'd write. Drink? There's a good whisky and a very decent brandy.'

'Brandy, thanks.'

Cale took the delicate glass and sipped. It *was* decent.

'This claptrap about the Dust Men turns out to be inspired. The only reason the fellow who runs security –' He gestured towards Cale to remind him.

'Moseby.'

'Yes – the only reason he started claiming the murder was committed by them was to deflect attention from an investigation by Arbell's steward, Saul Gaines, into his long-time habit of helping himself from the till, so to speak. Met Gaines at all?'

'No.'

'Very able man. What my more deplorable constituents would call a smart nigger. Very smart, as it happens. Anyway, he'd found out that this Moseby had been skimming supplies at the house for years, had deals with most of the suppliers to re-export about a tenth of everything that came in and sell it at fifty cents on the dollar. He's been pulling in maybe twenty thousand a year for the last ten years after everyone's been paid off. He hoped a big score like this Dust Men nonsense that he'd personally uncovered would save his neck.'

'And will it?'

'Well, Nick's pretty loyal to his people. Southern honour and all. It's done us a lot of good. This claptrap about a group of cunning

Negroes out to take revenge on the white man has caught fire everywhere in the South. It's even frightened the more half-hearted supporters of black rights in the North – and there are plenty of them. Handle this well and I might be able to put this whole issue back by twenty years.'

'You don't give up, do you?'

'What I want is to stop a bloody civil war that'll destroy the United Estates. I don't see how the coloureds are going to benefit from that. Given time, slavery'll wither away – I truly believe that. But it's too soon. We need to adapt the old servitude, make it more humane, with proper legal protections. But if Lincoln keeps trying to enforce the laws on emancipation, the South and the North go to war. That's all there is to it.'

By now Van Owen had become passionate. Catching himself out, he stopped talking and smiled. 'Perhaps I should have been a preacher.'

Cale did not respond for a moment. Then:

'Why are you telling me all this?'

'Who has brains better to pick than the brains of the great Thomas Cale? That makes sense, doesn't it?'

'Of course.'

'And nothing I tell you of my plans is worse than the things you already know. So, it's sensible to make use of you and sensible for you to be made use of.'

'A wicked thought shared is a wicked thought halved.'

'Something like that. So, what do you think of my strategy?'

'I'm not interested in your problems, I'm interested in *my* problems.'

'What would it take for you to *become* interested?'

Cale was up and with a knife drawn – a flash from the light of a mirror in the sun was slower. His alarm was inspired by the fact that the question came from the other side of the room. And there was no one there. There was a brief pause then a loud click and a panel of books opened to reveal a coal-black rectangle from which Nick Van Owen emerged.

'Don't be alarmed,' said the governor quickly. 'This is my brother,

Nick, who, as you can see, has an adolescent taste for making an entrance.'

'Could get him in trouble one day. And you.' Cale turned to the governor, pointedly not putting away the knife. 'How many other people have you told about me?'

'No one else – I assure you.'

'But I'm somehow not reassured.'

'Mr Cale,' said Nick. 'I know' – he paused – 'everything about . . . the business between you and my brother.'

'You mean that we conspired together to murder John of Boston?'

'I was trying to be circumspect,' said Nick. 'After all, walls have ears.'

'Then stop using my name.'

'Of course. My apologies. And for my sudden appearance. My older brother is right to rebuke me. It gives him such pleasure and I find it hard to resist giving him the opportunity to tell me off. May I sit down?'

Cale put away his knife. He didn't want to be outdone in style.

'We think it's a crying shame that a man of your abilities should be languishing in charge of a collection of the fat and the useless in a job of no significance.'

'I quite like languishing.'

'But for how long?' asked Nick.

'We want to offer you a promotion,' said Van Owen.

'I wonder what it is that makes me long for a fast horse and directions to the nearest border.'

'There's nothing stopping you. You could have done that weeks ago. So, given that for whatever reason of your own you've decided to come to Malfi, you might as well have as much power . . .'

'And money,' added Nick.

'. . . as possible.'

'Whose throat do I have to cut?'

Both men laughed, amused, but Louis van Owen a little uncomfortably. The governor placed a thick bundle of dollars on the table.

'Yours.'

'For what?'

'Information.'

'About?'

'What's going on in Malfi,' said Nick.

Cale was puzzled. 'What I'm told is that Nick Van Owen knows pretty much everything that goes on in Malfi.'

'Everything,' said Nick, 'but what goes on at its heart. My sister-in-law Arbell is an aloof person, a cold person. When the doors of her private apartments close, nothing comes out.'

'What do you want to know?'

'Things in the Estates are difficult – factions oppose factions in turn riven by factions. Arbell may be a chilly piece of work, but we think she's in contact with black and white suffragists in the North – more to the point that she's supplying them with the money to make their case. If so, we need to know. Her steward Gaines may be the go-between. He may even be an important man in the movement himself. If so, we need to know.'

'So . . . again . . . what do you want me to do?'

'Moseby just made up the notion that the Dust Men were after Denmark in the hope it would help him stay out of jail because she'd be so grateful. But it seems to me his hand was guided by the Fates themselves. Arbell's climbing the walls with worry. We want you to become Denmark's bodyguard.'

19

Lying naked on her enormous bed, seventeen-year-old Arbell Materazzi (heiress to an empire) held Thomas Cale in her arms (sold for sixpence, nobody cared how old he was), having banished all reservations about him. How brave he was in saving her life. How kind and generous he'd been towards her brother, dumb from birth and treated with contempt by everyone, even her father, for being an imbecile. How ungrateful she had been to harbour any doubts. How generous towards others it made him seem, allowing her to forget the sight of him killing half a dozen men in their sleep in saving her with no more emotion than if he were snuffing out a candle. She was almost burning with adoration as she made love to him that night, worshipping him with every inch of her lovely body. What graceful magic this worked on Thomas Cale's abraded heart, what joy and astonishment at the touch of her skin and lips to ease the weeping blisters on his soul.

'No harm can come to you. Promise me,' she said after nearly an hour of silence.

'Your father and his generals have no intention of letting me anywhere near the fight. I've no intention of going, anyway. It's nothing to do with me. My job is to look after you. That's all that interests me.'

'But what if something happened to you?'

'Nothing's going to happen to me.'

'Not even you can be sure of that.'

'What's the matter?'

'Nothing.' She held his face in her hands and looked into his eyes, as if searching for something. 'You know that picture on the wall in the next room?'

Cale thought about his answer carefully. 'No.'

She laughed. Everyone treated her feelings so carefully, as if she were a little china doll who must always be agreed with and treated as special. What a joy (for now) to be treated like just a girl.

'It's my great-grandfather – with his second wife, Stella. The reason I put it up there was because of a letter I came across when I was a girl, nosing about in some old family bits and pieces I found in a trunk. I don't think anyone had looked inside for nearly a hundred years.' She stood up and walked over to a drawer on the far side of the room, naked as a jay-bird and enough to stop the heart. How is it, he thought, that such a creature loves me? She rooted around for a moment then returned with an envelope. She took out two pages of dense writing and looked at them sadly. 'This is the last letter he wrote to Stella before he died at the siege of Jerusalem. I want you to hear the last paragraph because I want you to understand something.' She sat down at the foot of the bed and began reading:

My very dear Stella,

The indications are very strong that we shall attack again in a few days – perhaps tomorrow. Lest I should not be able to write you again, I feel impelled to write lines that may fall under your eye when I shall be no more.

Stella, my love for you is deathless, it seems to bind me to you with mighty cables that nothing but God could break. If I do not return, my dear Stella, never forget how much I love you, and when my last breath escapes me on the battlefield, it will whisper your name.

But, Stella! If the dead can come back to this earth and move unseen around those they loved, I shall always be near you; in the garish day and in the darkest night – amidst your happiest scenes and gloomiest hours – always, always; and if there be a soft breeze upon your cheek, it shall be my breath; or if the cool air fans your throbbing temple, it shall be my spirit passing by.

Arbell looked up, tears in her eyes. 'That was the last time she ever heard from him.' She scrabbled closer to him from the foot of the bed and held him tight. 'I am bound to you, too. Always remember that, no matter what occurs, I will always be near, always my spirit will be watching over you.'

Cale, amazed, did not know what to say. But in a short time words were no longer necessary.

The next day she sent him something he never could have possibly imagined existed in the world: a love letter.

All night long full of you – can't eat, can't sleep. I scold myself for being so ridiculous – see what a fool you've made of me! I want you, just want. I lay down on the cold marble to cool myself down and hoped it would reach my heart and make it numb. No such luck. I believe and believe that we have become one flesh, one soul. Let me tell you, sir, that the way you leaned your head gently back against the wall and looked at me when you thought I wasn't watching drove me out of my mind.

A xxxxxxxxxxxxxxxxxxxxxxxxxxxx

20

Texas weather at that time of year was of two kinds: roasty hot and scorification hot. Malfi was no exception. It was so warm by early morning in Rosewood township it felt as if a new word must be coined to describe the temperature that day (crematory? torrefying?). Ray Jackson was emerging from Lunsford the Grocer after another failure to get a job, this time delivering vegetables to the servants' kitchen at the Malfi house. Amazed at the furnace outside, he crossed the road to sit in the shade of Munros Barber Shop (Shave 10 cents – Haircut 15) along with half a dozen men. The only person moving in the heat was a boy of about twelve carrying a bucket of paste and a sheaf of papers. Panting and covered in sweat, he started pasting up the tenth poster of the morning, which presented a rather delicately drawn man who offered to give anyone who found him the sum of $50,000. Finished, the young boy moved on, looking as if he were about to have a stroke. Unusually, no one gathered to gasp in amazement because it was pasted up on the sunny side of the street and the size of the reward couldn't quite be made out from the shade of Munros.

Ray was working up the courage to take on the sun man-to-man when he noticed a middle-aged woman carrying a large and heavy-looking package. He was not the kind of person to merely watch a lady in distress, unlike the half-dozen men of varying ages nearby who seemed amused that anyone would be foolish enough to make such an effort on a hellish day like today. Ray walked over to her and asked if she needed any help, watched with unusual intensity by the unchivalrous men in the shade.

'What does it look like, boy?' said the woman, in a tone that brought a burst of laughter from the watching men on the other side of the street. She did not give Ray the time to reply and handed him the box, as if furious that he'd taken so long to offer. 'I'm not paying you,' she said, to the accompaniment of more hilarity. The box *was* heavy, surprising him that such a slight person had been able to carry it any distance at all. Determined not to seem a complete fool to his audience, he replied loudly enough for them to hear:

'And where would you like me to take your order of lead pipes, ma'am?'

'If it's too much for you, young lady, I can manage myself.'

Then she took off, leaving Ray to follow, helped on his way by the wind from delighted hoots of the layabouts in the shade. Har! Har! Har!

But they weren't the only ones enjoying Ray Jackson's discomfort. The three tiny sisters had also turned up to keep pin eyes on their great black hope and make sure the cat was stirring nicely in the pan as they brewed up the ingredients of the great mischief to come. And to enjoy the already fully dry wanted poster of Thomas Cale.

By now, Cale had found a narrow trail where he liked to do his thinking, his mulling walk, his pondering path. It had as little of interest to distract him as possible: no pleasing sunset, pollarded avenues or people passing the time of day. It started not far from the guardhouse, by a river where the water was muddy and full of rotting weeds, the grass dank, no ducks and ducklings, no white swans, no trout taking gorgeous dragonflies with a gentle kiss. Walking allowed him to inhabit a useful place where his most unpleasant thoughts could be kept quiet and he could sift the kinds of daily problem for which there was a cure.

This was where he worked out a way he might solve his most pressing difficulty: persuading Gaines that he disliked and was distrusted by the Van Owen brothers. As long as there was a suspicion that he had anything to do with them, there wasn't a chance of getting anywhere with this particular didoe. During these pondering sessions he often lost all sense of where he was, so that when he came down to earth he found that he'd walked nearly half a mile beyond his usual stopping spot. What brought him to today was the sound of two young black boys mucking about in a tree on the opposite bank with branches leaning over an incredibly noisy and powerful weir.

At first it made him smile to hear the unadulterated pleasure of their screams and shouts as they bounced the branches of the tree with all the exuberance of the youthful hooligan. But then the danger of what they were doing struck him.

'Hey!' he shouted at the boys as they bounced up and down on a branch in a jubilant delight at having something to break.

'*Get out of there! If that branch breaks, you little fuckwits, the weir'll suck you down!*'

The boys, startled, stopped and looked at him from across the river.

'*What are you going to do about it, Grandad?*'

'*You cheeky little bastard. What I'll do is let you drown!*'

There was a brief discussion, during which the two boys uncovered enough sense between them to realize that the man on the opposite bank, gallingly, had a point. Beneath them, the river boiled and surged with a malevolence they at once understood would indeed easily swallow a little boy or two.

But were these gurriers grateful? They were not. Carefully stepping back on to a solid bough and holding tight, they kept one foot bouncing on the smaller branches until they split and hung down enough to give them victory. Then they ran off, howling and screaming a series of disgusting insults concerning the size of his mother's genitals, his love of taking it up the bum and the imaginative hope that his ears turn to arseholes and shit on his shoulders.

Half an hour later, Cale was waiting outside a carefully disguised side entrance to Nick Van Owen's apartments, waiting to be let in to deliver the solution to the Gaines problem, which he'd solved just before he was subjected to so many vile insults by two children he'd been trying to save from drowning.

'I've had an idea,' said Nick Van Owen before Cale could say anything. 'I'll arrange for Gaines to be attacked while he's on his own, and you, just happening to be passing by, bravely come in and rescue him. It's brilliant. He'll owe you his life just as there's a bloodthirsty threat to Arbell's son.'

'Threat?'

Nick laughed. 'Shocking stuff – the Nowse have just come into possession of convincing evidence of a Dust Men threat to our golden boy. Seems they're getting their spies in places everywhere – Malfi most of all.'

'Nowse?'

'It's crow slang for the Board of Estate Security – means sneaky but smart with it.'

'Seems sort of convenient, a rumour like that.'

'It is, though, isn't it? No doubt based on information from a concerned citizen.'

'Will she believe it?'

'If it was about Arbell herself, probably not – but the threats to her spoilt little brat, what loving mother wouldn't be afraid? Besides, the Nowse don't care for me and my brother. She knows that, so she'll be convinced.'

'So why did they believe you?'

'People believe what they want to believe. The Nowse has one purpose: to root out plots and the agents of plots. So, we've given them a plot they *want* to believe. Find me a rat-catcher who's willing to tell his customers that there are hardly any rats. When people stop believing in witches, a witchfinder either has to starve or find another kind of witch.'

Cale made a point of considering what he'd heard carefully. 'It's a very good idea, rescuing Gaines.' In fact, Cale thought it was a terrible idea.

Nick looked very satisfied – what's better than the praise of the praiseworthy?

After the praise, the demolition. Cale tried to look conflicted about turning down the plan. 'But from what I've heard about Gaines, and what you and your brother have confirmed, I've a real fear he'll see through it. He's smart, clearly – he wouldn't have caught out Moseby. I fear its neatness would alert him – and all he'd need is a suspicion to put him off. He might be deeply grateful, but there are all sorts of ways to reward me without letting me into his inner sanctum. Do you see my problem?'

Nick Van Owen looked put out. A worrying pause then a truculent reply. 'Do you have anything better to offer?'

'To be honest, I haven't.' This was a lie, but he thought it undiplomatic to come up with a solution so quickly after having rejected the one offered by Nick. It would keep for a day. 'This is tricky, I admit. I don't see him as someone who'll come to judgement about something so important just on the evidence of one experience.' He could see Van Owen was about to reassert himself – but as he opened his mouth to reply Cale interrupted him. 'But I *do* have a first step to getting his trust.'

'I see,' said Nick, sniffy.

'He distrusts your brother as much as he distrusts you, yes?'

'Putting it mildy.'

'So, working on the useful notion that my enemy's enemy is my friend – often in my experience completely untrue – he needs to see your brother and me at each other's throats.'

Van Owen, his vanity fighting it out with the good judgement and intelligence not yet corrupted by a lifetime of getting his own way, considered this for some time.

'How?'

21

Inside the justly renowned Chapel of Light in Malfi lies the majestic granite sarcophagus of Aristotle Van Owen. Two female figures, almost identical, are kneeling in front of it, on this, the fourth anniversary of the internment of the great man now rotting down inside the elaborately decorated tomb. The two figures, however closely they resemble one another, are, in only one respect, utterly distinct. One, Arbell Van Owen, is a woman of flesh and blood, the other her image astonishingly realized in marble. Unlike the carving on the tomb, the standard decorative bombast of the wealthy dead – the statue is a masterpiece of the sculptor's art – according to the artist Theolokopolis, 'the most compelling depiction of grief of the last one hundred years'. But, as is usually the case with art, it presented a vision of the human spirit which ought to be true rather than one that actually is. In fact, Arbell had merely quite liked the much older, and rather ugly, Van Owen and had at first politely but firmly rejected his offer of marriage. But so powerful was his genuine love for Arbell and so increasingly enormous the sums of money and property he offered to bestow on her – including nearly all of his wealth upon his death – and so gently and sweetly did he deal with her constant refusals that in the end she relented and agreed to become his wife. At first, she was a little ashamed of herself for marrying a man for his money. On the other hand, it was a very great *deal* of money and she had never lied about her feelings for him. And given that in the years since the death of her first husband, unjustly executed by the Swiss for a defeat against the Redeemers that was certainly not his fault, she had never been able to find even a spark of passion for the endless queue of those who longed to marry her. The problem is that she was relatively poor and was deeply worried about providing for her son (not, it should be said, something that worried Denmark much himself). She also had to support a small army of dependent relatives who, having lost all their money and property when the Redeemers sacked Memphis, had failed to discover a role in life, there not being much call for people whose only talent was to tell other people to bring them things. Throughout the Four Quarters, this pathetic bunch were known as Wenwees, on account of their tendency to begin almost every conversation with the words, *When we were in Memphis* . . .

In the end, rather ashamed of herself, she gave in. But theirs was an amicable and affectionate union, much gossiped about – most famously for the widely believed claim that she had written into the marriage contract a clause which obliged her to share the bed of Aristotle Van Owen on no more than twelve occasions a year.

True or not, they got on well, despite the fact that she spent eye-watering sums of money turning Malfi into a powerhouse of the artistic and intellectual naissance that had so thrillingly galvanized the world since the collapse of that hideous cult of death known as the Redeemers, a philosophy now (everyone agreed) consigned to the dark ages of the past and the dunghill of history.

It was the fourth anniversary of Aristotle Van Owen's death and this was why Arbell was kneeling at his sarcophagus next to her marbellized self. Once the service was over, everyone who was anyone, including Governor Van Owen, trooped out, looking forward to yet another excellent out-of-doors banquet of a kind for which Malfi was renowned. There was no sign in Arbell of the profound grief embodied in the beautiful statue praying at Aristotle's decaying feet, only a quietly fading sadness over a now long dead but well-liked man.

Both the greatest cooks of the world, and the new priesthood describing themselves as chefs de cuisine, came to Malfi to make their reputations. The two groups, traditional and new, loathing one another with as much passion as the almost-vanished Redeemers once reviled the almost-extinct Antagonists. A frequent lodger at Malfi, Nick was well aware that Saul Gaines did not care for these gatherings, although as steward he was very much entitled and even expected to attend. Gaines would have been hard pressed to decide what he disliked most about these occasions: the carefully, and not so carefully, disguised hostility towards him, or the obsequious flattery from those who wanted to gain the approval of Arbell by demonstrating their lack of prejudice.

As soon as he decently could, Gaines took himself off to his modest office some five hundred yards from what the cooks called a picnic and the chefs a *fête champêtre.*

In order to get to his office, Gaines had to pass along a high, windowed corridor next to a rarely visited memorial garden, where, warned of his approach, Cale approached Governor Van Owen and loudly, but not too loudly, buttonholed him just as Gaines was about to pass.

The governor was playing with his springer spaniel, who'd jumped up on the bench on which he was sitting in the hope of being given a treat.

'I know, Patch,' said the governor amiably to the dog, 'that people think you care for me only for what you can get, but I know that it's true affection and loyalty.' He looked up at the approaching Cale.

'I do haunt you still,' said Cale. The governor looked back at the dog.

'You know what I love about you? It's not just your eyelashes the size of a giant cobweb or your big feet. It's that you don't whine when there's nothing more to be got from me. Off you go!' The dog jumped down and went off happily to sniff a hydrangea bush.

'I've put myself in the way of great danger in your service. I deserve better.'

The governor sighed.

'You think too well of yourself. You have *exactly* what you deserve, no more, no less. Besides,' he added, 'doing a job well is its own reward.'

Behind a pillar in the corridor Gaines could see Cale was incensed by the jibe.

'You and your brother are like plum trees growing over stagnant water – plenty of ripe fruit, but nothing but maggots and crows can feed on them.'

The governor remained completely calm in the face of these insults.

'They *do* say,' said the governor mildly, 'that crows fatten best in hard weather. So why not you?'

With that, he stood up.

'Come on, Patch,' he called to the dog, who, fascinated by the strange smell of badger urine and musk of fox, paid him no attention. '*Patch!*' Not wishing to seem too obedient but knowing on which side his bread was buttered, the dog urinated for a few seconds on the bush to show it and his master who was boss and, having demonstrated he was no lapdog, followed the governor. Cale stood watching them leave, intense loathing in his eyes. Ducking a foot or so down, Gaines ensured that he could not be seen through the window and thoughtfully made his way back to his office.

'FUCKING, FUCKING, FUCK, FUCK, FUUUUCK!'

Even those of you with very delicate feelings might have forgiven these hideous curses had you witnessed the fearsome blow the apprentice responsible had delivered to his middle finger while practising nailing a horseshoe to a piece of wood. From most in the stable, there was only laughter. From two visitors, there was only sympathy. One of them was Cale, in the stables to have his horse shod. The other was Saul Gaines.

It was a carefully calculated meeting. Nick Van Owen had ears and eyes everywhere, except in Arbell's private rooms, and Gaines was a creature of habit, taking his rides three days a week, at the same time.

While he waited Cale had been studying one of the horses – even the uninitiated would have been able to see it was something special. He seemed to be on the move even while he was standing still. For a moment, Cale was lost in admiration.

'He's the most perfect horse I've ever ridden,' said Gaines as he came up beside Cale. 'Sinews of wire and legs like a deer. He must weigh two hundred pounds more than any of the other thoroughbreds in this stable. Even his eyebrows have muscles. Are you a man for horses?'

Cale laughed. '*Out of brave horsemanship arise the first sparks of growing resolution that raise the mind to noble action.*'

'That may be so,' said Gaines, smiling back. 'I'm not sure riding has made me noble, but it has given me more pleasure than almost anything else. You're Savio, yes?'

Cale nodded.

'I'm Gaines, the steward here.'

'Yes, of course,' said Cale.

'So what do you make of us so far?'

'It's an extraordinary place.'

'Well, it's certainly that. I've been in some remarkable places, but nothing quite like this.' A pause. 'And how have you found the guards in the lower grounds?' Gaines tried to make this sound casual.

'Honestly?' Cale tried to play the straightforward man of work.

'I find it saves time.'

'Terrible. But the advantage of them being so bad is that the improvements are dramatic.'

'Glad to hear it.' They regarded each other with pleasure, an immediate affinity, despite the deep roots of suspicion common to both men.

'You were in Rus, I hear.'

'Hear?'

'Well, read. As the steward of Malfi, I make a point of looking over the references of anyone connected with the security of the place.' His position established, Gaines smiled. 'You know, I've always been fascinated by the revolution – how something so admirable, the freeing of the serfs from oppression, could go so horribly wrong. I'd be fascinated to pick your brains. Look here, why don't you come to dinner tomorrow?'

'Glad to.'

At that moment a beautifully dressed black woman appeared.

'At last,' she said, looking at Gaines. 'My mistress wants to see you.'

'Look, Cariola, I'm about to go riding. I'll be there in an hour.'

She smiled agreeably. 'She wants to see you *now*.' They held each other's gaze for a moment, Gaines irked, the woman's eyes full of mischief. 'Whether my mistress wants you because she's worried about the new shade of red paint on her fingernails or she's concerned about rumours that the world is coming to its promised end – it's all the same to you, Mr Gaines.'

Gaines smiled, good-humoured. 'I stand corrected.'

And so it was arranged. The first move in the great game was taken.

Later that day Gaines sent a message postponing their dinner for two days and then another delaying the meal for a further week. Did this mean he'd lost interest in Cale? Or did it have no significance at all beyond the fact that Gaines had a particularly difficult and demanding job, and by the look of it a difficult and demanding mistress? So, despite the frustration of the delay, he had the satisfaction of having his hostility towards Arbell confirmed – she was a spoilt brat. But a less patient Nick Van Owen ordered him up to his apartments to find out what was going on.

'Don't you think we should be careful about meeting here?' said Cale. 'There are too many eyes and ears in this place.'

'True. But they all belong to me – even the ones Gaines thinks belong to him. My brother is right – not the least irritating of his habits – Gaines has many talents, but his skills as a sneak are limited. So how did your meeting at the stables go?'

'Well enough. I'm to come for dinner next week.'

'And what's your plan?'

'I don't have one,' said Cale pleasantly.

'Shouldn't you?'

'It's always been my experience,' said Cale, still pleasant, 'and let's face it, what extraordinary experience that is, that when I hired someone who really knew what they were doing I'd leave the matter of plotting up to them, unless they very specifically and explicitly asked for my opinion.'

It was clear that Nick was not at all accustomed to being told by his hirelings to mind his own business. His expression darkened, and not just in the ordinary way of an employer defied by the employed.

'You were once a great man' – he paused to let this sink in – 'but no longer. If you think you can understand me and know my drifts this way and that . . .' He smiled. 'My quicksands are understood neither by you nor by anyone else. Are we clear?'

Cale leaned forward a little and spoke softly. 'I do not think so.'

Again a flicker of surprise from Van Owen. And again a swift and unexpected change.

'Then what *do* you think?'

'That you grossly flatter yourself.'

Van Owen stared at Cale for a moment as if he'd just started to grow a second head. Then he stood up and walked around the desk. Cale, uncertain, thought about pulling a knife. But Van Owen held out his hand.

'Until I met you,' he said, 'I never hired anyone but flatterers and people who were too frightened to tell me the truth to my face. Like all great men, I need an honest man who understands me and corrects my vices.'

It was not easy to surprise Cale, but he was surprised now. In the matter of garden-variety evildoers, he'd placed Nick right in the middle of the compost heap. This level of insight was not at all what he had expected.

At the dinner with Gaines a few days later Cale began to consider again if he was losing his touch when it came to reading other people. By reputation and their previous meeting, Cale had reckoned Gaines to be a man in command of himself. In a world where almost everyone around him was hostile to his unforgivable blackness, he gave the impression that while aware of this antagonism, he was pretty much indifferent to, and even mocked, their resentment. But tonight he did not seem the same man but distracted, as if he was trying to contain some great excitement. But so what? Perhaps he'd bought a new pair of particularly handsome shoes. Or received some great news. Cale told himself the same thing he'd told Nick Van Owen – stop thinking you know anything. At any rate, after a couple of drinks they both eased off and they mutually returned to the game in hand.

'When I was in Paris a few years ago I came across an interesting fellow, Vladimir Safranski, though everyone called him Vova. He was a fixer for the Boll Sheviks, at least that's what people said, and that he knew everyone right up to Stalovek himself. Come across him at all?'

It was the oldest trick in the book, but still a good one, thought Cale. If such a person did not exist and you claimed to know them, then Gaines's work was done. But even if you denied knowing them, the wisest move, it was hard even for a good liar not to give away a flicker of hesitation. Admitting that he knew Safranski, which he did, might seem to add to his credibility, but this had its problems. What if Gaines still had contact with him? A letter with a description would be a very dangerous thing indeed. Fortunately, Cale knew that Safranski had upset Stalovek with a clumsy joke about his weight and had vanished from his apartment one night, never to be mentioned again. At least not if you knew what was good for you.

'I met him a few times. But I didn't know him well enough to call him Vova.'

'What *did* you call him?'

'Mr Safranski. Friendly fellow, though, like you say. Mostly, people don't much care to chat with bodyguards.'

Gaines moved on as if it were nothing much, and a few more casual questions about Cale's time in Rus followed that weren't at all casual. But Cale had the advantage that he was able to lie about his time there, using the truth carefully pruned of anything useful. Gaines moved on in his interrogation, probing him all informal and nonchalant about his attitudes to the Van Owen brothers while Cale tried to do the same. It took some considerable skill to raise the subject overheard by Gaines of Governor Van Owen's failure to live up to his side of the (entirely fictional) bargain they'd struck. He mentioned it then almost immediately changed the subject, as if to say to Gaines: *I was badly done by, but I'm not the sort of retainer who'll whine about things so I'm not going to say anything more about it – however wronged I was.* The difficulty, and the pleasure, was to express his loathing and resentment of Van Owen without seeming to be the kind of unstable and therefore untrustworthy person dominated by loathing and resentment. But he set the hook tasty like.

After a while, Gaines came back for a careful nibble. Cale pretended to dismiss it. 'I had a friend who used to advise me: *Talk happiness, I've trouble enough of my own.*' He laughed softly at himself, as if for his foolishness in expecting the powerful to be grateful. 'If you want a great man to treat you well, be Patch, the lapdog.'

'He made a promise then, the governor?'

'He did.'

'But didn't keep it?'

A bit too direct, thought Cale. *Tone it down a bit.*

Cale smiled the smile of the rightly aggrieved. 'It was a private matter, and I gave my word to keep it so.' Having established that there were limits to the power that the treacherous would have over him and that he was an upstanding servant to be absolutely trusted, he tried some nosing of his own.

'What's your experience of the governor?' A bit on the nose, reflected Cale. Don't drink any more.

Gaines grimaced pleasantly. 'I don't know him that well. He has, I'm told, a great taste for women and is held to be a lively and pleasant enough fellow. He has a reputation for being able to broker a deal between people who'd rather die than talk together. God knows, it's a skill we need.'

'We?'

'The Estates.'

'The people we dislike,' acknowledged Cale, as if self-aware and rueful, 'can never be bad enough. Nothing can be more painful than hearing they have qualities to admire.'

A pleasant silence for a moment.

'You mentioned you fought against the Laconics during the White Terror.'

'Yes,' said Cale. Gaines asked a few questions, again with the main intention of finding out whether there were weaknesses or evasions in his response. Cale presented himself as a blunt soldier. In this, he was completely convincing.

When he left it was still light, just about, and in the garden he was pleased to come across Hetty Summerstone, arm in arm with a girl, eighteen or so. Hetty was neither pretty nor plain; her attraction lay in her expression – mischief and daring; but the other girl was extraordinary. She looked like the model for a beautiful woman in a painting he'd come across after he'd taken Ravenna in the war against the League of Cambrai. He'd forgotten the title or who painted it, but it had stayed in his mind for two reasons: the grey-eyed beauty of the woman in the painting and the sheer oddity of the fact that she was holding a large weasel.

Hetty looked at him, cheeky but not unfriendly, and Cale bowed slightly and said nothing. Hetty whispered something into the girl's ear and both of them laughed like children as they headed off in the direction of the maze.

As he turned into an elegant hermit's grotto that no hermit had ever lived in (the ones he'd come across were invariably smelly and mad), who should he discover having a quiet smoke on a bench but Nick Van Owen.

'I refer you to my previous comment,' said Cale.

'Don't worry, my dear Savio. No one ever comes here when I'm at prayer.'

Cale assumed he was joking. But after their previous meeting he was no longer confident that he had the measure of Nick Van Owen.

'So, did you and Gaines talk about us?'

'I'm surprised your ears weren't burning.'

'My ears are always burning,' said Nick.

'Flattering yourself again, I see.'

Nick laughed.

Cale continued: 'I confirmed what he already knew – that I think that you and your brother are a pair of bastards. But I revealed my trustworthiness by refusing to go into details. He thinks I'm honest – not a man for gossip – reliable in the face of provocation. Underneath the bluntness, a man of intelligence and understanding – if of a limited sort.'

'Offer you a job?'

'No.'

'We need to move on.'

'Good night.'

On his walk back to his rooms Cale indulged himself in thoughts about how little he understood about how things worked in the world but, still, how much greater that limited understanding was than the grasp possessed by almost everyone else. Nick, for example, in his belief that the matter of Gaines could be hurried. For

Nick, and for nearly everyone else, problems were a matter of scale. But just because a problem was of a huge size didn't mean it was difficult. The problem of how to beat one of the best-trained armies in history using peasants whose only skill was using shovels and wheat-flails was, of course, quite difficult – but it only took a couple of weeks to work out the basics of how to do it. It probably didn't take five minutes to come up with the idea of neutralizing the cavalry of the Cognac by destroying the viaduct over the Merida Valley and flooding it as they charged. But the problem of gaining the trust of a clever man like Gaines, bred to be suspicious and determined to keep everyone from his employer's circle he couldn't vouch for at the deepest level, was so tricky it was seriously beginning to get on his nerves. Several days went past and the brothers were becoming even more impatient. They had been successful in deepening the rumours about the threat from the Dust Men to Denmark Materazzi and clearly felt that they'd made Cale's job much easier by doing so. They were beginning to have doubts.

'Nice thing you did for Sarah Prince. She's not by any means a grateful person. Giving Sarah a helping hand requires the patience of a saint.'

In the cool of a Rosewood evening, Joseph Hanson had called out to Ray Jackson to wait up for him.

'It wasn't anything much, Reverend.'

'*He who would do good to another must do it in minute particulars: general good is the plea of the scoundrel.*' Hanson smiled. 'You see, young man, I bring my soap box with me wherever I go. How's the search for work?'

A pause. Then:

'Fine.'

'I know someone who might be able to help.'

Ray hesitated, caught, it seemed, between pride and weariness.

'Look, son, a young Negro in this world is going to find that too often every man's hand is against him. There's no shame in taking a helping one.'

Ride along, ride along with Thomas Cale,
The revolution he'll not fail.
With the blow from an axe and the reaper's flail,
For Caaaale and Stalovek!

The shepherd's crook, the reaping hook,
Has taken on a warlike look.
We've made a weapon of the plough,
For Caaaale and Stalovek!

(*The choir shouts as one*)
October! The Commune! Stalovek!

– 'Battle Hymn of the Proletariat'
(Music and lyrics by Aleksandr Mosolov)

The Philadelphia Inquirer.

A TRUE ACCOUNT OF THOMAS CALE'S MURDER OF THE ROYAL FAMILY OF RUS: THE LOVERLY TSARINAS

. . . Cale and his men crowded into the basement. Cale approached the Tsar. 'What do you mean by this?' said the Tsar.

'This is what I mean,' replied the drunken Cale, and shot him in the chest. He then shot the Empress in the head. Also drunk, the remaining executioners shot chaotically over each other's shoulders until Cale was forced to stop the shooting because of the caustic smoke of burnt gunpowder. A door was opened, and it took some minutes for the smoke to clear, during which time the killers could hear moans and whimpers inside the room. Only now could they see that while the Tsar and Tsarina and the heir apparent were dead, the young girls, though wounded, were still alive. They then set about these beautiful children with bayonets and rifle butts. It was not soon over. By the time of the last dying breath of beautiful 17-year-old Anastasia, twenty minutes of brutal horror had passed.

22

Cale was on his mulling footpath, allowing his thoughts to go a-wandering in the hope of further inspiration in the matter of getting close to Arbell. Today the riverbank was thankfully absent of naughty foul-mouthed boys and Cale slipped easily into the pleasant world of the daydream. At some point during this reverie his waking brain might have become aware of the intermittent sound of a woman singing, but if so it was as gentle on his mind as a drop of dew on the feathers of an Aylesbury duck.

So it was not until the young woman actually floated past him on the river and began picking up speed as she approached the weir that he came back to earth with a start. At first he thought the woman was a mannequin, a dummy thrown into the water by those naughty black boys, perhaps. But then she began singing snatches of a melancholy song:

> Come, my ladies, ladies, ladies, come;
> Good night, ladies; good night, sweet ladies;
> Good night, good night.

His next thought was that he was suffering one of the hallucinations that afflicted him during the various attacks of lunacy that plagued him from time to time. What he was seeing in front of him was what it appeared to be: a young woman being kept afloat on the river by her voluminous clothes and completely indifferent to the fact she was about to be swept to her death in the raging maelstrom of the fast-approaching weir. She changed song, more urgent now.

> Withhold from us our ghostly foe,
> That spot of sin we may not know.

Instinctively, Cale moved to help. Who wouldn't? But Cale was not only a terrible shot, he was also a sorry excuse for a swimmer. Alas, the thought of simply allowing the young woman to drown did cross his mind, and not for just an instant. Those tempted to judge might take into account that the last time he risked his life to save an innocent girl, he'd set in train a series of appalling events that led to the fall of several empires and the deaths of millions. So it was with a heavy rather than heroic heart that Cale jumped into the water and splashed towards the quickly sinking girl and after a few clumsy strokes grasped her tightly by the shoulder with his left hand.

The clothes that had once kept the girl afloat had now become soaked and were dragging her, and Cale along with her, down to the bottom of the river. All at once, the girl became aware of the watery death about to engulf her and panicked. She grabbed Cale around the neck with a vigour surprising in someone so delicate. It was then he realized that the drowning girl was in fact the young woman he had seen laughing at him and heading towards the maze arm in arm with Hetty Summerstone. More pressing than the recognition was that the immediate result of this embrace was that they both went under.

Cale may not have been a great swimmer, but he was certainly a great survivor and, without so much as a moment's consideration for the beautiful young woman, he delivered a blow to her stomach that would have winded a plough horse. It is a tribute to the power of panic that even this was not enough to loosen the girl's grip and a hefty second whack to her head – her ear, in fact – was needed to get her to let go. Gasping, coughing and spluttering, Cale resurfaced, a part of him considering whether to let the struggling girl go and make for the bank, whose sides were looking increasingly steep and muddy and offered nothing but spindly weeds to grab on to. Historians and moralists have often asked themselves whether Thomas Cale was an evil man with some generous impulses or a generous man capable of acts of appalling wickedness. But there was, of course, no time for any of that now. Some part of Cale was unable to leave the girl to drown and, furious, he reached down and grabbed her beautiful long hair. (Interestingly, she'd seriously considered cutting it short only a few days before. Oh, life-saving hair decision!)

Thrashing and gasping as he was dragged down by this soggy girl-anchor, Cale spluttered and flailed towards the bank as the current, desperate for a death and preferably two, urged them towards the whirlypool boiling on the other side of the weir. Cale snatched at the weeds on the bank but, like the cowards the name of weed suggests, they immediately surrendered their roots into his desperate hand. *Let the bitch go!* one of his inner advisors sensibly shouted in his mind's ear. How tempted he was. Another grasp of the weeds – another gutless capitulation.

A few seconds earlier, a minnow, startled by the flash of light reflecting from the sun through an amethyst given to the girl the day before by an unrequited love, turned, panicked out on to the mainstream of the river, where a waiting pike lunged at the little fish and gulped it down, flicking its mighty tail to cause a trifling eddy to move towards Cale and, by an eighth of a nib or a thousandth of a centipawn, shift him closer to the tree from which the naughty gurriers had hurled abuse upon his guiltless head. The branch they'd broken now hung lower towards the river – but not by much. A fraction more, and Cale could easily have grasped the saving branch and pulled himself and the girl to safety. But it had not quite fallen enough to save their lives so easily. But, by a fraction of a fraction his grip held good.

For a full ten seconds the pair of them hovered between all's well and eternity. And then he grabbed the branch up higher in a fingerhold. Another higher grab, then another. And there it was. Exhausted, Cale hauled himself and the waterlogged girl on to the bank and then, by degrees, up the muddy sides, three inches up and then two slippery inches down. Lungs filling with water, exhausted by the dreadful weight of the girl's wet clothes, slowly he began to lose the battle with the Kindly Ones as they stood by tittering to themselves. And then the strong hands of the two boys who had abused Cale so roundly the week before grabbed the girl and pulled her up. But Cale was finished and, as the girl was hauled to safety, he slipped away and, swiftly losing consciousness, sank below the water and was dragged with ever greater speed towards the weir. Did his extraordinary life pass before him as he sank – visions of pain and suffering, the destruction of the mighty, the fall of empires, the millions destroyed, the millions saved, the power, the glory, the agony and ecstasy? Indeed it did not. There were two last thoughts that crossed his dying brain: one was for the girl: *Stupid cow.* The other was for Arbell.

23

Tues morn

Darling Tom

All day filled with thoughts of you. A huge crack has appeared in the wall in the bathing room and I think I might fall down a great big hole in the earth crying out Save me! Save me, Tom! And you would, of course.

When you're not with me I begin to dry up like a grape left out in the sun – a wrinkly little parched raisin. My dearest sweet boy, it's driving me doolally, not seeing you. Thanks for showing me what courage looks like.

A

– Jenufer Smythe, *The Letters of Arbell Materazzi to Thomas Cale: Fact or Forgery?* (Atlantic)

It was unlikely, given how much practice she got, that Gladys (the beautiful, kind-hearted Gladys, I would like to say) made an error in failing to cut the thread of Cale's existence with her shears. More probably, the three weird sisters thought the world was a more amusing place with Cale alive and felt there was plenty of entertainment yet to be had from him. At any rate, he slipped over the weir and was rushed into the depths, where he was whirled around and around like a lump being churned in a madwoman's custard. He could easily have been twirled in the whirlpool of the weir for hours, but something in the interminably complicated swish of the dreadful vortex was disturbed by – who knows what? A little eddied nudge from that pike's tail again? An added swirl caused by a rolling rock disturbed along the riverbed that broke the rhythm of the tumbling water which seemed to have him in the grip of death? Well, whatever it was, it caused the unconscious Cale to be spat out by the spinning maelstrom and sent across the millpond, to be pulled to safety by the two boys who, by adding to their breaking of the branch, saved his skin for the second time.

Within half an hour, both Cale and the girl had been whisked away to the great house, the girl being vanished off to somewhere luxurious while Cale was respectfully helped towards a modest but adequate infirmary. An hour later Cale was recovering from puking up what seemed to him to be significantly more dirty river water than any human being had a right to contain when Saul Gaines arrived, very satisfyingly both deeply concerned for him and full of gushing admiration for him having saved someone who was clearly of enormous significance.

'You know, of course, who she is?' asked Gaines.

'I've seen her swanning about like God's gift, yes.'

Gaines laughed. 'You don't like beautiful women?'

'I don't like the beautiful in general. They seem to think being good-looking is an achievement of some kind.'

'She's Mona Afuentes, daughter of the ambassador of our former Nish masters. He's at Malfi to negotiate the normalization of relationships between us. I can't tell you the money at stake here. If she'd drowned here and for the reasons she threw herself in the water . . . well, I don't want to think of the consequences.'

'Threw *herself* in the water?'

'Ah.' A silence. 'I thought you knew.'

'I certainly did *not* know, because if I had known I'd have let the stupid fucking bitch fucking drown.'

Gaines grimaced sympathetically. 'What can I say? Except that I, personally, am glad you didn't . . .'

'Thanks. I'm so glad you're glad.'

'Play the cynic all you like. I can't tell you the importance of what you've done.'

Cale looked at him. 'Try.'

Gaines laughed again. 'Don't worry, your appalling lapse of judgement has won you golden opinions. But I must be off. There's still hell to pay. The ambassador wants to know why his beloved child tried to kill herself, and the explanation is as tricky as it gets.'

'Which is?'

'I *have* to go, but . . . Look, Savio, keep it to yourself . . . but it seems that the girl was sweet on Denmark Materazzi and the spoilt little fuckwit dropped her from a great height. I've got to go. Say nothing.' He smiled at Cale as if he were his horse and he had won the Derby. 'Outstanding.' And then he was gone.

It was probably too late for the whole thing to be hushed up. Governor Van Owen was right: if three people knew a secret, two of them had to be thrown over a cliff. Even when their own fates were at stake, it astonished Cale how frequently the traitorous blabbed, one way or another. And the people they snitched themselves to! Wives (bad enough), close friends (almost as bad) – women they paid to have sex with them (unbelievable!). Far and away the best thing to do (in general – assassination not included) was to be the first to claim the story and give it the meaning that suited you or which obscured the truth in some way. In the case of the suicidal girl and the heartless boy, his tack would have been to announce that she had fallen in trying to rescue a drowning puppy and had been saved by the heroic actions of . . . ?

Well, it depended. If you were skilled in such matters, you could readily kill two flies with one slap. If you had a cause that needed a push, you could splice it to whoever had saved the day. Speculating on the matter idly (he had nothing better to do), what if you wanted to calm the hostility between the coloureds and the whites: in this case, the black boys by the river bravely risked all to help in the rescue and should be touted around the place and showered with praise and gifts. On the other hand, the opposite effect could be created by – best of all, this – pushing the two meetings with the little gurriers together so that they hurled insults at Cale during his brave rescue, and when he struggled to the bank with his soaking wet cargo of gorgeousness the evil little bastards had robbed the exhausted couple of their belongings.

Why not be daring? A big lie is as readily believed as a small one.

The heinous little coons had urinated on the body of the woman, having knocked the brave rescuer out with a rock. There were usually people who would guess the truth – so don't hide the truth with lies to cover it up, just provide as many alternative truths as the market will bear. People will believe anything if they want to believe it. And avoid an argument about the facts. Make it a question of right and wrong. Did the boys truly piss on the young woman? Make it so that to ask for evidence that the crime took place is, just by asking, to show that you support the act of pissing on unconscious women. A politician needs to understand that you can fool some of the people all of the time and so those are the people you need to concentrate on. Never persuade, *incite.*

It's just as well I'm such a nice person, thought Cale to himself. *Otherwise, I could get to enjoy doing this kind of thing.* The truth was that he'd done this kind of thing on a fair number of occasions, villainy mitigated only by the defence that the people he'd framed had entirely (usually) deserved it.

It was just then that the door of his room in the infirmary opened and the world changed.

It was Arbell Van Owen.

Amazement. Awe. Dismay. Delight. Astonishment. Stupefaction. Disgust.

It's said that, in the jungly continent that's dark, there is an eel whose lightest stroke can shock the organs and the body's nerves so that the victim shakes and shivers as if the soul itself has been struck a blow.

Cale could feel the tremors in every cell vibrate in an agony of . . . what? There were once poets great enough to set before you in words how in an instant love and joy could blend with hate. But all the poets of that quality are dead.

Unbearably lovely, the gorgeous goddess bitch slipped into the room, a smile of sweet compassion on lips that on any other woman would be poutily preposterous in their ruby redness and plump and heady kissability.

'Am I disturbing you?' she asked. Oh, the mockery stabbed him in his bursting heart!

He had last seen her nearly twenty years ago. Now there was a bloom upon her that filled the room and, along with the room, his raging and resentful heart. This was what you took from me, you heartless bitch: eyes almond and brown, cheeks pink and feather soft, the hands that could have stroked, the breasts he could have kissed and the private paradise in which the horror of his life and world would have been eased away.

For God's sake, I hear you cry. This is just a woman, not paradise in the extravagant puff pastry of human flesh!

No doubt if he had spent the years since that too dreadful day in Memphis living with the real woman, hearing her stories for the fiftieth time, listened to her notions about the world, which were half-baked even when she was a girl, seen those milk-white bosoms tipped with coral pink ten thousand times, heard her pass wind, moan, whine, sulk – every one of you older than sixteen, man or woman, knows that universal plot, is utterly familiar with the unsatisfactory progress of that disappointing second act in the theatre of man and woman's married life. But wise, experienced, skilful and clever as he was in nearly everything, in the matter of love Cale was a child imprisoned in a cell to which only the wickedly divine Arbell possessed a key.

Still, it must be said, mere fleshly woman as she was, she was something extraordinary to behold. Seen a beautiful woman? Bleugh! Not like her. No sign now of the coldness for which she was renowned: all in that face was kindness and concern. Her figure: sculpted. Her waist: slender (though held in by a corset, it should be said). Her breasts: words fail again. Her fingernails: carmine red. Her teeth: like pearls, they were. Her eyes: they flashed. Her voice: low. Her breath: lily of the valley soaked in rain. Her neck: so long and sonsy zaftig that more songs than you could shake a stick at had been written about its luxurious curve. But her heart? His moithered soul protested, seethed and boiled: her heart must smell of bins, drains, putrid fish and rotten milk. But still what surface loveliness this whited sepulchre presented to the world.

'No,' he said, quiet and cold. 'You're not disturbing me.'

As he intended, his tone crimped her attempt to be the Lady

Bountiful. As someone who mattered in the world, she had become used to even tepid expressions of her goodwill being welcomed with gushing gratitude. Often, people became almost completely unhinged when they were presented to her. Although bemused that any human being should have this effect on another, she accepted that this worship of the celebrated was just a peculiar fact of life and she made a point of giving those overcome with, she knew, her non-existent divinity a chance to regain their composure and, if not, to pretend that there was nothing ridiculous about getting into such a stew. It was greatly to her credit that she managed to keep any hold at all on the knowledge that she had been born among the sanctified merely by accident of birth and nothing more. But still, to meet such a complete and total failure to be impressed by her was something of a shock.

'How are you?'

'Alive.' Oh, how satisfying it was for Cale to strike her down with an indifference that was as unfamiliar to her as the pangs of hunger or being contradicted.

The thought, of course, that she was looking at Thomas Cale had not crossed her mind. From the breath-choking moment when she had first entered the room, Cale's heart had surged with the certainty that, also somewhere in *her* heart, she would – indeed must – see him at once for who he was. It took these brief exchanges to realize this was not the case, something for which he was in practical terms grateful but in spiritual terms deeply affronted. How dare you not know me, you treacherous, ungrateful bitch? How can you stand there and not die with shame at what you did to me, you feckless cow?

But she did not die, she merely tried again.

'You were very brave. I understand it was a close-run thing. I am so grateful that you saved Mona. She's such a lovely girl, but very rash – very emotional.'

'Being distraught at the fecklessness of others is not something to be dismissed.'

A hit! A hit! A sneery, palpable hit! She indeed looked for a moment as if she'd been struck.

'Ah . . . no, no, of course not. I only meant she's very passionate and young and, well, not that there's anything wrong with passion, of course not.' This was ambrosia for Cale. 'She tends to see the world as utterly wonderful or as complete hell. Um . . . she's very young.'

But a very odd thing was going on inside Arbell – though it's only odd if you believe that we have one personality in our head as unvarying as porridge in a bowl. You and I know better: in every normal skull there is a crowd of, let's say, four or five who stand uneasily behind the sane and sensible leader of the gang. This leader does the talking to the world. The others, some of them gagged, look on in varying degrees of resentment, envy or desire.

Cale had been stripped to the waist because of a nasty scrape taken from his adventure in the whirlpool of the Watergate. The doctor, thankfully not convinced by the current fad for covering such wounds in badger fat, had told him to leave it to a coating of butter and the healing power of the air. As Arbell was having her polite but difficult interview with Cale, one of the more unruly maids-in-waiting in Arbell's soul (not a slut by any means, this maid, she just had something of a taste for strange) could not help noticing the enormous chest so marked with scars, the narrow waist almost as thin as a girl's but muscle-bunched and glistening like a coil of snakes. It was at once offputting and provocative. But then her inner slut was thrust out of her soul-room, perhaps by the snow queen who was said to rule that soul.

As for Cale, at last the more sensible goblins in his nature managed to get the upper hand over the devil threatening to spoil his foggy plans for Arbell.

'How is she?' he asked, grudging.

'Oh, she'll be fine, the doctors say.' She smiled, awkwardly attempting to make amends. 'All twelve of her doctors are agreed on that.'

'She's very precious, I hear.'

'Yes,' she said. 'Very. Her father dotes on her.'

'Is that so unusual, for fathers to love their daughters?' The devil temporarily got free of his guard. Arbell's eyes widened at this extraordinary behaviour.

'I should let you rest.' A pause. 'Goodbye, and thank you again.' And with that, she was gone.

How many meetings have there been in the history of the world between a betrayed lover and the one betrayed? Angry strangers who know all each other's secrets. After half an hour of chewing his liver Cale finally calmed down enough to realize how stupidly he'd behaved. But as acting stupidly often does, it worked out all right in the end.

When Gaines, inevitably enough, raised the question of Cale being hired as Denmark Materazzi's guard against the imaginary threat of those who would do him harm, she was persuaded easily enough.

'He is,' she said, having already given Gaines a blow-by-blow account of her uncomfortable first meeting with Cale, 'extremely blunt.'

'You mean rude.'

'Very well . . . he is *extremely* rude.'

'As you wish, madam,' said Gaines. 'In the admittedly extremely unlikely event that the Dust Men manage to confront your beloved son, I shall arrange to have a more ladylike son-of-a-bitch to keep him alive.'

There was not, of course, very much the startled Arbell could say in reply, and so that was that. Finally, Thomas Cale was exactly where he had plotted and planned to be. He had always mocked those of his opponents in battle who were hugely skilled in the tactics of war but had no over-arching strategy, no ultimate plan to make proper use of their brilliant manoeuvres. It is not, of course, wrong to sneer at others when they deserve contempt, but it will be considerably more painful when you are forced to recognize that you're no better. What on earth was he going to do now he'd succeeded?

Later on the same day, Saul Gaines had gone into hiding from the responsibility of running the greatest plantation in the South. It was almost four in the afternoon at Malfi and oven hot, with the only sound that of the crickets throbbing with such a racket it sounded as if each one must be the size of a cat.

Gaines was reading in the shade in a spot where the wind blew up from the lake – possibly the only cool breeze for a hundred miles.

'So, studying to be a great wise man?'

Gaines knew the voice and expressed his opinion of its owner by placing a bookmaker with insolent slowness to save his place. Then a very little smile, not looking up, and a shut of the book with a snap, the crisp sound saying everything that needed to be said.

'Interesting?' said Nick Van Owen, letting it be clear that he was utterly indifferent to the answer.

'Very,' replied Gaines, pretending not to understand the question. 'It's by Thomas Carlyle on the Negro question.' He smiled at Nick. 'He argues that the black races are distinctly and self-evidently inferior.'

Nick waited for some sort of disagreement, but Gaines merely continued, smiling: 'But I imagine you're familiar with it.'

Nick considered and then rejected the idea of claiming that he had read Carlyle.

'No,' he said. 'Can't say I am.' A silence, if there could be such a thing within the cacophonous throb of crickets. 'Though I have been reading 'bout slavery too. As it happens.'

Gaines raised his eyebrows as if they had been failing to make conversation at a tea-party and had mercifully just discovered they were both interested in growing geraniums.

'It really set me thinking,' continued Nick. He wiped the sweat off his neck. 'My God, it's hot. But I suppose you're used to it.' Gaines said nothing. 'The governor used to play a game, you know, at dinner parties. He'd ask people a question – *when was the last time you changed your mind?*'

'Used to?'

'Yeah. It upset people.'

'Really?'

'Yep. 'Cos they never had. They thought Louis was making fun of them. Which he was.'

Nick looked down at the lake as if he'd finished. Gaines did not bite. 'But now I see what he was up to. Me. I've changed my mind about slavery.' Another provocative pause. But no taker. 'See, I was reading an article, a long one, in the *Atlantic*. Know it?'

'Yes.'

'Just come out. This article I'm describing to you, it was about that country in Afrique that some of the freed slaves set up way back . . . um . . . Liberia.'

'I've heard of it.'

''Course you have. What'm I thinking? But this article, the one that just came out, it's real fascinating. It turns out I was wrong all along – about black people and white people being completely different. This article showed me, made me change my mind.' Another pause to unsettle Gaines. He didn't bite. But Nick was still enjoying himself. 'It turns out . . . in this article . . . that when the freed slaves got to Liberia they took all the best land from the natives, who they discovered were just ignorant and superstitious, and started calling themselves . . . what was it? . . . Americo-Liberians, and proceeded to make slaves of the locals, just like here. They passed laws that declared only Americo-Liberians could be citizens and passed some more laws saying the native blacks were just savages and ignorant heathens. Then they took to wearing bowler hats and the women to wearing crinolines so no one would mistake them for the natives. Made it illegal for one of them to marry a local. Then they murdered all the chiefs who tried to stop them and started using slaves themselves. And made a good living selling them.' Nick shook his head, as if wondering how he could have misread things for so long. 'Now I see we're not so different, blacks and whites.' Another broad smile. ''Course. I shoulda realized before 'bout how white and black people were just the same.'

He waited for Gaines to take the bait. He did not.

'Y'know, it's kinda interestin' how when you hear you black people goin' on about how wicked the slavers were and how terrible slavery is, and how bad white people are, you kinda forget to remember that every slave that ever there was brought to this great country was already a slave and made so by his fellow Africans, and that they was doin' so long, long afore we came along. Still doin' it, too. Ain't that real strange, Mr Gaines?'

With a sigh at the enormous heat, Nick strolled off into the Sally Gardens. Gaines watched after him for a while then went back to his book. Not for long, though.

'I'm sorry to disturb you, Mr Gaines.'

He looked up. 'That's all right, Reverend.' It was not all right, not at all, but Joseph Hanson was a serious man in Rosewood. 'How can I help you?'

'I can see I've interrupted your time for reflection. I'll be brief. A young man of my acquaintance, a Ray Jackson, has come to Malfi looking to improve himself. He seems to be a decent fellow and deserves that something be done to help him.'

'What sort of work were you thinking of?'

'Nothing too grand, Mr Gaines, just a position where he can show whether he has the stuff.'

PART III

I love you! Yes, from that very day
When you appeared before my eyes,
I sensed that a chain impossible to break
Tied us together.
In this kiss, may your soul forget for ever
All the sufferings, the sorrows, forget all pain!

– Jules Massenet, *Werther: An Opera*

Do I love you with all my heart?
I love you with all my liver,
And if I had you in my mouth,
I'd spit you in the river.

– Black folk song

24

Love flies by, and carries with it
Our tender caresses for ever.
Love flies far from this happy oasis
And does not return.

– Offenbach, *The Tales of Hoffman*

'I prefer,' said Nick Van Owen, 'to listen to my operas in German.'

'Really?' said Cale, not very interested, but a little surprised that, of all people, Nick Van Owen had a la-di-da side. 'Why's that?'

'It means I don't understand what they're saying. That way, I can imagine it's something sensible and not something utterly ridiculous.'

'Same here,' said Cale. 'Except I prefer not to hear the music either.'

'You don't like opera?' said Nick, amazed.

'No.'

'Everyone likes opera.'

'I think you'll find that they don't.'

'But they do, they really do. Arbell puts them on for the servants twice a week, once for the whites and once for the blacks. Everybody likes opera.'

But Cale not only did not like opera, he did not like talking about opera. And he sat silent.

'I want to know everything,' said Nick.

'What if there's nothing?'

'There's always something.'

'I'm not your gossip.'

'Don't underestimate tittle-tattle, Savio: the hedgehog knows one big thing but the fox knows many small things.'

Cale did not fancy this much. It made him feel like a sneak. 'Every time I pass information to you, it creates a chance for them to discover me.'

'I'll risk it.'

'But I won't.' Nick looked at him. A flash of something – more than anger at being told by an underling what he would or would not do. 'I can't remember if it was you or your brother who said that if you hired someone who knew what they were doing, you should let them do it.'

'It was my brother. It sounds like the sort of thing he *would* say. I'm more of the do-as-you're-damned-well-told persuasion.'

'I'm sorry, but that's how it has to be.'

'Are you sorry, Mr Cale?'

'I don't know why I said that, a bad polite habit.'

'I'm paying, I call the tune.'

'I risked a great deal to get inside Arbell's household. I'm not throwing it away in order to tell you who's taking it up the arse from who.'

'So nearly getting yourself drowned was part of a cunning plan, then?'

'No, it was a very stupid mistake, if you must know.'

Nick burst out laughing.

What an odd fellow he is, thought Cale.

'Is it wise to admit to stupidity while you're telling your employer to go and fuck himself?'

'Perhaps not. Take it as a compliment, if you like.'

'So, tell me,' said Nick, 'how many times have you done something stupid and it worked out?'

Cale smiled back. 'About the same number of times I've done something brilliant and failed, I suppose.'

'So your reputation for genius is undeserved?'

Cale looked thoughtful. 'Not undeserved, just misguided. The reasons people think, or used to think, I was a genius in politics and war usually thought so for the wrong reasons. But if they knew all the facts – the facts being that when you're the one making the decisions and the information you have is incomplete or just plain wrong, and there are ten ways of dealing with a problem that you don't know much about and ten people are sure they know what you should do, and you make the wrong decision, then you're defeated but still alive. Well, those are the moments of greatness. If people knew how I succeeded in what they think are my failures and failed in what they think of as my successes, they wouldn't think I was a genius, they'd think I was a god.'

Nick started to giggle like a sixteen-year-old girl. It took some time for him to recover. 'I suppose,' he said, pouring himself a gin, 'you've given that speech once or twice before.'

Cale passed over his glass for a refill. 'Once or twice.'

Nick raised his glass. 'Have it your way, then. To incompetence and failure!'

It was a little past eight o'clock, and Arbell was looking out over the lake as the sun was going down. The free-tail bats from the eaves of the great house, thousands of them, were already flowing towards the water to dip their jaws in the lake on their way out to the fields, plumes of smoke for miles around, to feed on corn and cotton moths.

'My late husband,' she said, 'rebuilt the roof so that the bats would roost there. Everyone thought he was mad. Bats were supposed to be bad luck. In five years, the crop losses from pests fell by three quarters.' She turned around. The person she had been talking to was Gaines, and they'd spent the last six hours going through Malfi's annual accounts. She smiled, a little wearily. 'If you're up when they come back at dawn, they race in like a tornado and then slow down by opening their wings like a great sail. It sounds like a thousand people blowing on blades of grass.'

Gaines smiled, noting that if she was not sad exactly, she was certainly melancholy.

'So,' she said. 'I'm a quarter richer than I was last year.'

'You are.'

A pause. And then, impulsive: 'I want to increase the wages of everyone at Malfi by the same amount.' There was only a silence from Gaines. But it was not a silent sort of silence. 'You don't want to be richer by a quarter?' she said.

'I would.'

'So *you* want to be richer by a fourth – but you don't want the same for everyone else?'

He considered this carefully. 'If I had to choose' – a little smile – 'I could manage my conscience to live with that.'

She laughed. 'So you think I should improve your already impressive wage by a fourth part but award everyone else nothing?'

'There is an argument to be made for doing exactly that – or very close. As you can see, I have managed your property particularly well this year.'

'Your vanity!' she said, laughing.

'It's not vanity at all.' He gestured at the array of ledgers on the table. 'The figures don't boast on my behalf – they only speak the plain facts. Saul Gaines, they say, is an outstanding servant who has improved on his service in the last year by exactly one quarter.'

'And what,' she replied, 'would you say if I were to keep your wages the same and give everyone else a rise?'

'I'd advise against it.'

'Would you?'

'Yes, I would.'

'Why?'

'You have the best-paid workers in the South – black or white.'

'And they've made me richer by their work so . . . fair shares.'

'Normally, yes.' He was no longer teasing. 'But these are not normal times.'

'Go on.'

'Give people a little bit more and it will be spent on better clothes or food or drink.'

'And what's wrong with that?'

'Nothing. But it will be gone in a month on buying a few tricks and a packet of bear signs. You need to keep that money and use it for bribes, flattery, the writing and publishing of pamphlets and all the rest involved in stopping the reintroduction of slavery.'

'I could sell land and do both.'

'Land that produces more cotton per acre than any other in the estate. Do that and you rob our cause of that revenue and put it in the hands of plantation owners who'd use it to put the chains back on every black in the South.' She looked at him – an odd silence. 'There's a war to fight. Put your money into guns, not butter. When it's over, then I'll help you to give your future away.'

'I wasn't,' she said, smiling, 'thinking of going quite that far.'

Gaines just laughed. 'That's a relief. I'm not sure I'm good enough to work for a saint.'

Outside, Cale was sitting near the Malfi library on a low sandstone wall turned honey-coloured by the sinking sun. Sometimes he watched the Malfi beautiful people doing their night passage along the Avenida Ponce de Léon but mostly he was thinking about what had happened at the river weir and how easily he might now be rotting down in a grave marked with the wrong name. He was approached by a tall and handsome young man with close-cut blond hair and dressed all in black.

'Would you mind if I interrupted you?' said the young man.

'I suppose it depends on what you want to interrupt me with.'

'To thank you,' said the young man.

'You're welcome.' The young man was surprised into silence. 'All right,' said Cale. 'What for?'

'Saving Mona's life.'

'Oh, yes.'

'And an apology for' – a beat – 'being the cause of it.'

This unexpected confession gave Cale time to cover the odd mixture of feelings that came along with his realization that this was Arbell's son, Denmark. The last time he'd seen him, his mother had been holding him in her arms and Cale had been raging against her treachery as he babbled away cheerfully.

'If it was you who threw her off the bridge,' said Cale, 'I'd say an apology was the least of your worries.'

Again the young man was startled by Cale's response, but then he smiled, gaining the measure of the man – though it was no happy smile.

'It seems she threw herself off the bridge *because* of me.'

'That's quite a boast. You must be very wonderful.'

He laughed. 'Not in the slightest wonderful. But she's very young and wasn't able to see me for the mediocrity I truly am – a personality in search of a character.'

This time it was Cale's turn to smile. 'Well, at least now she'll have the opportunity to learn.'

'Because of you. What you did showed great heroism.'

'You're not the first person to say that today.' Expecting modesty of some kind, again the young man was thrown. Cale laughed. 'You think I should say it was nothing, that anyone would do the same? Possibly, anyone would, but not me – I take my life pretty damn seriously. So if I'd known she'd decided to drown herself, I'd have let her drop over the weir and never given it a second thought.'

'I've heard that men of great courage often try to deny their virtues because they're afraid of having to live up to them and, feeling they can't be always heroic, are angry that they must live their lives as frauds.'

Cale looked at him. 'Read that in a book?'

'You don't approve of books?'

'I do, as it happens. But they're not much good without experience. The trouble is that the people who think rarely have experience and the people who have experience rarely think.'

'But you have both, I take it?'

'Yes, I do,' said Cale.

'I don't,' said the young man. 'All I have is books. The world is just an idea to me.'

'You're still young. If you want my advice . . .'

'I do.'

'Get out of places like this.'

'Isn't there plenty of life here? The whole world comes to Malfi.'

'True enough, I suppose. But it's nasty and it's narrow.'

'And the world isn't nasty?'

Cale laughed. 'You're not as stupid as you look. Indeed it is – but it's bigger, broader and, though I hate to say it, there is some good out there.'

'To be fair, there's good here too.'

'Then stay and be who you were meant to be. Which is . . .'

The young man held out his hand. 'Denmark Materazzi.'

Cale had been informed only the day before that he was to become Denmark's bodyguard, although with strict instructions to say nothing about it. The young man was not expected to take well to the news of someone constantly watching over him.

'Dominic Savio.'

'So why are you here at Malfi, Dominic Savio, if you despise it so much?'

'Because when it comes to my own interests, I'm a hypocrite.'

'Then we're brothers.'

'And because I have to be.' Which, of course, was a damned lie.

'And I suppose, there, we're different,' said Denmark. 'If I really wanted to, there's nothing stopping me putting all my goods in a handkerchief, tying it to a pole and going out into the wide world to learn about life.'

'You don't want to listen to anything I say,' said Cale. 'I'm just bitter and twisted and, recently, I nearly died.'

'Heroically – doesn't that make a difference?'

'What difference? Dead is dead.'

'Not a bad way to go. Even you have to go one way or another.'

'And be remembered? For about a week. Save the world and it might be ten days.'

'*Great Caesar dead and turned to clay, might block a hole to keep the wind away*,' declaimed Denmark theatrically.

'That just about sums it up. Yours? You look like the sort who might write poetry.'

Denmark laughed. 'Can't remember.' A pause while he got around to asking about something that derived from more than lazy curiosity. 'So what happened at the river – it frightened you. Stupid thing to say. Of course, it must have done.'

Cale looked at him. 'I suppose it is stupid. I've had a few close-run things in my time, and . . .' He grimaced, unable to find the words. 'The yobs at the Red Opera, you know about it?'

'I've heard of it, yes.'

'They used to sing a song to the unfortunates about to fight to the death:

We don't want to squeal
We don't want to blab
But soon you'll be lying on a marble slab.'

'Charming.'

Cale laughed. 'I just used to dismiss it as what you'd expect to hear from a bunch of hooligans. But that day at the weir I felt it, the beating of his wings, like I've never felt it before. That's when I felt the feathers on my cheeks. That you could *be* or not *be*. And there was nothing between them. Between existence and non-existence there was a gnat's wing.'

For a moment they sat in silence.

'Try not to be too hard on her,' said Denmark.

'Easy for you to say.'

'You've never despaired? Wanted things to stop?'

'I'm more your angry type. I prefer to break things.'

He looked at Denmark and felt an unexpected sympathy for the boy.

'Don't give it house room, that ending-it stuff. Things can always be worse. What if there's someone on the other side of this world waiting for you with a rope?'

Denmark smiled – sad again. 'An unpleasant thought.'

'Then keep it in mind next time you're thinking about throwing yourself in the river.'

Denmark laughed, this time with more of the good humour of the young. 'I will.' He stood up. 'Thank you, again.'

'If you ever do decide to run away, make sure that in this handkerchief of yours you take plenty of cash.'

'I will.'

He watched the young man walk away and, just as he was about to pass out of sight, he called out again: 'And wrap it up in plenty of money.'

*

Cale started another pipe and settled back to enjoy the sunset. But not for long.

'You ought to be careful about creeping up behind people you don't know,' he said. 'You can never be sure how they might react.'

Hetty Summerstone moved from behind Cale. She was wearing a curious dress that seemed part uniform and part some sort of formal costume, including a top hat and a fetching black veil.

'So,' said Cale, pleased to see her, 'just dropped by on your way to the Mad Badger's tea party?'

'Do you like it?' she asked, giving him a little twirl. 'I designed it myself.'

'I'd never have guessed.'

'Don't be mean,' she said, laughing. 'Has that Denmark boy gone?'

'I believe so.'

'Spoilt brat.' She waited for a comment, but Cale just looked at her, smiling. 'I suppose you're thinking who's she calling the kettle black?'

'The thought never crossed my mind.'

She regarded him carefully. 'I like you,' she said, and laughed at his surprised expression. 'Don't worry, not in that way.'

'Why not?' he said. 'I consider myself quite a catch for a young girl, if what you're looking for is a bad-tempered chuglet, completely charmless and with no money – though I am coming up in the world.'

'So I hear.' It was clear there were rumours going about and that she hoped to catch him out. But he did not react. 'Rather you than me wiping Denmark's tiny little bottom.'

'No idea what you're talking about.' They smiled at each other. 'What have you got against poor old Denmark?'

'His eyes are too close together.'

'Really? I've known some pretty narrow-spaced sons-of-bitches in the eye department. Denmark doesn't even come close. Has he spurned you in love?'

She called out loudly in derision. 'You know very well *that* isn't true.'

'You might just be going through a phase.'

'No, I'm not,' she said, laughing.

'I believe you.'

'So, you're going to keep us all from being murdered in our beds by the secret agents of the Dust Men?'

'Don't know who you've been talking to – you're going to have to take your chances, just like always.'

She looked at him, wide-eyed. 'You mean you wouldn't put your body between my pretty white neck and a black man's murderous knife?'

'I'm rethinking my policy on saving rich young white women. I've had a bad experience recently.'

Her face darkened and for the first time he saw her express hesitation and what looked like shame. 'I wanted to talk to you about that.'

Interesting, thought Cale.

'All right,' he said.

'Mona.' She looked properly guilty now. 'I'm the reason she threw herself in the river.'

'I see. And why's that?'

'Why do you think?' Some irritation here. Asking for forgiveness was unfamiliar territory for young Hetty.

'I don't know. I thought you'd come here to tell me.'

She could see Cale was not going to make this easy, and she was entirely used to things being made easy for her.

'I was . . . flirting with her.'

'She threw herself in the river because you were flirting with her?'

She gasped in frustration.

'All right . . . it was more than flirting. I was trying . . .' She couldn't bring herself to say more.

Cale was not so precious. 'To fuck her?' he suggested.

She sniffed. 'I suppose so.'

'And did you?'

A sigh this time.

'Nearly.'

'*Nearly?*'

'I stopped . . . you know.'

'Not really.'

'Because I . . . it's just that I only tried because she was so beautiful and everyone so adores her and the men positively faint when she passes by . . .'

'So you wanted to prove you could succeed where they'd failed?'

She looked at him. 'Yes. Horrible. I'm a horrible, wicked person.'

Cale thought about this as if carefully considering it. 'Yes, horrible and wicked . . . that just about sums it up.'

'But I stopped,' she said, 'before . . .' She stumbled to a halt.

'And?'

'I said I loved someone else and was just trying to get back at them and that I was very sorry.'

'Ah, the woman in the maze.'

'What?' said Hetty, confused. 'Oh, Sophie? God, no. I made it up about loving someone else. I thought she'd be less upset if I gave that as a reason. You know, she wouldn't take it personally.'

'And did she?'

'She was annoyed. I mean, we'd gone quite a long way when I got my attack of . . . consideration for others.' She laughed nervously. 'I mean, I didn't know what it was at first. I thought it might have been indigestion.'

Cale did not respond, as she'd expected, with a forgiving smile. 'So what was the real reason you stopped?'

She looked at him, eyes opening wide.

'I told you.'

'All right. I accept, probably, that a bad conscience was one reason. What was the other one?'

She looked at him the way a small girl looks at her mother when she's guessed she's been stealing biscuits, not realizing she's got chocolate smeared all over her mouth. *How does he know?*

Hetty looked down at the ground. 'Mona's only eighteen.' Now Cale was puzzled. 'I only like older women.'

A silence. Eventually, he smiled. 'Still, half of you was trying to do the right thing. That's a start.'

This was a little too far for Hetty. 'Oh, and I suppose you always do the right thing.'

'Me?' said Cale. 'Hardly ever.'

Another silence.

'So, it was my fault Mona nearly drowned and almost took you with her.'

Cale looked at her and she briefly looked back before turning away. 'So how do you propose,' he said, 'to make it up to me?'

She was, perhaps, too new to the business of admitting she was in error to have considered the demands of atonement. She seemed, thought Cale, intrigued by the idea.

'What do you want me to do?'

Cale thought for a moment. 'I can't think of anything at the moment but, some day, and that day may never come, I might call on you to do a service for me.'

She was, after all, a most intelligent young woman and was wisely suspicious of such an open-ended commitment. But what else could she say?

'All right.'

Cale smiled. 'And look on the bright side. You never know with these throwing-themselves-in-the-river types exactly why they do these things. It may have had nothing to do with you.'

Hetty looked at him, sly. 'Does that mean, if that turns out to be the case, I don't have to do you a favour when you want one?'

'Sorry,' said Cale. 'A promise is a promise.'

The next day, aware that the gossips had somehow got wind of the matter, Arbell told her son that he was to have someone following him about on a more or less permanent basis.

Denmark took the news about as well as any boy of his age would. A huge row followed of a kind as eternal down the ages as the song of the nightingale. He didn't merely storm off in a huff, he tornadoed, hurricaned and tempested out of the room in a whirlwind of rage. For thirty minutes he circled the grounds, then made his way up to

Cale's new rooms to give him the benefit of his views on bodyguards. He was informed by Cale's new maid that he had gone for a walk in the Seville gardens.

It took an irritable five minutes to track him down, with not even an 'excuse me' to break the thick ice between them.

'I want to make it clear to you, Mr Savio, that I'm not going to accept you, or anybody else, watching over me.' It was pretty clear that Denmark's hostility was deeply felt. This made it tricky for Cale. He needed to get close to Arbell, and the boy was his ticket. Denmark might get his way and put an end to the matter, but even if his mother put her foot down, a hostile Denmark could be a serious nuisance.

Denmark thought a little better of his tone – after all, Cale had saved Mona (now shuffled off to an expensive lunatic asylum for the disturbed wealthy) – and tried to modify his anger. 'With all due respect –'

Cale interrupted: 'You're a cunt.'

Denmark's mouth opened in astonishment.

Cale smiled. 'Isn't that what usually follows the claim of due respect? So why don't we get to the point?'

Winded by this, Denmark became more careful. 'I can take care of myself.'

'I wasn't thinking of helping you to take a bath.'

'Pretty damn near it. I don't want someone – even if I admire that person's courage – following me around all day.'

'Put it like that, I can't say I fancy it much myself either.'

'Then we're agreed.'

'Not really. Though I grant you it's easier for me – I'm getting paid, and very well. You're not so lucky.'

Denmark sighed irritably.

Cale shrugged sympathetically. 'As I see it, you have to lump it. For my part, I promise to be as unobtrusive as possible. I'm paid to keep you safe, not spy on you. That's a promise.'

Denmark was about to dismiss the promises of mercenaries but remembered that he was talking to a man of integrity and great bravery, still being young enough to believe that virtues were like cows and went around in herds.

'I believe you, of course. But I'm good with a sword.'

'What about large coloured men coming to cut your throat in the night?'

A snort of disbelief. 'Hobgoblins made up by the Van Owens.'

Not completely foolish, then, thought Cale.

'One important person in Malfi has already died in his bed.'

Another gasp of derision. 'Maybe a Dust Man with wings got to Almand Lord – but he'd have needed to join a bloody long queue.' He looked at Cale, cool and determined. 'I can look after myself.'

'What if I prove you can't?'

'What?'

'What if I prove that you can't look after yourself?'

'And how will you do that?'

'You can fence, I hear. Well?'

'Yes.'

Cale smiled. He liked the way he said this – matter of fact, not brash. 'We'll have three passes at each other. Best of.'

'And if I win?'

'I'll turn down the job and say I think the danger is overblown and that . . . you can look after yourself. I'll suggest improvements to security to keep your mother happy.'

'And what if they get someone else?'

'Nothing I can do about that. But it might work. What have you got to lose?'

By an odd coincidence, Ray Jackson had overheard much of this exchange from the other side of a hedge. Now a prentice under-gardener, he'd misunderstood the instructions given him – surprising this for such a quick study – and was pruning a Black Limbertwig apple tree. This was also odd because Ray had pruned a thousand of them when he was a boy in Virginia and he ought to have known that it was a month too early for this kind of cropping. Ray watched Denmark leave, a surge in his belly as if he were suffering a sort of indigestion of the heart from eating too often at a table filled with meals of ash and grit. There had been too many beatings, too much contempt. All his life he had been abhorred. How could he not have hated Denmark as he walked away, all white and gold, a boy who owned everything while Ray Jackson owned nothing. Soon, Ray might not even own himself.

FILED
Plurus Superior Court
Brumaire 33
Clerk of the Court
Deputy Clerk

THE INTERNATIONAL CRIMINAL COURT OF THE HANSE

BLANDINGS SMI STATUTORY
DEFENCE ADVOCATES

Qaz is this too late?

THOMAS CALE

Date: 12 Brumaire ME 1956

Sorry, Bolly, you lose (but you must be used to that).

Love
Piggers

VC

INDICTMENT 701 103

Clerk

Bail, $ no bail for all defendants

Laurel Beeler

This represents official notice to the defendant Thomas Cale (in his absence and under a Red Notice) and his solicitor Blandino & Smi that the Grand Jury has formally ruled that the case against him of crimes against the humanity under Articles 12, 18, 34a, 42c, 57, 58, 76 and 89 is deemed worthy of prosecution and must proceed to trial.

25

Dearest Tom

I feel like I've always really been a block of ice all my little life – the ice queen is what everyone calls me – nobody touching me or getting past my frozen walls. I need to melt inside you. You. You. You. Good or bad as you so entirely are. You are closer to me, young man, than my own breath.

No matter what happens, part of me is yours always always always and for ever.

Promise me you're burning these letters.

A

– Jenufer Smythe, *The Letters of Arbell Materazzi to Thomas Cale: Fact or Forgery?* (Atlantic)

'How are you, Mr Savio?' Arbell was all concern and gentle smiles, the treacherous, gorgeous bitch.

'Well enough, madam.'

'And have you completely recovered?'

Cale was having difficulty swallowing her performance as a Have-you-come-far? Lady Bountiful.

'In some ways better than I've ever been.'

She looked at Gaines, also uneasy, as he wondered why Cale was being so stroppy.

'Better?'

'Yes.'

'Why so?'

'Because I believe that after many years I've finally learned to keep my nose out of other people's business.'

Arbell looked at him, intrigued, it had to be said. Those who inherit power are often stupid and, given that they will have grown up being deferred to, they require flattery in the same way that those addicted to narcotics require increasingly vast doses merely in order to feel normal. But such people are not always foolish and will often acquire the odd renegade among their retinue to give life a little flavour. As long as the renegade knows not to go too far. Gaines was not sure this was the case with Cale, just as he was not sure how much of this sort of thing his mistress would tolerate. It would be interesting to see.

'If you hadn't interfered in Mona's business, she'd be in her grave,' said Arbell.

'True enough – but then I wouldn't have come as close to dying myself as it's possible to do and yet not die.'

'But how would you feel now, if you'd let her drown?'

'I'd feel very disappointed with myself, madam, and weep for my lost honour.'

She smiled. *She's intrigued by him*, thought Gaines,

'So, surely, you'd do the same thing again – save the girl and your self-respect?'

'Tell me this, madam, suppose God sent me back to a few seconds before I saw Mona Whats-her-name but with foreknowledge that she had chosen to kill herself and, being a difficult God, telling me only that it'd be touch and go whether I drowned myself trying to rescue her. What should I do?'

She thought about this for a moment.

'I suppose . . . I don't know . . . I suppose I'd say you' – she paused – '*I*'d still be obliged to try.' She laughed. 'But when I say it aloud I want to say that talk is cheap.'

But Cale wasn't going to be charmed by this snake. 'Yes, madam, it is.'

She held his eyes for a moment and then looked at Gaines with, thought Cale, very much the same know-all smile of the self-satisfied trollop as in that painting everyone was always going on about.

'But,' she said, 'it's the wrong answer to the wrong question. Nobody ever *does* have foreknowledge. We're always in the dark when it comes to choosing, and we can never be anything else.'

'That's a good answer, madam, and not just clever but true. So we don't try to gaze into the future when we choose – we look into the past. Isn't that so?'

Arbell smiled with a lightness that infuriated Cale with its warmth and good nature.

'Why do I feel,' she said to Gaines, 'that Mr Savio has been preparing a trap for me all this time?'

Cale didn't give Gaines the chance to add his opinion. 'If it is a trap, then the conclusion will be false – if it is true, then it can't be a trap. The truth, in the end, is always plain.'

'Very well. Yes – we look to the past when trying to make a choice in the present.'

'And, what else *can* we do, after all? But in the question of risking my life to save the life of others, that's not what I've been doing. If I had been doing what you admit is all we can really go on, our past experience, then by saving that girl I behaved stupidly in the light of that past experience. And bravery is only real bravery when it emerges from understanding, otherwise it's just bluster and swagger. Evil men show courage all the time in doing evil – the wicked defy odds, risk everything – will risk their lives to save their evil friends. Is that bravery?'

Intrigued but definitely wary.

'I see your point. Perhaps we need a new word to describe courage shown in pursuit of wickedness. I can concede that. So, what's the past experience that should have taught you the correct action when it came to saving or not saving Mona Fuentes?'

'Understand, madam, that I'm not boasting when I tell you this.'

She smiled again. *Stop doing that*, thought Cale, *you lying slut.*

'Of course not.'

'Twice in the past I saved people who were innocent of any blame for the danger they were in. I risked a hideous death to save one and I nearly died saving the other, pretty much as close as I came to drowning in that weir.'

He stopped when she had expected him to continue.

'As far as I can see it, from what you've told me – which isn't much – you did a good and brave thing in defence of two innocent people. They were entirely innocent, yes?'

Cale smiled, vindictive. 'No one is entirely innocent, madam.'

'You know very well what I mean.'

'I do. I apologize. And also for not giving you all the facts. You see, the thing is, the rescue of those two innocents had disastrous consequences for me, and many others. My experience speaks very clearly – though not clearly enough for me to listen, apparently – and it shouts that while great evil actions have terrible consequences, so do great good ones. It's now clear to me that it's our actions that the fates care about, not whether they're good or bad, only whether they can be made to give them pleasure. That's why the Laconics call the fates the Kindly Ones, to flatter them, because they're such enormous bastards.' Gaines was shocked by the language and was about to tell him off when Cale got there first. 'My apologies, madam. I'm afraid I've let my anger at the young lady make me forget my manners.'

'That's very understandable, Mr Savio. To be honest, I wanted to box her ears myself.' She paused, awkward. 'It's become clear in the end why she tried to kill herself. It had nothing to do with unrequited love for anyone.' Another awkward pause. 'It will be difficult, I imagine, for a stranger to this peculiar country to understand. Indeed, I hardly believe it myself. This is a matter' – she shook her head just a little, a most affecting sight, so delicately did the soft locks of her hair tremble, so beautiful the slight turn of that exquisite and legendary neck – 'terrifying for the people involved . . . for Mona's family. You see, she tried to kill herself because she thought she was tainted by being a demi-meamelouc.' She groaned with exasperation, as if even knowing about this reflected badly on her. Gaines helped her out.

'A demi-meamelouc is someone who –'

Arbell interrupted. 'I had to have the term explained to me by Mr Gaines. I'd never heard of it . . . or imagined that such a notion could even exist.'

'A demi-meamelouc,' said Gaines, returning to his explanation. Now it was Cale's turn to halt Gaines.

'. . . someone who is one thirty-secondth black.'

It is always a pleasure to astonish the room. Arbell and Gaines looked at him with their mouths a little open.

'How on earth did you know that, Mr Savio?' said Arbell.

'Perhaps I'm not as stupid as I look.'

The tone was self-deprecating – a joke at his own expense – but the look on his face did not exactly match. *How insolent he is*, thought Gaines. Whatever the truth of the matter, the exchange between his mistress and Cale was all going somewhere peculiar.

'We have a meeting with your brother-in-law in five minutes,' said Gaines.

Cale nodded to Arbell by way of a bow and went to leave. She stopped him.

'But what you said a minute ago . . . about not protecting innocence in the future. How does it apply to my son? Does it mean you'll refuse to risk your life for him?'

Cale ground his teeth at his gobby stupidity. 'It's completely different, madam.'

'But I don't understand how. He might be threatened by something terrible. Why should you put your life at risk for another innocent?'

'Because I wouldn't be sticking my nose into the business of the Kindly Ones.'

'How so?'

'Because it *would* be my business.' He looked at her directly. 'I will protect your boy as if he were my own.'

Gaines was yet again puzzled by the change of tone. But it convinced Arbell – and it was indeed, he had to admit, entirely convincing, for some reason.

'Before I let you go, Mr Savio, my son is unhappy about having you as a guard.'

It was another question. He smiled. 'I'll persuade him.'

He bowed and was off out the door. But he was not fast enough to get away from Gaines.

'Savio!'

Sighing, Cale stopped, collected himself and turned. Gaines was not pleased.

'What was that all about?'

'I don't know what you mean. She asked me questions, and I answered honestly.'

'Don't play the blunt soldier with me. Why were you behaving like a pillock?'

'I'm not familiar with the term.'

'It means someone who behaves in the pillocky way you were behaving in there – are you drunk?'

'No.'

'Well, that alarms me even more. You went in there thinking you might be rude but that you were a man of unimpeachable integrity – and somehow you managed to leave her wondering whether at the first sign of trouble you're going to leave her pride and joy to get his throat cut.'

More teeth-grinding from Cale.

He sighed with what he hoped looked like reluctant regret. He knew he'd made a bad mistake, even if it was not quite the mistake that Gaines believed it to be. But he was a skilled liar, of course. 'I was still angry with the girl for nearly getting me killed – and not a word of thanks from her or her father.'

Gaines grimaced with sympathetic exasperation. 'Yes, well . . . her father is a twenty-four-carat shit. Spaniards like him are mad for pride and you knew about what had happened. So he . . . well, he can't bear it that anybody knows the truth.'

'Particularly a common thug like me.'

Gaines looked at him. 'As it happens, he was a lot more insulting about you than that.'

They both smiled – both relieved for their very different reasons.

'I have to go,' said Gaines. 'Are you all right?' This meaning *have you got your head on straight from now on?*

'Right as rain,' said Cale.

'There's something else.'

'Yes?'

'From now on, you must never speak of anything to do with my mistress or her son to anyone for any reason.'

He looked at Cale intently. He seemed not to have any reaction at all. Gaines waited.

'All right,' said Cale.

'You don't want to know why?'

'If you want to tell me, I'm very happy to listen.'

'This place is full of Nick Van Owen's stoolies. You should consider that anyone not allowed in Arbell Van Owen's private apartments to be a snark, and if not a snark then a fink. Clear?'

'Clear.'

'Good luck with Denmark – you might find it harder to win him over than you think.'

'How much?'

'What?'

'How much do you bet me?'

26

Hamlet's Lament:

Ophelia – should have loved you, not my mother
Ophelia – didn't mean to kill your brother
I stabbed your Pa, which was against the law
(And forgive what I did with Marie the whore
involving a bottle and a cucumbore)
I am a rogue and peasant slave
Deserving of poison and an early grave
Under the cold earth I must go
Eee-Ay-Eee-Ay-Eee-Ay O

– Song: 'Hamlet's Death' from *The Tragical Comedy of Hamlet and His Father's Ghost* by Francis Formby & George Bacon

There will be no question of Hamlet and his Uncle's Ghost being shown in Hustone. If the vulgar herd want to listen to that disgusting little ditty about cucumbers, they'll have to be content to hear it in degenerate Malfi. But not for much longer – the fancies who flock to that place don't yet realize that the wind of change is blowing through the South. A cold wind for them.

– Llorde Reith, Mayor of Hustone, Ordinance 417

Cale was not the only one to have his card marked that morning. A couple of hours later, Cariola opened the door of Arbell's apartments with a delighted flourish to announce someone in a tone that would have been regarded as acceptable at the Last Judgement.

'Miss Hetheria Summerstone for you, ma'am.'

Cariola, eyes smiling, had stopped abruptly, causing Hetty to bump into her and so feel even more nervous than she'd been in

Arbell's anteroom, where she'd been left, as a matter of policy, to stew in her own juice for half an hour.

Cariola, her eyes now full of a pantomime cold disdain, turned back to Hetty. 'You are to wait until you are called!'

Startled at being spoken to in such a tone by a maid, Hetty stepped back as if she were a little girl being scolded by a teacher (not that Hetty had ever paid much attention to teachers, however much they told her off. But this was no headmistress about to reprimand her. This was Arbell Van Owen).

Cariola turned back to Arbell and opened her eyes with delight at such a lark. 'Do you want to see her now, ma'am?'

Laughing, if silently, Arbell signalled her to let the poor girl in.

Cariola pushed open the door and, giving Hetty her best look-what-the-cat's-dragged-in face, nodded her forward. Hetty walked uneasily into the room. Cariola closed the door. Arbell stared at her, making it clear she should leave. Cariola ignored her.

'Thank you, Cariola. That will be all.'

Cariola stared back insolently. The two women looked each other in the eyes for several seconds, then Cariola turned down her mouth to make clear that she couldn't be bothered with this nonsense and walked out.

'Come in, Hetheria,' said Arbell, voice temperature a little above freezing. 'Sit down.'

Hetty's inner gang of rebellious young women had been scattered by the severity of her summons: a furious knock from two uniformed servants with grim faces: 'You are to come immediately, no matter what.' Then the wait in the anteroom and the performance from Cariola. But Hetty was made of insolent rather than stern stuff – her life had not been difficult enough for the truly unyielding to enter her soul. Nevertheless, she was no pushover.

'Nobody calls me Hetheria. My name is Hetty.'

If the history of great starers is ever written, it is certain that Arbell will vie for a long chapter with many illustrations of, in no particular order: her cool stare, her warm stare, her indifferent stare, her you-have-my-permission-to-adore-me-from-afar stare, her (very rare this one, seen only twice) you-can-adore-me-from-as-close-as-it's-possible-to-get stare. What Hetty was given at full blast was Arbell's who-said-you-had-permission-to-even-breathe-in-my-presence? stare.

Hetty sat down as if someone had given her a sharp tap on the back of both knees.

'I've called you here to talk about Mona Fuentes, among other things.'

The last puff of wind spilt from Hetty's sails. A guilty expression flushed over her face, all the more touching because of its rarity.

'I'd no idea she'd do something like that. I promise, if I'd known . . .' Her voice trailed away, her expression changed, the guilt modified not by shame exactly – alarm, perhaps.

'If you'd known what?' said Arbell. But in fact she felt sorry for Hetty now it was clear she blamed herself for Mona throwing herself into the river. It was helpful that she was so uncharacteristically contrite. It also made it a good deal easier to raise, for Arbell at any rate, the awkward question of Hetty's sexual disposition. It should be clear that Arbell was much more alarmed by any possibility she could be accused of disapproving of tribadism than by tribadism itself. Moral disapproval of such things was irredeemably bourjeois and she considered herself, as an aristocrat and a woman of the world, to be above such conventional pieties – a conventional piety, however vulgar, that was shared by virtually everyone in the United Estates; along with a deep religious devotion, a horror of sexual deviance was perhaps the only thing that united all of the Estates – white, black, slaver or abolitionist.

'When I was your age,' said Arbell, a little less coldly, 'the two of us had a great deal in common.'

An astonishing idea began to rise in Hetty's breast – along with the guilt and the now diminishing alarm. Was Arbell, the cold and beautiful and utterly unobtainable and utterly delicious Arbell – about to admit that she, too, had once been, perhaps still was, a player in the game of flats?

'Just like you, Hetty' – a pause and a softening – 'I thought I knew everything. I thought I knew exactly what my place in the world was – a very important one – and that this very important place was an entirely natural and inevitable place and it would last for ever. And then, in a single day, a single afternoon, as it happens, it all came crashing down around me. And a very few years later, it happened again.'

Poor Hetty. A fair bit of collapsing was going on around her at that moment. Now Arbell was really beginning to feel sorry for her. But there was a job to be done.

'You need to be more discreet, to be more careful, for your own sake and for the sake of other people.'

Now the guilt over Mona flooded back, and Arbell could see it, even if with mixed feelings. 'Both of us live in a world of extraordinary privilege.'

'I know that,' lamented Hetty.

'Do you? I don't think so. Not if your behaviour is anything to go by.' Hetty looked like an increasingly deflated balloon. 'The thing about privilege is not that it makes you arrogant – though it does – it's that it makes you stupid. And it makes you stupid because it makes you believe that nothing can change. But it can. This country is coming to the boil about slavery.'

'I'm against slavery. I don't want to see it return,' wailed Hetty.

'I'm sure all the black people of the United Estates are delighted to hear it.' A beat. 'I'm sorry, that was unkind. I'm not just giving you an earful' – Hetty's eyes opened a little at such a coarse phrase from Arbell – 'because you need to start thinking about the needs of other people. I want you to understand that the world you know can vanish overnight. And if it does, then the fact that you don't care who knows that you . . .' At this point, Arbell became a little flustered herself.

'That I love other women,' said Hetty. A little of the balance of power between them shifted in Hetty's favour. Arbell gestured her agreement – rather awkwardly, it had to be said.

'Look, Hetty.' Now very soft indeed. 'The world can be very cruel – horribly cruel. Change might be coming. You must be more careful.'

Two large tears collected in the corner of Hetty's eyes and spilled down her cheeks. Arbell now felt she'd been too harsh. 'But I have one piece of news for you which will cheer you up.'

Hope springs eternal in a young woman's heart, particularly the heart of a force of nature like Hetty.

'Mona Fuentes trying to kill herself . . . it had absolutely nothing to do with you. I promise.'

'Really?'

Arbell was touched to see, and a little surprised at, the depth of Hetty's relief. Not so careless of others, after all.

'Really.'

'Oh, thank God!' She was at once a little ashamed at letting her act slip (effortlessly lovely, effortlessly witty, effortlessly without a care in the world). The mask went up again, but not entirely. 'It was so terrible having to think badly of myself.'

Arbell smiled, not too much but enough. 'Tea?'

Tea would be wonderful.

They sat and drank together, Arbell all lightness after the telling-off. Hetty was entranced, as she was meant to be. After ten minutes of being friends, Arbell came to the second point of the interview.

'I know, Hetty . . .' It was the first time Arbell had ever talked to her in such an intimate way. Hetty was thrilled: to be the sudden focus of Arbell's affection was a wonderful thing. 'I know, Hetty, that you are a true friend of the coloured people of the Estates.' This was true enough, if overstated rather. But Arbell's assertion was so artless Hetty was at once in agreement that, yes, she was a true friend. 'And I know you want to do something practical to avoid the terrible prospect of their enslavement.'

Hetty was certainly against any such thing, but the notion of the specifically useful made its way even through the mist of her new infatuation with Arbell.

'But what can *I* do?' she said.

'That's what I wanted to talk to you about, Hetty.' A skip of the heart from Hetty, despite her alarm. 'Your father loves you very much. Yes?'

'Um . . . well . . . yes.'

'He adores you.' Hetty stared – a rabbit in the light of Arbell's flame. 'And your father is a man with great influence in the South . . .

an influence he's yet to make use of. And yet I know he's no friend to the idea of re-enslavement.'

'He isn't at all,' said Hetty, trying to reinforce her new-found fervour in the cause of the Negro. 'He doesn't want to see slavery back in the South. But he thinks that Congress is against the South and he doesn't want to be of any help to the Northerners who are so vile about us. He's in a difficult position. So he's waiting and hoping it will all blow over.'

Arbell nodded thoughtfully to show she was completely understanding of the problem.

'I want to convince him that there are many in his position. He's not as isolated as he thinks.' Let me be frank with you, my dear,' she said, not at all frankly. Another fluttery glance at Hetty, another thump of the heart. But infatuated though she was, Hetty was no fool and struggled mightily to regain some of the control she was accustomed to having under all circumstances. She broke away from Arbell's seductive gaze: *Stand up for yourself, you lecherous mopsy!* She summoned up a confidence she hardly felt.

'You want me to try and influence him.'

A pause and another seductive look from Arbell that somehow said clearly: *How impressed I am by your cleverness.*

'Would that be possible?'

It was about four o'clock, and Cariola had decided to teach her ungrateful mistress a lesson for not allowing her to be present when she took down Hetty Winterstone a peg or two. She would make it clear she couldn't care less about the matter by deciding to go missing for an hour. An early caminado was in order, a Spanish term for a walk undertaken by a young woman in order to give others the undeserved privilege of admiring them. But there was no one worth looking at her anywhere to be seen. Then she remembered there was some sort of muzik burlesque taking place in the open air on the other side of Malfi – popicok about a young man who can't make up his mind about anything, his long-suffering girlfriend, and a ghost. So she walked and found herself so enjoying the solitude she made it all the way to the stream that marked the end of the park, some two and a half miles away from the house. She slowly became aware of a sawing sound, a heavy rhythm back and forth. Curious, she peeked into the line of willows that Ray Jackson had been pollarding for several days. As she moved around the willow that seemed to hide the source of the noise, Ray came up close behind her – but not too close.

'Hello. You are the Konpayel elegan to the owner of this place.'

She looked at him as if he were a fence post that had decided to speak. But this was a palpable hit, and she was flattered and intrigued – no easy thing for someone so used to flattery. He had called her Arbell's elegant companion; Ray, being familiar with the attitudes of spoilt ladies' maids, knew how the idea of being a servant, no matter how significant, rankled with these special ones.

'Is it possible,' she asked, as if to her lady-in-waiting, 'that this person is talking to me?'

This was a good deal less harsh than someone who knew Cariola would have expected from her on being addressed in such a way by a mere servant, black or white. But he was well spoken, much more so than she would have expected of a gardener, and very handsome. Given no one was nearby to expose her to gossip, she had decided to be intrigued. It might be amusing. She was also softened by his calling her elegant. She was always described as beautiful but felt this was so obvious that it counted as evidence of stupidity. She liked elegant much better.

'You know that if they discover you've accosted me in such a way, they'd tan your hide.'

'No, they wouldn't,' he said, without boastfulness.

'Really?' This smiling confidence made Cariola laugh.

'No one on God's earth will ever lay a hand on me.' He was going to say *again*, but stopped himself in time.

A little snort of disdain at this gallantry – but not too much.

'Where are you from?'

'Butt's . . . Georgyer.'

'If I were you . . .'

'Ray.' He smiled his most charming smile. It had some effect.

'If I were you . . . oh dear, I've forgotten your name already . . . I'd arrange to be from somewhere else.'

'You want me to lie about myself?'

'Why on earth would *I*' – she emphasized her *I*-nessness – 'want you to *do* anything at all?'

'Because you like me, perhaps. I am a remarkable person, you know.'

Again, it was the matter-of-fact and modest way he said this that sent the tiniest of flutters along her spine.

'Are you, *really*? Don't tell me . . . you're an eccentric millionaire who's wandering around the South pretending to be a half-wit gardener.'

Ray roared with laughter. An alarm bell of the tinkliest kind went off in Cariola's brain. *Don't you dare have anything to do with him, you foolish slut!*

'AHOY! HOY! AHOY! HOY!'

This peculiar shout of warning was soon followed by the even more peculiar sight of Denmark barrelling around the corner on his latest toy, a velocipede – a two-wheeled device, one wheel in front of the other, with a seat in the middle and a bar handle for steering. Pushed along by his feet, and coming downhill, Denmark was travelling at a tremendous lick. Fortunately for the chirpsing pair, he had just enough control to miss them – though not by much.

'*Sorry!*' he shouted out cheerfully, and vanished from sight behind a row of huge mimosa trees.

Cariola gasped in irritation as she watched him and then turned back for more entertainment from her alluringly impudent gardener. It was as if she'd turned into a bitter wind. Ray's expression had changed utterly from that of the alluringly impudent chancer of a few seconds before. It was as if his face had become infused with a hate and bile that flushed under his skin like black water under ice. He barely seemed to see her as he stared after Denmark. It was as if, in a second, any moment his hatred would split his skin from top to toe.

'What's the matter?' she said. He did not reply.

Quickly, she started to walk away, and this seemed to bring him back.

'Wait!' he called.

But she did not wait. She walked more quickly, so quickly that her walk turned into a run, something she had not lowered herself to do since she was ten years old.

'Cariola, please!'

The Hanson Lodging House was one of the few two-storey buildings in Rosewood if you were black or an enlightened white, Muntown if you were not. The way the black township of Rosewood had been talked about to Cale, he had been expecting something squalid and menacing; it had clearly evolved in its higgledy-piggledy streets from a shanty town, but it was pleasant enough and clearly on the up. The Lodging House was used by the emerging class of black salesmen and businessmen as somewhere welcoming to stay while attempting to get a piece of Malfi's affluence for themselves. Tough as it was to get their feet under the table, there was a following wind at Malfi through Gaines – with the approval of his mistress – to give a fair stake of the opportunities to black as well as white: a source of much resentment among white businessmen, who regarded favouritism to anyone but themselves as a deep injustice. It should be pointed out that Gaines had no favourites – a black trader who offered inferior goods or services was heartlessly received. Black merchants came to the Hanson Lodging House not because it was cheap – it was merely reasonable – but because there was nowhere else that would have them that was not one step up from a dosshouse.

There were four of these tradesmen in the small lobby and they took to Cale's arrival with surprise, quickly disguised. The woman behind the counter, if she was confounded in any way, hid it very well.

'Can I help you, suh?'

If it was not asked as politely as the words themselves might imply, there was a wariness here he couldn't put his finger on. And why would he?

'I'm looking for two boys . . . twelve, fourteen? Name of Hanson. I don't know their first names.'

The wariness was replaced by alarm. 'They're not here.'

Cale could more easily place fear when he heard it. 'It's nothing wrong. I came to thank them. They saved me from drowning in the weir pool.'

She relaxed, her face softening in such a way that she could only be the boys' mother – first relief, now pride.

'We didn't think anyone would come.'

Cale was surprised. 'The girl's family haven't been' – he was about to say *to see you* but caught himself: 'in touch?'

The faintest of smiles on her lips, more enigmatic by far than the one on the famous painting of that bland hausfrau in that puffed-up painting in the museum at Paris.

'In touch? No, they ain't been in touch.' The secret smile faded, but very slowly.

'Perhaps they don't know how to find you.'

'P'raps.'

A pause.

'Are the boys likely to be back soon?'

'You think I might be deceiving you?'

This was a tricky one, this woman.

'I just came to say thank you.'

She looked him over for a moment. 'They've gone to Santa Anna for a month.' A pause. 'Or two.'

Cale nodded, as if thoughtful. 'Are they your children?'

'They yare. I'll tell them you said to thank 'em for what they did.'

Cale tried a little enigmatic smile of his own. 'Well, you see . . . Mrs Hanson?' A nod. 'I'm a very vain sort of person – though you might not think it to look at me.' A smile from her, not quite so secret. 'And the thing is, I value my hide, the one your boys saved, at a higher price than you might think could be altogether justified. A "thank you" doesn't flatter me enough. My pride demands that the boys have a reward that reflects my significance in the world as I see it.' He took an envelope from his jacket and put it on the counter. It was deliciously thick. But was it thick with oners or fifties? Mrs Hanson wondered. However, she had too much class to open it and count. Cale thought it was only right to put her out of her curiosity.

'There's $500 there.' Her eyes widened. He pretended to

misunderstand. 'I can see you're surprised that I value my life so cheaply, but the truth is – that's all I've got.'

She was about to reply when the door opened, and she looked straight past Cale in a way that made it clear it was no salesman that had entered.

'Joseph,' she said, voice delighted. 'Just right, this is Mr . . .' She turned to Cale.

'Dominic Savio, Mrs Hanson.'

'This is Dominic Savio. He's the man who saved that young girl down at Millers pond and that the boys pulled out of the water. He's come to thank the boys.'

Joseph Hanson was a head taller than Cale, and muscular with it. He looked at Cale, smiling, and took his hand.

'I'm pleased to meet you, Mr Savio. And pleased that gratitude should be properly expressed for the boys' courage. You've restored my faith somewhat in my' – a mocking pause – 'fellow man.'

His voice was as sonorous as you might expect from such an imposing figure. But the way he spoke intrigued Cale. It was not like the county informality of the ordinary blacks he met, nor was it the way that Gaines spoke, indistinguishable from any educated white man. It was careful and precise, clearly learned by someone who had taught themselves, but it was not stilted or pompous. Stately was the best he could come up with.

'I told Mr Savio that the boys are away.'

Joseph Hanson looked at Cale. 'Well, it's a pity they're not here to accept your recognition of their courage personally. It would have been good for them to hear it. But I will write to them to pass on your thanks.'

'He's done more than thank them, Joseph. Mr Savio has given the boys $500.'

It took no very great understanding to see immediately that Joseph Hanson did not approve. It was as if a dark cloud had materialized above his head.

'My wife and I appreciate the trouble you've gone to in order to recognize the courageous act undertaken by them to save your life and that of the young woman – but their behaviour was that of ordinary decent people, and that is what we are, Mr Savio. We cannot be paid for doing what's right. Our decency does not come at a price and I will not teach my sons that it does.' He walked to the counter, picked up the envelope and handed it back to Cale. 'I will pass on your thanks to my sons, and that is all.'

Later that night in bed, Cariola thought about the strange events in the park. Now she felt ridiculous, and even ashamed. She had overreacted – and to what? She had been flirting with a lowest-of-the-low servant and he'd looked sideways at His Highness as he nearly ran them over. His reaction had been a little wild – she'd already played down just how wild it really was – but even Denmark's mother would hardly blame someone for being resentful of her reckless little darling nearly breaking his neck as he went about his green-fingered business. So Cariola tied a millstone around the neck of her alarm and drowned it in the depths of the forgetful sea. But Cariola was sensible in many ways. That was that for Ray Jackson.

The following morning, Cale and Denmark Materazzi, stripped to trousers and close-fitting undershirts, were in a little-visited courtyard of Malfi facing each other, both of them holding rapiers. It was early in the morning and the sun was tinting the lichen-mottled tiles of the roof surrounding the space with a gorgeous red.

'Go on, then,' said Cale.

Denmark moved gracefully back and forward in a movement that would have looked precious if he had not spent so many years practising to make it second nature.

Cale stood still and watched. Denmark stopped – a thought had struck. He looked at Cale directly in the eye.

'I won't be tricked,' he said.

'I don't need to trick you.'

Denmark was not satisfied. 'Best of three passes. If I win, you turn my mother down.'

'For God's sake, it'll be dark before we finish. You need to learn to get on with things.'

'Say it.'

'If you win, I'll turn your mother down.'

'Best of three passes.'

'Are you trying to bore me into a mistake or what? Yes, the best of three passes.'

Then Denmark attacked, careful not to expose himself and in order to check the quality of Cale's skill. A few strokes, the sound of kitchen knives being sharpened. Then back to the start – Cale still as a stump, Denmark like a forward-and-backward-moving crab. Then again. And again. A longer pause – then Denmark attacked with speed and *tring! tring! ttring! ting!* Cale moved back, then to one side, then coming close – but Denmark was fast and away. Then he was back, the blade dancing all around Cale's body. And then a hit. Directly, classically, in the chest. Precise and deadly.

Denmark leapt backwards. Cale let his rapier fall to his side.

'Yes!' shouted Denmark, smiling affably and removing his protective mask.

Cale did not react one way or the other. 'Again,' he said.

This time a little longer. But the same result – a hit to Cale on the left upper chest.

'Again.' This time the longest exchange of all. But the result was no different. The point took Cale an inch to the left of the faded heart printed on the padded chest plate.

Denmark moved back to his starting place and did something slightly foolish with the blade, whipping it crossways and saluting his defeated opponent and smiling, but not insufferably, just with pleasure.

'What do you think?' said Denmark.

Cale looked thoughtful as he removed his gloves and placed the rapier in a rack of five different blades.

'Who knows?' said Cale. 'Perhaps tomorrow you'll win.'

'What do you mean? I won three to love.'

Cale grimaced doubtfully, mocking. 'Not really.'

Denmark laughed. 'I hit you three times – you hit me no times at all.'

Cale looked at him. 'Give me your hand.'

Denmark looked suspicious.

'Don't be such a baby. Give me your hand.'

Denmark held his right hand out and Cale took him by his index finger, guided it down to inside his left thigh and poked the young man's finger into a small cut in the material.

'Before you hit me the first time, I used this' – with a twinkling smile, he seemed to magic up a small knife in his left hand of the kind used for peeling potatoes – 'to expose the deep artery in your leg. If I'd gone and actually cut you, you'd have bled out in about twenty seconds.' Then he moved Denmark's finger to another small cut in his vest at the top of his right arm. 'Cut into here . . . unconsciousness in about fifteen seconds.' Then he took his finger to the padded breastplate and jiggled it up and down in the slash along the embroidered heart. Then up to his collar bone and another cut in the undershirt. 'Two seconds, perhaps.'

Denmark was appalled. 'All of them before I hit you?'

'Long before, I am afraid.'

'I thought I was good at this,' said a mournful Denmark.

'And so you are – but your kind of fencing is a game, an art. *This*' – he held up the ugly potato knife – 'is neither.'

'Teach me.'

'I thought you could look after yourself?'

'Touché,' said Denmark, smiling. 'I was wrong. Teach me.'

'And put myself out of a job? I don't think so.'

'I'll pay you to teach me.'

'How much?'

'How much do you want?'

'I thought you believed the Van Owens were scaremongering about the attack on you.'

'They are. You know that as well as I do. Or better.'

What did he mean by that? thought Cale. *Best ignore it.*

'So why go to all the trouble?'

'Because I want to,' said Denmark. 'Well?'

'If you really want to learn how to kill another human being, it will be unpleasant, I can promise you that.'

He was taken back by this. But not wanting to seem weak, the words were out rather too quickly to be entirely convincing. 'I wouldn't want it any other way.'

Cale looked him over. He liked Denmark, but this ridiculously privileged boy might just as well have been born on the other side of the moon. He smiled, not altogether generously.

'It's your money.'

It had been several days since Joseph Hanson's rejection of Cale's generosity. There are few things as mortifying as expecting to be received with admiration and gratitude for your magnanimity than to have it dismissed as an insult reflecting only your lack of moral style. Cale's nose was out of joint. He was annoyed even further by the enormous breakfast laid out for him in the small sitting room, despite his constant demand that the first meal of the day should consist of two boiled eggs and battered hominy grits – a porridge made of corn which, despite the horrible name and that it was not at all gritty, he'd come to enjoy. Both the sight and the smell of what looked like more food than even the most energetic glutton could manage in a week made him feel queasy: fried chicken in gravy; tripe in green tomatoes – as nauseating as it sounded; pork knuckles in lard – a sin crying out to the Heavens for vengeance; and, thank God, a watermelon, the only thing he could face that particular morning.

The door opened, and the maid came in.

'Sarah,' he whined, 'how many times do I have to tell the kitchen I don't want all this' – he looked at the assortment of baked, fried, boiled and stewed dead animals assembled on the table and words failed him – 'stuff.'

'Can't say, Mr Savio.'

'Can't or won't?'

'Can't.' As it happened, she could explain very easily the array of food, ridiculous even by the excessive standard of Texas breakfasts. Knowing Savio to be ignorant of the ways of the South and realizing from Sarah that he thought nothing in Texas made any sense, the kitchen rightly calculated that he would tend to assume this deranged plenty was normal. The reason for their excess was that the kitchen – and Sarah – were able to take home anything uneaten by the guests at Malfi.

'Preacher's come to see you,' said Sarah, anxious to change the subject.

'Preacher who?' Assuming this was someone's name.

'Preacher Hanson.'

'Joseph Hanson – who owns the hotel in Rosewood?'

'Sure is, suh.'

'What's he want?' he asked, sure this visit would only mean more grief.

'Wants to see you, suh.'

'About what?'

'Didn't ask. He's the preacher.'

'You mean a sort of priest?'

'No. A sort of preacher.'

He sighed. Even the watermelon looked now as if it were covered in an invisible chicken gravy with fixings.

'Bring him up.'

Five minutes later Preacher Joseph Hanson was sitting in a chair looking slightly – not too much, only slightly – ill at ease.

He had politely refused the offer of breakfast, hiding his astonishment that one person should be able to eat such a vast amount at one sitting. A silence. Then:

'Sarah tells me you're a preacher?'

'I am.'

'That's a sort of priest, I suppose.'

'Indeed no, Mr Savio. We reject the false prophets of the whore of Byzantium.'

'Whore of Byzantium?'

'The Pope.'

'Sounds as if you don't care for the Redeemers.'

'They falsely claim a devotion to the Hanged Redeemer. He came to save mankind with love and kindness, not with cruelty and oppression.'

'I see,' said Cale.

'I've come,' said Hanson, 'to apologize to you for my lack of charity the other day.' If Hanson thought Cale was going to meet him halfway, he was mistaken.

Cale just watched him.

'Anger arising out of pride is a fault of mine. I cannot deny it,' he said, with a hint of the pride that he was condemning in himself.

Still no attempt by Cale to take any of the blame.

Hanson could not help himself from trying to regain some lost territory. 'Of course, I still do not believe that my boys should be paid for an action that should only be expected from a Redeemist.' It startled Cale, this new word. 'But I was wrong to be so ungenerous when you clearly meant only to do the right thing . . .' A meaningful beat. 'I am sorry, sir.'

A pause from Cale while he let the big man squirm a little.

'Think nothing of it, Mr Hanson – a misunderstanding among strangers. Let me at least offer you a cup of coffee. Or would you prefer tea?'

'Coffee would be very fine, Mr Savio.'

Cale stood up, smiled and raised a finger to indicate he had something amusing to show him. Treading softly, he walked over to the door and opened it suddenly, like a magician demonstrating the materialization of a young woman in a previously empty cabinet.

Sarah, who'd been listening at the keyhole, launched into the room and was only just able not to fall down on the floor. Cale pretended not to notice.

'Sarah! Just the person I was looking for.' Sarah stood upright and looked at Cale with the expression of a dutiful servant awaiting her instructions in an attentive and helpful manner.

'Coffee for two, if you would.'

Sarah gave a little bob of acquiescence, a curtsey entirely out of her normal behaviour, and quickly made her exit.

Cale turned to Hanson. He'd hoped that his playful kindness towards Sarah's wickedness would reflect well on him with the preacher. He was right. Hanson was smiling.

Cale went back and sat down. 'No man,' he said, 'is a hero to his servants.'

'I try not to think about that,' said Hanson, who employed ten of them at his lodging house. 'I have agreed with myself to maintain the illusion that they always talk about myself and Mrs Hanson with the most profound respect and affection.'

Now they were enjoying each other.

'Are you from Malfi, Mr Hanson?'

'My wife is. She once belonged to the present owner's late husband.'

Cale had now been in the Estates for more than eight months and he knew cruelty and evil as well as any slave, but it startled him still to hear someone talk about the ownership in such a matter-of-fact way. But of course, it was a matter of fact.

'Did you know her husband?'

'Everyone agrees he was a kind master. He emancipated his slaves before the law was passed.'

'But you disapprove of him?'

Hanson thought about this for a moment. *Rare, this,* thought Cale. *He thinks before he speaks.*

'Disapprove? No. Slavery, in my opinion' – and he clearly meant this – 'is, perhaps, unique among all human evil in that it corrupts everyone it touches – good, bad, indifferent, wicked – the owner and the owned.' Now this was interesting. Victims, in Cale's experience, usually saw themselves as victims.

'I couldn't but notice, Mr Savio, your reaction when I spoke of the Redeemers. You've come across them, I think.'

'I was brought up by the Redeemers.'

A silence. Then, softly:

'And are you still one of them?'

A gasp from Cale, a sort of laugh, unmistakably distilled from two parts loathing, two parts rage, three of disgust with a tincture of ill will and an overall bouquet of spite and malignity, hostility and pique, with undertones of grudge and the aftertaste of malevolence and gall. Hanson knew these odours well enough, had breathed them out himself, but here was something of rare intensity. He smiled – the brotherhood of loathing.

The two men realized they had something in common and might

have more. But it would have to wait. Both had business to attend to. Cale invited Hanson to dinner. Hanson laughed.

'You're not from around here, Mr Savio.' Cale pretended not to understand what he was saying.

'Is it so unusual for one man to eat with another?'

'It isn't done.'

'Let me see you out.'

They walked down the corridors of Malfi in an easy silence.

'I was once,' said Cale, as they came to the nearest door into the outside world, 'locked up, by accident I want to assure you, in a lunatic asylum. It took hardly any time to start taking the craziness for granted. It turns out you can get used to anything.' He held out his hand. 'It looks like I have to go away' – he was going to say *with Denmark* but stopped himself – 'for a few weeks, but when I return, please come to dinner.'

'Denmark! A word.' He had just emerged, late morning, from his room. 'Don't pretend you haven't seen me.'

He turned and smiled. 'Salutations, Mother!'

'You know you're having dinner with me tomorrow.' It was not a question.

'Wouldn't miss it. Morning, Cariola.'

She looked at him, smiling and a little dismissive.

'I forgot to tell you,' said Arbell, 'to ask you . . . to ask Mr Savio if he'd like to join us.'

'Expecting an attack on me during the fish course?'

'Just do as I tell you, is that too much to ask?' He was a little surprised at yet another invitation for Cale. She was not slow to pick up on this. 'What's the matter, Denmark, do you think your mother is too much of a hothouse flower for your friend?'

He considered this for a moment.

'Yes.'

'Let me tell you,' said his mother irritably, 'by the time I was your age I'd been at one of the most terrible battles in three hundred years and seen everything I'd ever known collapse around my ears.'

What he thought was *My God, Mother, sing another song.* What he said was 'I stand corrected.'

'You should watch your tongue, little boy.' This time it was Cariola's turn to have her say.

'I've already got a mother to keep telling me off, so I don't need you sticking your ten cents in every time she has a go at me. There must be loads of people you need to irritate on the other side of the building.'

'Stop squabbling, both of you.' But she was not finished with her son yet. 'Did you write to Mr Tenedor to thank him for the tickets?'

'Yes.'

'No, you didn't.'

'Then why ask?' With that he began to mime being pulled back into his room. 'Oh, no!' he called out. 'I'm being pulled behind this door by a mysterious yet impossible-to-resist force.' He opened the bedroom door and was dragged back by invisible hands, closing it in front of him. 'Aaaargh! Aaaargh!'

'Write that letter!' shouted his mother through the door.

She sighed, the sigh of mothers through all the generations back to the very first.

'Strange boy,' said Cariola. 'You don't think, do you, that he was starved of air when he was born?'

'Honestly,' said Arbell. 'You're as bad as he is.'

'You can either come out from behind those bushes voluntarily or I can come in there and get you.'

There was a pause, wisely not a very long one, followed by a rustling, a trip, an unladylike swear word – it was clearly a woman – and then her appearance with an expression of someone both innocent and wronged. 'Mrs Hanson.' He enjoyed her awkwardness. 'What can I do for you?'

'How'd you know?' she said, advancing on to the path, as if it were entirely normal for a respectable preacher's wife to be residing in a bush at seven o'clock in the evening. 'How'd you know there ain't sumptin' I can do fer you, Mr Savio.'

'Is there?'

'No.'

She cleared her throat, as if to wipe the slate of the previous exchange clean from the board.

'I wanted to talk to you 'bout Mr Hanson's conversin' with you concernin' ma boys.'

'He came to see me two days ago to apologize.' A beat and smile. 'Up to a point.'

'Hmmmm,' she said. Oddly, this communicated entirely clearly that she had absolutely no interest in her husband's apology, up to a point or otherwise. 'We gots to have a talk 'bout that money, Mr Savio.'

'He made it very clear he still wouldn't accept it.'

'So he tol' me.' She was clearly not impressed by what she'd been told. 'My husband's a proud man. Me, I'm a proud woman. But they not the same thing. You get my meaning?'

'I'm not sure I do, Mrs Hanson.'

'My boys deserve that money, jus' like you said.' A pause. 'So I gots to ask you for it.'

'Ah . . . I see.'

She looked at him thoughtfully.

'You worried 'bout offendin' my husband?'

'Yes.'

'Then don't say nothin. Leas' said, soonest mended.'

Another pause.

'I don't have it with me.'

'Imagine not,' she said. 'I reckon I'll be hiding in these bushes at the same time' – she looked at him – 'tomorrow convenient?'

'You can always come to the house.'

'Lots a people with big noses and bigger ears at the house.'

27

'By treating serious things lightly and light things seriously, Herman Melville in his so-called pantopera Oswald the Assassin has made a cynical musical folly of execrable history and against all standards of artistic seriousness. We rise to what ought to be great tragedy and fall to the depths of low comedy and vulgar action in a haxdy-daxdy disregard for good judgement and sound taste. He is admittedly a talented composer, but a man with scant education and negligible conscience.'

– Oliver Notes, *Atlanta Daily*

Opinions about Thomas Cale were many and varied: he was the worst of men; he was the best of men. He was misunderstood and had actually done many great good things; he was misunderstood and had actually done very many terrible things. In all this there were as many opinions as there were stars in the sky: he was tall; he was short; he was ugly; he was beautiful beyond all men; he was an oaf; he was a charmer; he was by temperament cruel but he could be kind; he was by temperament kind but he could be cruel. The one thing of which he was never accused was stupidity. But you have now seen that he was very stupid indeed.

Bluebeard kept the bodies of his many wives in a cellar. Rocastle kept his mad wife in an attic. So long as they kept the door locked, they were model fathers, model citizens and even model husbands. But while Cale, better than most, had kept his inner madwoman penned in a dungeon, bastilled with bars that were thicker than a giant's thumb, Arbell Materazzi had the key to break her free. He had better get himself under control, or who knew what would happen? But maniacs, once out, usually develop a taste for making a break for it and getting up to who knows what dreadful mischief.

That night Cale gave in to a second ration of the black stuff and fell asleep, smiling and muttering and singing to himself the irritating tune he'd heard from Oswald and which he could not purge:

Mumble mumble flee mutter mutter love
Mumble flower mutter poison mutter mumble
Come into the garden mumble mutter
Night has mumble flown and poison mutter
Honey love and poison flowers mumble mumble mutter mutter

He woke up feeling terrible and had two fingers of brandy, which made him feel worse. He drank two jugs of water and made himself sick then took two grams of St John's weed out of his locked case and tried not to notice the waxed paper of wormwood crystals that were as likely to throw you over the cliff as drag you back from the edge. This was the medicine of last resort given to him by Sister Wray, but the last time he'd taken it he'd been a powerful man with two people at his back to cover for him, no matter what. The simple fact was that he was no longer important enough to risk going mad.

Ten minutes later he felt better than he had any right to and left his delightful two-room apartment to go down to Denmark's suite of rooms, where the young man was enjoying breakfast.

'Help yourself,' said Denmark, gesturing towards the elegant sideboard laid with bacon, sausages and grits; eggs in three types – wrecked, coddled, sunny side up; sweet bread and toast.

'I've already eaten.'

'Suit yourself. Sit down. Coffee?'

Cale nodded. A flunky poured. Denmark looked him over thoughtfully. 'I'm not sure I've ever seen anyone quite that shade of white before. What would you call it? Plague White? Cream of Eternal Rest?'

'Never mind my complexion, sonny, what are you doing today?'

The flunky was deeply shocked. Denmark laughed. 'I want to ride up to the old quarry for a swim. Do you ride?'

'Well enough.'

'Do you swim?'

'Very droll, your enormity.'

The flunky was exhibiting signs of severe palpitations. He emitted a slight squeak. 'Thank you,' said Denmark. 'That's all for now.'

With a mixture of relief and pique, the flunky left.

'What am I supposed to call you, by the way?'

'In public, I quite like Your Enormity, but it would cause less comment if you kept it to sir. In private you can call me what you like, as long as you realize that I'm quite a sensitive little flower and I'm prone to tantrums if someone disagrees with me even a little bit. What should I call you?'

'Savio.'

'Not Dominic?'

'Nobody calls me Dominic,' said Cale, which was true, as far as it went. 'Besides, to call me by my first name makes me sound like your pet dog.'

'Savio it is, then.'

'And after we ride and you swim?'

'I'll read here for an hour or two. Are you a reader, Savio?'

'I didn't used to be, but I am now, when I get the time.'

'Well, I read a lot, so you'll be able to catch up.' He looked at Cale, sly. 'Let me guess, you like a nice romance – love betrayed, a foundling girl, a heartless villain, a tearful reunion and a happy end.'

'I'm ashamed to be so obvious. You don't like a happy end?'

'I do in my life – I want endless sweetness and joy and never to be crossed in anything. But in my books I like misery and pain and sorrow and a miserable death for hero and villain alike – no marriages, and lots of funerals and plenty of despair. That's me. That kind of thing makes me feel deep.'

Cale could not stop himself laughing. He was a charmer all right.

'Then it's lunch with my mother – so you won't need to work until three, when I'm supposed to attend *Barbra Seville*.'

Cale looked puzzled. 'It's a new opera by Bret Harte – one of those new pantoperas. Looking forward to it.' He noticed Cale's mild look of disapproval. 'Not an opera fan?'

'No.'

'I promise to change your mind.'

'I doubt that.' A beat. 'What's a pantopera?'

Later, making their way out of the grounds and towards the old quarry, Cale asked if Denmark wanted him to ride behind.

'Do you want to?'

'It's up to you, sir.'

Denmark looked thoughtful. 'Thanks, Savio.'

'For what?'

'Sometimes I do like to be on my own. In fact, I probably like it too much.'

'It's not possible to like being on your own too much,' said Cale. 'You have double the pleasure: you have the benefit of being on your own and the joy of not being with anyone else.'

This started Denmark cackling away. 'There is a third good thing about being on your own,' he said. 'Other people don't have to put up with you.'

'You know, sir, that never occurred to me.'

They didn't say much on the journey, but from time to time Denmark kept bursting into laughter.

When they arrived at the east side of the old quarry half a dozen coloured boys were already swimming there, splashing about, laughing and abusing each other.

'Damn,' said Denmark.

Cale felt an oddly unpleasant sensation at the back of his neck. He'd enjoyed liking the boy. It felt good to tell himself that he was above the pettiness of taking out his loathing of the mother on the guiltless son. It made him feel less like a sneak or a stalking madman. But then Denmark had been so easy to like: clever, self-mocking, self-aware (up to a point) and, always something easy to respond to, he was clearly impressed by Cale. 'It's an extraordinary thing,' IdrisPukke used to say, 'but I always feel like praising a man who has praised me first.' But now this handsome, clever, witty young man was showing he was deeply uneasy about sharing a lake with a handful of boys having a good time just because they were black. Looking troubled, Denmark began to undress. By now the boys had noticed the two white men. Slowly, the fooling about stopped and all six made their way to the rocks, pulled themselves out and stood, naked, watching the pair of them. Stern-faced, Denmark stood on a ledge about eight foot off the surface of the water. He sighed heavily. Then he called out to them, 'Don't go! Just carry on. It's absolutely fine. Please!'

But the boys stared back, sullen as they pulled on their clothes and left.

Denmark watched them and after a moment dived into the clear slate-grey water and swam up and down for about twenty minutes, pausing only once to invite Cale to join him.

On the way back they barely spoke at all, just the once.

'I told Moseby to put the word out that anybody who wanted could swim in the quarry. I even talked to Nick Van Owen to make sure he did as he was told. He said he would.'

'And you believed Uncle Nick?'

'Thank you for reminding me. You're right. I really am that stupid. I expect people to do as I ask, because they usually do. I've lived here long enough to know that not even the spoilt-brat son of the owner of Malfi matters a pile of Lucy Bowles racoon shit when it comes to this *thing* of theirs.'

'I'm not from around these parts,' said Cale, feeling sorry for the boy. 'Do I take it that racoon shit is not highly regarded?'

'You know, Mr Savio, I came to the Estates when I was five years old, and it's not that I disapprove of the way the Southerners disdain the Negroes – I mean, I do disapprove, believe me –'

'Of course you do,' said Cale, 'even as you benefit so handsomely from that disapproval.'

He looked at Cale. 'I deserve that, sure I do. But not as much as you think.'

'Don't pay any attention to me,' said Cale, genuinely sorry for tormenting the boy. 'I'm just a washed-out cynic.' Then, softly: 'You were saying.'

A pause while Denmark tried not to sulk. 'You see, the thing is, I've been here most of my life and there's something more about this black business other than it being wrong.' A sigh of exasperation.

'What also really bothers me is that I still don't understand what it's about.'

A group of twenty or so middle-aged worthies, men of great influence in the South, were sitting around a table in one of the more splendid rooms in Malfi – which was saying something. They were all regarding Arbell Materazzi with the amiable condescension of the gentleman Southerner who is just about to make a very large amount of money from someone who should have had the sense of her sex to allow a man to do the negotiations for her – although not the black man sitting next to her, of course. They had a point. The deal that Arbell was about to sign with them to provide extensive land for the development of a railway from Galveston to Topeka and then all the way to Chicago was very much a licence for those involved to print money. They knew, as even a woman should have known, that in many ways she had them over a barrel. The extensive land she was leasing, accompanied by a somewhat inexpensive loan, offered by far the most economical way of driving a railway line through the South. The deal was not bad for her; she would become even more fabulously wealthy because if it, but she could have negotiated very much harder. It was as easy as candy and especially satisfactory for these great men of commerce in that she was generally held to be particularly good at business.

'If we're all agreed, then, gentlemen.' They were agreed all right. How could the promise of so much power and influence at a bargain price not be delightfully amiable?

She stood up, the men also rising as she flowed to the door and used a trick she'd overheard when she was a young girl at dinner with her father and her Uncle Vipond, according to some the wisest (and most devious) politician who'd ever lived: *Whenever you want to devastate your opponents, give the appearance of coming to an agreement which satisfies their desires. Then leave. But as you reach for the door handle, turn as if it were something you'd forgotten and then deliver the real point of your being there.*

'Of course, gentlemen, it goes without saying that my investment in the railway and great fortunes that will come to you and those you represent from that investment are entirely dependent on the stability of the United Estates as a whole. A successful vote for re-enslavement in Congress would result in the immediate withdrawal of my offer.'

Later, Arbell and Gaines, full of self-satisfaction at their cunning plan, were drinking a very nice bottle of Pol Roger (it resembled a very great Chablis, with a note of white truffles and chocolate).

'To Arbell Van Owen,' said Gaines, 'who has committed her purse and not just her mouth to a great cause.'

Then she laughed – such a wonderful sound, thought her steward. 'I'm so sorry, Mr Gaines, if I've given you the impression that I'm a saint. I've seen ruin, and I don't want to experience it again. I still intend to make money from this railway. While I want to see good done in the world, I think constantly of myself and constantly of my son.'

'And nothing else?'

She looked at him for a little while. 'Just one other thing.'

A beat. But then his expression changed. 'There is something else I need to talk to you about.'

'Yes?'

Another beat, not the same.

'You might find this . . . upsetting.'

'Oh?'

He took a large piece of paper from his pocket and handed it to her. It was the wanted poster advertising the reward for Thomas Cale. If the air in the room had been made of glass, it would have been glass vibrating from a high-pitched sound just before it shattered.

'It doesn't mean,' said Gaines, 'that he's anywhere near here, or even anywhere in all the Estates of America. The Hanse have been posting these everywhere in the world, as far as I can find out. Many people think he's dead.' She didn't say anything or react in any way. She just examined the picture. Then, softly:

'I'd never have recognized him. A long time ago.' A pause. A deep frown. 'Is this a true likeness?'

'Whatever you say about the Hanse, you could never accuse them of not getting their facts straight.'

'I suppose so,' she said, absent. She looked at the poster for a few moments longer. Then she folded it and handed it back to him. A silence.

'Something else,' he said.

'Yes?'

'You won't like it.'

'I know I never like it when you say I won't like something.'

'Compensation . . . we should support it.' His expression was one of defiance, as if his statement was something unspeakable that nevertheless had to be spoken.

'How can slave-owners who no longer own slaves be compensated for losing something they don't own?'

'I hadn't thought of that,' he said. 'Now that I hear your response, I'm sure you can simply point it out to the former owners of slaves, who will be utterly cowed by your reasoning and withdraw their demand for reparations instantly.'

They stared at each other. There was some turbulence here.

'Well?' she said at last, grit between her teeth.

'We should make a deal with Louis Van Owen. He thinks compensation might sway the vote his way.'

'His way?'

'He doesn't want secession any more than we do because he thinks the South will lose.'

'He also thinks he can return your brothers and sisters to slavery under another name.'

'That's another fight.'

'Are you sure?'

'No.'

Another silence.

'You said I'd have to make deals with devils when I started this. I didn't realize you meant with the actual Devil.'

It was time to back away.

'You don't have to decide now. Mull it over. We'll have plenty of time to talk about what to do . . . or not do . . . on the way to Washingtone.' A pause to let the sugar go down. But he could not resist. 'If you decide to pursue it, I'll see about setting up a meeting with him.'

[illegible] that the [illegible]
[illegible]. Chauffeur folded it and handed it back to [illegible]
[illegible]

'[illegible],' he [illegible].

'[illegible]'

'[illegible] like it.'

'[illegible] instead you may want something [illegible]'

'Compensation? [illegible]' [illegible] expression [illegible] everything [illegible] to be [illegible].'

[illegible]

'[illegible] of it all,' he said. 'Now [illegible] I [illegible] the former [illegible]'

[illegible] There [illegible]

[illegible]

'It's [illegible].'

[illegible]

[illegible] he [illegible]

'That [illegible]'

'[illegible]'

[illegible]

[illegible]

'You [illegible]'

[illegible]

PART IV
Washingtone

'And upon that woman's forehead a name was written, and that name was a mystery. But that woman was Babylon the City, the Mother of Harlots and all the Abominations of the Earth.'

– The Second Book of the Community of the Redeemer

28

Arbell's journey from Texas to Washingtone to help sway the vote on the reinstatement of slavery had at first been slow, a six-horse carriage and roads that varied from excellent to terrible. Riding with her from Dallas through Botón Rojo and Biloxi was Denmark, watched over by Gaines and a leery Cale, all heading for Mobile to catch the new trainline that now extended from the capital all the way to Atlanta. Before Mobile, much of this expedition passed through a countryside bathed in white. Nothing, besides perhaps a stretch of arctic snow, presents such unspoilt loveliness than when the cotton buds have flared in late July. A few decades before, that wonderful sight would have had the added interest of a harvest moon casting a magical pallor on the fields of exhausted slaves dreading the visit to the weigh-station and the whip in case their pickings should be light. And if they picked more than they were expected to, poor beasts, then they must pick the same the following day and face the lash if they did not.

A few hours after the train moved them out of the South, the beauties and horrors of nature and of natural man were slowly replaced by the beauties and horrors of his Northern brothers' love of machines: the farms were planted by machines, the crops harvested by them, the grain threshed by them. The people who served these devices in the fields were more often white than black. They had crossed more railways and canals in the last 150 miles than there were in the Southern estates combined. And in the night, in the far distance, to the east and west and north, the glowing satanic mills of the foundries belching out pig iron for the industrialization that cotton was ecstatic to defy.

Arbell did not pay much attention to any of this. Her journey was mostly inward; brooding on the knowledge that what was to take place in Washingtone was of such bigness that perhaps no occasion in history had ever been so weighty: to the death of thousands (perhaps tens of thousands – even, God forbid, hundreds of thousands), there was also the death of a nation, the ownership of millions, and the wiping out for ever from the world of that peculiar institution of one man one vote.

How had the United Estates come to this? I'll tell you.

It is, of course, a question that has been the subject of many books and will be the subject of many more. Morality was against it; history was against it; that the revolution had been fought on the grounds of the equality of all was against it; the North, with all its vast wealth and military power, was against it; the majority was against it; the world was against it. Everything was against it. Slavery had been consigned to the dustbin of history.

But a wicked king (a magical, wicked king) had arisen to put a spoke in the wheel of social progress. And his magic wand came in the shape of a technological device that multiplied the money a slave could make for a master a hundredfold: the cotton engine. With this contrivance, His Satanic Majesty brought the promise of vast prosperity – but only if there were slaves. And this was why the Southern estates, where money could now be grown on a bush, wanted their niggers back.

And this, broadly speaking of course, was why that summer in Washingtone the reintroduction of the legal right for one human being to own another was coming to a vote the result of which, whatever that result, was most likely to bring ruin and hatred to the Estates for generations, if not evaporate it for ever.

Another gloomy traveller towards Washingtone that same day was Louis Van Owen. He was coming to see that his wonderful grand fudge was probably doomed. Why, oh, why couldn't the South see that a freedom for the black peoples guaranteed by high-sounding laws written in misty phrase and airy generalities could easily be undercut by local estate laws and general chicanery? What made him so defeatist now was that one important underpinning of this fudge was the introduction of compensation to the slave-owners for the loss of their human capital. His hope had been that money would grease the passage of a final legal emancipation down the throats of those who claimed they faced ruin if slavery was not reintroduced. But it now seemed clear that there was little chance of the North agreeing. There were two reasons for this. The first emerged from those in the North generally more amenable to compromise in the matter of slave ownership. At first there had been a cautious welcome for the idea – but then they'd consulted the numbers and the numbers had shouted back: *two and one half billion dollars!* Ruinous. Impossible. Why spend a sum of money that would bankrupt the estates, when in all probability the South would blink first and back down; or be made very easily to back down if they started a fight? Van Owen had exasperatedly pointed out that whatever the cost of compensation it could very easily be dwarfed by the cost of a war which would bring blood and destruction, along with the expense and very possibly the end of the United Estates itself. And with the end of the United Estates (he found himself becoming quite emotional at this point for some reason), the greatest experiment in the rights of man would perish for ever from the earth. Emotional or not, it did no good.

But for many others money was not the issue. For the true abolitionists, this was a matter of the highest principle: they would not accept that the terrible wickedness of slavery should be rewarded. Belatedly – blame his black soul for this, not his intelligence – he was coming to realize that this was not an issue of blood or treasure, it was about what was Good and what was Right. And both sides thought they were Good and Right. Nothing, not even death and terrible destruction, let alone Louis Van Owen, could defy such a hideous marriage of moral certainty. His great plan was being crushed between the determination of the North to enforce the end of slavery in deed as well as name, and the equal determination of the South to have slavery back in name as well as deed. His soul inhabited the world of the deal, but at some point reality had changed its mind; now he was lost in the world of the crusade. Poor Louis was cursed with a problem. He did not dislike black people. Nor did he like them. But he did not, and never had, understood the Negro *thing* that flowed through so many of his fellow Southerners. It did not seem quite enough to describe it as hate; it was something else he could not quite, in the end, after a lot of thinking, put a name to. But, possibly, perhaps, if he had to do so, he would call it rage. But what were they angry about? Perhaps it was fear. But if so, what were they afraid of? They were just Negroes, after all.

Arbell was also caught up in the iron jaws of compromise, but jaws with rather different teeth. On the one hand, she, too, wanted to feel that the issue of slavery was, in essence, simple: a matter of right and wrong. Unfortunately, she also knew that life had no essence: life was all made up of fog and knots. Life had no more of an underlying order than a rat's nest. Mulling the complicated difficulties involved in preventing re-enslavement, she wondered if she might even be risking becoming something of a rat herself. In all sorts of ways, she could make things worse, given the nature of good intentions and its horrible ally, the law of unforeseen consequences. And though the cause was noble, the means to bring it about was going to be dirty. Over the next few days she was going to be involved with an awful lot of cheating, lying, bribing, shaking hands with and smiling at the loathsome and the vile, and in coming to an accommodation with them swallowing some of their vileness and loathsomeness and living with the taste in her mouth for ever and ever. She had always believed in the notion that to do a great right you must sometimes do a little wrong. But now this seemed merely sanctimonious. Now she understood that the demands of reshaping the world were a good deal harsher. If she were to try to bring an end to slavery for ever in the United Estates and make a deal with Louis Van Owen on compensation, it would be to do a great right by doing a great evil. But for all her agonizing, Arbell had bigger problems than she recognized. Her real problem was that she was losing touch with the spirit of the times. Now, for once, she and Louis had something in common. But they were intelligent. Perhaps one of them, at least, could change.

And so the two of them came to Washingtone, burning, burning.

Washingtone! Had there been a city like it since the days of Babylon? For some, it was the home of the future, where the great Congress of the capital city was the mother and the father of votocracy. But for many of its visitors Washingtone is of all places the most detestable. Everywhere, on lawns and side streets, parks and boulevards, were animals of every kind: hogs, sheep, goats; cattle as well as dogs and cats roamed freely, eating the garden plants and stripping the newly planted trees – and with them, of course, piles of animal dung dressing the landscape everywhere. With the dung came a blizzard of flies and, on account of the fact the city was built on a swamp, the flies were escorted by clouds of mosquitos. Needing a holiday just like anyone else and finding Washingtone very much to their taste, the occupants of Hell over-summered there and always in the same place. Beelzelbub, Lucifer, Mammon and Satan reigned there, and their temple was the real centre of politics in Washingtone: Willards Hotel.

Willards was home to a dozen political parties as confused and peculiar as their names: the Fusionists, the Know Nothings, the Know Somethings; there were the Temperance Men, the Hindus, the Anti-Masons; and there were three types of deimocrat – Hard, Soft and Half Shell. It seemed there was a new one every day – but all of them were here this particular summer to decide in the foundry of equality whether or not the slaves who had been freed only a few years before might now be brought back into bondage.

So it was this, the very existence of the United Estates, that brought Arbell and her retinue to Washingtone and past that hostelry of the infernal on Pensylvanier Avenue. She was no stranger to the place, but Denmark gawped as their caravan moved on through the city, which looked as if it had been invaded by an enormous but unruly country farm. They were halted on F Street for fifteen minutes as a march went past demanding that the Union be preserved. Every twenty yards there was a balloon with red-and-white posters plastered to the curves: REMAIN! The balloons shouted to the world: REMAIN! REMAIN! From among the crowds watching the procession bawl and trumpet its way through the city were the opposition, heckling and booing and throwing the odd dead cat. Balloonless as yet, they waved the flags of the Carolinas, Texas and Tennessee and in between each one a flag that shouted: LEAVE! LEAVE!

Only as they passed through the centre did the animals thin out, to be replaced by a zoo of people of every kind, drawn there to see what they might profitably do. There were wrisly lollygaggers, handy dandies with pure boys in bowler hats, egglers in braces, gum bashers looking for Eisen Howers and Three Pounders calling out their goods against the cry of the tock mongers; there were tooled-up Thumbriggers and Gum-bashers looking for a job of work. Then it was down through Bourse Street, and there the splendid financiers in red weskins smoking pure perique and negotiating wimpies with pretty horizontals and gorgeous tantalizers.

That night, ensconced in the unfinished mansion on Constitution Street, the racket dimmed, but only by a half – the bleat of goats and bellow of cows and squeal of pigs was replaced by the squabbling bark of dogs and cats battling the larcenous foxes coming into town to gobble up the chickens that hadn't made it home to roost.

Then there was the night smell. After dark the gong farmers and honey dippers fought over who would take the shit from the city middens down to the dock for five dollars a load. It was barged downriver to a remote location, to be dumped in time for the tide to bring it back the following day to rinse the Washingtone waterfront with excremental sludge.

Denmark couldn't make his mind up whether he was fascinated or repelled and found it hard to get to sleep. If he'd known what was coming, neither he nor Cale would have slept at all.

29

Denmark woke early next morning and pulled the curtains to reveal the sight of the two guards who'd been outside all night at Cale's instruction. Next to the guards were two goats eating a hydrangea bush. One of the goats stared at Denmark, chewing away as if thoughtfully considering what he was worth.

'Bleeeeeeeauh!' said the goat, dismissively.

'You, too,' replied Denmark.

Breakfast was a dismal affair because, although Gaines had sent a selection of Malfi cooks ahead, they'd taken a wrong turn at Columbus and got halfway to New Madrid. They would not arrive for at least another two days, which was why Arbell and Denmark, along with Gaines, were staring miserably at a selection of corn breads, slightly stale; hard-boiled eggs and stew: the coffee resembled coffee in that it was hot and brown but otherwise almost completely devoid of flavour other than a hint of warm dishwater.

'What's on the menu for dinner?' asked a forlorn Arbell.

Gaines consulted the list in his inside pocket. 'Uh . . . *frizzled beef . . . soused calfs' feet*' – he sucked his teeth disapprovingly – 'that should be apostrophe s not s apostrophe . . . followed by shad, roast tongue and udder, followed by stewed fruit and custard.'

She looked at him then smiled. 'You're teasing me.'

'Ah. Unfortunately, madam, no. I'm afraid I don't have the kind of imagination that could summon up roast tongue and udder.' Her face fell rather charmingly. 'But shall we eat out?' suggested Gaines, so anxious not to disappoint her in anything.

'What about Denmark?'

'What about me?'

'It won't be safe in public.'

'I agreed to having a guard go with me everywhere on the assumption that I'd actually be going *somewhere* where he could guard me.'

'Please indulge me,' said Arbell.

'I already have,' replied Denmark, in a bad temper. Arbell turned to Cale, who was the only one at the table eating the breakfast without any fuss. If, as a child, you have eaten rat and regarded it as something of a treat, then not even roast udder held any terror.

'Is it safe for my son to eat in public?' she asked, making it pretty clear what answer was required.

Cale looked her in the eyes, working hard to mask his loathing. How much he hated the redness of her lips, despised the turn of her throat, abhorred the fine delicacy of her cheeks.

'No,' he said.

She turned, triumphant, to her son. 'See!'

A snort of derision from Denmark. 'He's only saying that because he's too lazy to do his job. He wants the easiest life possible. Even if the Dust Men exist, which I doubt, they exist down in the South, not here. Ask him if it's safest to lock me in a basement without any windows.'

'That's not a bad idea, as it happens,' said Cale. 'In fact, I highly recommend it.'

'You see!' said Denmark. 'The whole thing is ridiculous. There's no point in my coming.'

'Which,' said his mother, 'is exactly why I didn't want you to come.' She turned to Gaines. 'If I have to eat frizzled possum hung for a week, then so be it. We stay here.'

There was a bad-tempered silence, broken eventually by Cale. 'Oddly enough, once you get used to the idea of eating stew for breakfast, it's really not that bad.'

No one was amused. After more stew of the non-edible kind, Arbell tried to mollify her son.

'I had a letter last night.' He looked at her warily, knowing the softened tone meant some bribe was on the way. 'It was from Martin Luther. He wants to come and talk to me this morning.' Another pause for the bait to take hold. 'I'd like you to be there.'

30

There was certainly no doubt in Alexei Comsky's mind that the execution of the Royal Family was solely the idea of Thomas Cale, who argued that, as long as they lived, they would be a rallying call for opposition. When Stalovek objected to the execution of the children, Cale remarked that he might as well hand over the keys of the Kremlin to the White Rus and then they could all go home. Of the twenty-three members of the Central Executive Committee, eighteen voted for the executions and the remainder, led by Stalovek, angrily voted against what the latter called 'an act of infamy'.

– Andrew Napsley, *Necessary Murder in the Boll Shevik Civil War* (Orden and Orden)
104–7 ME 1974

There are many ridiculous ideas about anger, the most idiotic being that you can rise above it. There are, of course, examples of people who have conquered anger in themselves, but they inevitably suffer one of two fates: they end up dead in a ditch, the victim of the anger of someone else; or they do not end up dead in a ditch, but only because they have been protected by someone who, fortunately, hasn't risen above their capacity for wrath. When you use peaceful means to counter violent people, it is not the violence that goes away.

Consider anger, rather, as if it were a precious but powerful medicine whose curative powers depend on careful use and the correct dose. Too little and you die of the disease, too much and you die of the cure. This is why the Greeks have two gods of war: Ares, insanely destructive and brutal, and Athen, careful, proportionate and the wisest of all the gods. Athen – quite interesting, this – is a woman. Sadly, the human heart is careless with anger and prone to leaving the lid off the bottle or storing it in one with a misleading label.

Of course, there are a great many very angry people in the world, some of them, like Cale, for very good reason, but he also possessed a unique ability to put his anger to good (or bad) use. Still and all, when it came to such anger, leaks were inevitable. The trouble is that sometimes, even for the cowardly angry man or woman, something small can get dangerously out of hand. And anyone, after all, can have a bad day.

It was the day after he'd been accused of idleness by Denmark and they had, in accordance with the heir to Malfi's wishes, met to continue his training by Cale in the skills of what Denmark still thought of as dirty fighting and Cale merely as fighting. It was early and Cale had found a place in the grounds behind a former pigsty which protected them from sight and sound.

As Cale bound each one of his hands separately with coarse bandages, Denmark, already uneasy at his ill temper of the day before, grew more uneasy still at Cale's refusal to catch his eyes.

'I just wanted to . . .'

'Who do you trust?' asked Cale as he finished tying off the bandages on his hands.

'What?'

Cale lashed out and fetched Denmark a hefty blow in the chest. 'Answer.' For the first time, he looked Denmark straight in the eye. It was not a pleasant experience. The young man felt something unfamiliar in his stomach – the feeling that comes from being out of your depth. But he was, after all, Denmark Materazzi and, despite being a largely unspoilt person, he was still spoilt. Entitlement still hung around him, and entitlement's first cousin – invulnerability.

'Oh,' said Denmark – sarcasm to cover his doubt, 'you want me to learn that I should trust nobody.'

Another hefty thump from Cale, one that landed with more than irritation.

'I asked you a question.' Cale circled around him. Another blow – harder than the last. Denmark's attempts to block were so poor Cale's fist had landed and was back at his side before he could react.

'I don't know what your problem is. I'm not playing.' He turned and walked away, but the lightest flick from Cale's right foot knocked his left heel against his right and he fell. Cale moved to block the only way out.

'You see, Denmark, you have to understand that, one day, no matter how much power or money or anything else you have, there'll come a moment when you won't be able to walk away. Until then, you're going to be a baby. You've paid me to make you not a baby and I take my responsibility seriously. As long as you think you can rely on someone else other than yourself you're a nothing – different from all the other nothings in the world who know they're nothings only by the fact that you think you're special.'

'I don't think I'm special.'

''Course you do. You look special. Everyone treats you as if you're special.' Another blow to the chest, but so powerful it sent him crashing to the ground, winded.

'So, who do you trust, arsehole?'

A few moments to catch his breath. 'Not you.'

This time, a kick to the face. As intended, Denmark was more astonished than hurt.

'Who do you trust?' Another kick with his boot on the other side of his head.

'My mother!'

'Liar!'

Another kick. Denmark stood up and stumbled back. 'I do trust her. Fuck you!'

'*Every mother's heart is a dark continent which her children can approach but not explore.*'

'What?'

'You'll learn.' A pause. 'What about Gaines?' This time, Cale moved in with a fist and another right to his stomach.

'Well?'

'I don't know.'

'Liar!' Another hefty blow to the side of the head. Then another and another – stunned, Denmark collapsed to the floor.

Cale looked down at him – terrified, the boy looked back. Cale reached into his jacket and made much of pulling out a dagger in a sheath – not long, about six inches. Carefully, he eased the blade out of the cover and dropped the sheath on the floor. He walked over to the boy, who tried to get up but took another ferocious blow to the side of the head, falling back on the ground. Cale got on top, raised the knife, and brought it down with enormous power. Denmark blocked it with his right hand on Cale's wrist, Cale's weight pressing down on him. A moment. Then Cale began to push downward. A terrible gasp from the boy as he realized he was going to die – inevitable, horrible. He pushed back with all his strength, sickened, terrified. What was happening? Stop! Stop! But the knife, completely in Cale's command, moved down towards his heart as if it were impelled by a machine – slow, implacable. Eyes dead, Cale pushed on, the knife point eighth of an inch by eighth of an inch making towards the skin, the flesh, the heart.

Stop! Stop! Eyes wide. This is not happening. And then the final push – a scream as the knife with a sudden push hit him in the heart.

But of course, you realized, of course you did, that this was part of a lesson of some kind. At the last fraction of a fraction of a second Cale turned the knife and lightly touched Denmark on the chest. Then, eyes still flat, he stood up.

Perhaps you can be too frightened for weeping and sobbing. Breathing – why did his heart not stop? – breathing as if it were life and not air that he was breathing in, Denmark stared, wild-eyed.

'Who do you trust?' said Cale.

The boy gawped.

'Who do you trust?'

Still, the boy stared.

'The answer, half-wit, is that until now, you've always trusted absolutely everyone. Not any more.' He stepped back, his eyes softening thoughtfully. 'No need to thank me,' he said, and walked away.

That night, very late, he slipped away and met the Van Owen brothers in a back room at Willards Hotel with its entrance in a side alley.

The brothers had been spending eighteen hours a day in meetings in Washingtone, making deals, twisting arms, offering bribes, blackmailing, taking temperatures in the matter of just what the various interests in the South were actually prepared to do rather than talk about doing. If there had been babies available, they would have drowned them in kisses (not that even the most neglectful parent would have taken a baby, not even the ugliest, within ten miles of Willards).

Louis had a particular task to accomplish. He had realized that his plan to prevent a civil war by killing John of Boston then negotiating an enlightened form of serfdom with his weak-spined successor had been a complete failure. He'd run the pennant of ugly compromise up the flagpole of American votocracy – and no one had saluted. At one level, he was appalled at the irrationality of this rejection of a bipartisan middle way, given that the alternative was a niagara of blood at best or, at worst, a niagara of blood and the destruction of the South along with it. He wished he'd been right about Lincoln being spineless. What a long-lived and peaceful votocracy needed was men with a weak will – wishy-washy fudgers, the faint-hearted and fearful. You could usually trace all the ills of this world to someone with a vision, someone determined to do what was morally right, even if the Heavens fell. Well, now they were going to fall. No point wasting energy wailing about it. Time to accept the inevitable and work to survive what was to come with as much of his power, and as much of the South, left intact, as possible. The first stage in this reinvention was to change the view of him among mad-for-slavery Southerners as an unprincipled wheeler-dealer willing to trade away to wicked Northerners the great heritage of the South, its tradition, its identity. These people were unquestionably fools, but they were not stupid. The wrong kind of sudden conversion might result in them seeing him as no more than your typical politician-type weathervane. So he decided to take his lead from a proclamation by the Hanged Redeemer he had always been sure would come in useful one day: *There shall be more joy in Heaven over one sinner that repents than over ninety and nine righteous persons who do not need to repent.*

He would present his past efforts at compromise as the misguided efforts of a man willing to go the extra mile for love of country in general and the South in particular. He was now admitting he'd been wrong and (vital this) that others had been right. But no more. In defence of his heritage, he would imitate the action of the tiger, disguise his Southern generosity with hard-favoured rage. Fortunately, in Nick, he had one of secession's golden boot boys as an ally. But he mourned the passing of his skills, the cunning strategy for the cunning opponent, the give and take in which more can be taken than given, the subtle deceitfulness, the hoodwinking. The deal. All this was gone with the wind. The future was now clear: passionate intensity. Don't persuade your opponents, inflame your supporters.

Move on. Besides, they had more than one dog in this fight. Neither Louis nor Nick had any intention of moderating their plans to get Malfi back into the hands of the real Van Owen family. Nevertheless, despite all this serious business, Nick would not resist the chance to taunt Cale when he arrived.

'We've missed you, Dominic Savio.'

'I'm touched.'

He dropped Cale's wanted poster on the table. 'Lotta otha people missin' you, too. Seen this, have you?'

This was his little joke, given that the poster was all over the United Estates in general and all over Washingtone in particular. It looked to the brothers as if Cale's reaction was pretty much what they expected: a wry amusement, a cool one, at being mocked. But though he'd now seen the poster many times, he was very much the opposite of cool.

'Handsome young feller,' said Nick, gesturing at the drawing. ''Cept for the scar.'

'Do you know who it is, Mr Savio?' said a smiling Louis.

'No idea,' said Cale.

'I suppose he looks a bit like you, in a bad-light kinda way,' said Nick. 'But I guess somebody up there likes you.'

'I've often found that to be the case,' said Cale.

'More than we do,' said Nick. 'We're kinda disappointed in the fact that all the information you've given us so far amounts to a huge pile of steaming pappakak.'

'He means,' said Louis, 'we haven't heard from you when hearing from you is really all of what you're about.'

WANTED

BY THE HANSE FOR CRIMES
AGAINST THE HUMANITY

THOMAS CALE
$50,000 REWARD
ALIVE NOT DEAD

Distinguishing marks: unmistakable scar
extending sideways from the middle of his left cheek
Reward posted by Pinkerton's
The National Detective Agency

APPLY WITH INFORMATION
TO ANY LOCAL OFFICE

'If you wanted regular-type communication,' said Cale, 'you should have sent me a crate of pigeons. I'm making my way to be trusted.'

The thing is that Cale was in an awkward position. His explanations for having provided so little in the way of information were just excuses. Whatever his increasingly confused intentions concerning Arbell, he was not at all unclear about his approach to the brothers. There wasn't much doubt that Louis had tried to have him killed (or probably not much doubt) and he'd certainly do so again if it suited him. He must keep them sweet while giving them as little as possible. But it was clear he must hand over something useful.

'I'm the bodyguard to Arbell Materazzi's son, not her confessor.' A pause. 'She's beginning to warm to me . . . but she's intelligent and cautious. You can't rush these things.'

A slight grimace from the governor. 'How disappointing.'

Cale realized he would need to show more value for money. 'Gaines is more important to her than I realized.'

'*How* exactly?'

'He's not just an advisor or a go-between, she trusts him . . . completely. He has real influence.'

'How?'

'Instinct.' A snort from Nick.

Cale looked at him. 'My instinct kept me alive in circumstances that would have rolled right over you as if you weren't even there.' He turned back to Louis. 'He trusts me a good deal less than she does. But again – patience.' He threw in a few more pacifiers: that Denmark was allowed to attend some of the meetings Arbell was having. Then, lyingly, that Denmark was going to ask that Savio be allowed to attend these meetings but that he, Cale, had advised him to wait for the right moment.

This seemed to satisfy the governor, up to a point.

'You must have gained some impression of what she's up to, no?'

'In my opinion, she's doing something smart.'

'Which is?'

'To find out what the thinking is on all sides – the extremes and the middle – who's leaning one way, who the other. She's mapping the terrain. Then, once she's got a true sense of where everyone is . . . then she'll put every bit of influence she has and a lot of money into stopping secession.'

'I know all this. I want to know the details of what she's going to do to block us. She could, possibly, perhaps, swing this thing.'

'Then the sooner I can get her to trust me absolutely, the better. Push too hard and I'll be out on my ear.'

'What I think,' said Nick, 'is that she's made up her mind already. She's a nigger lover, always has been. I say we get her out of Washingtone and back to Malfi. As long as she's here, God alone knows what she might be able to do. Money talks.'

'It's all very well saying that,' said Cale. 'Why should she leave? She won't go because I say so.'

'There's one thing,' said Nick, 'that she cares more about than spooks, and it's her precious little brat. Persuade her that little Lord Milktoast's in danger. Get her out of here, Cale, or I might start to doubt that you're entirely sincere about helping us.'

'I accept the need, Mr Cale,' said Louis, 'for a certain patience. But it wouldn't do to rest on the notion. This thing is in the balance. Something small might shift it. So Nick is right. Get her out of town, Mr Savio. We have a right to expect it.'

Cale walked back to the house on Constitution Street smoking a cigarillo and thinking about the only lie he'd told the Van Owens that was important to him. He recognized too well the portrait on the poster sketched by Riba: it was Vague Henri. She'd drawn it for Cale as a gift about twelve years ago, as if Henri had aged along with both of them. Of course, she'd unquestionably saved Cale's life by claiming it was a likeness of him she'd drawn herself and so could vouch for. But he couldn't bear to look at it, which was why she'd kept the portrait for herself. Despite the fact that Riba had done him such a great service and had taken a huge risk in doing so, he found it harrowing to see Henri's face everywhere he looked. If he'd lived, everything might have been different. Perhaps not.

Distracted then, Cale eased his way back into the house without disturbing the guards. If he'd not been so preoccupied, he might have been troubled by the ease of doing so. On the other hand, he was so skilled in the business of creeping about heavily guarded places up to jiggery-pokery that it was not especially surprising. Having made his way back up the stairs, he emerged on a landing, walked on like a little mouse in the absolute dark, only to turn a corner and run straight into Arbell.

She screamed, and so did he. She was just startled, but Cale, of course, had a lot more to fear from people creeping about in the dark.

She was carrying a small table lamp and, after the quick shock, a short laugh of relief followed. His reaction was a touch more complicated – a bit more like the weir at Malfi which had thrown him round and about while it considered killing him. It was not helped by the fact that she was wearing a dressing gown, maidenly enough, but which revealed those creamy shoulders and that swanny neck. And most terrible of all. She smelled. She smelled of herself twenty years ago. Oh, the time-devouring talent of whiffs and musks to take us decades back to Heaven or Hell. His treacherous conk was returning him against his every will to his lips on her lips and his flesh on her flesh.

'Oh, Mr Savio,' she said, grinning at him and so fetchingly bashful (stop it! stop it!), 'you've caught me out.' She showed him the half-eaten peach in her left hand. 'I'm so greedy I couldn't even wait to get back to my room.' Now (don't look! don't look!) he noticed in the yellow light a drop of peach juice trailing gently and terrifyingly from her lower lip to her chin. Feeling it tickle, she wiped it off with another laugh. 'I didn't bank on our protector watching over us all. Don't tell on me.'

'I won't,' he said, then dropped his head in acknowledgement of her formal status (that'll teach you). 'Goodnight, madam.' He walked off into the dark. *Thumpetty thump thump* went his heart. *Pitter patter thump* went hers.

The next morning Denmark Materazzi did not appear for their scheduled practice behind the old pigsty.

Cale walked over to his rooms, exchanged pleasantries on his way past the guards he had chosen himself: 'How's the wife?' 'Your boy's cough better?'

He knocked on Denmark's door and went in without waiting for a reply. A butler was serving breakfast.

Denmark stared at Cale for several seconds, considering his considerations. He decided. He waved the butler out.

'Leave.' The irritable tone upset the servant, who flounced out of the room with more affronted dignity than the Duchess of Pique herself. The door shut with just the merest hint of slam.

'You're late,' said Cale.

'What?'

'Late. Tardy. Overdue.'

'You think I'm having anything more to do with you – you bloody lunatic.'

'I don't understand. Have I offended you in some way?'

'Leave.'

Cale looked surprised – although there was no attempt to hide his insincerity.

'I've no idea what you're upset about.'

'I thought you were going to kill me.'

Cale pretended that understanding had dawned. 'Oh, that. You paid me to do that to you.'

Denmark seemed about to burst with indignation. 'What?'

'It was in our contract. You asked me to teach you everything I know.'

'I didn't want you to try and kill me!'

'What are you whining about – you're still alive, aren't you? But my mistake. I honestly thought you understood that all the fencing you learned from your camel-shit fencing-masters was about as useful in a real fight as knowing how to dance the Spanish cakewalk.'

Denmark's good sense could be observed fighting it out with the terror and humiliation of the day before. Time, thought Cale, to step back.

'If it's any help, I thought you did pretty well.'

'Well?' A slight alleviation of his inner steam. Just right. Denmark had been offered a way out. Would he take it?

'I've seen a lot of people at the point of death – been there myself. A lot of them piss themselves – or worse. For a little boy in the middle of his wonderfulness realizing it was all going to be taken away, as if he was worth absolutely nothing at all' – he sniffed – 'I was impressed.'

Denmark began to boil a little less violently.

'You did all right.'

Denmark's stare was diminished – uncertainty now.

'Look, old son, I realize when you asked me to teach you what I know, you thought you were getting some yob to teach you to gouge out an eye or bite off an ear.' He smiled. 'And we'll get round to that. But it just won't do – teaching. Talking. Telling. You have to *know*. On your pulse. In your guts. You have to know what it means to lose everything. To look down into the nothing and see it staring back.'

Cale sat down and helped himself to a kipper.

'See – you haven't had my disadvantages. So, I gave you some.' He smiled. 'Don't thank me. I just wanted to give you a little help on the way down – a letter of introduction, so to speak, to Lord and Lady Nothingness. Just to help you on your way.' Another smile. 'And then I pulled you back. But there you are' – he chewed thoughtfully while he spread a little more butter on the remaining kipper – 'the ingratitude of princesses.'

Despite himself, Denmark smiled – a little weakly, to be sure. Cale let the silence live for a bit.

'I know you think you showed you were a coward. And that's what I was trying to show you. But you weren't – being a coward, I mean. A lot of that, what you felt, it was your body being a traitor, not your spirit. People don't realize – people like you – that there are, in a manner of speaking, two types of courage. Soul courage, for want of a better phrase – and body fear. 'Course you were afraid. But it was your body that really let you down. When death comes for you, all those emotions come piling in at once in a way they never do any other time. Most of what fucked you up was that your body couldn't handle it. Why should it? I've seen Inuktun children swim in waters that would kill a grown man who wasn't used to it in seconds – Andeans living up a mountain running around while I could barely catch a breath and had to be carried back before I dropped dead. See, you can get used to anything – mostly. But we're bodies more than souls – if that. Next time, it'll be easier.'

Denmark looked at him, almost persuaded.

'But next time I'll know. That you're not going to kill me, I mean.'

Cale finished the last of the kipper and smiled at the boy. 'Will you now?' he said affably.

31

It's not clear why Napsley takes the claim that Thomas Cale was the instigator of the murders of the Rus Royal family at face value. The accusation came from Alexei Comsky, a loyal Stalovek supporter of many years standing, who later became notorious for his claims that his boss had invented, among other things, dynamite and the electric light bulb. Whether Stalovek, 'the greatest mass murderer of the last hundred years', would have been emotionally disturbed by the execution of the royal children is questionable. On the other hand, the more reliable Nadezhda Krupskaya did say that her husband, who claimed he was present when the committee voted, told her that it was Cale's idea but that Stalovek had supported it and persuaded more doubtful others by declaring, 'Good riddance to bad rubbish.'

– Anne-Marie Watson (ed.), *The Normal and Abnormal: The Political Decision-making of Stalovek and Thomas Cale in the Rus Revolution* (LoCarnstein and Hart)

'Martin Luther has arrived at the main gate,' said Gaines.

'So,' replied Arbell, and he noticed she was a little nervous, 'we finally get to meet the great man.'

'He's a good man, yes, I think so. His greatness remains to be seen.'

'Got out the wrong side of the bed this morning?'

'Not at all. I respect him. But we need leaders, not saviours.' She stared at him. After a little, he relented. 'I am a little on edge, I admit. I'm worried about Louis Van Owen and his attempt to reposition himself as born-again Southerner. Those who want to secede are powerful, but they are not burdened with too much in the way of intelligence. I don't want his brains at the service of their bestiality.' A pause. 'Perhaps they'll see through him.'

It was a question. Her face fell a little.

'No. They won't. It's true my brother-in-law could persuade a turkey to join him for Thanksgiving. But there's more to it than that . . . the Good Book tells us that Heaven rejoices more over one sinner who repents than the righteous ninety-nine who don't; what it doesn't tell us is that the same is true for the devils in Hell. They'll believe him, all right.'

'Let me ask you a question, madam, and if it offends you, then nothing I say can come to any good.' As Martin Luther paused, everyone in the room from Gaines to Denmark and even Cale, sitting unobtrusive in the corner, was alert and tense. What on earth was this imperious black man going to say? The only person who did not look concerned was Arbell Van Owen, née Materazzi, who was trying not to smile.

'Suppose, madam,' continued Luther, 'suppose you yourself were black.' He paused. 'I'm sorry – does that idea offend you?'

She no longer suppressed the smile.

'When I came to Malfi thirteen years ago all the women looked at me in my olive skin and said, "She's got a touch of the tar brush in her, that one." When I heard about it, I had to ask my late husband what it meant.' She looked at Martin Luther openly. 'He did not spare me in his translation.'

'And do you? Have a touch of the tar brush, I mean.'

Even if there was not a gasp to be heard, there was one to be sensed. She laughed – a silvery sound that sparked a ripple of loathing in Cale's heart it was so beautiful.

'Not as far as I know, Mr Luther, but it's said that the Materazzi women are as cold as they're beautiful. Who knows whether my ancestors looked for women more agreeable, whatever their colour?'

Luther looked at her as if appraising a fine horse on whom he might consider making an offer.

'Are the Materazzi women as beautiful as you are yourself?' His tone was matter of fact, not at all flattering.

'Oh, much more, I was always considered rather plain. When I was little, my cousins used to tell me that I was so ugly my father was going to palm me off on to the Governor of the Mudfart Islands.'

There was astonished laughter at this. Luther threw back his head and a high-pitched giggle emerged – odd coming from such a majestic head. After a few seconds, he stopped and looked at her carefully.

'So how would you feel . . . if you were black?'

'I'd be very angry.'

'A good answer,' said Luther.

'I'm not sure it is,' said Arbell. 'The Helots were slaves – worse than slaves here, in fact. The Laconics would send their most violent children out to kill them as a rite of passage. When they offered freedom to any Helot who would fight with them against the Redeemers they gathered together the five thousand who volunteered – and they massacred them all, on the grounds that slaves with that kind of courage were a threat to be eliminated. That, on top of two centuries of cruelty, made the Helots insane with anger – and look what happened to all that rage: they put the half a million Laconics who survived the war into the prison camp at Taygetos and murdered every one of them.'

A considered silence from Luther. Then:

'I do not believe in violence for that reason. The black peoples of the Estates must be cunning before they are brave. Intelligence will set us free. And a certain patience. I believe another way can be found – but that way depends, I would say, on the friends that can be found and on how much those friends are prepared to put their backs into doing what's right.' He looked at her gently. 'So how much of your back are you prepared to put into it?'

'All I can. But not if there's violence. If there's violence, you'll lose. There aren't enough of you. And the support you have in the North, I think, will vanish. Then you'll have nothing.'

'My mistress,' said Gaines, 'will do everything to sway the vote against the reintroduction of slavery. And by everything, I mean money as well as persuasion.'

'You won't find us lacking,' said Arbell.

'And if your persuasion fails?'

'Wait until we do,' said Gaines.

Luther sat back. 'What about your brothers-in-law? What will they think when they find out what you're doing? And they will find out. You know that, don't you?'

'Leave my brothers-in-law to me,' said Arbell.

After everyone had left, Arbell remained in the room to talk about the meeting with Gaines.

'So Mr Gaines, what did you . . .'

There was a knock on the door and a servant entered with a note for Gaines.

'Excuse me,' he said, opening it without waiting for her permission.

Truth was, Arbell was a little put out at being set aside by Gaines just for a note. But when he looked up, she could see it was serious.

'I don't know whether we've been saved or damned. At any rate, you don't have to worry about the right or wrong of making a deal with Louis Van Owen on compensation. It seems he's seen the light and joined the secessionists.

32

It is a sad reflection on the general uselessness of poets that they have universally failed to improve on a convincing manner of representing the sound made by the human body while it is being kicked, punched, thumped, thwacked or pummelled: namely aargh! Oof! Uh! Whiff! Oooh! Ugh! And so forth. Shameful. You must imagine then the sound of a healthy eighteen-year-old male wrapped in a collection of pillows and bolsters tied around his body with string and being struck repeatedly by a powerful-looking thug in his thirties. Denmark would stand up, take a punch or a kick, make one of the dishwater sounds noted above and, usually, fall over.

After five minutes of this, it became increasingly clear to the young black woman watching and wincing from her hiding place that the pillows and bolsters were not as effective as they appeared.

After ten minutes of this punishment, Cale told Denmark to take a rest and remove the pillows.

While he did so, Cale went over to a satchel resting against the wall of the pigsty and rooted about for a moment, then returned to Denmark, who was still breathing heavily as he removed the last pillow from his stomach. He could see Cale was holding something and was, of course, suspicious. Cale opened up the palm of his right hand.

'What's that for?'

'It's a pig's ear,' said Cale.

'I know what it is – what's it for?'

Cale took out the knife he'd used a few days before. 'Remember this?'

Denmark's expression made it clear he remembered it very well.

'I don't think you do. Or not well enough. See, you and me, we're going to go through it all again.'

'I know you're not going to kill me.'

'Do you really?' Cale stared at him grimly, like a man who might possibly have been paid lavishly by mysterious forces to slaughter the young heir to Malfi for reasons unknown. Then he smiled. 'You're right. I'm not going to kill you.'

'Then what's the point?'

'The point is, old son, that while I'm not going to kill you, I am going to stab you. Not very deeply. And not where anyone will be able to see. We don't want Mummy asking questions. But somewhere painful, certainly.'

'You're a bloody lunatic,' said Denmark.

'You're paying for this, so who's the lunatic? Just say and we'll stop.'

Denmark looked at him, wary but curious in an anxious sort of way. 'And the pig's ear?'

'We're going to wrestle. I'll put you down like I did before and I'm going to push the knife in the fleshy bit at the top of your right breast.'

'No, you're not.'

'I'm going to put this pig's ear in my mouth, and if you can bite it in half – all the way, mind – then I'll stop.'

'I was right the first time – you are a bloody lunatic.'

Cale shrugged. 'When you thought I was going to kill you when I was looking in your eyes and pushing down on to your heart with my knife, you were completely powerless. Yes?'

'All right. Yes.'

'No, you weren't. You still had your teeth. You could have bitten my nose off. And that's true because I put my fetching little snozz right where you could get at it.' He smiled. 'But it never crossed your mind, even at the point of death, because you're such a big fucking lady's blouse.' Then he jumped at Denmark and he was down in a second. Cale, knife raised, Denmark holding his wrist, trying to stop the slow movement of the tip towards his chest. Cale completely in control as he moved half-inch by half-inch, closer and closer. Then Denmark bit the pig's ear in Cale's mouth – but it was hard and gristly and didn't tear. The knife came closer and closer, his eyes moving between Cale and the tip of the blade until it was two inches from his chest. Cale eased back, but only slightly. Denmark, wide-eyed and grunting, the hideous gristle between his teeth. A jerk nearer from Cale – an inch left between the tip and his flesh. More pressure – more grunting. And then a sudden guttural yawp from Denmark and the ear tore along a quarter of its length.

A moment's more pressure, then Cale stopped. Denmark was staring at him with something that looked like madness in his eyes. Cale stood up and backed off as Denmark got to his feet. They looked at each other, both breathing heavily. Cale looked down, keeping Denmark in his sights.

'What do you think?' said Cale, nodding at the half-severed ear.

Denmark said nothing for a moment. Then he threw up.

'You did all right,' said Cale, as the retching continued. 'Next time, you probably won't be sick at all.'

Five minutes later – pale and clammy – Denmark was well enough to think about returning to the house for a (foodless) breakfast with his mother.

'You sure you want to keep doing this?'

Denmark looked at him, pale but insolent. '*I am in blood stepped in so far that should I wade no more, returning were as tedious as go o'er.*'

Cale considered this. 'Some poet say that?' he asked. 'I hate poets.'

Cale had a most peculiar, not to say unique, relationship with the man who at that time was the centre of all attention, Chancellor Abrahan Lincoln, a politician of no great distinction who'd been pitched into the very centre of things by the assassination of John of Boston. Now, courtesy of Thomas Cale, however reluctantly, he was the First Man of the United Estates and had in a few months managed to unify the Estates in at least one regard: he was loathed and despised by everyone.

'We might not be dealing with Lincoln for much longer,' Gaines had told Arbell the day before their meeting. 'All four of his most important Cabinet colleagues think they could do a far better job. Gutierez is worried about what he calls our Chancellor's painful imbecility and is plotting to topple him at once; Chase wants to replace Gutierez; and Todd wants to get rid of them both.'

The day before, in yet another of Arbell's endless meetings,

Cale – and Denmark of course – had listened as James Cooper, one of the most powerful politicians in the Estates, had spoken at length on the Chancellor's deficiencies: 'Loyalty to our Chancellor' – he spoke the word as if Lincoln had won the office in a card game – 'simply does not exist. He has no admirers, no enthusiastic supporters – no one, in short, to bet on his head – a head which appears, by the way, to have been taken from a scarecrow and stuck on the body of the boneless wonder belonging to a fairground that's gone out of business.'

References to Lincoln during the previous week's meeting had been less colourful but not very flattering either. He was, went the consensus, 'weak, easily influenced, if not corrupt, in hock to special interests, and spoke in public in phrases that sounded as if they had been rinsed in dishwater'.

Now the man Cale, Oswald and Van Owen had made the defender of the rights of mankind itself was sitting at the head of the table and speaking with a calm authority that contradicted the universal low opinion of him. It should be said that Cale was less easily influenced by general bad opinion – not so much because of his capacity for open-minded fairness but because the general opinion of his own influence on the world ran to very much worse than looking like he was assembled from a series of circus exhibits and that he was a terrible public speaker who no one admired.

'We have a tremendous nigger problem to solve,' Cooper had stated just before he left, with scant regard for the presence of Steward Gaines, and it was this tremendous problem that Lincoln was speaking to now.

'The truth of the matter, ma'am, is that the United Estates has never been a nation – it's merely a loose aggregate of communities ready to fall apart at the first serious shock. This is, here and now, that first serious shock. We're a cat's jump from a terrible disaster. You know that, ma'am, better than I do, that a great society can collapse and not take any time about it.'

Cale liked Lincoln better all the time. The look on Arbell's face when reminded that the Materazzi empire had disintegrated in a few weeks was as if someone had pinched her heart. If no one else could see Arbell wince, Cale could sense the tremor all the way to the bottom of her soul.

'But surely, Chancellor, it will either be one shock or another. If the vote passes, or if it fails.'

Lincoln looked at her carefully. 'People think that I have no principles, that I'll always take the line of weakest resistance. And you know what? They're right. I'd bow and scrape to Old Scratch himself if I could prevent a war that will probably drown a generation of our young men in a bloody deluge of a kind the human race has never seen before. And if it does, then government by, for and of the people will perish from this earth. And then where will your Negroes be?'

'*My* Negroes, Chancellor?'

'I stand corrected, ma'am – they're very much my Negroes – and with all due respect to Mr Gaines here – I can't tell you to what degree I wish they were not. If I could take all the black peoples in the Estates and send them back to the place from where they were so ignominiously and shamefully stolen, I would happily do so.'

'But you can't.'

'No, ma'am, I cannot. If I can save the United Estates as one country and have to endure the injustice of reinstating slavery, then that is what I will do. Even if that happens, I have no doubt that in time, sooner or later, the Negroes will be free at last. But if the unity is destroyed by keeping them at liberty, then they'll be free to inherit a wasteland.'

'But it's wrong,' said Gaines.

'I don't choose between right and wrong, sir, I choose between one wrong and another. And I choose the least bloody. I understand that you do' – he corrected himself – 'that you *must* see this differently.'

There was a long silence.

It was broken by Denmark, who had been told firmly and clearly to keep his mouth shut.

'What if the vote to extend emancipation for another five years goes against the South and they withdraw from the United Estates?'

His mother looked at him irritably. The Chancellor smiled, a little grim.

'We must hope that before it comes to such a withdrawal, the South realizes that it's too large to be a lunatic asylum.'

When the meeting finished Arbell walked over to her son and looked him directly in the eyes, in no very good mood.

'You've got too much to say for yourself.'

An hour later, as Denmark was having tea with his mother, he was still stewing over the rebuke. Time for reprisals.

'Have you seen those posters of Thomas Cale all around the place?'

Arbell looked at her son. There is no word for cold that could possibly do that look justice.

'Yes.'

A pause. Then:

'Is it true he laughed when my father was executed?'

'No.'

'What was he like?'

'I can't remember.'

And with that she got up and left.

33

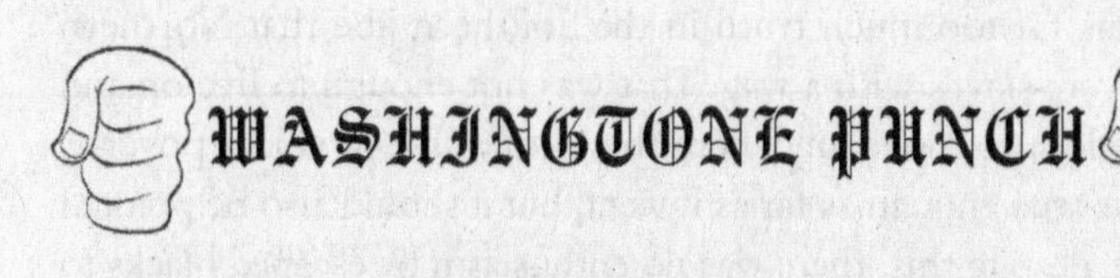

Science has long taught us that while the Arachnid species can be deadly poisonous to the individual, it cannot cause general harm by the spreading of fatal diseases. But science has been corrected. We know now of one particularly mephitic variety which most certainly has that evil property: *Morbidium spideriensis* – more usually known in the vulgar dialect as Louis Van Owen!

THE WEB
IS SPUN
FOR YOU
WITH
INVISIBLE
THREADS

Sensible people who would not contemplate leaving our sacred Union a year ago are now being infested in Washingtone by two foul diseases spread by this creepy-crawly: Secessionitis and Nigrum Slaveownia.

Watch OUT, our Southern Brothers!!! The Dallas Spider aka Louis Van Owen, whose voice once dripped with the poisoned honey of false compromise, is now seducing you with his calls for the breaking of this great Union. This spider-man is leading you to a GREAT DISASTER!!!!!

That night, Saul Gaines walked into a room barely a mile and a half from Arbell's rented mansion but another world away in every other sense. It was a slum for free blacks who were free in the sense that they were not owned and that they did not work for nothing – but there was far too much truth in the Southern jibe that Northern blacks were slaves with a wage that was not enough to live on and the freedom to move anywhere they could live in abject poverty. This was true enough as far as it went, but it should also be pointed out that, despite this, there was no enthusiasm by escaped blacks to return to the paternal kindness of their former masters.

Still, the building was a dreadful dump by any standards. Gaines was led by a middle-aged black man – in his late twenties, as it happens – who regarded Gaines in his expensive clothes with a mixture of hostility and curiosity. The man knocked on a door indistinguishable from a dozen others on the fourth floor. A soft voice called out.

'Come in.'

His guide gestured for Gaines to go in. The door closed behind him. It was surprisingly comfortable looking, given the ratrun of the building Gaines had walked through to get here. It was well lit by a couple of decent paraffin lamps, had a good fire and all was neat and clean. In the corner was a young man, mid-twenties perhaps, dressed simply and not just well but with astonishing . . . not elegance . . . such a word might suggest decoration or vanity; rather he wore his clothes with a kind of graceful severity, refined and cool and precise.

'Sit down, Mr Gaines.'

There was nothing proud or threatening in his tone or manner – all was courteous and restrained. And yet this was Malcolm Brown, a black man regarded by all Southerners and many Northerners who wished to see slavery abolished for good in the Estates as a dangerous fanatical zealot, a revolter and corybantic extremitarian alarmist ready to see every river in the United Estates from the Mississippi to the Tiber foaming with much blood.

This was by no means the first time the two had met but, in any case, Brown was not a man for small talk. They were soon at the meat of what had brought Gaines to the slum.

'It's criminal, no?' said Brown. 'To ask a man not to defend himself when he is the constant victim of brutal attacks?'

'Perhaps it is. But I'm asking, nevertheless. The vote is in the balance and we can't lose a single one – and we'll lose more than that if there is any violence from you.'

Brown's eyes, always cool, grew cold.

'It does you no credit, Mr Gaines, to tell me that I'm a man of extremes, unreasonable and a violent nut-head. I get enough of that hypocrisy from white men as it is. We believe – *I believe* – in peace, and I believe in courtesy. I believe in obeying the law and I believe in respecting everyone – but if someone puts his hand on me or on my wife or on my children in order to make them slaves, I'll send that someone to the cemetery. Do you think that such a position is unreasonable, Mr Gaines?'

Brown had him in an awkward position.

'No, Mr Brown, I don't think it's at all unreasonable.'

Brown smiled. 'So, we're agreed?'

Gaines laughed. 'No, Mr Brown, we are not. You may be right.' He stopped, then: 'No, you *are* right. But we do not have the power to resist violently.'

'If you're not ready to die for it, put the word *freedom* out of your mind.'

'I didn't say anything about dying, I said *failing*. In my opinion, there will be plenty of opportunity for dying to come. If the South loses the vote, there'll be a civil war. That's what's scaring even our white supporters in the North.'

'I'm concerned with the cause of black freedom, not the political union of the United Estates. Nor the death of white men.'

'It can be made the same cause.'

'And if the vote is lost and the blacks in the South are to be made slaves?'

Gaines looked thoughtful. 'Then you can put a hundred barrels of gunpowder under Congress and I'll lend you a match.' A long silence. 'So, do I have your agreement to stay in the shadows until the vote?'

'You have my agreement to abstain from action.'

'Meaning?'

'There'll be no violence. But I will not be silent.'

'I would prefer both. Just until the vote.'

Brown smiled again. 'You are mistaken in your strategy, I believe.'

'I see. Possibly. But ten days of silence isn't too much to ask, is it?'

'It may or may not be. But it is unnecessary. I will not be presented to the world as a violent fanatic. At some point, any man who believes in freedom will do anything under the sun to acquire it – or to preserve it. But even if I were the violent madman that people believe, I would have my place – my importance, if you will – in the scheme of things. Until I came along, Martin Luther was regarded as an instigator of race hatred, an extremist ready to bring terror to the United Estates to get what he wanted. Now, because of me, the whites of the North thank the Lord for Martin Luther. All change needs is a monster to shake up the smug and the undecided. Someone, if you will, to break into the house and murder the plantation owner. It concentrates the mind wonderfully, Mr Gaines, to have something worse waiting in the wings. So, over the next few days I will be attacking Mr Luther and every weak and shameful demand he is making – and no one in all his life will ever have helped him so much.'

'And will Martin Luther understand what you're doing?'

Brown considered this – a problem of great difficulty. He smiled, barely.

'The last time we met, three days ago, he gave me the impression I had his complete support in this matter.'

After a few cool pleasantries Gaines went to leave, but as he went to open the door Brown spoke again, as if he'd just thought of something.

'I hear rumours you're involved with a move for compensation.'

Gaines turned back into the room.

'Yes.'

'This move . . . it involves compensation for our black brothers and sisters for all their terrible suffering.' Gaines did not answer, because it was not a question. A smile from Brown. 'Thought not.' Another beat as they looked at each other, one of those speaking looks. 'Drop it,' said Brown, quietly but not gently. But it was loud enough to Gaines – at least as loud as the sound of a last nail being hammered into a coffin.

It would have been wise to pretend to Brown that whatever he had heard about the matter, it was a mischief-making rumour about exploratory talks, long abandoned because of hostility to the idea of reparations to blacks. But he didn't want to give him the satisfaction and left without saying anything.

34

Tom my love

Even when I'm with you I miss you terribly. What an idiot you've turned me into. Catching myself in this ridiculous state, I could kick myself.

Thinking about you, I had to splash my face with cold water. If you don't put your hand on me I shall most surely rot to death. I feel like boiling water forcing up against a lid, rising up and down and spitting and spilling over. Help.

I want you here with me sitting on your lap then I'll show you what I mean.

– Jenufer Smythe, *The Letters of Arbell Materazzi to Thomas Cale: Fact or Forgery?* (Atlantic)

So, given the stakes, everywhere was uproar. And not just for those who belonged to the Union. The Spanish Empire that had ruled the place for so long was in a torment of two minds, although very clear on their third: to shit in the hat of the United Estates in whatever way that might cause it to collapse in the most violent chaos. The revolution had not just cost it the United Estates and all its vast revenue, it had created a massive unrest in their other possessions – an empire so vast it was one on which the sun never set. It was of profound importance to the Spanish that no country that had freed itself from them should demonstrate that it was more advantageous to be outside the Spanish Empire than part of it. That the United Estates had thrived after kicking them out was a chicken bone in the empire's throat. Predictions throughout the world from the wiser heads of the established nations had been clear that the Estates would collapse economically without access to the great markets of the Union of Spanish Nations. The predicted disaster had failed to materialize.

Given that the Spanish were loathed equally by the North and the South, it was not easy for them to decide which side to support. In the end, they decided on both at the same time, in order to maximize their chances for making mischief. A civil war, the bloodier the better, would do very nicely to discourage the others.

The problem was that, for every prediction about what would happen in a civil war, there were a dozen others that flatly contradicted it – and each other. It would be over by Crimble. It could be many years. There was no doubt an agreement would be reached. There was no question that all attempts at a solution would fail. The South would incontrovertibly win. The South would undoubtedly fall.

Opinion-formers of every kind were unequivocally clear that this would happen, or that it would not. Wiser heads, aware of the complexities of the situation, firmly stated that though this might happen it was possible, perhaps probable, that it might not.

From Holland to the Hanse, from Cathay to the Nordic League, everyone took a greedy interest in the United Estates, greedy for its cotton so they could thrive, or greedy for its cotton to fail so there was a market for its own – inevitably inferior – product.

And so, there were a very considerable number of fingers diddling in this particularly scrumptious pie, and all of them very dirty. So, you can imagine then just what a ferment of malice and bad faith was creating a veritable twister and dust devil of delinquency and all-around malfeasance in every room (those that mattered, of course) the length and breadth of Washingtone.

It is the way of wicked conspiracies, poisonous and rotten as they are, to abort themselves or be born misshapen and deformed and die to be disposed of in the ditches and the drains. But one of them, ugly and disfigured as it was, slouched off into the night and made its way towards Arbell and her most cherished son.

We have already witnessed the difficulties of finding the right sort of wrong sort of person to carry out even carefully planned political murder. Washingtone was stuffed now with every kind of fanatic and hothead able to choose badly; every single cad, swine, chawbacon, riffraff, plotter, planner, toe-tagger and homicidal maniac had made their way to Washingtone from the troubled nation's collective supply of drains and swamps.

So, it should not be imagined that the six desperadoes making their way over the easily penetrated walls of Arbell's Washingtone residence were of the crack variety – nevertheless, they were big and ugly enough to do great murderous damage, fired up, as they were, on zeal or money or Kalamazoo black. Cale was responsible only for Denmark and strictly forbidden from interfering in the completely separate security provided for the rest of Arbell's household (politics is everywhere, of course). The mansion was large but protected by wooden fences and bushes. Who can say whether it was incompetence or bribery that prevented the building of better defences or the provision of a more carefully organized set of watchmen?

The six murderers arrived too early and should have waited until two o'clock in the morning for the attention of the guards to flag and there was no one about to keep an eye on them other than equally lack-lustre sentinels like themselves.

But they were lucky: a dose of the Washingtone runs had put half the guards to their beds so the detail that night was four guards short; the guards were working double shifts. Six of them were dead in the first rush of the attackers and only one of them injured in reply. Washingtone was a noisy place, even late at night – shouts, laughter, songs and horseplay punctuated the hours of dark on a continuous basis. By the time there was enough of the noise of violence to signal to Cale that something was wrong, the killers were already in the house and heading for Arbell's room. That's where the good and bad luck that spins extravagantly around each one of us moved fortune to favouring Arbell. She was with Denmark and Gaines, discussing the day's politics over an unappetizing meal of bottled rutabagas and fricasseed shad. It was then that what might have been just rowdy street noise alerted Cale to the possibility that something unpleasant was up. He stood, drawing his knife, and quickly gathered a loaded pistol from his coat.

'What weapons have you got?' Gaines and Denmark had a knife each. More shouts. *Stay here, or try for the basement and its thick doors?* Move. He gestured to the three of them to follow him out of the decorative but flimsy door. A mistake, as it happened. Not that he could have known. As they emerged into the corridor, five men – firm-handed with long knives – emerged up the broad main stairs.

Cale turned and shoved Arbell heavily back into the room, and went to do the same with Denmark. Denmark pushed his hand away.

'Come in here now!' Arbell shouted at her son. But there was no time.

'Lock the door,' said Cale, and slammed it shut and turned to face the killers on what, unfortunately, was more a landing than a usefully restricting corridor. The men slowed as they formed a line of five to face a line of three, of whom one, Denmark, looked like he was made of full-cream milk. Now they thought the odds were five against two and a half. Cale aimed the pistol at one of the men. On his face, horror. Cale pulled the trigger. *Clack!* Misfire. Where he'd been unlucky, the attackers had been incompetent: they'd fired the three pistols they had between them in the first rush outside. Cale moved out of their line of three and made a deliberately clumsy pass at the biggest of them. Seeing Cale was an amateur, he stabbed at his unguarded chest, only to take a cut which opened his throat, his heart breaking from the shock even as he fell. But now Gaines was locked in an ugly embrace with one of the men and the two were careering into walls and chairs, struggling for control of the knife.

Three against one and a half. Pulling Denmark with him, Cale, wide-eyed and breathing like a kitchen bellows, moved to cover Gaines from a stab in the back. The attackers were wary now of Cale as their biggest man shuddered on the floor. Cale tried stabbing at the man fighting Gaines but was blocked by one of the killers. The three remaining murderers looked handy.

'Help!' he shouted. 'Here! Help!'

This might or might not have been a good idea. It alerted any guards still left alive but also urged the killers to get on with it in case anybody came to the rescue.

And to the rescue they came.

One of the cooks from the basement ran screaming up the stairs with a cleaver and launched himself at one of the men. But he simply stepped aside, grabbed the cook, stabbed him in the back and dropped him howling to the floor.

The third man threw himself at Denmark and the pair swirled around in an ugly dance. Cale tried to help the boy, but the two other men moved to block him. They shuffled forward, one covering the other. All Cale could hear of Denmark was shouting, but whether in fear or anger it was impossible to say.

Ten yards away Gaines was in an ugly scrabble on the floor, wrists and hands still locked. Cale backed away, trying to encourage a careless strike from one of the two advancing men. But luck twirled in their favour. Cale moved slowly to give the Tiny Ones time to change their minds. They did.

The door opened and Arbell burst out, holding a stag's head she'd taken from the wall. Screaming, she raced at one of the men, pinning him between its antlers and knocking him into his companion. It was not much of a nudge, but Cale was on him as he went off balance, took him through the eye with his knife. The horns of the stag had snagged the jacket of the second man and when he tried to hurl it away it swung back and cracked his shins, the hefty weight unbalancing him. Cale's knife took him under the chin and upwards through the roof of his mouth. But the knife was now jammed in his jawbone. He didn't waste time trying to free the blade but left it embedded, took his victim's knife from his dying hands, and walked over to Gaines, now exhausted – and a second or two from having his chest opened by the man on top of him. Cale stabbed him through the ear: the only place he could strike one blow with certainty that the man would die instantly.

'Denmark!' It was Arbell.

Cale turned. Denmark was still struggling. The killer still had his knife, but Denmark had lost his. They had come to a kind of veranda, open to the outside air. The two men crashed against the low wall and, accompanied by a cry from Arbell, fell into the dark.

'How do I get down?' asked Cale.

'Stairs . . . at the end . . . please!'

Cale ran to look over the veranda wall into the dark but could see nothing. Then the sounds of a struggle and a terrible scream. He ran on, found the stairs. On the ground now, slowly, he moved forward, watching, knowing what must have happened. Then, a movement in the bushes. A hunched figure, pulling a body out on to the lawn.

Denmark stood up, wavered for a moment, then collapsed on to the body of the man who'd come to kill him. Cale grabbed him and pulled him away, giving what looked like a dead man a kick, just to be sure. Holding the boy up, he noticed the knife in the chest of the man and then, with considerable surprise, a terrible bloody mess on the left side of his head.

Denmark came round in an instant, as if smelling salts had been put under his nose.

'Denmark! Denmark!' his mother called desperately from the veranda above.

'I'm all right. I'm all right.'

Arbell said nothing more. Gaines ran up to her and she sank down to her knees and began to weep uncontrollably.

Denmark took a deep breath. Then another and another. He and Cale looked at the corpse or, more specifically, the ragged edge of his missing ear.

'You weren't supposed to swallow,' said Cale.

Denmark was not in a laughing mood. They could hear his mother's sobs wracking her beautiful frame. 'Better not to say anything about the ear,' said Denmark. 'It would be difficult to explain.' This time, he smiled. 'You take the credit. Tell her you found me as he was about to kill me but you got to him first. She'll love you for ever.'

Cale looked at the young man. This time, he was the one not smiling.

There was, of course, much weeping and embracing as Arbell held on to her son as if she'd never let him go. Both Gaines and Cale stood by, both delighted at the boy's astonishing deliverance (as well, though probably more, at their own), and awkward at being so close to such an intensity of terror, loss, joy and love of the kind, perhaps, that only a mother can feel for a son.

So intense was it that Denmark began to feel awkward himself; he was clearly about to tell his mother to stop fussing when a surprisingly stern warning glance from Gaines prevented him. But then the famously aloof Arbell reasserted herself, clearly with a terrible effort, sniffing and wiping her eyes in a manner that might have touched even Cale, had she not been the object of all his most profound loathings.

It was to Cale that she turned and embraced him with a hug almost as crushing as the one she'd given her son. As to the emotions felt by Cale, you must imagine for yourself. Only the most delicate Eri silk separated him from the skin that had once astonished a heart choked with pain and rage. In varying degrees, Cale had not been properly alive in the years before he was first naked with her and being kissed by those lips.

Perhaps Cale's intensity of emotion makes you feel ill at ease. One thing may be to blame: terrible envy that someone else has been touched by such rapture, but not you. But if jealousy is causing your heart to itch, let me offer you a cure. Consider what it means to be dragged out of hell, taken to paradise, then expelled by the very creature who took you there.

Then she let him go. 'Thank you. Thank you. Thank you,' she said, and turned back to her son. Fortunately for Cale, despite being shook to the very depths of his soul (as poets are accustomed to saying), Denmark and Gaines were so astonished at Arbell's behaviour that they did not notice the odd intensity of his reaction.

Despite his own so recent experience of the beating wings of that cat-hearted angel who will one day visit all of us, Gaines was alert enough to notice that the man who had come so close to killing Denmark had most of his left ear missing. He also noticed that there was a smear of blood on Denmark's face and no obvious wound to explain it. He also noticed that, despite the assumption of everyone that it was Cale who'd killed the assassin and bitten off his ear in the process, there was no blood on his face. On the other hand, that Denmark had performed such a dirty and hideous act was absurd. It was not that Gaines disliked the boy or had any lack of respect for his courage, but that someone brought up as heir to Malfi, educated, witty and refined, did not go about the place biting off bits of people. It's all very well saying that when you eliminate the impossible, whatever remains, no matter how improbable, must be the truth, but in the face of a nicely brought-up young man, a dead villain twice his size and a teeth-severed ear, the implausible was easily rendered unthinkable. Nevertheless, he continued to, if not exactly think it, then to keep turning the cat in the pan, as his father used to say.

An hour later, the bodies had been dragged into an empty room, the brave cook was having his wounds treated, and the floors and walls were being mopped of blood. An assortment of guards – those still left alive – had been re-deployed, reinforcements called for, and a major bollocking delivered to the Master of Security. All the main actors – emotions now heavily repressed – were once again gathered in the room where this most dramatic evening began.

At first they dispersed some of the boiling emotions by everyone talking excitedly about the bravery of everyone else. When he heard about his mother's intervention with the stag's head, Denmark was delighted at his mother's courage and ingenuity, but also pleased to have a way of distracting them from asking too many questions about events after he'd fallen over the balustrade. But, of course, Gaines pushed for details.

'Can't really remember,' said Denmark. 'I suppose I must've winded him as I landed on top of him – but I banged my head on his at the same time. All I remember is I staggered out of the bushes and my hero' – he smiled at Cale – 'was standing over the body.'

'But,' said Gaines, 'there must have been quite a struggle before Mr Savio finished him off. You know, the ear and everything –'

'Mr Gaines!' It was a sharp and irritated Arbell who brought the interrogation to a halt. Gaines, Cale noticed, was as much affronted as chastened. He winced or grimaced or something, but then gave in.

Arbell turned to Cale, who was seated close to her, and put her hand on his, failing to notice the shudder that passed through him.

'I will always be deeply grateful to you, Mr Savio. If there is anything I can ever do for you, know that it will be done.'

There were many responses from Cale to this – the one uppermost, if only to drown out some of the others, was: *As if I'd trust any promise of yours, you lying, treacherous bitch.*

With her other hand, she held on tightly to that of her son. From time to time she lessened her grip and he pulled it away, but she only, unashamedly, grabbed it back and held it all the tighter.

Gaines, definitely disgruntled and not hiding it as well as one might expect, changed the subject to what they should do next, a question which obliged them to ask who might have been responsible.

'Unsurprisingly, there was nothing on the men to give them away.'

'Two of the five men were black,' said Cale.

'And?'

'*And* nothing. Two of the five men were black.'

'Three of them were white,' said Gaines.

'And two of them were black.'

'Perhaps we should go to bed, get some sleep and discuss this when we're all less fraught.'

'I don't think we have the time,' said Gaines. 'My point is' – he took a deep breath – 'that their colour doesn't tell us much one way or the other. Whoever did this was trying to muddy the waters.'

'So who benefits most from the death of these two?'

'No black man, that's for sure – and if you're going to point out again that two of them were black, nobody's saying there aren't black scum as well as white.'

'I fought against the Montagnards,' said Cale. 'They believed that to come to a reasonable agreement with those more powerful than you was to commit slow suicide because you'd always lose out in the end. What you had to do was to make your opponents mad with fear about how unreasonable you were. Then they'd beg you to take your freedom.'

'And did it work?' asked Arbell.

'Too early to say,' replied Cale. 'As to the chances of Malcolm Brown, or some of the black alarmist groups being behind this – I don't know how reasonable or fair-minded I'd be if someone wanted to own me or mine. I can see that might make a person unreasonable.'

'We may be angry, Mr Savio,' said Gaines coldly, 'but we're not stupid.'

Cale realized he had let things get a little too warm.

'The thing is,' said Gaines, 'this country has more factions than it has cows, and more willing stirrers than Mother's little helpers in a kitchen. This could be the Spanish wanting to set the whole country at each other's throats. Could be the Fire-Eaters, terrified they'll lose the vote to leave; could be the Black Hand or the Negromaniacs.' He looked at Arbell and regretted what he said next even as he said it. 'For all we know, it could be the Van Owen brothers. I'd put nothing past those two.'

'I'm going to bed, even if nobody else is,' said Arbell abruptly. She looked at Denmark. 'Please get some sleep.'

Denmark, of course, was in no mood to go to sleep. It is, after all, not so easy to kill a man at the age of eighteen, particularly if you've had to bite off his ear in order to do so. Oblivion, on the other hand, was very much in order. He walked over to the tray of drinks on the side table and took up a half-empty carafe of brandy. Daring his mother to protest, he raised it towards her, appearing to ask permission. Wisely, she bit her tongue. Smiling, Denmark waved them goodnight and vanished out the door.

Arbell stood and held out her hand to Cale, who took it as yet another squall blew through his guts. She said nothing, looking into his eyes as if trying to transmit directly what she felt. She turned to Gaines. 'We'll speak later,' she said.

'I'm afraid, ma'am, we have to make a decision.'

Arbell turned to Cale to see what he had to say.

'Whoever did this wanted to create a great fuss,' he said. 'So, it seems to me the thing to do is not to give it to them. Mr Gaines and me, we should get rid of the bodies and, whatever the rumours, deny everything.'

She looked at him. She may not have been a Thomas Cale when it came to skulduggery, but she had experienced a great many rises and falls in her life. Besides, her trust in him now filled the room to bursting.

'Do what you think best.' In a moment she went white. 'I'm shattered. I have to sleep. Goodnight,' she said, and swept out of the room, ignoring Gaines, as if he were an icicle on a Dutchman's beard.

With Arbell gone, the two men – Gaines awkward, Cale mildly anxious – looked at each other.

'Drink?' said Gaines.

'Why not?' said Cale. 'Whisky, if you have it.'

Gaines grimaced. 'The whisky's from Omaha. The brandy, on the other hand, is from Spain.' Gaines was not above a little snobbery when it came to the Old World.

'I'll stick to whisky. I'm sure I've had worse.'

'Suit yourself.' Gaines poured one for Cale and a brandy for himself then drank it in one. 'That cheeky sod Denmark took the best stuff. Still, he's had to do a lot of growing up tonight.'

More than you think.

They drank in silence. Waiting.

'Thanks,' said Gaines, 'for saving Mrs Van Owen's life – and Denmark's.'

'I'm paid to look after Denmark,' said Cale affably. 'As for saving yours, I agree it was very kind of me.'

Gaines smiled, but he didn't respond to Cale's invitation to thank him. *Interesting*, thought Cale. *I wonder what that's all about.* Perhaps Gaines was tired of being grateful. Perhaps he'd noticed – he must have done – that, for all his efforts to save Arbell and Denmark, and for all her posturing about the equality of black and white, he was the only one who had not been passionately embraced by Arbell. It was a delightful thought for Cale that underneath her no doubt sincerely held beliefs there hid a tiny little bigot who could not bring herself to embrace a Negro.

'Will you sort out somewhere to drop the bodies?' asked Cale. 'I don't know this part of the world.'

'Me neither,' said Gaines, glad to be off the subject of gratitude. 'But I know a man who does.'

'We need to search them first. You never know.'

But Cale's careful check of the men in the corridor turned up nothing useful.

'What about the one Denmark killed?' said Gaines, as if he meant something by the question. Cale did not reply but started walking along the passage. 'Don't forget his ear,' Gaines called after him as he turned down the staircase.

It follows from the notion that we see what we expect to see that its opposite can also be true. Cale's search of the body was, of course, painstaking, and having finished and found nothing at all, he tucked the ear, which he had had some difficulty finding in the bushes, into the dead man's top pocket. It was only then that he looked directly at his face.

All shocks are unpleasant, but the ones that inflict the most pain are those which suddenly reveal that everything from now on is utterly different from what went before.

He recognized the man. He did not know him well. He'd barely spoken a dozen words to him. And that some time ago. His first name . . . Alex or Albert or something. His second . . . on the tip of his tongue . . . his second was . . . Petrov. No . . . Boshirov. He was pretty sure it was Boshirov. Stalovek liked to use him to murder foreigners because he was blond and didn't look like a Rus at all.

'Find anything?'

It was Denmark.

'What are you doing here?'

'Don't know.' A beat. 'I've drunk half a bottle of brandy and it might have been water.'

Five minutes later, Denmark was letting Cale into his rooms. Denmark sat on the bed, Cale on an overstuffed, mildly uncomfortable chair. There was an odd silence.

'So,' said Cale, finally. 'How are we?'

Denmark smiled boozily. 'We . . .' he said, and paused: 'are alive.'

'Yes, you are. You're alive.' Another pause. 'How do you feel?'

Leave now! How did they find me? How?

'I don't feel anything.'

'Really?'

'You expect me to be all sad and weepy because I killed someone who was trying to kill me?'

Cale looked thoughtful. 'It's quite something – killing a man.'

How did they find me? Leave now! Leave now!

Denmark held out his hand palm down. It was shaking, and clearly so – but not as badly as it had every right to be. 'There,' he said, 'steady as a rock.' He looked at Cale. 'So how does Nogbad the Bad feel about killing people?'

'I've killed a great many.'

'Did they deserve it?'

'Well, they were all trying to kill me in one way or another, so that's how I've always thought of it.'

Leave now! Leave now!

'Do you – deserve to die?'

'Definitely.'

'You don't seem to be in much doubt.'

'It's been a while since there was any uncertainty pertaining to my value to humanity.' Cale smiled. 'Is *pertaining* the right word? I heard someone using it the other day and I thought: I like that word. I must find a way to use it.'

'You're changing the subject.'

'Which is?'

'What's the point of living if your life has no goal, no purpose?'

'It never seemed to matter, not having a goal in life, not to me. Just staying alive seemed enough. I can't speak for others.'

Now! Leave now!

'And is that enough, just to survive?'

'It is for me.'

'Are you being clever?'

'I thought I was just being honest. I can't rule out the possibility that it's clever as well.'

Leave right now! Now! Now! Now!

35

Cale was not the only member of the household having a late-night chat. Gaines was in Cariola's room. She was dressed in a thin cotton nightdress barely short of transparent.

'What have you got to say for yourself?'

'What can you mean, Mr Steward Saul Gaines?' she replied, comically fluttering her eyelids. 'I'm just a simple maidservant afraid for her reputation.' She raised one leg on to the sofa on which she was sitting, allowing the cotton to whisper down her thighs.

'You told me that Savio was just teaching the boy to wrestle and such.'

'He was.'

'He was teaching him how to kill. And kill dirty.'

'What do I know about killing?' she lied, and put on a field hand's accent. 'I jus' a poor black guhl, sah. Don' know nothing 'bout nothing. Anyway, from what I heard, Savio was the one who did all the killing, saved you and the boy. What's the matter, jealous?'

'You're being even sillier than usual.'

'If you say so, Massa Gaines.'

'Your father didn't beat you enough.'

Cariola wafted her hand rapidly in front of her face as if to cool herself down because his words so excited her.

'As it happens, Mr Gaines, it's true that I've been a very bad girl of late and I could do with some arduous chastisement. I think you need to take your belt to me.' She sighed as if filled with remorse, shifted her left leg slowly so he could observe the turn of her bottom, her eyes widening in invitation.

Gaines looked. Who could say what his heart was doing?

Cariola burst into laughter.

36

There are times that do provoke
The notion life is but a joke,
And a man will think that jest
Is aimed directly at his chest,
And no one else, and no one else, no, no one else.
But he bolts down all at hand
As an ostrich gobbles sand
For you really cannot hide
From its punches in your side
And the thing that seemed momentous
Now seems a touch pretentious
A joke, a general joke, a common joke.
Ha ha ha ha ha ha ha ha ha ha ha ha ha ha ha
ha ha ha ha ha ha ha ha ha ha ha ha ha ha ha
ha ha ha Ha ha ha ha ha ha ha ha ha ha ha ha ha!

– ***Herman Melville, Oswald the Assassin: A Pantopera***

It is a belief among the Janes, a race as spiritual as they are violent, that each person is followed by an angel with fifty arms. In each of their one hundred hands they hold a dice with fifty sides, and every time they make a decision, trivial or important, the angels roll the fifty dice with their fifty sides to see what the consequences of that decision will be. The number arrived at is multiplied by itself and instantly checked against the same number in a great book in Heaven. Next to that number is a decreed fate which sets out the result of that decision. But the dice are loaded in a mysterious way so that the consequences of trivial decisions are usually trivial – the decision to open a door, for example, results almost always in the sight of someone eating cucumber sandwiches: the decision to kill the king, however, usually results in disaster for either the king, his assassin or both (the hand that wields the knife seldom wears the crown, and all that). Oddly enough, the most unpredictable of these kinds of decisions – trivial or important – is the trivial. Mostly, indeed almost always, choosing to cross the road ends in safe arrival on the opposite side. But very rarely, when the multiple dice are rolled a multiple of times, the result is strange and has extraordinary consequences. A bottomless hole opens up in the road as a person crosses, a hole caused by hidden floods beneath the ground, and that person is swallowed up, never to be seen again. Sometimes in mid-highway a bolting carriage runs over that person and mangles them beyond recognition. A person in the act of crossing the road rescues a girl from the horse, a naughty princess who has run away from her chaperone and whose father is so grateful he rewards the road-crosser with a place in court, where his previously unrecognized and unused talents take him to the most powerful position in the land next to the king, which, in time, leads the road-crosser to hatch a plot to kill that king. You get my drift. It's worth taking into account, and I'm sure you have, that everyone else on the street also has one of these gambling angels at their back. In other words, the world of events is mostly predictable, but often not predictable enough for this predictability to be of very much use. This is the reason why experts in matters of what is happening in the world, even the ones who really are expert, are so often wrong.

Consider then the decisions being made, few of them trivial, the day after the attempt to have Arbell killed along with her son. For many days her angel had been rolling the dice as, of course, had the angels of everyone else in Washingtone. Standing over this maelstrom of chance, Arbell was faced, if only in one sense, with a simple choice. Go or stay.

It should also be pointed out, as is usually the way with God's helpers, that not all of the fifty-armed angels were doing the will of their Lord but were instead rebelling against that will.

*

Arbell desperately wanted to stay to do what she could to help save the Union of Estates so that its vision of the rule of the people should live and that the former slaves should not be rebound in chains. Accepting she was merely one person – although a very rich and powerful one person – it was tempting to be humble and ask whether she – being one person – could really do much to stop the mighty forces of money and freedom on the move around her. If she had been exaggerating her influence, then it would have been much easier to take her adored son and run away. However, the nagging voice of conscience also told her that in such a finely balanced conflict, with so many decisions to the left and right being made in the days before the vote, she could unquestionably influence those decisions. She might make no difference; she might be vital. But she could not lose Denmark. It was not possible. Who could blame her, then, for persuading herself that as well as being a supporter of the cause of freedom, she was also a risk to it. Had she been murdered by secessionists, then the fires would have been lit. Better for her then, perhaps, to leave. Better for the cause, better for her and, most important of all, better for Denmark.

When Cale insisted that it was too dangerous to stay in Washingtone he was pushing at an almost open door.

But it was a long and vulnerable road back to Malfi. So better to stay. Poor Arbell calculated the risks all through the night and the next morning. But unfortunately, she did not know about the fifty-armed angels next to her and their fifty-sided dice. Poor Arbell knew only of dice with a mere six sides thrown by angels who had only two arms to throw them with. This, then, was the maelstrom in her mind when she brought Cale in to decide on what to do next. She got to the point.

'Is it really any safer for us to leave than stay, Mr Savio?'

Cale thought carefully about his reply. Running back to Malfi was not what his demons had been screaming at him to do, given that Stalovek's agents clearly knew how to find him, as long as he stayed with Arbell. Their advice involved stealing a bag of money and a horse and not stopping until he fell off the ends of the earth. But at

Malfi he could at least retreat to a place where he could triple the number of guards and introduce all sorts of extreme measures with the excuse that he was protecting Denmark. Then he could think things over. Something might turn up. His demons pointed out that the something that definitely would turn up was another of Stalovek's murderers. But he would not listen.

He thought about her question – or gave the impression he was thinking about it. Then came the reply of the blunt soldier.

'Yes,' he said. 'We must leave.'

It was the right tack – not that the other tack would have failed – because she had been going back over the pros and cons (throwing the dice with one hand) for the past eight hours.

'Why?'

Since he was a very little boy in the hell of the Sanctuary, Cale had been a devout follower of the principle that a truth that's told with bad intent beats all the lies you can invent.

'Last night we had four times as many men guarding the house as before the attack. I went out past the guards and came back in again without being challenged once. This place can't be defended with any certainty.'

'Probably after their failure last night the scum behind it won't be so keen to try again.'

'Possibly.' Cale managed to make it clear what he thought of this as an argument.

'What,' said Gaines, 'if you had all the material and men you needed – money no object? Could you protect Madam Materazzi then?'

A pause.

'Possibly.'

'Not very helpful, Mr Savio,' said Gaines.

'It's the best I can do.' A beat. 'I'm told there was an attempt on the life of Malcolm Brown last night. Is it true?'

Gaines looked awkward. 'Yes. He's dead, I'm afraid.'

Arbell looked at him oddly – clearly this was big news, why had he said nothing to her?

'This place is about ready to explode,' said Cale. 'We should leave.'

'There's no connection. Brown's murder didn't have anything to do with the vote on slavery. It wasn't white alarmists. He'd split a few months ago from the Justice Nation when he found out its leader had been despoiling young women. Three men from the Nation shot Malcolm.' The truth was that, while appalled by Brown's death, Gaines was also a little relieved. He sincerely admired his nobility of character – it was, thought Gaines, exactly the right word: *nobility*. But Brown dreadfully frightened those many white people who were going to swing this vote, white people who were disgusted by slavery but did not in any way think that a black person was or ever could be their equal. And they must not be frightened. Not now. This is not to deny that he was ashamed of being relieved. But relieved he was.

'It doesn't matter. This house isn't safe, this city isn't safe. I say leave now. Whoever wants you dead for whatever reason knows where you are every moment of the day. Murderers in Washingtone are five for a bag of horseshit. But I'll bet there isn't a single decent tracker within fifty miles of here, so we're better on the move than standing still. Though, of course, like all bets, it could be wrong.'

Then he was dismissed. Two hours later he was recalled and told to prepare to take the family back to Malfi. In the intervening time, a delegation had turned up from one of the cohorts of twenty votes that had made up its mind to oppose the motion to de-emancipate the slaves. The leader of the cohort was a man of fixed religious beliefs; once his word was given, it was set in steel. Now she felt she could leave in good conscience. But she would have left anyway. It was not possible to risk her son's life. Not when the man she knew she could trust absolutely with that life had so clearly told her she must.

But Arbell had one more task before she left: to go to Congress and listen to a speech. That Tuesday afternoon was about as pleasant as you might expect on a sweltering day in a city built on a swamp next to a river swimming in turds. The voice addressing the packed assembly trying to make up its mind whether to launch a civil war on a tide of human blood or send four million people back into inhuman bondage was a voice of sweet reason and compromise. It came from the acting Congressman for Texas, Louis Van Owen, whose sudden presence in the House was due to a bribe to his predecessor to become too sick to continue his responsibilities.

'I stand before you at a time when we have gathered together to consider the matter of indenture for the black races. Many on the other side of the house' – boos – 'many on the other side of the house wish to maintain that this is a question of the rights of all human beings, as set out in our great Constitution. But our revolutionary forefathers did not in their great wisdom, a wisdom that must be acknowledged by all of us if we are true members of this United Estates, they did not so rule in that greatest of all statements on the rights of man that the Negro should be included in that remit, except on a temporary basis, and in doing so clearly signalled that Congress should have the right . . . nay, the responsibility . . . to revisit this provisional ruling in the light of experience. And so our Supreme Court has ruled' – *Boo! Yah! Monstrous! Lackeys! Infandous!* – 'If our forefathers had not been uncertain as to its rightness, they would not have passed that great decision to their successors. And so the decision which I believe we will make next Monday is clearly in line with the traditions of those great men. We do not choose to enslave free men, which would be infamous and against every law of God and man we all in this House hold so dear' – UPROAR! – 'so dear. We only vote to no longer continue that temporary arrangement. We merely reassert the law, as the Founding Fathers clearly ruled was the proper thing to do, should we so choose by a legal demoscratic majority. There are many objections by many persons to a vote of non-ratification, but those objections cannot be based on the idea that in so voting we are in any way voting against the founding document of this sacred nation' – UPROAR!!! – 'But I have a deeply felt request for those who, in accordance with their conscience, refuse to vote for ratification . . . and this request comes despite the threat to their ancient freedoms from the overweening power of some of the Northern estates . . . I ask them to accept that, sometimes, in some places, the indentured work of the Negro has not always been conducted in a manner consistent with humane values. We must now promise to treat the Negro fairly.'

There was a rumbling in the house, as if from a distant storm, interesting in that it came from both sides of the house.

'I do not,' he said, 'apologize for saying so. We in the South must do better.' Now there was a distant hissing from the abolitionist, as if a large snake were uncertainly warning of something unseen approaching through the long grass. 'What I say to you today, as men of goodwill, is that those of us who argue the need – the *necessity* – of a return to indentured work, that we do so with humility in acknowledging that things must change.' Now there was hissing *and* rumbling.

'What I propose to you today, in all good faith, is a new covenant with the black peoples, whose work is so essential to the Southern way of life. In the past, good masters ensured the fair and kindly treatment of the black labourer – as it was not only proper but wise to do – he nurtured his Negroes so that in return they would not just be *able* to provide a good day's work, but willing. What we must offer is a legally enforceable code to guarantee the just and fair treatment of the Negro. Laws that guarantee fair treatment, fair conditions and a regard to their health and prosperity. Laws that recognize that the indentured Negro may have a family and that the past practice of ignoring this fact must – I repeat, *must* – be modified in the light of human decency. No one will then be able to say that the Southern black man is anything but profoundly better off, profoundly happier, profoundly more justly treated than the supposedly free Northern Negro, who labours in dark and satanic mills in conditions and for wages not fit for a dog.'

More hissing and rumbling.

'I beseech those of you who would vote to deny our ancient Southern rights to consider the consequences of their attempt to force their will on their fellow citizens. Accept it, and the happiness of the Negro in this country is assured. Accept it, and the unity and prosperity of this great union is confirmed.'

Van Owen drew in a deep breath.

'But refuse and there will be a letting of blood such as this world has never seen, a great and terrible crucifixion of our youngest and bravest men – and we will also see mankind's most noble experiment in all of history – rule *by* the people, *for* the people, *of* the people – perish for ever from the earth.'

At this a huge explosion of boos, cheers and hurrahs, and shouts of triumph and abuse. It took the Speaker of the House almost ten minutes to bring order.

37

> Opera is the most peculiar art form there ever was: four or five of them are among the greatest works that the human imagination has ever created – the rest are little better than pantomimes.
>
> – IdrisPukke, *Why I am So Wise*

> Ha! Ha! Ha! Ring-a-ding-ding!
> The bells of Hell go ting-a-ling-a-ling!
> Ho! Ho! Ho! Bo hoo hoo!
> The Kindly Ones have come for yoo!
>
> – 'The Laughing Song of the Fates' from *The White Devil*

The following morning Cale had Arbell and Denmark on the road early, leaving the bulk of the household to pack up and follow as and when. With one carriage, a plain one carefully chosen, and a dozen guards, they could move quickly, having only the family to protect.

Two days into the journey and, having settled Arbell and Denmark into a basic enough hotel in Lynchburg, Cale went down to the bar in the lobby where he could keep an eye on the stairs, the only way up or down, and ordered a large glass of the hideous local Indian ale. Gaines was waiting for him, as arranged. It could be the case, thought Cale, that Gaines had asked to have a drink with him out of gratitude – after all, he had reason to be grateful. But then having a reason to be grateful didn't mean that people always were. Too often he had had reason to recognize the unattractive truth so drearily repeated by IdrisPukke: *The difference between a man and a dog is that a dog won't bite you when you do him a kindness.*

Cale approached and Gaines put down his book. Cale picked it up and read out the title.

'*Researches on the Variations in Human Nature* by Christoph Meiners.' He smiled. 'So . . . you're studying to be a great wise man.'

'Studying to know the mind of my enemy,' said Gaines.

'Sounds harmless enough . . . the book, I mean.'

'Professor Meiners . . . I'm happy to say the *late* Professor Meiners – he died in agony from a strangulated hernia, I believe . . . is a great favourite among those few Southerners who can read without moving their lips.'

'Not a very nice man, then?'

'The professor split mankind into two divisions, which he labelled the beautiful white race and the ugly black race. Black, ugly peoples are distinct from the white, beautiful peoples by their sad lack of virtue and their terrible vices. Negroids, he says, have unduly strong and perverted sex drives, while only white peoples maintain the perfect balance of desire and intelligence.'

Cale considered this for a moment. Then:

'I'm just an ignorant soldier, of course, but I *can* say I've known a great many ugly white perverts in my time.'

'Are you?'

'Am I what?'

'Just an ignorant soldier.'

They looked each other over for a moment.

'You know something, Mr Gaines, I'm going to reject the professor's argument.' Cale smiled. 'You're a fine figure of a man, if you don't mind me saying so.'

'Perhaps I'm ugly on the inside.'

'I can't comment. I don't know you well enough.' His smile turned sly. 'I do know you haven't mentioned that I recently saved your life.'

'Some things are better left unsaid.'

'I agree with that wholeheartedly, Mr Gaines. It's just that *thank you* isn't one of them.'

Gaines laughed. 'Thank you. And I mean that very sincerely.'

'Don't mention it, Mr Gaines. I'm sure you'd have done the same for me.'

Gaines threw his head back and laughed even more loudly. He

was about to add something when a middle-aged man, slightly the worse for wear but not too much, approached the table.

''Scuse me, suh.'

Cale, always suspicious, took a quick look around. Nothing untoward.

'Yes?' Polite but not friendly.

'Do I know you, suh?'

It was very much not a question Cale ever liked to hear. He smiled.

'No, I don't think so. I've a good memory for faces – I'm sure I'd remember yours.'

The man looked troubled. 'Me, too – I've a good memory for faces, and I'd swear to God I seen you before.' Cale just smiled pleasantly, trying not to look like himself. 'Were you with me in the ships at Mylae? Stetson's the name,' he added. 'Were you?'

'No, I was never at Mylae.'

'I think it was,' kept on Stetson. 'You know Mylae, the battle?'

'I know of it,' said Cale. 'I hear it was a bad business.'

A look of inexpressible desperation took over the man's face. 'Yes . . . was a bad business. The cunts used wire on my friend.' A beat. 'Don' want to say no more.'

'I'm sorry,' Cale said, as if apologizing for the unpleasantness of the battle and for not being there.

The man stared, eyes moving back and forth over eyes, nose, forehead, chin.

Cale stood up and grimaced, still apologetic. The rest of the room, lacking anything else to do in a bad hotel in Lynchberg, started to take an interest. Gaines was riveted.

'Well, it's been a long day. Time for bed.'

'How about the fight at Finnsburgh? Yes, I think it musta been Finnsburgh.'

It was not that Cale recognized the man, but it was plain enough he'd seen Cale at Mylae, commanding the thirty thousand troops who went in and the twenty-eight thousand who did not come out again. At Finnsburgh there were only ten thousand but, if anything, it was an even bigger disaster. Whoever the old soldier was, he was either exceptionally tough or exceptionally lucky to have escaped either, let alone both.

But Finnsburgh had been ten years ago, Mylae even longer, and Cale looked, very deliberately, different now. In addition, he hoped, the sheer unlikeliness of Thomas Cale – *the* Cale, Cale the Emperor, King Cale, His Satanic Majesty, and so on and so forth – the impossibility of this angel of destruction being in a dull hotel in nine-horse Lynchburg drinking a glass of beer in the middle of the week, well, implausibility protected him. It looked bad leaving so early on in their tête-á-tête, but if the drunk put a name to his face in front of Gaines he wouldn't lack the nous to connect nothing with nothing. And if he mentioned it to Arbell . . .

'Nice to have met you, sir. Goodnight.'

'I'll come with you . . . pretty tired myself,' said Gaines, who had considered plying the man with more drink but thought better of it. It wouldn't be wise to annoy Cale over what was almost certainly nothing. Still, he couldn't resist a dig as they made their way into the lobby.

'He seemed very sure he knew you.'

'He did, didn't he?' said Cale. He moved to go towards the stairs. 'I thought you were tired.'

Gaines smiled. 'I have to sleep in the annexe with the other Negroes. Sleep well, beautiful white man.' And with that he walked out of the hotel entrance.

The next morning there was no sign of the old soldier, but Cale breathed a good deal easier the further they got away from the town.

The odd thing about the journey was Arbell. Throughout the drive back to Malfi the famously aloof Arbell, object of unimaginatively poisonous feelings bubbling away inside Cale, chattered away to him like a starling, as if, indeed, they were not just old friends but good old friends of the deepest kind.

A soul alchemist would have given a unicorn or a mandrake with eight legs to have been allowed to measure the mixture of Cale's angry heart as it was fed the kind and admiring words, the sweet and musical laughs and, most terrible of all, the soft touch of her hand on his as she leaned in towards him to emphasize a point or punctuate a laugh.

But was this water dripped into acid, or was it healing ointment to a deep and festering wound? Not even that soul alchemist would have been able to tell from his face what was going on. The odd tremble could have been the carriage lurching on terrible roads – but if she noticed, and she did, rather than putting her off, his refusal to be charmed by her in the way that everyone always was when she made the effort seemed only to intrigue her more. What a challenge for someone who expected to charm if that was what she chose to do?

This then was how Thomas Cale now seemed to her. As for how she seemed to him, it would be to describe every single killing swirl and gyre of the vortex that had nearly drowned him in the weir at Malfi.

On the road again the following day Denmark began singing, finding himself as delighted at the prospect of returning to the sanity of his home as he had only a few weeks before been delighted to set out for the excitement of Washingtone. His voice, though not strong, was pleasant, and Cale found himself humming along to one of the melodies from Stendahl's *Doomed Lovers*: '*Devo punirmi, devo punirmi, se troppo amai . . .*' (For those of you whose Italian is not as good as it should be: 'I must punish myself, I must punish myself, if I've loved too much . . .')

But during the last hour before their entry to Atlanta, Cale's sense of contentment soured. Every half-mile or so along the road there were posters for an opera new to the South which, according to the poster, at any rate, had been the sensation of the North the season before. The dominant artwork was a tall, sinister figure in black wearing a white mask with a tastefully stylized and carefully draped naked woman in one arm and the bony skeleton of death in the other. It was the title of this opera that ruined his day.

As you can imagine, Thomas Cale was referred to by a great many names, few of them flattering: Vinegar Tom, King Funeral, Crazy Tom, Cale the Witty (or Cale the Sneery, depending on the translator), Spider Tom, Young Sly, and so on. But one of them in particular got under his skin for reasons he could not quite put his finger on, perhaps because it referred to the days on which the terrible mania descended on him, the madness of retching and torment that had afflicted him since he was fifteen years old and which famously left his face drained of all colour: the White Devil.

'That looks like fun. Why don't we go tonight?' said Denmark.

The Atlanta Opera House was a rather highfalutin' name for a place which advertised itself as the Goober Grand Ol' Opry and hosted musicals and melodramas. Even on the rare opera nights, the productions were what the high-minded aficionados of proper opera referred to as musical burlesque. But now some preposterous American critics asserted it should be the basis for a virile revolutionary music of the Estates they called Pantopera. Pantopera – the name had originally been created as a term of abuse by the hoity-toity – had no respect for tradition or good taste; it was a ragbag of base comedy, vulgar melodrama, cheap romance, songs and arias of dubious relevance, incomprehensible storylines, ludicrous coincidences, pantomime, terrible tragedy, appalling horror, risqué lyrics, as much nudity as could be got away with, swashbuckling, comic songs by ridiculous clowns, fights, tears, intrigue, treachery and lust. In other words, it was realism at its most realistic. To Cale's surprise, Arbell was enthusiastic – clearly, she didn't know that this was one of Cale's nicknames and that the musical in question had Cale as its central character.

'Ever since I heard of Pantopera I've been dying to see one. Will you come, Mr Savio?'

Gaines regarded him with envy. He would be offered no such choice; attend he must. But Cale did not refuse. He wanted to see her reaction when confronted by his name and his actions, no matter how disturbed and ludicrous they were bound to be.

'Interesting coincidence,' said Gaines. A pause.

'What is?' said Denmark.

'That's what the slaves used to call cotton in Alabama . . . the White Devil.'

So that night, Cale, wary yet intrigued, made his way into the box hired for the evening as Denmark and his mother chatted away in excited anticipation of the gaudiness to come.

The orchestra – Gaines would have dismissed it as one very small step above a band – began to tune up for the night's performance. The sad pule of the bumbulum, the throaty grumble of the coud, the plaintive cry of the shawm, the lamenting howl of the zampogna and the sigh of the sackbut all contrived to sound like the animals in a zoo being slowly fed into the gears of a giant water mill.

But then! The conductor struck up the music and the ear-murdering pandemonium at once burst into a thrilling wall of ecstatic sound as the overture advertised the range of pleasures to come. And what strange delights they were for two members of the audience – about to embark on one of the oddest experiences of their lives.

38

The White Devil

Although Mozart's music for *The White Devil* has become justly famous as a concert piece, the accompanying drama – by journeyman playwright Bile Shex-sphear – has always been regarded as so vulgar and absurd that there has been no dramatic performance for many years. However, some fragments of this original libretto have survived and give a sense of the piece. Explanatory text has been added to make sense of this remnant.

Act I

The aftermath of a great battle. A young boy, Thomas Cale, can be seen holding a lamp and robbing the dead and dying of armour and jewellery. He gleefully sings while pulling the teeth from the mouth of a dying soldier.

CALE

Oh, what a peasant rogue am I.
(*laughs, delighting in his wickedness*)
For hours have I been hiding in the woods,
Waiting for the battle bloodily to end
That I might bayonet the wounded
And steal whatever I can find.
Ha! Ha! Ha!

Cale is captured by the victorious Redeemers but is saved from execution by the scheming Lord Redeemer Bosco, who sees in Cale a depth of wickedness that might be used to further his own deranged plan to do God's bidding and completely destroy mankind.

Cale is taken to the Sanctuary and trained in every act of martial violence but also to be a great general, brilliant and ruthless, even though he is only fifteen years old.

BOSCO

Oh vile Mankind, poisoned by Eve
and Adam's wilful choice to taste the fruit forbidden
by the Lord's command. Now He directs me utterly
to remove you from the earth. Cale is my chosen
instrument. He have I beaten into shape, hammer of God,
anger incarnate, rage personified in flesh. Mercy he does not
know, nor love.

But after attempting to rape an innocent maidservant and killing a pious and kindly Redeemer who tried to come to her aid, Cale flees the Sanctuary with his catamites, Vague Henri and Kleist and arrives in the great city of Memphis. A comic scene follows: a vulgar youth farts out of a window at his love rival and receives a red-hot poker to his naked bottom.

Act II

Opens, a year later, with one of opera's most moving love songs, the aria 'Rompere il vento e sossiare me', as the beautiful Arbell calls out for the return of her beloved, the young Duke Conn Materazzi.

ARBELL

I yearn for you, my love,
And though a princess,
Yet still a girl.
A girl standing before a boy,
Though royal,

Asking him to love her,
Break the wind and to me blow.
Return to me,
Or let me die untouched.

In the time that has passed since Cale has arrived in Memphis he has plotted and murdered his way to become an advisor to the Chancellor Vipond himself. But Cale burns with vile lust for the sixteen-year-old Princess Arbell. A comic scene follows: a character is chased all over the stage by a bear. He exits pursued by the bear.

Along with his catamites Vague Henri and Kleist, Cale resolves to ravage the princess and flee to the Boll Shevik enemies of Memphis and offer to betray all their military secrets. Cale attempts to dishonour Princess Arbell, but the young Duke Conn Materazzi returns and delivers a terrible beating to her attacker. The Duke rushes to console his beloved – but Cale has been feigning death, escapes and flees to safety with his catamites. A nightwatchman comes on stage and tells jokes – some very dirty.

Act III

Cale makes his way to Switzerland and worms his way into the affections of the notorious deviant King Zog. Having charmed the lovely Artemesia into believing him to be deeply misunderstood, she discovers Cale's disgusting true nature and Cale has her murdered by Vague Henri (his catamite) to hide the truth.

As the Redeemers surround the Swiss in Spanish Leeds, Cale excels himself in infamous treachery and betrays Conn Materazzi, now leader of the Swiss forces, to the Redeemers, who defeat him at the battle of Bex. Desperate for someone to blame, King Zog condemns the guiltless Duke Materazzi to death using perjured evidence from witnesses suborned by Thomas Cale.

Asleep one night, the wicked King Zog spontaneously starts to smoulder. In the morning his servants find he has slowly baked to death.

Finally, Arbell could endure this drivel no more. She stood up, Gaines with her, and turned to leave – but stopped, clearly surprised that Denmark had not moved. She stared at him and he looked back at her politely, as if to say, *Is something the matter?*

With a maternal gasp of irritation, she swept out.

Cale and Denmark – each a weir-pool of churny emotions – went back to their pantomime. After half an hour, the climax. But here something odd happened: after the infandous nonsense of the last two hours came a bizarre change of tone. In the last scene, the arrival of the Hanged Redeemer, sent by God to deliver judgement on Cale, the dreadful writing and clumsy comic scenes inserted to satisfy the vulgar vanished, and in their place Bile Shex-sphear's writing took wing and brilliantly began to match the sublime music.

As Cale is about to flee, having sung an aria cursing God, Questo mondo è una catacomba, *from the castle walls The Hanged Redeemer enters.*

THE HANGED REDEEMER

O Wicked impertinence to rebuke your god,
Question and reproach him not!

CALE

Be gone you cringing wretch who fawns and servilely
Adores the throne of the eternal tyrant you call Lord.

THE HANGED REDEEMER

(recoils ten paces huge at these prodigious insults and vile blasphemies)

Heretic wretch! Now from this hour down to the infernal pit I drag thee chained. Merciful God sends only suffering and pain mankind has power to bear. Heaven is for thee too high to grasp the mystery of His eternal ways. Silence, ungrateful rogue!

CALE

What from that despot god should I be grateful for? Babe innocent, I was –

THE HANGED REDEEMER

(interrupting)

No child is innocent but born of sin –

CALE

(interrupting)

A child is innocent in everything! And yet you gave me wolves for teachers, grievous wolves. All the days of my life, thistles I ate and also thorns; Vinegar I drank instead of mother's milk.

THE HANGED REDEEMER

Oh thankless cur!

CALE

Thankless for what I say again? Possession of the leper house in which you made men live? A house

of desolation filled with grief, where agony and heartbreak wait on us.
Tears for drink we have, stone for bread. Brutal our lives and short . . .

THE HANGED REDEEMER

. . . God gave you life, censure him not . . .

CALE
(*gasping with scorn*)

Did I request my maker from the clay
to mould me man, did I solicit Him
from darkness to promote me, or here place
me not in some earthly paradise but only hell?

(*sneering*)

The gift of such a life I sought not. Tell your lord,
inexplicable His loving kindness is.

The Three Fates emerge from behind the Hanged Redeemer, forks in hand glowing crimson with heat. They start to surround Cale.

THE HANGED REDEEMER

Drag you to Judgement before the throne of God these daemons shall. Consider now what you will say to your revengeful God.

CALE

Say? What I will say is this: I come, oh God, to hear you plead for my forgiveness.

THE HANGED REDEEMER

Oh vile! Your downfall now should make you beg.

CALE

O execrable Son of God – What though the
field be lost today? Of this be sure:
All is not lost; my unconquerable will,
And study of revenge, immortal hate,
My courage never to submit or yield.
My sentence is for open war 'gainst you and
Heaven's brutal king.

The Three Fates close in. From his pockets, Cale produces a bomb.

CALE

This from my science minion I have caused to be construed.
Vile groveller, farewell. Burn you in Heaven for eternity.

He throws down the bomb. An explosion confounds the Hanged Redeemer and the Three Fates. The smoke clears. Thomas Cale has vanished.

THE HANGED REDEEMER

God has ordained your breaking loose from me this day.
Everything you do from now is done with his foreknowledge
and command.

(a pause triumphant)

Futile is your escape, O foolish Cale. Your punishment has
only just begun.
Hear this, His judgement and His penalty.

Whichever way you fly from now is Hell. Yourself is Hell and in that lowest Hell a lower
Hell still threatening to devour you opens wide, to which the Hell you suffer seems a Heaven.

The Hanged Redeemer casts his cloak enormous around his shoulders and sweeps from the stage. The Fates hop up and down in fury then explode.

As soon as the performance had ended, to a mixed reception of cheers, hurrahs, boos, various types of rotten fruit and a dead cat, Cale told the young man he'd be back in five minutes. When he returned it was more like ten. They walked off into the night.

'So, where did you go?'

'A policeman wouldn't ask me that.'

After a teasing pause Cale pulled something from his jacket. It was the white devil mask his dramatic double had worn on stage to spy on Arbell as she was about to take a bath, dressed in a crowd-pleasingly semi-transparent nightdress.

'How in God's name did you get hold of that?'

Cale laughed. 'The day I can't relieve a bunch of warbling mimes of their property, they'll be nailing me into my coffin.' He held the mask over his face. 'What do you think?'

'It would be too obvious,' said Denmark, 'to point out that it suits you.'

'In that case, I may never take it off.'

'Why did you come, given you can't stand opera?'

'I was curious to see what they made of Thomas Cale. I fought in a couple of his campaigns.'

'What was he like?'

Cale thought about this and should have obeyed his initial reaction to change the subject. But he couldn't.

'I'm not saying he always conducted himself entirely in agreement with the standards of the Society of Concerned Mothers against Drunkenness and Vice – but there was a lot more to Thomas Cale than he's been given credit for.'

'*Was?*'

'I heard he was dead.'

'The Hanse clearly doesn't think so.' Cale shrugged. Denmark took the mask from Cale, placed it in front of his face and burst into song. *'I, the Infandous Thomas Cale, am wicked and vile in every way.'* He dropped the mask and started teasing Cale.

'You're not worried at all, praising the man who had my father killed? What if I told my mother?'

'You know, I always suspected there was a weaselly little snitch creeping around inside you somewhere. Look, good or bad, just about everything I ever heard about Thomas Cale sounds like nonsense to me. What I heard was that he refused to give evidence against your father at his trial.'

'My mother said that was just a pretence – so it didn't look like he was behind it.'

'Did she now? And did she tell you that he saved your father's life at Solsbury?'

'Really? Never heard that. You sure?'

'The only things I'm sure about are the things I was there to see for myself – and not always then. But the man who told me about it was as straight as the day's long. He said your mother begged Cale to go and rescue your father, and though his friends tried to stop him, because your father had always done him a bad turn when he could – well, this man said Cale was devoted to your mother, saved her life twice, and he said nothing but went off to what his friends told him was his certain death.'

All the time Cale was laying down this heroic melodrama – not to say it wasn't true – part of him had been screaming at him to put his tongue in his pocket. But twenty years of resentment and that night at the opera proved to be too much. 'So, I ask you – why would he do that and then work to have your father killed?'

'Perhaps he changed his mind.'

39

There has always been a mystery concerning how the notoriously terrible writing of *The White Devil* by Bile Shakespoor managed in the final scene to come close to matching the wonderful score by Mozart. This mystery has finally been solved. It is now clear that Shakespoor stole the scene from an unpublished manuscript, *Aiden Lost* ('Aiden' being an archaic term for 'Heaven') by the Antagonist poet Joan Milton. In this poem, Milton justifies the necessity for a loving God to expel Adam and Eve from Paradise into a world of pain, suffering and death in order to punish and yet save mankind for the sin of eating the apple of knowledge.

It seems that Shakespoor destroyed the manuscript of *Aiden Lost*, keeping only the final section, which was recently discovered among his papers. It is now clear he stole many beautiful phrases from this surviving section to transform the quality of his writing in the last act of *The White Devil* (though his transitions are often characteristically clumsy). He added insult to injury against Milton by perverting her words to attack her idea of a benevolent God and instead present mankind as a tragically abused victim of divine tyranny.

All we can do is lament both the dishonesty and the vandalism of Shakespoor for the loss to civilization, if the surviving remnant of Milton's *Aiden Lost* is anything to go by, of a great poet.

Borrowed Robes: Cultural Appropriation and Artistic Theft in the Popular Culture of the Four Quarters (ME 683 – ME 741
Author: Stearn Vileass. Pub: Barfe and Barfe London)

That night, very late and no one about, Cale was walking up and down the hotel garden having a smoke, his mind drifting this way and that, unaware that he was being watched.

On the balcony, dressed in a light cotton shift to help soften the steamy heat of the night, Arbell considered the man below. A bead of sweat, salty and pure, condensed between her breasts and gently rolled, tickling as it went, before it touched the white cotton and was absorbed. God does not have a soul, of course, being God. It was therefore necessary in Bosco's mind to remove any trace of one from little Tom, so that he could be restored to the manifestation of His wrath that he needed to become in order to wipe out sinful humanity. It was the sight and touch of her skin that recalled him to life. Imagine a world in which there were no women, only pain, then think what it might be like to see Arbell naked for the first time (girlish, slender, graceful, lithe). Perhaps you can understand how struck he was, never to be the same. Now, as she watched him unseen her breasts hung heavily where once they had pointed; her hips curved where once they were straight; her belly round when it had once been scant. But no one would have been able to say which one – the young girl or the woman – was more astonishing to the male gaze. Who knows what good it might have done to Cale to see her naked like this again, and her happy to see him, welcoming him into her loving arms? And then, of course, there was the long neck, blue-veined, tapering, the beads of sweat that formed on the surface of her throat that would have tasted to his kisses of Otto of roses, salty lemon, cassia.

She watched Cale for some time as he walked, but felt rather that she was the observed – something of great power was watching over her and those she loved. At a time when she was so agitated by the dangers to come, here was a presence commanding enough to protect her from anything, no matter how cruel, a spirit she could rely on even if they were walking through the valley of the shadow of death. She moved to go back to bed, passing through the dimmest of lights from the single lamp behind her just as Cale looked up and caught the silhouette of her lazy, plump breasts, the slight tummy and the long legs.

Inside the room, barefoot, she felt a surge of wonderful joy and began to dance, whirling and whirling, her arms spread wide, in a way she hadn't danced since she was a little girl. Does any poet that ever lived have the words to describe what was going through Cale's heart as he watched her dance to the measure of life itself? I have not. You must imagine the best you can.

New-York Daily Times.

SUPREME COURT – RE-ENSLAVEMENT
VOTE TO GO TO CONGRESS!!!

TERRIBLE BLOW TO FREEDOM!!!!

Read and Reflect!!!!! The CLAWS of the Van Owens extend malign reach!!!!!

By allowing the vote to re-establish slavery to come before the Congress, the Supreme Court has made a judgement which is baser and more iniquitous than anything we have before conceived of. We dare say there are many in this city who would rather shed their own blood than once again see a Negro stood up for sale on Broadway.

Dallas Herald.

JUDGEMENT OF THE SOLOMONS

Our forefathers instituted the Supreme Court in order for it to rule only on the most difficult questions that face our unique votocracy, the kinds of question that might break our nation but for the wisdom of those chosen to guard our freedoms from all who would destroy our great union. The judgement of this assembly of five honest and able men has been to demand that a vote be taken in Congress. Taking a vote will show that the greatest court in this land, or any other, prefers *reason and right*, *justice and truth*, over *passion and prejudice*, *ignorance and envy*!

40

Thurs aft

Nobody speaks to me the way you do, which I love (and hate). I'm always surprised by your tenderness to me – surprised because you're such an ill-tempered bastard! There! You don't have to worry about me idolizing you and not seeing you as you are. I know who you are.

Why aren't you with me? Boo hoo!

Destroy these letters. Keep me in your heart instead

A

– Jenufer Smythe, *The Letters of Arbell Materazzi to Thomas Cale: Fact or Forgery?* (Atlantic)

Hurricanes! Volcanos! Earthquakes shook the United Estates when the decision came down. In a moment, the years of endless talk were over. Something momentous was going to take place. Words were now fastened to hard facts: victory, freedom, right and wrong were on a stony path leading away from windy rhetoric to secession, and from secession to war. The Supreme Court had set a date in four months' time for the vote and members of the Congress were heading in and out of Washingtone and back to the estates that had elected them for the better striking of plans and plots, dubious schemes and dark conspiracies. Arms were twisted, threats made, deals struck. Both Lincoln and the Van Owens between them promised more important jobs than there were stars in the sky. What did the black peoples of the United Estates think? Hardly anybody cared.

As for Cale, he had deadly worries of his own to deal with. He had decided for now to remain at Malfi. His other option was, of course, to run. He'd decided against this because being on your own in the world with Stalovek's scum after you was no place to be if you could avoid it. In Malfi, on the other hand, he was surrounded by two sets of walls and two sets of guards. The belief that the assassins in Washingtone were after Arbell and Denmark meant he could lock Malfi down with improved defences and enough guards to keep out a weasel. He was also reassured by the attackers in Washingtone. They were thugs, not professionals. Even Petrov was merely competent. Stabbing someone unprepared in the back was his style. Staying here was the safest option, however dangerous. As life-or-death decisions go, this was certainly plausible. Whether it was correct or not is another question.

Although there was plenty of work to do organizing his safety, Cale quickly confirmed dinner with Joseph Hanson. This was not just politeness or, which was certainly the case, that he was looking forward to talking to Hanson again, but the anxiety of someone who, when he'd been on the lower rungs of his rise in Spanish Leeds had often heard socially superior persons amused by his proletarian frankness say that they must invite him to dinner. But the invitations had failed to arrive. That is, until months later, when it became clear he was going to be a very important person indeed. He did not want Hanson to think of him, even for a short while, as such a person.

It was a long Sunday afternoon before Cale's dinner with Hanson, a week after they had returned from Washingtone and a few days after the great decision of the Supreme Court. Cale and Denmark were spending an enjoyable half-hour in the garden shade squabbling about everything from whether pith helmets were made out of actual pith to whether diseases were caused by germs or by bad air. There followed an almost equally enjoyable pause, broken after five minutes by Denmark.

'If there was a war, could the South win?'

A moment for thinking. 'Depends. Probably not . . . Very probably not.'

'How very probably?'

A sniff. Reluctant. 'If determination and the will to fight is the same for the both sides, then the side with fewer men than their opponents and less rich almost certainly loses. But like I said, depends.'

'On?'

'It's a bit hot for this.'

Denmark was not to be put off. 'So you've never thought about it, a man with all your experience of war?'

'Not seriously. Why would I?'

'All right, what's your not-serious view?'

'You're going to hold me to this. I know you.'

'Don't be such an old woman. Like you said, it's too hot and we've got nothing better to do.'

Cale took a puff of his cigarillo. 'Anyone want to see the North collapse – I mean, want it badly?'

'The Spanish. But the Nish don't take well to humiliation – they want to see the South go under too.'

'As badly?'

A pause for thought from Denmark. There was something here.

'No, you're right. Perhaps not. The North is where the trade threat and the political threat come from. Too risky for the South, though. Divide and conquer is the Spanish way. Swapping rule by the Nish for rule by the North wouldn't be smart, would it?'

Cale shrugged. But it was becoming clear this was not something he'd raised just because it was too hot to do anything else.

'So, you're definitely saying the South can't win.'

'I don't remember saying that. They almost certainly can't win – not if they don't get a big power to support them. And you've ruled that out. But it's possible . . . possibly it's possible.'

'So without the Nish or someone like them, what can they do, General Savio?'

Another sniff of reluctance. 'Two things – and I'm talking without the weeks of thinking this needs.'

'Can we just get on with it?'

He did. And it was something of a torrent. 'First, I'd keep negotiating with the North and let them think I was weakening, backing down in the face of a war, going the extra mile for peace. Then I'd attack Washingtone with . . . say . . . half of the strength I had. The geography of the North and South permits such a sudden attack. I think it could be done. Surprise is worth an entire army . . . more. Take Washingtone, and perhaps Lincoln, and his government with it. Then' – he grimaced with all the uncertainties involved.

'Let me guess . . . you'd put Lincoln and the rest of the Cabinet up against a wall and shoot them?'

'Certainly not,' said Cale, as if this mockery rather hurt. A pause. 'The first thing I'd do, if I'd taken the city and Lincoln, is to be generous. Very. Treat the populace with all the Southern charm they can swallow – including Lincoln and his Cabinet. Get the news-sheets in and make sure the whole of the North knows how unnecessary all this is. Then with utmost humility explain to the people of the North that all the South wants is a deal to keep slavery . . . not slavery, its *traditions,* its *identity* . . . in the South . . . not expand it, mind you. Add some small changes to the Constitution to guarantee the rights of every estate – you know, the rights everybody here keeps whingeing about. Be good for the North, too, freedom for all from over-mighty government. And then offer to withdraw.'

'Sounds plausible,' said Denmark, smiling. 'For God's sake, don't tell my wicked Uncle Louis.' He thought about this for a minute. 'And if it didn't work? Or if it did and the North refused to do a deal?'

'Much the most likely outcome – either one,' said Cale. Then he was all decisiveness. 'Then I'd withdraw from Washingtone and burn the city to the ground. Take everything that wasn't nailed down. If I had Lincoln . . . shoot him . . . the Cabinet . . . and every administrator in Washingtone. Then I'd keep a small well-trained and well-supplied formal army in the field, avoiding big battles and anything that might be decisive.'

Denmark looked at him. 'I thought decisive battles were what wars were all about.'

'Did you, indeed? I'll give you this to think about: decisive battles decide things.' He moved on, speaking even more rapidly now. 'I'd turn the rest of my army into irregulars, give them general instructions, nothing too specific . . . broad aims. Let them get on with it – living off the land in the North. But continue with the executions of every official – mayors, sheriffs, even bank managers. Anyone who controls things, down to the most ordinary level. Burn everyone out of everything. But be kind to women and children. So no home-burning in the winter. Extreme ruthlessness matched with extreme kindness. I've always thought that would be an interesting strategy. But it would have to be a long war . . . the South has to keep casualties low . . . bleed the North until it's too exhausted to go on.' He smiled, reliving old talents and old glories, perhaps.

Cale could see Denmark was taken aback by all this. He was silenced. Cale laughed. 'You did insist. Sorry now?'

'But you wouldn't actually do this? And don't try to make me think badly of you. I'm wise to that. Tell me honestly.'

Cale stopped smiling and a look of something Denmark was not old enough to put a name to crossed the older man's face.

'Would I kill tens of thousands of innocent civilians to preserve the right to own another human being? I absolutely would not.'

Denmark smiled.

Cale continued: 'Would I kill thousands of innocent civilians to preserve the right *not* to be owned by another human being? I absolutely would.'

He let the boy consider this for a few minutes as they sat silently in the shade as the sun put in one last effort to boil every living thing in Texas.

'Mind you,' said Cale cheerfully, 'even that probably wouldn't work. The best chance for the South is to get backing from the Spanish.'

'And once the South wins, it should be prepared to go to war with them.'

'Yet again you demonstrate you're not as stupid as you look.'

Denmark nodded sagely at this.

'But the more I think about it,' added Cale, 'from a Southern point of view, I'd say your wicked Uncle Louis used to have the right idea . . . probably . . . fudge and twist and delay and obstruct.'

'Do nothing . . . allow nothing to be done . . . do not allow anyone to do anything.' A pause. 'I said that.'

'No, you didn't.'

Another pause. Then:

'No, I didn't. But now I understand it properly . . . which is almost as good.' Denmark stood up. 'God it's hot! I have to drop in on someone. Birthday.'

At the same time, Cariola was lying on a carpet under a cottonwood down by the lake, her head scandalously resting on Arbell's stomach. Around them lay the remains of their picnic, arranged in celebration of Cariola's twenty-eighth birthday. The two of them were not just celebrating a birthday, however, but that back in the world of Malfi they could shake off the restraints of an outside world where they had to preserve the appearance of white mistress and black maid whenever they were in company. Here, everything was different. Arbell's power was such that she could keep the reality of the outside world at bay. Whatever happened, when the vote came in, Arbell could rule this place as she liked.

There was not much left of the food – all creole, of course, given the day: crab salad, salpicon of ham and Prince's hot chicken. Most enjoyed were the two bottles of white Chablis of terrifying expense laid down in Arbell's late husband's cellar. The wine had taken its effect and both women had been asleep for the last hour and only now were waking up.

'Get Eugene to carry me back,' murmured Cariola.

'I will not.'

It was then that Denmark burst out from behind the cottonwood where he'd been hiding.

'Drunk again!' he shouted.

For a second they were startled. Then the pair of them burst into laughter.

In the governor's mansion both Nick and Louis were learning the truth of someone or other's observation (Napoléyon? IdrisPukke?) that no news is ever as good or as bad as it first seems. There were still plenty in the South mad for war, and the same number in the North. But the judgement of the Supreme Court had sobered up a good many. Now that it really was coming to a head there was a cooling off among enough people in Congress and enough voters in the country for the snivelling hand of compromise to get a look in. Deals were being discussed in midnight rooms. There was talk of settlement and conciliation. Lines in the sand were being erased. Louis was in two minds about all of this, given that fudge and mist were his preferred options for dealing with any crisis. Where, he wondered, were these spineless prevaricators when he needed them to put together his own deal? It was too late for him to turn tail again. He was bound to play hazard on this one, even though he didn't know what hazard was. It was something his father used to say. But just in case, he began to mull over his options.

Nick, on the other hand, was boiling with rage.

'You need to calm down, Nick. You'll do yourself an injury.'

Cale had been out riding with Denmark, these days accompanied by a dozen armed men to make sure no harm came to him, which is to say no harm came to Cale. They'd had a mildly bad-tempered exchange when Denmark had wanted to stay out riding while Cale said he had a meeting to go to.

'With who?'

Cale drew a large nose in the air in front of his face.

'You go, I've got the guards. Go – I can look after myself,' said Denmark.

'Why can't you do as you're fucking told for once?'

In no very good mood they returned to the stables and squabbled a bit more. Cale had started on his way back to get ready for dinner with the Reverend Hanson when he remembered he needed to arrange with the horsemaster for a dozen horses to be ready the following day. Coming around a corner into the stables, he bumped fairly heavily into a black servant.

'Sorry, suh!' said Ray Jackson.

'My fault,' said Cale. 'Should've looked where I was going.'

There was something vaguely familiar about the man he'd knocked into, but the moment came and went in an instant.

'So, Mr Hanson,' said Cale, 'how did you become a Redeemerist?'

'Redeemist.'

'Right.'

'The sufferings of my past are now like a dream, Mr Savio. But the Redeemer, peace be upon him, so tempered my heart away from the hatred caused by too much suffering that I cannot explain my faith without explaining something of that suffering.'

'Of course.'

'Please understand I don't say this out of a fear of being tedious. I can flatter myself well enough that there are enough villains here to entertain even the most sensational appetite. But I'd not have you think that I am one of those who feeds on their past misery. I can feel sorry for those whose afflictions have poisoned everything for them – but I cannot be one of them. Do you understand me?'

'Understood.'

He laughed. 'Very well. If you're sitting comfortably, I shall begin. I was born the property of Dr Josiah McPherson at the end of our antecedent century in Port Tobacco. My earliest recollection is of my father appearing one day covered in blood and beside himself with rage and suffering. The overseer had brutally assaulted my mother and, seeing this, my father had sprung like a tiger on to the man, in an instant mastered him, and would have killed him like Moases did, but for the entreating of my mother and the terrified promises to say nothing from the wretch who attacked her. It was a promise' – and he said this with a particularly intense emotion – 'like all the promises of the cowardly and debased, that was kept as long as the danger lasted. The penalty was one hundred lashes on my father's bare back and to have his right ear nailed to the whipping post then have it severed from his body.' He looked at Cale. 'Have you seen a flogging, Mr Savio?'

'I have,' said Cale.

'Then I will not need to describe the fifty lashes delivered by the blacksmith, big as a house, and the pause to check his pulse so my father might live to work again and remain a valuable property; the go-ahead of the next fifty, the cries dying out, fainter and fainter as my father grew too weak. Then the nailing of his ear, the pass of the knife, and the bleeding member left fastened to the whipping place.' A pause. 'Did you know your father well, Mr Savio?'

'My parents sold me to the Redeemers for sixpence.'

'Before his whipping and maiming my father had been a good-humoured and light-hearted man – his banjo-playing was the life of the farm. But from that hour he was utterly changed – sullen and morose and dogged in his pain; his heart, so full of the milk of kindness, was to wormwood turned. Nothing – no threat, no punishment – could make him step away from brooding on the wrongs done to him.'

'You blame him?'

'Blame?' He considered this carefully, clearly anxious not to acquit himself too easily. 'You think me harsh?' This was a thoughtful question, not an accusation.

'Not for me to judge,' said Cale, smiling. Hanson joined him.

'Do you judge your parents?'

'I have laid my parents aside and never think of them.' A thoughtful moment. 'So, I suppose the answer is yes.' More smiles. 'I once expressed my rage at the hell they'd sold me into to a friend, a mentor of a peculiar sort. He'd no sympathy for me. He pointed out that if I hadn't been bought by the Redeemers for sixpence, I'd've been raised up scraping a living from near-dead soil and never being sure where the next meal was coming from – so I should consider myself blessed.'

'I agree with your friend.'

'I thought you might.'

'I do not blame my father. I blame the doers of evil who destroyed his soul.' A silence. 'But I refused to share his fate. It's what I said to you earlier, and to which you took such exception.' Cale knew exactly what he was referring to. 'Evil corrupts everyone it touches, perpetrator and victim alike.' He stopped and corrected himself. 'No, not alike. But it corrupts all it touches. Or tries to. If you become the victim of evil and nothing more than that, then whether you are innocent makes no difference. It has destroyed you in this life.'

'But not the next?'

'They sold my father into the place that every Negro, west and east of Tobacco City, fears more than anything: the Deep South. The coloured people of the Deep South tell a joke about Brother John Henry. Like to hear it?'

'Please.'

'The Devil, exhausted by his wickedness, hangs himself. But on account of a trick played on him by Brother John Henry, when the Devil tried to buy his soul in Jackson the Devil leaves him his two most prized possessions: Hell and Mississippi. What does Brother John Henry do when he learns of this bequest?' Hanson paused for effect. 'Full of joy at his good fortune, he decides to rent out Mississippi and move to Hell.'

Laughter from Cale as Hanson smiled with pleasure.

'I was born in the Upper South, where Negroes are looked on the way I'm told sheep farmers regard their flocks: as a burden barely worth the trouble and expense of keeping. But in the Deep South, by which I mean this part of the world, there's a hate for black peoples that goes into the make-up of their very souls. They must own us, these creatures, in order to be what they are most fully, and they must hate at the same time for the same reason. And this is the source of all their pain. The chain they want to replace around our ankles also winds around their necks.' He laughed at Cale's surprise. 'I shock you, Mr Savio, that I should talk of my oppressors' agony.'

Cale shrugged. He did not exactly care to show that anyone had surprised, let alone shocked him. He must push back. 'This must be that forgiving of people four hundred and ninety times that I read about in the Gospels.'

'And how many times would you recommend, Mr Savio?'

'Most of the time . . . once is probably too many.' Hanson laughed. 'But you were explaining the nature of your oppressor's agony.'

'"Explaining" would be too great a boast. Not even I am so proud. The soul of a white Southerner is like the interior of the Dark Continent from which my ancestors came.' He smiled broadly. 'It can be approached, but it is best left unexplored.'

'Yes, I was forgetting. Nick Van Owen' – a look of distaste from Hanson – 'at a dinner where I was in attendance, rather than one of the invited, Van Owen took some pleasure in pointing out that there could be no slave trade at all without the black princes and their subjects who stole your ancestors from their homes and sold you to the evil white slavers.'

'He's absolutely right. It's true. It cannot be denied.' *What an interesting man he is*, thought Cale.

'We demand that we Negroes are the equal of any white man. And so, we are: equal in malice, cruelty, greed and hypocrisy. No Redeemist can think otherwise. We are, all of us, sinners and, given the power over others, we would be as cruel and heartless as anyone. It is another example of how evil corrupts the victims of oppression – it makes them think that being oppressed makes them good and noble. Just because, *Mr'* – the term was never used more disdainfully – 'Van Owen is a vile human being doesn't make him wrong.' He looked across at Cale. 'Were you present when you were sold for sixpence?'

'Might have been – too young to remember.'

'A blessing of sorts.'

'No doubt.'

'Soon after the flogging, my father was sold and never heard from again. The plantation owner died and all of us were sold, too – our teeth were inspected, we were made to run up and down in front of our buyers, our bodies examined. My mother and me were bought by different owners. I can shut my eyes and see her agony. The iron entered into my soul that moment, young as I was.'

'That's something I do remember,' said Cale.

'I'm sorry?'

'The second – well, the seconds – it took about ten. I was nine years old, perhaps. I'd been given a beating with a rope the width of a man's arm. After, I was feeling pretty sorry for myself.' A grunt. 'I don't know why I'm making light of it – what I was feeling was the most horrible pain and suffering. And then it was as if someone pulled a plug of some kind in my belly and I could feel all of it – all the pain, misery, fear, everything – just drain away. I can feel the sensation now – like water draining out of a hole in a bucket. And then I felt nothing. It was wonderful. Like you, I knew what it felt like to be made of iron.'

'The Kommitee have asked me to commend you for the information you provided about Dominic Savio's visit to Washingtone. I think there's a better understanding now of how important you can be to the struggle in the United Estates.'

Ray Jackson, sitting opposite, did not react to this praise in the way that people normally do to flattery. 'The scuzz in Malfi is that someone tried to kill the Duchess and her son. That so?' he asked.

'What are you to them, or they to you, to worry about whether they live or die?'

'She hasn't done me any harm,' replied Ray, languid, refusing to be told what to think. 'Done others a lot of good.'

Ray's handler put his hands together and touched his lips with the tips, as if he were praying. Then:

'In Bolshevism, the goodness of a wealthy and powerful person is meaningless – beautiful clothes on an irredeemably ugly body. Arbell Materazzi is a decent enough person, I grant her that – but whether she knows it or not, like all reformers of the unreformable, she wants to preserve her interests by putting into practice the notion that in order for things to remain the same things have to change.'

'Is it unreformable? Just because you say so?'

'History says so, Ray. Try reforming the situation if you will – then history will show you that, a hundred years from now, blacks will still be poorer, will still fill the jails, die younger, still be inferior. A Southern lawman kills a Negro for giving him lip, ten to one the white policeman gets away with it. But things *will* improve – you'll be second class instead of third class. Is that fate good enough for you?' He shrugged. 'I know it isn't.' He smiled at Ray, admiring and full of understanding. 'The well-meaning reformers are more dangerous than the pantomime villains of this world.'

'But you didn't try to kill Arbell in Washingtone, did you?'

'No.'

'You wanted to kill Dominic Savio.'

'Yes.'

'Why?'

A careful pause to signal that he was exceeding his authority. He wanted Ray to know that he held him in such high esteem that he would say things that should not be said.

'Dominic Savio is a threat, a serious one, to the revolution here and in Rus itself.'

'In what way?'

'You must understand, Ray, that the Kommitee can't be loose with information, not if we want Bolshevism to succeed in America. What if you're caught?'

'But your way, I'm still a black man doing the bidding of white men. What's changed?'

'What's changed is that you're working for the freedom of the coloured peoples in the United Estates. On your own, what can you do but complain and be destroyed and forgotten? It's only with Bolshevism that freedom is possible.' A long moment to let this sink in. 'That's why you have to kill Dominic Savio.'

41

Mon morn

Tom

I think of you FAR TOO MUCH and I'm going to stop doing it. Ten minutes a day is your lot from now. I'm unmovable on this. I will read improving books instead.

A

Mon morn 10 mins later

Darling Tom

I've completely changed my mind. You've seen and endured so much ugliness I can't bear it. But I can love you enough to make up for it. I can. I really can!

A

– Jenufer Smythe, *The Letters of Arbell Materazzi to Thomas Cale: Fact or Forgery?* (Atlantic)

Get Thomas Cale to plan a war and he will build into his scheme an understanding that all his plans are required to do is fall apart less slowly than the plans of the general he is attempting to defeat. Rarely in life do plans succeed in a way that resembles their original design – much, or at all. And most of the time, of course, there is no design or strategy. Mostly in life there are just events which have a shape as hard to make out as the animals in the game of Inky-Winky: perhaps there's a pig in there somewhere, but it could just as easily be a rat.

So – consider the cunning stratagems in operas and in books, then consider the blot of ink and ask yourselves (when everything is ended here) whether what has taken place is the result of human intention or is merely accidental blotches on a page. If tragedy is the working out of the inevitable in human affairs, there is no such thing as tragedy.

Ah, love! A most peculiar thing. The desire for a particular woman is the very essence of the absurdity of the entire world and all its longings in that it promises so excessively much and delivers so pathetically little.

Through those summer months Cale and Arbell often met, as they were bound to do. Consider the turmoil in his heart, nothing unusual in that particular storm: how many men and women experience love and hate for someone who once told them they were everything to them but then decided, on careful consideration, they were wrong. Such feelings are so commonplace they are of no interest to the serious mind. The love he felt for her drew him, however reluctantly, to her side; the hatred drove him away with pretty much equal force. So in her company he was reserved and seemed to show considerable coldness towards anything she said or did. Not always, though. From time to time his love would shine like the sun through a gap in the clouds on an otherwise rainy day. Then he could be briefly witty, clever, wise – interested in everything she had to say. And then in a moment the sun was gone and the intriguing man who'd saved her son and whose fierceness seemed to enfold them both and promise to protect them from the worst withdrew from her and stood engrossingly apart. She found herself kept at a cool distance then suddenly felt the heat of his close attention. Is there a man or woman who cannot be unbalanced by this push and pull? It was not a trick to make him fascinate her. But if it had been, it would have been a trick of magical effectiveness.

A few weeks after their return to Malfi, Denmark wanted to go to the stables to see a new foal whose parentage had caused general excitement about the chances of his being a champion racehorse. The discovery that Arbell, along with Gaines, were already in the stables put Cale in an immediate bad temper. He was not in the mood for the hurly-burly caused by being in Arbell's presence. She greeted him with great cheerfulness, as if genuinely not just pleased by his presence but excited. He merely bowed his head in reply, a movement so slight and graceless that an attentive person – Cariola, for instance – would have seen that Arbell was genuinely hurt by his response. She turned back to the foal to cover her upset and pretended to listen to Denmark and Gaines discussing the possible virtues of the ungainly-looking newborn. She took a full five minutes before she glanced back at Cale to see if he was still in the stables. Cale was resting against a tower of pack hay. She did not recall ever having seen anyone having taken that colour: his face was the grey and white colour of cold bathwater. His lips seemed to have been drained of blood.

'Mr Savio,' she said, moving to his side. 'You're unwell.'

For a moment it seemed that he'd faint, but he took in – or rather forced in – a huge breath and steadied himself. Quickly, she called up her carriage, which had been waiting to take her away to some duty or another ten miles away, and despite Cale's weak protests had him delivered back to rooms in the house, with a concerned Denmark, to make sure he was taken care of.

In five minutes, he was lying on his bed and looking as if there was some chance that he could yet be numbered among the living. Within ten minutes, his colour had returned enough to show that whatever it was had passed, and certainly he looked well enough to be taunted by Denmark.

'Just as well,' said the boy, 'that you have such an ear-biting, throat-slitting reputation, or it might look bad for a bodyguard to have the conniptions like that.'

'Why,' asked Cale softly, 'don't you take a long walk off a short pier?'

'So, what's the matter?'

'Swamp sickness – caught in the Kulagash.'

'Never heard of it.'

'I'm sure,' said Cale, breathing out the last remnants of the attack, 'that the people of the Kulagash would be devastated if they knew.'

'You're clearly feeling better,' said Denmark. 'I'll leave you to rest.' But he didn't leave. 'Does it happen often?'

'Not often. I'll be fine in a few hours.' It was, of course, nothing to do with swamp fever and it was very far from over. For the next few hours Cale retched and heaved himself into a state of complete exhaustion. As always with these onslaughts, he never actually vomited. Whatever poison was being ejected, it came from some world halfway between the world of things and the world of ghosts. But it had been a long time since he'd been this bad.

For a decade, all there was to remind him of the terrible madness of his younger self was the occasional tremor and, once a year or so, the odd minor quake. But nothing as bad as this since he'd left the lunatic asylum at the age of sixteen. For now, it was over, and he spent the rest of the day lying on his bed like a man who had barely made it to shore from a horrible wreck.

Later that night, there was a gentle knock on the door.

'Come in.'

It opened to reveal Arbell carrying a small basket of peaches.

The tuning fork located somewhere in his belly began to vibrate.

'How are you?' she asked.

'Fine.'

A beat.

'Denmark tells me it's the return of swamp fever.'

'Yes.'

'I understand it can be very unpleasant.'

'Yes.'

'Well, you must take your time to recover.'

'Yes.'

'Are they looking after you well?'

Another beat.

'Yes.'

'I thought you might like a peach. They gave them to us at the unveiling in Laredo.'

'Unveiling of what?' The merciful release of a question. She looked regretful and forlorn.

'I can't remember. They did tell me what it was. But I forget. Shameful, I know, but I unveil so many things.'

A smile between them. Hers shy and a little mischievous.

'Perhaps you could send me instead next time. I've always longed to unveil something.'

'Agreed.' She put the peaches down on the side table. Another smile. 'I'll let you get some rest.'

'Thank you.' A pause. 'For the peaches.'

'Don't eat them all at once.' Then an awkward moment and an awkward couple of words to go with it. 'Take care.'

She reached over to his hand, which was lying on the cotton sheet, and squeezed. How attractive a strong man – a dangerous one, even – can be when he's laid low and needs some tenderness. But something besides tenderness appeared at once in the room. As she leaned forward one of the buttons on her blouse, all crisp white linen and maidenly, gave way under the pressure of a few too many honey cakes during the previous month. It popped open to reveal the swelling of those blue-veined curves and for a second, possibly, the slightest edge of a pink rose-coloured nipple. The man did not live who could look away. And of course someone who all her life had been the observed of all observers knew instantly when the gaze was on her. She glanced down (a glance barely perceptible) then straightened up, both of them pretending that nothing had taken place, that nothing had been shown, nothing that had been seen had been seen. But it could be said that she had not straightened up as quickly as she could have done and he had not looked away as swiftly as he'd wanted to.

Another smile. There was a sound in the room, but only the breathless Tiny Ones could hear what it was: the sound of two hearts pounding at the same speed.

As for Cale's thoughts when she'd left, you may look for them in the wind.

As if this wasn't enough turmoil, he was talking later that afternoon to Denmark when there was a to-do across the courtyard as two carriages, pretty grand, pulled up to the main entrance to be greeted by Gaines in his best bib. An entourage got out, to the accompaniment of much high-style glad-handing and bobbing and nodding.

'Who's that?' asked Cale.

'Oh God,' said Denmark. 'I forgot. It's the new ambassador for the Hanse. I'm supposed to show my face. Damn!'

'Why're they here?'

'Why does anyone come here? They want Her Majesty's influence.'

'Over what?'

'Cotton. They want to get their noses in the trough – you know, the new Topeka railway line.'

This was a relief.

'And they wanted to ask for her help in finding Thomas Cale, but Ma said she didn't want to discuss it.'

That night Cale was retching like a landlubber who no longer had anything left to puke on the tenth day of a storm at sea. When it finally passed he was both exhausted and still in a fine state about Arbell. Angry (how dare she!). Bowled over. Mad.

It was all too much. He took ten drops of Mexican black in a glass and a few more for good measure, and within five minutes beautiful insensibility took him to the soft black shores of tranquil seas.

Three hours later he woke up. On the other side of the room, his greatest of all friends, Vague Henri, was sitting in a comfortable chair and, between smiles, eating a large cream cake from Frau Kuchen's patisserie in Spanish Leeds.

That Vague Henri should be eating a cake, by far and away his favourite food, from a shop two thousand miles away was certainly odd, but a good deal odder was the fact that Vague Henri had died in his arms nearly twenty years ago.

'Am I dreaming?'

'Hard for me to say.' He smiled and took another luxurious bite.

'Still like them?' said Cale.

'How could anyone not like cake?'

'And girls?'

Vague Henri smiled again. 'The only thing better than cake.'

'You've made a decision, then?'

'It's taken twenty years in the Underworld, but I've finally decided in favour of girls.'

They both laughed, old friends who were so close that neither time nor death could prevent them picking up where they'd left off so many years before.

'Have you come to take my soul?'

It was a sort of joke, but not really. Vague Henri's face altered immediately.

'No. The opposite, in fact.'

'You've come to give me one?'

Vague Henri didn't smile. 'It would be wonderful if that was possible. But it ain't. I've come to help you with the one you've got.'

There was a pause.

'There's nothing wrong with my soul.'

This time, Vague Henri laughed loudly. 'We both know that isn't true.'

Cale smiled. 'Nobody's perfect.'

'Nobody's perfect.'

'I'd say I was more sinned against than sinning.'

'That's fair enough. Probably. The trouble is, I can't tell you how many people in Hell with a hot poker up their bum are screaming the same. Time to buck your ideas up, mate.'

A silence. Then:

'Or?'

'Someone will be along to talk about that later. But now you need to listen to me.'

'Go on, then.'

'What are you doing here, fool, moithering after her again?'

'It just happened.'

'No, it didn't.'

'No, it didn't.'

'Time is short, Thomas. They're coming.'

'Who's coming?'

'Time you weren't here. You can no more dig up your love for this woman and make it live than you can dig me up and take me out looking for girls and cake. All you'll find in this place is death. Leave now.'

'I want to go. But I can't.'

'I don't have time to argue with you. Leave her or die. And you can't afford to die, Thomas, not yet.'

'I . . .'

Then Vague Henri vanished in an instant with a strange, melodious twang and a lingering smell of lemons.

Cale sank back on the bed. *It's a dream. Just a dream.* Then, as if he'd taken another dose of opium, he was sucked back into the black sea.

It might have been seconds or several hours later, but in a moment he woke up – instantly alert with every hair on his body upright and screaming in alarm. *Don't move!* Another scream, but this one silent and to himself. His eyes moved at the speed of lightning all around the room as he tensed, ready to jack-in-the-box to his defence against whatever wicked thing had come into his room and woken him. Very slowly, he felt the sheet and blanket covering his feet begin to move downwards off the bed as if being reeled in by some monstrous but careful fisher of men.

Little by little, ynche by scruple, the sheet and blanket were scrolled over the foot of the bed into the mouth of whatever sneaky gargoyle was pulling the bedclothes and Cale himself into the very bowels of Hell.

BOO!

A cry from Cale.

Up from the foot of the bed burst a figure in a cassock and hood holding a glinting scythe the length of half the room. Cale screamed in terror – the figure screamed back high and full of malice and hate. And then.

Gradually, the scream from the figure of death turned into a laugh. Then, with a flick of its arm, the reaper threw back his hood to reveal a grin so broad it might have split a real face entirely in two.

'You!' said Cale.

'Well,' said the figure. 'There's no arguing with that, is there? And to think that there are some people who still claim you're a moron. Not many, I admit, just a few of those who know you well.'

The creature threw the scythe across the room, where the blade, being made of painted cardboard, immediately bent in two. He smiled.

'What do you think of the get-up? A touch obvious, I know, but it startled the shit out of you all the same. No need to answer. I can tell by the smell.'

'What the fuck do you want?' said Cale, his heart slowly returning down his throat and to its more usual resting place.

'Not to be here, that's for sure,' said Poll – for yes, indeed, those of you who have loyally followed the appalling journey and all-round horrible life of Thomas Cale, it was her. Poll, the wooden-headed mannequin that (which? who?) was the most peculiar part of the treatment given him by the mind-doctor Sister Wray in saving him from eternal madness. For herself, Sister Wray was wise and gentle, but in her arms she always carried Poll the dummy, who deeply abominated Thomas Cale and never lost the chance to ridicule the boy.

'She sent me – Sister Wray – to tell you something.'

Cale had regained the appearance of a man in control of himself. 'And what would that be?'

A wooden wink and a wooden smile to go with it. 'What if you should die tonight? Isn't that what the Redeemers used to shout at you before you went to sleep?'

'What of it?'

'This is a warning about what's waiting for you if that most long overdue felicitous event should take place.'

Out from her capacious cassock Poll produced a ragged-looking rope tied carelessly into a grubby noose.

'What does it mean?'

'You know what it means. But if you don't understand, I wouldn't tell you even if I could.' Another woody smirk. 'Though, as it happens, I can.'

'What must I do to prevent it?'

Poll sniffed: the sound of sherry sucked through sawdust.

'You must not die,' said Poll cheerfully, and vanished, but not with a twang, melodious or otherwise, but leaving behind the faint smell of phellinus contiguus.

42

It seems clear from the newly discovered minutes of the Rus Central Executive Committee meeting that July that neither Thomas Cale nor Stalovek were present during the discussion relating to whether or not to execute the Rus royal family. Neither are their signatures on the warrant of execution. Of course, this does not entirely rule out the possibility that in reality they were at the meeting. Both men were powerful enough – and wise enough, given the brutally botched nature of the murders – to have arranged that their involvement not be recorded. It is also incontrovertibly clear from the archives that when the executions took place at the House of Special Purpose Cale was thousands of miles away in Petrograd.

– Lucas Okotie-Eboh, Inside the
Stalovek Archives (Atlas)

'. . . then opportunity knocked for me when the plantation overseer was caught in an infandous fraud that had been going on for years. So, the owner put smart nigger Joe Hanson temp'ry in charge.' Hanson laughed. 'At least, that's what he thought. In two months, he was earning twice as much from that plantation as he ever had. No more talk of being temp'ry, I can tell you.'

They were both interrupted for a moment by a pair of hummingbirds come to take water from the river. A buzzing hover, a sip, delicate as a duchess, then they were off.

'And did he reward you for all your efforts?'

'He did not. My master was too much of a brute to show any gratitude. But once a week, a Sunday, he let me go free to wander for an hour or two. I went into Newport Mill and saw some people at a meeting there, listening to a white preacher who had a great reputation in those parts, a Mr McKenny. Well, they wouldn't let niggers inside, but at last I got to the front door and I saw him with his hands raised to Heaven and calling out to the people: *The Redeemer, the son of God, tasted death on the gallows for every man – for the bondsman, for the free; for the man in chains of gold and the Negro in his chains of iron.*'

Hanson looked at Cale and laughed. 'I couldn't believe it and yet, in an instant, Mr Savio, I did believe the Redeemer died for me, an abused creature deemed by others to be nothing but an animal fit only for toil and degradation. I was astonished by joy in that moment, and that joy has never left me.' Then his face fell. 'Except for once.'

What happened on that one occasion was going to have to wait, as Hanson had to be off to a prayer meeting.

It had been a warm afternoon, made bearable by thick cloud and a breeze, but the wind had dropped and the cloud dispersed so it quickly became insufferable. Cale decided to take the longer but much shadier path to the house through the woods.

Halfway into the trees, he was thinking of nothing very much – cotton-gathering, as the locals had it – when he was possessed by a vivid sensation of danger. He turned as a dreadful pain exploded on the top of his head, caused by a glancing blow from a heavy, pick-like device used in the Malfi kitchens to break down large blocks of ice. Had he not moved slightly, it would have lodged itself very nicely in the centre of his brain.

It takes practice not to collapse after you've taken a heavy crack on the head but, unfortunately for Ray, pain and injury were old friends of Thomas Cale. Despite the terrible hurt to his head (lovely little stars in his eyes bursting like a fireworks display), Cale jerked away, holding out his right arm to fend off another blow.

Startled at his miss, Ray hesitated – would-be murderer and victim stared at each other. Although unused to killing, Ray was familiar with a fight and rushed at Cale, swinging the ice-pick with such speed it would have split his skull in two. It should be said that if the first blow had missed, this would be a remarkably dull account of a fight to the death. But Cale was in no condition for a fight as he staggered – just – out of the way of the second strike. The fight to live was a pantomime: stunned victim, skilless youth. Another blow – Cale dodged back but slipped and fell, left arm hitting the ground and holding him half upright as a third blow arrived at his head, blocked by his forearm and agonizing pain. Rising, he pushed the young man away with all the power of someone staring into the nothing.

Even in such a frantic state Ray understood that he could only lose by being rash. He waited, hesitated – something in between. Cale rose to his full height and slipped on the grass under his feet. Ray started forward but Cale balanced himself and moved away and his killer, wary, held back. Waited. Waited. What do the soon-to-die think of? A thousand things, perhaps, but the sense uppermost in Cale's mind was the unbearable smell of mint – it was Texas mint, not grass, in which he'd slipped. It seemed to clear his mind a touch. Ray, seeing him blink, thought he was ripe to kill and ran forward, ice-pick above his head, as Cale remembered his knife, pulled it out, dropped to one knee, allowing Ray to impale himself on the blade.

But O, O, O, that abominable cry. How many times had he heard that shriek, the pain, the horror, and the knowing? He drove the knife into Ray's belly as hard as he could, dragging him to the forest floor using his weight to force the blade home. A shove. A cry. A shove. Another cry.

But then he stopped, one forearm pinning Ray's wrist above the hand still gripping the ice-pick as if he'd lose his hold on life itself by letting go. Cale wanted to just lie on top of him, taking no chances trying to get up while Ray was still alive and could strike at him. But it was life or death to know who of all the many whos that wanted him dead was behind this. Carefully, leaning on Ray's wrist, he pulled himself half up and looked at his assassin's face. There would be no trouble here. Eyes wide, breath shallow, this creature was nearly gone.

Cale stood up, put his foot on Ray's wrist and, with great difficulty, prised open his fingers, pulled away the ice-pick and threw it into the bushes. He went behind Ray, put his hands under his arms and, with a great cry of agony, pulled him over to a Spanish oak and sat him against it.

Cale stood back and looked him over, eyes blurred from the horrible stench of mint burning in his nose.

'I know you, I think.'

A couple of shallow breaths.

'Been working . . . at the house.' A smile. 'Watching over you.'

'What's your name?'

Ray thought about not answering. Then:

'Ray.'

'Why did you try to kill me, Ray?'

'You're an enemy of the people.'

Cale groaned. *IDIOT! IDIOT! WHAT DID YOU EXPECT?*

'Who sent you?'

No answer this time. But a terrible spasm of pain made Ray clench his teeth. Cale waited for it to pass.

'You're a dead man, Ray, but you're not taking me with you. So you're going to tell me who your handler is or I might just as well have let you put whatever that thing is right through my head.'

Ray stared straight ahead.

'Torture is a very bad thing, Ray, a very bad thing. But you're going to have to talk, or I'm going to have to die. I'm sure you understand.' Another spasm. 'A belly wound like that . . . take you a long time to die. A lot of pain. If you want, I'll help you get it over quick. But you have to tell me what I want to know.'

Another gasp. When it passed Ray shook his head.

Cale sat down next to the dying man and lowered the knife to a point in the middle of his knee. He gave it a light jab. Ray cried out.

'Hurts more than you'd think possible, doesn't it? You're in a lot of pain now, but an inch-long jab into your knee just here results in the most hurt you can feel in the human body. Please tell me about the man who sent you. The only person in this world who wants this less than me is you.'

Jackson clamped his teeth and shook his head to tell himself, rather than Cale, he would not talk. Cale groaned – irritation, remorse, exasperation, shame.

'This is senseless, Ray. No one can take this pain – not me, not anyone. Your great leader Stalovek would sing like a fucking canary.' Then, querulous: 'This is your doing, not mine.'

Still Ray forced his lips together, his wound agonizing.

Cale placed his hand over his mouth, knowing that it would only muffle what was to come. Then he carefully positioned the blade on Ray's knee and pushed. You may in your life have heard a person scream. But probably not like this.

43

While this horror was playing itself out, just half a mile away Gaines was in the Jardin de Los Claveles reading through a stack of Southern newspapers whose front pages had today taken a leap forward in the mixture of false news and real hysteria in reporting a fire in the three-horse town of Waxahachie.

The Southern Watchman.

WAXAHACHIE BURNS!
NEGROES AND ABOLITIONIST
ARSONISTS SEIZED!

National Intelligencer.

FIRE OVER THE SOUTH!!
AFRICANITY MUTINEERS!!!
CALL FOR SLAVERY NOW!!!

Dallas Herald.

TEXAS ON FIRE!
VIGILANTS CALL TO ARMS!
3 NEGROES HANGED!!
DEMANDS THAT CONGRESS REPEALS
ABOLITION NOW!

Nick Van Owen was wandering around the grounds of Malfi looking for mischief when he came across Gaines, who looked as if he was growing more dispirited by the minute.

'Ah, Gaines. I was hoping to find you.'

Gaines looked at him with all the contempt an unmoving face can provide. Nick was delighted to be the cause of so much carefully hidden loathing.

'What can I do for you, Mr Van Owen?'

Nick pretended to be a little put out that his friendly overture had been met so coldly.

'I was just wondering about your view of some surprising and very scientific evidence I've just been reading.' Gaines turned his head slightly. It was invitation enough for Nick. 'I was reading in the *New Washingtone* an article by Dr Samuel Cartwright, a most eminent scientist, about a mental condition that afflicts people of colour – drapetomania. Heard of it?

'I believe not,' said Gaines.

'Well, it turns out that this is a disease of the mind that causes slaves to run away.'

'Really?' said Gaines, as if this were a most fascinating idea. 'You mean, a sort of morbid desire to be free?' Nick laughed. He and Gaines had one thing in common: they understood each other. 'So,' continued Gaines, 'it's just as well we don't have slavery in the United Estates any longer.'

Nick looked worried. 'I can see that, Mr Gaines, but will that be the case for much longer? I fear there is bound to be an outbreak of drapetomania when Congress votes against continuing the Emancipation Act.'

Gaines smiled. 'Then we must hope it votes to make the Act permanent so that your fears go unrealized.' He smiled. 'I'm very sure it will.'

'Are you indeed?'

'Yes.'

A pause. Then:

'Dr Cartwright also argues that black skin is certainly a form of non-contagious leprosy.'

Gaines again considered this carefully. 'Dr . . . ?'

'Cartwright.'

'He's most certainly wrong about that.'

'How can you be so sure? Do you have a qualification in ailments of the skin you haven't told us about?'

'No,' admitted Gaines, 'but I have always found questions of skin colour absolutely fascinating and I've read widely on the matter. Leprosy turns the skin white, Mr Van Owen.'

He excused himself with the very slightest of bows of the head and walked off.

Nick watched him leave, not obviously put out.

'That's one smart nigger,' he said softly to himself, and sat down to enjoy the sunset.

The long day was closing, too, in Malfi's Panford Memorial Park. The susurrus of the crickets was warming up and in half an hour would be deafening. The early bats were flying overhead for the night's feed. The lovely song of the Mozart bird, so beautiful, so sweet, was informing any possible competitors that a hideous dismemberment would be in store if they dared to make an appearance. On a bench in a quiet corner of the park sat Jackson's handler, a gentle smile at all this beauty softening a countenance usually so stern from being focussed on the class struggle, the weak against the powerful.

He was dead, and had been for nearly twenty minutes.

In his room, Cale had just finished tending to the nasty but small gash on the back of his skull, one which, fortunately, could be hidden by his long, thick hair. His head hurt so badly he wondered if the blow from the late Ray Jackson had cracked his skull. He was staring at himself in the mirror. If he had been thinking, it would have been to tell himself to leave or die. But he was not thinking.

44

Oh the human heart is small,
Not wide or thick or tall.
And whether for saint or sinner,
Not sufficient for a dinner.
But even though it's slight,
To feed its appetite,
The whole world's not enough
(which is why our lives are tough).
La la la la la la la laaaaa, la la la la la la la laaaaa

– *Polly Perkins in the West. A Pantopera* by Mark Tweain

Hettie Summerstone was a frequent visitor to Cale's rooms, often with flowers she'd stolen from the wonderful gardens, and she gossiped about the nature of art, her favourite operas and her latest conquests – and in the most eye-watering detail. She was a welcome distraction with her hummingbird wit and starling chatter, all spiced with a sharpness of mind and a delight in everything naughty. She kept him from thinking one thing in particular: *Leave. Leave. Leave.*

'Have you seen Jehovine Lara Hopko? No? She's the wife of the Puritain ambassador – the one with the white bonnet and the ear flaps.'

'I like her – she wants to ban opera.'

'That's the one!' she said brightly. 'I mean, my God, she looks as if butter wouldn't melt, but the filth she comes out with when she has the sugar hiccups. You know what that is?'

'I can guess.'

'And the noise! I had to put my hand over her mouth in case they called the constables.'

As Hetty opened the door to leave she discovered Arbell just about to knock. The mistress of Malfi looked so gorgeous in a yellow silk day dress with a cleavage only just enough this side of good taste that Hetty almost had a case of the sugar hiccups herself. Realizing that Hetty was going to find an excuse to stay, Arbell dismissed her with a generous bribe: tea the following afternoon. Off she went, both frustrated and full of hope for the next day. Arbell came into the room to find Cale arranging the mix of flowers and glorified weeds Hetty had snatched from the garden to show her concern for his health.

'I'm worried she's going to lead you astray,' said Arbell.

They laughed, which nicely covered the noise of whatever was pulsing between them. She watched as he carefully placed the flowers in a vase, paused, then moved them again.

'I'd always hated lilies before,' she said. 'But just using one or two with – is that grass? – well' – she smiled – 'I've entirely forgiven them.' He laughed. 'What a surprising person you are, Dominic Savio.'

'You find it strange that a desperado like me enjoys flower-arranging?'

'Oh dear,' she replied, seeing he was amused rather than annoyed. 'I can't say right for saying wrong.'

'No,' he said. 'It's true. I can prove that even the wicked can have a talent for the lovely and delicate. I learned how to do this from Albert Speer.'

'I don't know the name.'

'No loss. As mass murderers go, Speer was notable because of his irritating – but I admit quite interesting – habit of wringing his hands and weeping about how terrible it was that he was obliged for the safety of the people to slaughter this person – or, more usually, several thousand persons. He fancied himself as a man of culture.' He corrected himself. 'No, that's unfair, he *was* a man of culture. He had a master flower-arranger from Japan to teach him all this stuff. Cost him a fortune.' He smiled at her. 'So, there's nothing contradictory about being brutal while also having a beautiful soul.'

'I think you're beastly.'

'Why?'

'You want me to think you're even more interesting than I already think you are.'

'I'm sorry to disappoint you,' he said, but smiling. 'Too subtle for me.'

She looked at him shrewdly. 'I doubt that. But I've been wrong before about people.'

'I can imagine,' he said. She laughed – delighted by his cheek.

'Why are you so horrible to me?'

'You'd prefer I was more respectful?'

'I didn't say that.' She smiled. Smiles cannot have sides, of course. But if they could, it would have been one with as many facets as your more expensive kind of diamond – all sparkly and twinkly and wanting to be owned.

'You like taunting me, don't you?'

'I shall stop immediately.'

She stood up and looked at him. And what a look it was. 'I didn't say that, either.'

Then, conscious of her beauty and utter loveliness, she swept enjoyably out of the room. Don't blame her: she *was* beautiful and utterly lovely.

Shaken, Thomas Cale went back to his flower arranging.

LEAVE! LEAVE! LEAVE! LEAVE! LEAVE! LEAVE! LEAVE! LEAVE! LEAVE! LEAVE! LEAVE! LEAVE!

45

Clever enough, I suppose, in the way that a skilled servant of any kind is clever but otherwise a nasty little boy on the make.

– King Zog on Thomas Cale, quoted in *Blundering to Victory: A Reassessment of the Military Skills of Thomas Cale Loraine Cornwall* (Pingüino)

Tues night

I am so sorry sorry sorry I was a monster last night when I woke up and shouted at you for looking at me when I was lying naked on the bed. I'm spoilt – Princess Brat – I know. I get angry when I'm frightened. I'm so scared when I think about what would happen if they find out. I could promise you anything you wanted to make it up, but I can't give you anything you don't have already. Just now I looked up into the night all weepy and missing you and feeling like a harpy – then I see there's a round-looking object staring down at me and throwing the palest light I've ever seen on the world. Probably it's the moon.

I lack you. You will never leave my mind or heart. Sorry, sorry, sorry, sorry, sorry, sorry, sorry, sorry, sorry, sorry, sorry, sorry, sorry . . .

A

– Jenufer Smythe, *The Letters of Arbell Materazzi to Thomas Cale: Fact or Forgery?* (Atlantic)

'Oh, come in, Mr Savio.'

Cale entered the room. The table was laid for five but with a much simpler assembly of extravagant cutlery than usually accompanied formal dinners at Malfi. 'Have you been in *el gran comodor* before?'

'No.'

'It sounds impressive, but it just means "the big dining room" in Spanish. Thank you for coming a little earlier than the others.'

A note he received from Arbell an hour ago had set his oil-and-water emotions simmering. What did it mean?

'Drink?'

'Sherry,' he said. 'A Bar Badillo Versos, if you have it.' He knew perfectly well that she did not. A single bottle cost more than a thousand dollars – if you could find one in such a sherry wilderness as the United Estates had become since independence. He wanted her to see from his sophisticated palate that he was not just a blunt soldier, but her ignorance about the finer points of sherry meant the request was lost on her.

Her face fell as she looked at the drinks cabinet. 'I'm sorry, I don't think . . .' Her crestfallen expression at having disappointed him would have penetrated even a heart of stone. 'Perhaps you could see what we have.'

He appraised the bottles in the manner of a wine connoisseur asked to give their opinion on a selection of alcoholic cordials made from parsnips, sprouts or potato peelings. He made his choice – a perfectly acceptable amontillado – and poured it into one of six rather beautiful crystal copitas.

'What can I do for you?' This was asked by no means with the coolness it appeared to be.

'It . . . this is difficult . . . I don't really know how to talk about it. I'm afraid of losing your good opinion of me.' Do men's hearts flutter? This man's did. 'You must know that Denmark's life is more precious to me than my own.' He merely stared. 'But I'm trying here to balance his safety with his future – but also my own. And what I have to say is . . . you have, or could have, both of them in your hands.' She swallowed heavily. 'So I wanted to ask . . . well . . . to consult you, really, about whether it would be safe to leave Denmark in Malfi while you performed a great service for us both.' One more awkward pause and then: 'I need you to take something for us to Mehxico City.'

'What?' The tone startled her.

'Do you really have to know?'

'I do.'

Life is not always easy when you're charming, rich and powerful. Generally, people fall over backwards to say yes even before you've asked the question. So they're not at all equipped for the word *no*, or the threat of it, even.

'You know how we lost everything after the fall of Memphis and the death of my first husband?'

'I do know.'

'So I understand how things can change without warning.' A pause for him to sympathize. Nothing. 'But we have a warning now, with a war coming, perhaps. I want to be prepared. I want to put some money aside where it's safe. Things might get ugly for both of us if the vote goes badly. We might have to leave quickly. I need someone I can trust. You. I need you to take . . . jewels, mostly . . . and deposit them in the Banco Inbursa.'

'What about Denmark's safety while I'm gone?' A pause to let the stab hurt. 'And yours, of course.'

'For myself, I'll take the risk. But that's what I wanted to ask you. Is it safe for you to leave Denmark before the vote . . . or after . . . or at all? I want to know what you think. You must realize how much we depend on you.' She reached over and touched his arm. If it burned, he didn't show it. Of course Denmark and Arbell were perfectly safe. The question for Cale was whether it was safe for him. On the outside, there were the Hanse and Stalovek. On the other hand, if he decided to make a break for it, doing so with a fortune belonging to Arbell Materazzi was a wonderful opportunity. Taking her money and betraying her at the same time – what justice! What an act of retribution! How this would redeem him in his own eyes! Coming to Malfi would no longer be the act of an idiot driven by . . . whatever it was driven by.

'I understand you completely, madam.' More barbed wire. 'Let me think about it.'

But already he'd decided that it wasn't enough, the money and the betrayal. But what would 'enough' mean? Yet again, he felt as if it wasn't eight pints of rancid water he'd swallowed when he nearly drowned in that hideous watergate but the entire weir, down to the last shutter-sluice and fish-ladder.

Then the door opened and the other guests started to arrive, among them Gaines, who looked put out by Cale being there on his own. As for Arbell, the troubled plotter was in an instant swallowed up entirely by the vivacious host.

The food, she cheerfully explained to Cale, would be quite different, probably, from anything he'd eaten in the Estates. 'Or,' she added, 'perhaps anywhere else.' It was part of popular legend that Cale had eaten things so strange during his campaigns in the East that some of his soldiers had immediately dropped dead the moment they saw them. If this sounds unlikely – especially given that the kind of people who were on campaign in the East with Cale would have eaten their own mothers if nothing else had been available – you can still be sure Cale had good reason to be disdainful of Arbell's mild boast. But he turned out to be wrong.

First up was transparent soup – it looked like a broth of beef bones, a consommé of a kind he'd eaten at dreary banquets, most in his honour, from one department of the Four Quarters to the other. But it didn't taste like beef or anything else. It was pleasant enough – it was just odd. However, he refused to ask, and the assembly declined to explain but just got on with it.

Arbell was considering the question of Cale's table manners. She was a noticing sort of person and what she was noticing now was something odd about Cale's way of eating. For someone who went to some considerable effort to present himself as a rough soldier, he had the table manners of a duchess: he broke his bread directly on to the table and not on to the side plate and buttered only a small piece at a time. He dabbed his mouth frequently with his napkin and placed the salt he took from the (tastelessly) elaborate silver salt cellar on the side of his plate rather than sprinkling it generally over his food. It was not that she cared so much about such things (although if anyone ate with their mouth open or slurped their soup in front of her she was shocked by the spasm of loathing that filled her heart), but that it was so unusual to see such delicacy of manner. It brought her back to her childhood in

Memphis to see such easy refinement. It was very odd in a small way. Intriguing.

The unfamiliar dishes kept coming. There was Fish Pond – some sort of seafood chowder, though again he couldn't place the taste – then Pork Griskin, which looked like the fried fingers of an unusually fat baby.

When they'd finished the Griskin, Cariola smiled, provocative, at Cale, who'd said very little through dinner. She waved the waiting servants forward.

'Now, Mr Savio,' she said, 'this is my favourite pudding of all puddings. I *do* hope it's agreeable to you.' The young maid arrived at Cale's side and placed a plate with a delicate china bowl with handles in front of him. 'In your honour as a stranger in these United Estates,' said Cariola, 'I offer you: Globes of Gold Web with Mottoes around them.'

Everyone realized there was some sort of mischief here. Gaines and Denmark were amused at what Cariola was up to, but Arbell, who knew her rather better, looked at her not at all twinkly. There was nothing for Cale to do but go along with it. He lifted the porcelain bowl.

In the middle of the plate there was a ball, transparent, probably made of boiled sugar. Inside, there was a frothy white foam, custard or ice-cream of some kind. With great skill the surface of the globe had been criss-crossed by the cook with an elaborate pattern of thin gold leaf. Expecting the mottoes were some sort of peculiar Creole concoction designed to put him down a peg or two in some way, they were instead exactly what she said: mottoes. Around the inside rim of the plate were two sayings written in chocolate in an elegant italic.

'Go on, Savio,' said a delighted Denmark. 'Read them out.'

With a sort of smile, though it was not that exactly, Cale read the first.

'*The point of the needle is the easiest end to find.*'

From the puzzled expressions of the three watching, it was clear that now they, too, were the object of whatever it was that Cariola was up to. There seemed an edge to her, and a sharp one, but no one knew what she was driving at. But Cale went on to the second motto.

'*The goat's business is not the sheep's affair.*' He stared at Cariola and she stared straight back.

'What does it mean?' said Denmark, uneasy that his friend was being maligned in some way.

An entirely false look of surprise from Cariola – a little hurt innocence.

'*Je blague.*' She shrugged. '*Un petit blague.*'

Denmark translated.

'She says she was just having a little joke.'

Cale raised his eyebrows affably, took a large spoon in his right hand, turned it over and gave the sugar dome a sharp blow, much harder than it required. He scooped out the ice-cream and put the over-large spoon deep in his mouth.

'Delicious,' he said.

Arbell eyed Cariola, meaningfully might be the word.

'The next time we do this, *cher*, I'll have Cook make my favourite dish for you – cat stirred in the pan.'

'*Pourquoi tout le monde est-il si sérieux?*'

'I don't think I like Globes of Gold Web with Mottoes around them,' said Denmark. 'I wonder if the kitchen has any bear signs going spare.'

'What are bear signs?' asked Cale.

'A sort of fried dough pudding,' replied Arbell, still staring at Cariola.

'Why bear signs?'

'Because they look like dollops of bear shit in the woods,' answered Denmark, pleased with himself.

'Remind me never to eat one,' said Cale.

'Don't know whut yure missin',' said Denmark.

'Some of us,' observed Arbell, as if it were a minor point hardly worth mentioning, 'are trying to eat.'

Later that night in the bedroom, Arbell was sitting while Cariola combed her hair. She gave the brush a yank.

'Ow! *Tu ne pleures pad und dinde.*'

'So sorry.' A beat. 'What was that all about at dinner?'

A gasp of dismissal. '*J'aime pas la manière qu'il te regarde.*'

'What?'

'*Ou konnen ekzakteman ki sa m ap di.* I don't like the way he looks at you.'

A heart murmur.

'What are you talking about?'

'*Li vle pou fuck yu.*'

From heart murmur to heart attack.

'Don't be disgusting.'

'Mrs Van Owen,' said the respected senator for Louisiana, 'I know it's hard for you to understand the feelings of the Southerner on the peculiar matter of slavery, particularly when so many people take the actions of a few bad masters and exaggerate and lie to tar the rest of us. But the South was once a land of grace and plenty. I dare to say that no society in history was ever more generous and hospitable. And what do ignorant Northerners want to do? Infect the Negro with suspicion and hatred, where there was once an order and mutual loyalty between the white and the coloured peoples.'

This was no time to be disagreeing. She let his lament play out. But he wasn't quite finished.

'Let me tell you, Mrs Van Owen, the South would never have agreed to a union of the estates if they had believed it was impossible to get out.'

A look of regret filled Arbell's lovely face. 'Senator, please believe me,' she lied, 'this is a hard-headed question of commerce. It's not my right to look into men's souls and tell them if they're worthy or not. But if, as I truly believe, the South secedes over the question of slavery, then there'll be a war, and if that's what happens the cost of this railway and all the prosperity that must flow from it for the South will be lost. The Malfi fortune is at stake here. I'll pull out if there is a vote to secede. I can't do otherwise.'

'A great many men will be ruined if you do that.'

'Rather them than me, Senator.' Her face softened, but she still looked grim. 'I know you fear what's to come and I know that there are many who are mad for war. I know you are not. That's why I need you to use your influence to persuade the doubtful.'

In five minutes, he was gone. Arbell walked to a heavy curtain covering a niche and pulled it back. Gaines was standing behind it.

'Peek-a-boo,' she said, a touch weary. 'What do you think?'

'I think even the doubtful are learning to keep their mouths shut. It's going to be a pretty damn close thing.'

'Yes. Go and make sure the senator is on his way out the gate and then go and bring in the next one.'

46

Sweetheart. Tom

Sometimes holding you is like hugging an earthquake. But I'm not going to be afraid of all your anger. From now on I intend to stare you in the eye and not flinch. But I also want to put my arms around you so that no harm will ever come to you. I believe I shall always love you. Have whatever you like from me. It's yours. But sometimes I feel powerless to love you enough. So much of the time you're either sad or angry.

A

– Jenufer Smythe, *The Letters of Arbell Materazzi to Thomas Cale: Fact or Forgery?* (Atlantic)

Ah, love! Delightful love. How wonderful it is to feel love for another who feels an equal love for you. And how ghastly it is for everyone else to watch it going on. Is it revulsion for so much extravagance? Of course. Is it envy? Probably that, too. Is it a sense of doom (these violent delights have violent ends)? Possibly. But mostly I'd say it's fear. Of what, you ask? You know exactly what I'm talking about. Fear that you also have inside your brain the terrible worm of such a love as this: mad and fatal, ruinous and full of pain, to turn your life and sanity into a toxic hell – the honey of poison flowers and all the measureless ill.

But let us leave off love for now and turn to the subject of war. Or, to be more precise, the subject of the coming war between the North and the South.

Ah, war! Terrible war! Odd that there should be so much of it when nearly everyone agrees it's hell, a last resort, futile, a waste, a tragedy, and so on. And yet we can never give it up. Sooner or later, everything comes down to blows or the threat of blows. People, nations, only decide to talk because somewhere, however far away or in the shadows, a fist of some kind, a threat, is in the process of being made. The Laconics, to be fair, consider war and conflict to be the natural state of things. It's hard not to concede those horrible bastards had a point – as long as it is understood that war can rage over a cup of tea and a cucumber sandwich.

'Why don't we move to declare secession now?' asked Nick Van Owen.

'Because the point for now is not to secede and start a war we have every chance of losing but to convince Lincoln and the rest of them that we are determined to do so if they don't give us what we want.'

'I'm not afraid. Nor are my allies.'

'Lincoln knows there are Southerners who *are* afraid of what secession will mean. He knows we can't be certain of enough support yet to take the whole South with us when push comes to shove. So why should he concede?'

'Those sobcows and pusillanimous cocksuckers just need the wind to be in the wrong direction to find an excuse to do nothing. We have to do something to make them jump – declare secession and they'll come into line.'

'You could be right.'

'I am right.'

'You could be. But that only brings us to the next problem.'

'More excuses!'

'Not so. Ever heard of someone being killed with cotton, Nick?'

'Do we have to do this? You always try to make me look like an idiot by making me ask you to explain what the fuck you mean.'

Smiling affectionately, Louis Van Owen looked up. 'You're always telling me a Southerner is worth three Northerners in a fight, but the trouble is that there are five times as many of them – and they have an economy built for making things, things like firearms and cannon and the shells to go with them. Cotton may make us rich, but it makes a very poor weapon. Know how many factories in the South can make cannon, Nick?'

'Oddly enough, no.'

'One.' He stared at his brother. 'I'm telling you – even if we can make the Southern doubters agree to secede, the only chance we have to beat the North is in the first year, before they can adapt their factories and their factory workers into making a factory of war. We need money we can put our hands on now; we need to bring the wealth of Malfi to support the South in that first year, or we'll lose. We have to get rid of Arbell.'

Nick gasped with irritation. 'We've been trying to get her off the pot for years. What's changed now?'

Louis smiled. 'Me, Nick, I've changed. I've been too obliging. It's time to squeeze Thomas Cale to do his job and find out something useful.'

'And what if there isn't anything?'

'Then we make it up.'

'And if we don't succeed with Arbell and we can't get the votes?'

'Then we fail.' A pause and a grim smile. 'Or something turns up. No, I take that back. Two things have to turn up.'

'Not funny, Louis.'

'Who's laughing?'

Unknown to Louis, someone was laughing, and they were doing so in that very room. The Tiny Ones had been earwigging to all this gloom and doom, squawking and honking with merriment as they did so. They knew exactly what to do.

It is unclear whether the Tres Mujeres Maliciosas have the power to simply move events and persons at will. But where would be the fun in that? Being small and in possession of the bigger picture, what polishes the star of the three of them most of all is to climb into the ears of those they want to influence, being so tiny, and whisper and mutter to them in their dreams. So it was that Louis decided on the risky strategy, given his brother's unreliable temper, of sending him back to Washingtone with a strict instruction not to get involved in any overt action but to confine himself to shaming the fence-sitters into acting like Southern gentlemen of honour, standing up for freedom and tradition, unique identity, etcetera, etcetera.

In this, Nick was successful at first, but it quickly became clear that it was working only on the lower-hanging fruit. The majority of holders of the votes required still hung back. Lincoln intended to defeat the vote against the extension of slavery, and there would be no compromise; then it would be civil war or a complete climb-down by the South. The problem with a secession undertaken only by some Southern estates was, in Louis's view, that it was bound to end in defeat. The only chance for success was if all the Southern estates withdrew from the Union at the same time and put all their energy into the first twelve months of the war that would inevitably follow. It all looked very bleak. It was then that something turned up, helped by the tiny sisters muttering in the ears of two very peculiar people: Galusha Burlingame and Nick Van Owen. It used to be widely believed that history consisted of the actions of great men; whether this is true or not, I am not wise enough to say – but I can confirm that from time to time it is most definitely the actions of odd and inadequate men. Consider the Great War of Europa that started in Sarajevo in '18 and ended in Berlin in '45. Millions died, and the map of the world was redrawn because a lower-middle-class person of no special or interesting qualities shot an aristocrat of no special or interesting qualities. No matter how many powder kegs there are in a cellar, without a spark, they may just sit there and do nothing, get damp or be discovered.

And then this vital spark was struck during a session of Congress some five days before the final vote on extending or revoking the abolition of slavery was to take place. Into that great vault strode Galusha Burlingame, leader of the most extreme of the groups against slavery, who regarded anything less than disgust and loathing for the slightest compromise with the South as proof of absolute and unforgiveable degeneracy.

His personal loathing for Louis Van Owen was intense because he feared the effect of his recent conversion from mealy-mouthed fixer to born-again defender of ancient Southern freedoms. Burlingame saw that Louis was adding intelligence and strategic insight to the otherwise brutally stupid rhetoric of Southern re-enslavers like his odious brother. He'd become convinced that only the most savage and unrestrained attack on his opponent could rescue four million black people from the prospect of a life in Hell itself. Taking the podium in Congress, he looked out over his fellow representatives of the only democracy on earth and felt that the triumph of good over evil rested on what he would say next.

'It is worth remembering, my fellow congressmen, that the fall of mankind was not the product of a horned beast with a pointed tail stinking of the pit which is eternal, but a softly spoken snake –'

Hurrahs and boos.

'. . . I say again –'

Shame! Resign! Nigger-lover!

'. . . I say again . . . the fall of man came by way of a softly spoken reptile. The newly elected Congressman for North Texas – an appointment on which we congratulate him most sincerely –'

Huge laughter, a volley of boos.

'. . . most sincerely . . . like his illustrious, creeping, slithering predecessor, cannot open his mouth but out of it flies a shameful assault on truth. It used to be greased in the poisoned honey of reasonableness and generous compromise, where a slave becomes a person held to service and a child sold on the auction block a symbol of the traditions and ancient freedom of the noble South.'

Boo! Hurrah! Resign! Ahoy! Hoy! Rubbish!

'But now this phoney moderate for vicious oppression has revealed himself as a born-again convert to insurgency and instead of coming to us with a forked tongue dripping in poisoned honey, now he approaches us with a knife behind his back: his brother, a consanguineous evildoer who out-Satans Satan in rancour and malignity, leading an army of murderous robbers and hirelings plucked from the vomit-filled drains of Dixie.'

At this a volcano of cheers, catcalls, jeers, hoorays and all the rest. This time there was no order to be restored and, despite the early hour, Congress broke up in a ferment to resume the following day.

But the known chaos predicted turned into unknown unpredicted chaos as the consanguineous evildoer who out-Sataned Satan, otherwise known as Nick Van Owen, was heated into a boiling stew. Possibly Burlingame should have taken his breakdown of Nick's vices (rancour, meanness and malignity) more seriously than he did. It is the fate, perhaps, of phrasemakers to be better at coming up with insults than at grasping the consequences of their being right.

That evening Burlingame was in the library of the Congress writing a leading article on Chancellor Lincoln while brooding on a conversation they'd had at the White House half an hour before.

'I grant you, Mr Burlingame, that making compromises with the South on slavery is a dirty and disagreeable matter,' said Lincoln. 'But, sir, the world is more often than not a dirty and disagreeable place. I do not want, with all my heart, for there to be such a thing as a slave – but I do not want in all my heart to lead this Union into a war that may forever destroy the belief in democracy and which will undoubtedly slaughter and cripple young men in their tens of thousands. I don't have to choose between good or evil but between one terrible evil and another.'

But Burlingame was having none of this loose talk. For him, there was a line, and slavery crossed it. Any sacrifice was worth making to ensure that no human being could own another. While he was selecting something for the article from the wide range of insults he had coined for Lincoln (weak, spineless, immoral) Nick Van Owen came into the sparsely populated library carrying a thick gutta-percha cane – and if you do not know what gutta-percha is, I am very sorry for you.

'Mr Burlingame,' he said.

Lost in the process of carefully weighing up whether to call the Chancellor 'a small man in an era of great events' or as 'having no more backbone than a bowl of custard', Burlingame looked up with more puzzlement than alarm at the powerful figure standing in front of him.

'I have read your lurchid speech twice, and it is a jousty libel upon the South and upon my brother. Take this.'

Burlingame tried to stand but as he rose to his feet Van Owen raised the cane with its heavy silver handle and struck him a terrible blow between the eyes, one so violent that Burlingame lost his sight almost immediately. He collapsed to the floor under his seat, which was attached to a short track that allowed it to slide back and forth but which now trapped him and prevented him moving away from the blows of the cane. Finally, with a great bellow, he stood up, ripping the chair from the floor, and with his eyes obscured by blood, staggered into the aisle, desperately trying to protect himself from the blows to his head, face and shoulders. Then the hefty cane snapped – but, undeterred, Van Owen picked up the heavy end with the silver handle, grasped the blinded Burlingame by the collar and proceeded to stab him over and over in the face.

Unconscious, Burlingame slumped to the floor and Nick let him fall so that he could more easily deliver a series of hefty kicks. But someone had called the sergeants and on seeing them enter the great library hall Nick delivered one final kick to Burlingame's head, threw the broken cane down with an insolent flourish and walked calmly away.

47

New-York Daily Times.

**SPIDER FROM TEXAS BEHIND
OUTRAGE IN CONGRESS!
SOUTH CELEBRATES!! FIREWORKS
AND BONFIRES!!
BURLINGAME CLOSE TO DEATH!!!**

Be under no doubt, Louis Van Owen, posing as the spider from Texas, is behind his brute brother's attack. That rarest of things, a Southern patriot, Sam Houston described the infandous Texas governor: he is as ambitious as Lucifer! Make no mistake, this grotesque violence in our sacred Congress is a bid by the vile Van Owen family to become leaders of the South. Look behind the growing mutterings and gabbling for secession below the Dixon–Mason line and behind them will be the poisonous appendages – THE FANG AND THE WEB – of this Union's greatest apostate and heretic.

News of Nick Van Owen's entirely spontaneous act of brutality spread across the entire union within days.

When he'd first heard about what had happened, Louis Van Owen was furious, fearing a wave of sympathy for Burlingame and revulsion at his brother's thuggishness from those who otherwise supported the cause of de-emancipation. He was wrong. The long history of the abuse of ordinary Southerners for being morally inferior, a group who regarded themselves as both God-fearing and morally graceful, built up such a wellhead of resentment against those who wished the slaves to remain free that all restraint snapped. Nick's expression of hatred mirrored their own. They knew that the government in the North despised them, that it delighted to use its power to do them down in every way; it did not care about them, did not worry about them. All they worried about, all they cared about, was the blacks. At last someone was standing up for them against those who despised them. The North did not listen to Southern reason and now Nick Van Owen had shown them it had better get used to listening to Southern force.

Rallies were held throughout the South to celebrate Nick's straightforwardness in giving a Northern wretch the kind of beating he so richly deserved for attempting to deprive the South of its God-given right to be itself. It was barely possible to move in the grand hallway of the governor's mansion for the hundreds of canes which had been delivered to replace the one broken on Burlingame's back.

It made Louis Van Owen laugh, if painfully, that in one act of brutal stupidity Nick had turned the torch of secession – already burning bright – incandescent. Before this the South had been prepared for war, but now it was mad for it. The South had nothing to dread. At the end of Nick's boot the South had finally remembered what it was. In him, the South had discovered a hero – a man who did not persuade his enemies but gave them a good hiding. Nick might have been one of the privileged rich, but he spoke the language and carried out the wishes of every dirt-poor Southerner with his arse out of his trousers to teach a damned good lesson to those of the Northern moral supremacists who looked down on them as deplorables. As far as Nick was concerned, the move to independence for the South was all over but for the shouting. Louis was not at all sure about this, mostly because he was losing faith not just in his own powers of guessing what was on the other side of the hill but in the idea of believing that any such guessing was much more than luck. It wasn't, after all, that he had ever believed he was always right, just that he was right very much more often than he was wrong. Examining his failure to negotiate a deal for the creation of a South where the blacks were slaves in all but name, he was not so much worried that he had failed but that he couldn't understand why or how he might have managed things better. Perhaps most of the time things just happened, driven by some invisible hand. Perhaps it was just hindsight that caused people to believe that things had a shape, a cause and an effect. All of us took our belief in the power of wise or foolish actions to change things because we exaggerated our occasional successes. Perhaps, mostly, things happened, good or bad, for reasons that, mostly, were beyond human understanding. *Perhaps only God knows*, thought Louis. But unfortunately for Louis, he didn't believe in God.

But whatever the causes, Southerners in ever greater numbers moved to the Van Owen ticket and those politicians who until now had been astride the fence had no choice but to move with them to hail the leadership of the brothers – one a man of renowned cunning, the other a dauntless man of action. For them, the great fear of Northern power had burnt off like a morning mist for no greater reason than an act of deranged brutishness. By popular acclamation, the brothers were now leading a South at last committed to the cause of Southern freedom without reservation. There were other Southern men of power who had their eyes on the same prize and were ready to do everything to stop the Van Owens from claiming that throne. But for now, the times were against them and they must drink it down and offer their support and hope against hope that something turned up. But the Van Owens, by means of some good judgement, some luck and, of course, the help of the teensy-weensy hagsfish of Fate, were now on the rise. The Bill, the death of hundreds of thousands, the freedom of millions, the collapse of votocracy, the future of a great power, all of them hung in the balance.

48

At the same time, in Malfi itself, Arbell and Gaines, for now unaware of the great shift in their affairs, watched from the Balcony of Sighs overlooking the lovely-smelling camomile lawn in front of the house. Cale was preparing to give a fencing lesson, having been tricked into doing so by Hetty Summerstone after she had primed him with a gift of a box of decent cigars.

'What in God's name do you want fencing lessons for?'

'I'm worried,' she replied, 'about defending my honour.'

She had now turned up with a dozen of her hangers-on. This had obliged Cale to split the irritation by calling in Denmark to help.

Three of the young women had cow eyes only for Hetty, five were fluttering their peepers at Denmark, who was driving them to distraction by being very severe on them, the remaining four were beating fast for Cale, and not just their hearts were going pitter patter.

Arbell watched this set with a careful attention. Gaines noticed her look and could not quite make it out.

'It seems,' he said, 'that Mr Savio has admirers. Are you one of them?'

She did not reply at first.

'What do you think of him?' she said at last. 'Be honest.'

'Savio?' A good deal of thinking followed. Then. 'He would be good.'

'Would be?'

'Yes. But something comes between him and the light.'

She replied with an odd murmuring sound and then smiled. 'But that's what excites them.'

'No doubt you're right. But they're just little girls who don't know anything. They're full of romantic illusions about healing the damaged soul of a demon lover.'

She laughed. 'You surprise me, Mr Gaines. It almost makes me wonder if you have such longings yourself.'

He was unphased. 'Me, ma'am? Not at all. My preference is for predictable girls. Give me a homely meat-and-potatoes sort of creature – the kind who can't have their head turned by strangeness.'

He looked at her, one of those strange, speaking sort of looks. She wondered what it meant.

'I think you're being very harsh on Mr Savio.'

'Perhaps. But whatever it is that's eating him, I wouldn't want to meet it. It would, whatever it is, burn up an excitable little girl without even knowing she was there.'

After this charade was over Cale was on his way back to his rooms when one of the Van Owens' Malfi stoolies approached him in an empty corridor.

'The Misters Van Owen ain't real pleased with you, Savio. Reckon yure ass is in a sling. They want to see you pretty damn quick – in your nightdress, if that's what yure wearing.'

Cale considered the man calmly, as if taking in the threat. Then he thrust his hands at his face. 'Boo!'

The startled minion leapt back and pulled a knife.

Cale laughed, all affability. 'Tired of life, are you?'

It is not by any means true that your typical bully is a coward. The thing that all bullies really have in common is a taste for certainty. It's the act of bullying that's always the same, in that the pleasure is always in the drama being entirely familiar, like a much-loved story. Someone laughing at you when you have a knife and they don't might suggest this could be a story with an unwelcome twist.

Nick's stooge thought better of it. 'Lucky fer you the Van Owens want to deal with you personal. You be laughing on the other side a yure face tonight, Savio.'

He threw a piece of paper on the floor and backed away. Out of reach, he turned and swaggered off.

The note instructed Cale to meet the brothers at a hunting lodge owned by Louis about ten miles west. Wary, naturally enough, of turning up in the middle of the night in a remote hunting lodge at the invitation of the brothers Grim, he arrived as if he hoped to sell enough knives, knuckle-dusters and hand guns to start the impending civil war.

'Don't you trust us, Tommy?' said Nick as Cale sat down and ostentatiously placed a pair of Millers three-shot pistols in his lap. Cale pretended to be surprised.

'These?' he said, gesturing vaguely at the instruments of violence on display. 'Just body jewellery, really. Where I come from, if you arrive at a meeting and you're not armed to the teeth, people think you don't take them seriously. So, what can I do for you?'

'Perhaps you could tell us something useful,' suggested Louis.

Sarcasm was not Nick's way. 'Arbell fucking Materazzi is holding the balance, Tommy. She's got the money strings on just enough cockless caitiffs ready to sell us down the river when the going gets tough. It's time you did your fucking job. We need something scandalous to use against her, and we need it now.'

Cale traced the shape of one of the Millers with his right index finger. A silence followed.

'You must excuse my brother. He's very passionate about the South.' Louis looked at Nick with all the silent fury he could manage. 'Unfortunately, it makes him objectionable from time to time.' Nick looked at Louis as if he would burst. But he said nothing. 'Please ignore him. We'll deal with Arbell ourselves. I have something very much more important for you to consider.'

'Yes?'

'We intend to win this vote.'

'Yes.'

'If we do, there'll be a war.'

'So I hear.'

'In the light of an independent South being formed very shortly, it could be an almost miraculous answer to all your prayers. And ours.'

'My prayers?'

'For a place safe from your enemies – of which there are very many and all very determined to have your hide. The South will have a hard job to defeat the North. So what do we have but a marriage made in Heaven? A great general particularly renowned for defeating the odds and a country that would protect him for the rest of his life if he helped that country to survive.' Louis smiled, all affability again. 'I never saw the hand of God so clear in anything.'

This was true enough, of course. What better opportunity could he hope for than that Congress should vote that the Reverend Joseph Hanson and his wife must become slaves again?

There were three things on his mind.

Whether he should accept.

In what way could he warn Arbell.

Or whether.

FILED
Plurus Superior Court
Brumaire 33
Clerk of the Court

THE INTERNATIONAL CRIMINAL COURT OF THE HANSE

BLANDINO & SMI STATUTORY DEFENCE ADVOCATES

Boll,

So sorry this comes to you so late in pre-trial. It should have been delivered with the last packet of discoveries. Can't get the servants! It's from the notes the bureau confiscated from the files of Cale's head doctor, Sister Wray. Though it won't do you any good, sport.

Piggers

PS Cale has now been spotted in the Belgian Congo, Formosa and (again) the United Estates.

34th Nivose 1956 ME. **NOTICE OF DISCOVERY.**

Priory, 15th VENTOSE 783

Today Thomas C told me about a series of strange psychic visitations he'd experienced as a child, quite common at first, from about the age of five, and slowly diminishing in number as he grew older. They always took place at night when he was in bed and consisted of episodes that lasted around a minute, in which he began to feel a pleasant sensation growing swiftly into an ecstatic burst of joy in the world. Then it faded away, leaving him with a deep sense of peace and happiness. They were usually, although not always, he said, triggered on nights following an unusually severe beating. At the age of twelve or so these strange bursts of exhilaration and happiness ceased altogether.

At the time I could not bring myself to explain what these extraordinary visitations were. I've come across such experiences before in the young, though rarely, and never described with such intensity. All of these children, girls and boys alike, have one thing in common: they experienced unusually strong physical and emotional attacks on them by an adult of a force intended to deprive the child of their distinctive character and as a result destroying or severely damaging the ability of that child to experience joy in life. The somatist Daniel Schreber called this process 'Soul Murder'.

But my fear for TC is terrible – what happened to him in the house of desolation in which he was raised has perhaps inflicted an irreparable injury. These great bursts of intense emotion arise from the soul itself crying out for life in the same way that the old olive tree in our garden when I was a girl sensing its death sent out a profusion of green shoots from the base of its trunk in a desperate attempt to live again. The lemon trees in our orchard, starved of water during a terrible drought, responded to that killing thirst by increasing the number of flowers in great profusion.

These are miserable thoughts, which, of course, I cannot talk to him about. My hope for him lies in my ignorance. I have been studying the effect of such cruelty on children for thirty years and am humbled by how little I really know. He may yet be recalled to life. There is always hope for us.

(Soon after this THOMAS C left the Priory and did not return.)

49

Darling Tom

I sit in my day room wondering who I am, wondering about all that's happened between us, wondering what's going to happen! It fills me with dread that they'll find out. Please don't be angry when I tell you that my world is one I love. My father loves me. My brother. People are, I agree, too good to me. You have nothing to give up from your horrible past. But Memphis and the people in it are so much of my life. Don't be angry, as if I don't love you enough, because I do. If you really do love <u>*me*</u> *try to understand, please.*

I feel as if when I'm with you I can never give you enough love to make up for all the wickedness inflicted on you – you demand everything I have.

You've opened up my little world so much – but you frighten me because because because because . . . I fear for myself that I'll just blow away in the terrible storm of all your suffering.

A

– Jenufer Smythe, *The Letters of Arbell Materazzi to Thomas Cale: Fact or Forgery?* (Atlantic)

We have all heard of, may have experienced, the long, dark night of the soul, the bitter watches of the night, and what-have-you. In poetry, soul-misery takes place in dramatic settings, the fretting mise-en-scène of a dark and stormy night, a rain-lashed cliff: but in real life despair sweeps over a man or woman anywhere, perhaps especially during a conversation in a living room, or walking down an ordinary street. Heartbreak and grief had dropped by on Cale in the middle of a pleasant Texas afternoon, sitting in the shade of a cottonwood on a bench in the delightfully tended gardens of Malfi. Of course, we all of us do our best to walk on the surface of the world, the best place, after all, for us to be. But now and again the crevice opens up and causes us to stumble; in this case, the crack in the earth yawned wide and swallowed Thomas whole. There we are again: not even the well-armed can stop entirely the bombast poet lurking in all of us. Now that the brothers Grim had put their hands on his shoulder, it seemed to shake him so that all the doubts and resentments that had begun to settle into the sediment of his peculiar soul had been given a stir. A choice had to be made: for Arbell or against.

Cale was not aware he was sitting in the Van Owen family garden. Or perhaps he knew and did not care. It was not surprising, then, that Arbell was coming to the same spot, shielded from the sun and from others and carefully placed to take the cool wind coming off the lake. Seeing him there, she stopped. There were large rocks around the bench, not native to the place, brought from Rollright to the east, where (depending on who you talked to) they had been placed thousands of years ago by the Clovine people and were used either as an altar for sacrificing children to their god, or for highly accurate astronomical calculations.

Sitting on the bench, he looked, she thought, much older than the rocks themselves. Strange currents tugged at her heart. Most women have the sense to avoid, of course, these granity types of men. Or boys. Perhaps it was the same unclean spirit calling to her that she thought she'd cast out when she was seventeen and cut the rope connecting her to the young Cale and watched him fall. Now, just a ghost of that former ghost, it lightly rattled her windows and softly tried the door handles to see if it might come in. But she was no longer seventeen, of course, and was about to leave when Cale turned to look at her.

That look. If only she could have read a few words of what it had to say. Now she must stop.

'I'm sorry, Mr Savio. I didn't mean to disturb you.' She was apologizing to someone sitting in her own private garden. What was it about him that alarmed her but also drew her on? As for Cale, what must it have been like as he was drowning in his misery to see the person who had first poured oil on these most troubled waters and then set it alight standing in front of him uneasy and curious and only a few feet away?

Strangely enough (and what is stranger than the human soul, as some poet must surely have observed at some time or another?), seeing her there calmed him a little. Like cures like, according to the nonsense of the homeopaths. The bully or the tyrant from our childhood pasts met as an adult is often forgiven, or nearly so, when met again – they and they alone have experienced and know the past that others who love us very much can never know. How rarely such encounters result in blows or angry words.

'Join me,' he said. 'The breeze is very fine.'

Shyly, she sat beside him, but as far away as possible on the curving bench.

'You look,' she said, trying to be light-hearted, 'as if you were thinking weighty thoughts.' She expected the polite thing – a denial.

He looked at her. *I don't like the way he looks at you.*

'Yes,' he said. 'Very weighty thoughts.' There was humour in his reply, a provocation to the convention of well-mannered conversation, but something more. She laughed a little nervously. *Those dark eyes*, he thought. That long neck of the swan he had so often dreamed of wringing.

'Whenever people say that about me – you know, that I look deep in thought,' she said, 'I'm usually thinking about what's for tea – or just nothing at all.' He appeared to consider this awkward chatter carefully.

'No,' he said, 'it was particularly weighty.'

'If you've uncovered the meaning of life, I hope you'll share it.'

'The meaning of life?' he said, 'Oh, I knew that a long time ago. I was thinking of something much more important.'

This was startling and intriguing – as it was meant to be.

'Are you going to tell me?' she said sweetly.

'The meaning of life?'

'We could start with that, of course.' Now she was more at ease and able to restore some of the proper balance to the conversation. It's not the fault of great men and women that they're used to being the centre of attention, to being the ones with the reins and the whip in their relationships with others, however light the touch. If everyone defers to you on all occasions, who could stop themselves from being spoilt? The truly great, of course, *long* to be teased – although not more than that, nothing at all sharp.

'I can't tell you the meaning of life,' he said.

'I thought you claimed to know what it was.'

'Not *claimed*,' he said casually. 'But to tell you is too great a responsibility.'

She laughed at him. 'You're worried that your wisdom will devastate my mawkish woman's illusions?'

'I don't for a minute think your illusions are mawkish.'

She laughed again. 'Now there's a back-handed compliment.'

'Not at all. I know enough of your history to catch that you've seen how hideous the world can be.'

'The world isn't all hideous,' she said. 'There are the people you love, children, good food, good conversation, the beauty of the world. Not very original, I know, but true.'

'Yes,' he said, 'all of these things are very good.'

'So, the meaning of life is that some of it is very horrible and some of it is wonderful.' He looked at her but gave nothing away. She smiled. 'Clearly, that's not your secret.'

'Clearly.'

'So, tell me.'

'No.' A pause. 'But I will tell you a story about wonderful things.'

'I'm listening.' She was smiling, but the currents were on the move again, dragging at the sand beneath her feet.

'A man dies,' said Cale, 'and he wakes up in a place of great beauty. The air is full of birdsong, like the birdsong here, but the very best birdsong that ever there could be. All around there are flowers, but the most colourful flowers, and that most wonderful of all sounds, the sounds of masses of children playing, and there's laughter of all kinds – belly laughs as well as the tinkling laugh of beautiful women knowing they're adored.'

Arbell laughed once more.

'"Welcome, welcome," says a giant creature with wings like a peacock's tail, an angel, presumes the astonished man. "I hope you're refreshed by your sleep. If you are hungry, eat. If you wish to talk, everyone will take pleasure in what you have to say. Do as you please, go wherever you please. All the desires you have ever had, from the most trivial to the richest and deepest, are available to you. Welcome to eternity, my friend."'

'What is it that makes me think you have something in store for me?'

'Well, madam, if you let me get on, the sooner we'll get to where we're going.'

'Sorry.'

'So he tries everything out, and it is as beautiful as the angel described, but even more wonderful. Indeed, everything is wonderful – the food is wonderful, the conversations are wonderful, the women are wonderful – clever, kind and compassionate, and sweet as they are strong.

'And this goes on for a thousand years, and then a thousand more, and then a hundred thousand years of all these wonderful things, and then a million and ten million. And now he is filled with terrible, terrible despair, a dreadful anguish; all the food has been eaten a million, million times, the conversations with the greatest minds in history had a million, million times, all the love that can be given or felt – a million, million times. Utterly wretched and desolate, he seeks out the angel and says to him, eyes full of grief and terrible weariness and hopeless boredom, "Angel, I wish to die, to be lost in the dark, extinct and void, and become nothing. Release me from Heaven. I beg you." The angel's face fell with a terrible distress. "Oh dear," he said. "Oh dear, oh dear, I blame myself. I'm so ashamed. I thought you knew. I really, truly, thought you knew." "What is it?" said the man, a terrible dread growing in his ruined soul. "Oh dear, oh dear," said the angel. "My good fellow, my good fellow, I really thought you understood. This isn't Heaven, dear boy. This is Hell."'

Arbell's mouth – that enormous mouth, lips so full that on anyone else they would be ugly – her mouth gaped. Then she burst into laughter, loud and not at all the tinkly bell, like the laughter of the beautiful women in Cale's story, but a laughter from deep in that slightly – very slightly – plump belly of hers.

'That is,' she said, when she managed to stop herself, 'possibly the most wicked story I've ever heard.'

He smiled – she'd blown something really quite terrible away in the afternoon. 'I thought you'd like it.'

They sat in pleasant silence for almost a minute.

'Have you thought any more about Mehxico?'

Cale made a thoughtful grunt, as if to say that he'd thought of little else. Given that he was haunted at all times by the admittedly distant presence of the Hanse and that shit Stalovek, this was true enough. There was also the golden offer made by Louis Van Owen.

'It makes sense – of course it does – for you to make plans to run away.' He could sense her shift awkwardly at this way of putting it. But for all the pleasure of the past few minutes, he couldn't resist. 'I think it might be done. Malfi is shut up pretty tight. But the problem is me leaving for – what? – three weeks there and back. When I'm there, I can't be here. To make it a reasonable gamble I'd need to find someone – more than one – to take my place. That'll take time, if it's possible at all. It's not easy to find someone with my abilities, or anything like them.' A pause. 'Does Gaines know about this?'

'Yes, of course.'

Why, of course, he thought.

'Send him to talk to me. We should begin the search as soon as possible.'

'I don't understand, Mr Savio,' said Gaines, who'd arrived in a peevish mood, 'why we can't use Pinkerton's. They have a good reputation. The Hanse use them.'

'You've done a lot of work as a bodyguard, have you, Mr Gaines, work you've never mentioned before?'

'No, of course not, but . . .'

'No buts, Mr Gaines. You bring Pinkerton's in here and you bring the Hanse in with them. One week later and the Hanse will have swept up every bit of dirt in Malfi. Why do you think they're so good at doing deals and getting people to stick to them?'

'If you don't want my opinion, why did you ask to meet me?'

'I don't want to leave Malfi at the moment.' This was true. 'I still need to be here to bed in the extra security.' This was not. 'I've heard of a small agency in Dallas, Giteau's – they've a good reputation, so I hear. I want you to go and see them. I'll give you a list of questions and an idea of what to look for. Depending on what you find, I'll bring them here and see for myself.'

Gaines did not at all care for the role of Cale's flunky. But this was important business so he had to lump it.

'I'll make the arrangements,' he said, with as much ill grace as possible.

'When you have a date, I'll go over things with you.'

Gaines got up to leave. As he put his hand on the door knob, he turned back to Cale. In his studies, hungry for advice, Gaines had read that the important things on your mind in a conversation should be left to the last minute, dropped in, as if casually.

'I meant to say to you . . .'

'Yes.'

'When you talked about this business to Mrs Van Owen the other day . . . in the garden.'

'Yes.'

'Well, the thing is – and please don't take this the wrong way – it's her *private* garden. People want to talk to her all the time – usually to get something out of her. She needs somewhere to be alone with her thoughts. Everyone knows not to go there. But, of course, you're new here. I'm sure you understand.' He smiled and left.

Of course Cale understood about being constantly on display, always being the object of those on the make or just desperate. He valued being alone now more than almost anything. But, of course, it was a dagger into his heart that she'd sent Gaines to let him know his place.

In Dallas, there were vastly more important matters being managed than this nonsense. Louis Van Owen was trying to work at his desk when the door burst open and in walked Nick, arrived from Atlanta and meaty with news.

'We have them. Both of those cocksuckers – Peasegood and Chavez.' He smiled. 'We're close, Louis. Fuck Lincoln and fuck Arbell.'

Louis stared at him. 'That's what they told you, Nick. I'd say that we've a promise of ten votes from people who say they're going to vote for us and who're facing ruin if Arbell drops this railway idea. If we don't make our sister-in-law get off the pot, we could lose easy. Don't believe otherwise.'

Nick looked as if someone had confiscated his toy soldiers. Louis walked to the window and stared out miserably over Dallas.

Did he see his countrymen bleeding in their thousands? Did he see his country laid waste, the cities ruined, the buildings eyeless? Did he see the bodies of young men crippled, minds broken? Did he see the wives without husbands, the children without fathers?

'For God's sake, Louis, you look as if you're off to a funeral.'

It took Louis some time to answer, knowing that it would be unwise to speak while feeling such a deep hatred for his brother. He felt sick with loathing, for Nick, for all Southerners, for every black man who ever lived, for himself most of all. He'd looked up the word *hazard*. It was a game using two dice in which the chances are complicated by completely arbitrary rules.

But even being sick to the stomach couldn't stop him from making plans.

'I want you to go to Malfi and get an answer from Cale about joining us.'

50

> Do I contradict myself? Tra la la.
> Well, then, I contradict myself, tra la la.
> I am large, tra la la,
> I contain multitudes, tra la la.
>
> – Whalt Witmane, *The Wanderer, An Opera*

In one of Shagspur's plays – I forget its name – there is, for once, a mildly entertaining conceit in which a man and woman, hostile to one another in the way of a cat and a dog, are tricked by mutual friends into believing that the other is besotted with them. As a result, thinking themselves beloved, their animosity is replaced by gratification, and gratification by love. It also works, of course, the other way around. The anger of Thomas Cale was implacable and yet it had been, in some measure, soothed by his conversation with Arbell in the garden. Now, believing himself betrayed again, his fury at her returned more poisonously than before. But Cale was being taunted not by moronic friends, as in the Shagspur play, but by the crafty Fates who took such joy in their shenanigans with Cale. But not even the Fates completely control events. Even the Kindly Ones are subject to accident and chance. Even the furies are gripped by the iron law of unintended consequence.

While Cale seethed, Arbell fretted. It is the fate of the well-to-do, the powerful and the intelligent to be aware that everyone – not always excepting the spouse and the children – is presenting a mask of lies to them and that this mask is always smiling. If you are only rich and powerful, this may be very agreeable, or merely all you've ever known. It used to be said of King Zog that he was under the impression that the outside world always smelled faintly of new paint.

Quick-witted Arbell liked deference up to a point – but her appetite sickened with too much of it. And hence her pleasure in the cheek of Cariola. But Cale had come to promise the taste of something very different from beloved insolence – dark, clever, hidden, extraordinary. There is a kind of woman – rare, of course – who is drawn to such qualities in a man. Who can say why?

But having tasted the pleasure of an equal conversation between vast unequals, she wanted more. It is pointless, by the way, to criticize her for being aware of their inequality – it was a plain fact. Unaware of Gaines's decision to warn him off, her lovely nose was out of joint to discover that Cale was now avoiding her. People did not reject her advances – she was Arbell Van Owen. This unusual state of affairs threw her much more than she was prepared to admit. The result was that she found herself – or rather she did not find herself – pretending that she was not keeping an eye out for Savio. But Savio being Cale – and poisonously angry – making himself scarce was something he was particularly good at.

To Denmark's considerable irritation, she started to drop in on him at unusual times. He was no more keen than any young man to have his mother poking her nose into his affairs, assuming, as the young are prone to do, that anything that happens must relate directly to them.

After the fifth such visit Arbell got what she wanted. Denmark had been due to go out riding with Cale in attendance – in fact an excuse to visit that hidden space in the woods where he could continue his lessons in brutality. Not for the first time, he'd overslept. While he was half dressed, Cale had arrived and was – in no good mood – waiting for him. There was a knock at the door.

'Could you get that?' asked Denmark, pulling up his trousers.

'I'm not your butler, boy.'

This was not the kindly irritation with which he often talked to Denmark, a sign of his great and growing affection for the boy. He was in a doubly bad mood that morning, afflicted both by the business with Arbell and also by reading the news in the *Post* about his formal indictment by the Hanse – as well as the wrong but still worrying reference to his having been seen in New York. In practical terms, the indictment changed nothing; there were a great many determined to deal with Thomas Cale. At least, the Hanse would, when it passed sentence – an inevitability – ensure an execution as civilized as it's possible for an execution to be. This was a great deal more than any of the others would offer.

Denmark realized he'd annoyed Cale when he was only trying to tease him. He was wise enough to say nothing. Just a little remorseful (boorishness showed a lack of style), Cale went to the door. You can imagine the look on both of their faces when he opened it, so I won't go into the tiresome details of her fake surprise and his entirely sincere loathing.

'Oh!' she said, as if his appearance was the last thing she expected. 'Good morning.'

He turned aside and let her walk in, pointedly not replying.

What was she to make of this? But she continued on through the anteroom and into Denmark's bedroom. He wasn't pleased to see her either, but not quite rude enough in the presence of another to say what he would have done if they'd been alone – something along the lines of: *What in God's name do you want, Mother?*

'Good morning,' she said again, even more cheerfully, to show that greeting him was entirely the reason she'd come at such an ungodly hour.

'Morning,' said Denmark. 'Got to wash.' Then he was gone into his bathroom, leaving Cale and Arbell alone for the first time since that afternoon in the garden.

There was one of those silences that in the South are so quiet they say you can hear a frog pissing on the cotton. Arbell was confused by the intensity of anger in the room as well as by her intense need for friendship with this man. Being rich and powerful for most of her life and therefore not having to beat around the bush with people, she merely said what was on her mind.

'I'd been hoping I might see you in the garden again. I really enjoyed our conversation.'

The Hunterians – a people much given to sailing – have another hugely original metaphor. When someone is filled with powerful emotions of anger or pride and some discovery happens that reveals them to have been mistaken in blowing themselves up, they refer to it as 'having the wind taken out of your sails'.

Cale's spinnaker, so ballooned with the gales of humiliation and ire, spilled its wind in two shakes of a lamb's tail. He was so astonished that he showed no caution.

'I was told my presence in your private garden was an intrusion I was not to repeat.'

How satisfying was that opening of her mouth, the gasp of astonishment.

'No!' she said. 'Who on earth told you that? It's not true. I know nothing about this. Who told you that?'

Nobody, of course, likes a sneak.

'Where I come from it's not done to snitch.'

She was not much impressed.

'This isn't telling tales out of school, for goodness' sake. Someone who's plausibly claiming to speak for me can cause terrible mischief.'

'No mischief was intended, I'm sure of that. I'm asking you not to press me.'

A beat. At first angry then quickly accepting – she had, after all, inadvertently already offended Dominic Savio badly. It shocked her how deeply she wanted him to think well of her. Mysteriously. Oddly. Passionately.

'All right. Besides, I can guess.'

It's sensible, of course, to trust no one, but even if you're a powerful person and one with many spies in Malfi, like Nick Van Owen, this is a position that sometimes presents problems. He could not go to winkle out Cale in his rooms. He did not want to send him a message through one of his stoolies, who, by definition, were treacherous because they were supposed to be Arbell's servants. Knowing Cale's usual haunts, he was obliged, therefore, to wander around the grounds trying to find someone who was equally determined to avoid him. It was while Cale was on his way to see Gaines in his office that he saw Nick on a path just below him, clearly on the lookout for someone. Just ahead was one of a number of niches built to offer shade and refuge from the heat, and he made it into its deep shadows before Nick climbed a stairs to his level. Nick was about thirty yards away when he saw an extraordinary sight: an old black woman with her face thickly but badly painted white calling out to Nick Van Owen. 'Yoohoo, Nicholas, my dear,' she shouted. 'Yoohoo, it's Mrs Wade Hampton II.'

This was such an extraordinary thing that Cale risked revealing himself by moving forward out of the shadows to see Nick's reaction. It was not what he expected. Nick Van Owen smiled with what looked like genuine pleasure and said, 'Nelly Hampton, how are you, old thing? It's been far too long!' He took her hand, also covered thickly in white make-up, and shook it warmly.

'Oh, Nicholas,' she simpered, 'still so handsome. All the ladies are quite in love with you, particularly after you gave such a good whipping to that dreadful Burlingame. Well done, young Nick. I've been telling all the ladies to warn every man that if they do not hasten to battle, they'll shame them by rushing out to fight those Yankee darkie-lovers themselves.'

'Well, Mrs Nelly, I . . .'

'Mima! Mima! You leave that genumen alone, hear.' Another black woman in her twenties rushed past Cale's hiding place, raced up to the pair, grabbed hold of the old woman and gave her a hefty slap around the face. 'Bin lookin fer you this last hour!'

The old woman began to wail. But Nick's face went dark. In a rage, he pulled the young woman away and landed a hefty blow to the side of her head. Mrs Wade Hampton II stopped wailing, and the young woman started.

'I hear of you so much as looking cross-eyed at Nelly again and I'll have the hide off your back. I'll know about it if you do, and I'm a man of my word.'

Nick turned to Nelly. 'Now, you go along with this person and I'll make sure you're treated with the respect due to you from now on.' He looked back at her assailant. 'Understand me, girl!'

'Yes, suh,' whimpered the woman.

'Thank you, Nicholas, thank you.'

'That's all right, Nelly, you go and get out of this here heat, y'hear.'

'I will, Nicholas, I will.'

With that, the younger woman took her, very gently, by the arm and led her away.

Fortunately for Cale, Nick hadn't spotted him, and he walked off searchingly in the opposite direction. He gave him five minutes and made his way to his meeting with Gaines. Things between the two men had been distinctly cold of late, but Cale was so amazed at what he'd just seen he couldn't stop himself asking Gaines about it.

'Oh . . . that's, umm . . . can't think of her name . . . she was ladies' maid to Aristotle Van Owen's first wife, who was a Hampton, big family in the Carolinas. After she died the poor thing went loco. Started putting on the white make-up and claiming she was a white woman from a grand family. Aristotle paid for her to be looked after in a house at the far end of the grounds. But she breaks out from time to time.'

'And Nick?'

'Must have known her when his sister-in-law was alive, I suppose.'

How very strange people are, thought Cale. Being wise, you are no doubt wondering if he was also thinking about himself.

'You want to be careful, Savio, about thinking that Nick Van Owen has a soft spot. It's more likely he's kind to her because he's just as crazy as she is.'

Hanson had eaten twice more with Cale when he came to a difficult decision. This did not sit right with him, to be a recipient of another's generosity without making an effort to repay that kindness. But he also felt the anxiety of refusal. Negroes in Texas did not invite white people to dinner. Anxiety bred a certain resentment. He was as good a man as Dominic Savio, so why should he be obliged to be ill at ease? It was unjust. Who did Dominic Savio think he was, giving him such anxieties? Then he would catch himself and be exasperated. Then he would put it off. Then he would find himself stealthily becoming offended again. Then finally he could stand it no more.

'Come to dinner, Mr Savio.'

Fortunately, Cale, being bought for sixpence and not being from the madhouse of the Deep South, did not notice that a, to him, entirely ordinary invitation had burst into the conversation, impelled by such colossal force.

'Thank you,' he said, and continued on with his story about his frequent visits to Moscow Zoo to visit Thom and Victoria the gorillas.

For the first half an hour at the Hanson Lodging House even Cale was aware that there was an odd tension in the air. The Hansons, Mr and Mrs, both believed that there was no reason to be uneasy, but they were. The truth was, they felt a little honoured by Cale's presence and disliked the sensation. *Why should they be honoured?* they said to themselves. But they were. A white man, one who was in daily contact with both the Mistress of Malfi and her son, was in their parlour, about to break bread with them. It was nothing and yet it was something. It was significant.

Not for Cale, however, for whom it had no significance at all, which was really rather stupid of him. Or rather touching. At any rate, as they began talking and eating, the Hansons began to forget centuries of history and soon put the complicated things they were feeling into one of the many outbuildings that our souls have created to make life bearable – or possible.

Once dinner was over, Matilde Hanson excused herself in order to attend to the guests at the Lodging House and shut the place down for the night, and Cale and Joseph Hanson were left alone, smoking and drinking the excellent wine Cale had brought. It seemed now that Hanson was finally at ease, a last hurdle of intimacy having been jumped, and in his own home he was ready to say what had been on his mind for many weeks.

'About two years after I found the Redeemer, or he found me, things went from bad to worse at the farm, where I'd become overseer in all but name. I'd made a great deal of money for my master, but he used his wealth for drink and gambling and got into debt. Then he was dragged into a lawsuit over property and, day after day, his affairs grew more desperate. He was as good as ruined. Then one night in January he came to my cabin, and a more wretched creature you could not imagine, groaning and wringing his hands. "Oh Joe," says he, "I'm ruined, ruined, ruined." "How so, Massa," says I. "Joe," he went on, "there's only one way I can save anything." And he looked at me like a motherless child – alone, lost, abandoned. "You can do it, won't you? Won't you?" And then he did the most uncommon thing. I don't believe I was ever more astonished in my life. He stood up and he threw his arms around me; misery and suffering had levelled all distinction between us. Weeping, he held me, and then, taking me by the shoulders, "I know I have abused you, Joe, but I didn't mean it. Take pity on a poor wretch." Still he avoided telling me what he wanted.'

Hanson had moved his head to one side as if looking at all this, thought Cale, as if it were being played out on an invisible stage on the other side of the room. Now he looked at Cale directly.

'You'll think that I was a fool, Dominic, to have a moment's pity for such a man. And you'd be right. But that's what the Redeemer demands in return for his love, and nothing less. How many times must I forgive a man? Seventy times seven is the answer, Dominic. He died on the gallows for all of us sinful men. To refuse my master would have been to refuse the Redeemer himself. *Depart from me into the eternal fire for I was hungry and you gave me no meat. I was naked and you clothed me not, sick and in prison and you did not help. For what you fail to do for others, even the wretched and the man of sin, this you fail to do for me.*'

Hanson sat back in his chair, the power of his emotions making him breathe a little harder as he tried to compose himself. Gripped as Cale was by the revelation to come, you will need little understanding to guess how unconvinced he must be by the idea of forgiving anyone four hundred and ninety times. But he was not just being cynical – he did not doubt at all that Hanson deeply believed in forgiveness; but there was something stranger at the heart of what had touched Hanson about his master's abject state. The thing is that it was only Hanson himself who had given Cale the key to understand the terrible force that along with his compassion for the naked, hungry, criminal, slave owner begging for his help was drowning him: the horrible charm of being begged to help a brute whose gratitude and regard he craved.

'So, what did he want you to do?'

Hanson, off in his own world for a moment, grew alert. He took a breath, as if he were about to try and lift something heavy.

'"Promise me you'll do it, Joe," that's what he kept asking me.'

'Do what?'

Hanson smiled. 'He was determined to have my promise first because he knew how much pride I took – my great weakness – that when I gave my word it was as good as done, no matter how hard the doing of it. I said to him, at last, "If I can do it, Masa, I will. What is it?"

'"There's only one thing that can save me. I've lost the case and in two weeks every nigger I've got will be put on the block and sold. You too, my boy."'

Again, the darting look in Hanson's eye. 'I don't want you to think, Dominic, that I was just filled with the compassion of the Redeemer for my wretched owner. It was what I feared almost as soon as he'd come into the cabin.' He looked intently into Cale's eyes. *So, Thomas, wrong again. Hanson was well aware of the poison that was working its glamour on him.* But Cale was wrong in another way this time. Hanson's fear was of something else.

'You have to understand,' Hanson continued, 'and you said it to me yourself a few weeks ago, there's always another circle in Hell. The bondage the Negro was sentenced to in Maryland was bad enough, but everyone in the estate feared worse: being split up from children and wives and being sold into the ninth circle of Hell in the Deep South to Georgier or Mississippi. He wanted me to take all his slaves to his brother's plantation in Kentuckee.' He gasped with disbelief. 'He was telling me to take all his niggers and run away to slavery in another estate. Don't think I didn't balk at that – a thousand miles with eighteen Negroes in the dead of winter to an estate where I knew the way as well as the journey to the moon. "You'll be all right, Joe, a smart fellow like you." And when I still recoiled he worked on my fears of being sold into Mississippi. Worked on me, he did, for three hours. And at last I gave my consent. What he proposed was that he'd do his best to hide what money and land he could and join us in Kentuckee and we'd start again, the old life in a new plantation. A fresh start. My pride, again, was aroused at this great responsibility, and because my master's other Negroes trusted me as someone who had stopped the worst of the beatings on the plantation and alleviated the miserable conditions that used to afflict them . . .' He stopped. This was hard for him. 'Well, no difficulty arose in regard to my authority and the rightness of the journey to Kentuckee. And, besides, the dread of being sold off and separated, or sold down South united them.' Another silence.

'To cut a long story short, Dominic, it was no summer progress. A cold going we had of it, in the very dead of winter, just the worst time to take such a journey – the ways deep, the weather sharp. But we had no shortage of places to stay. In all the taverns along the road there were places for Negroes to be kept as their white drovers took them to be sold here or there. When these drovers saw a Negro was in charge of such a group and that he left them unchained at night, they were astonished. They weren't suspicious at all or hostile – they'd invite me to join them for a drink. And always the same compliment, and always from me the same pride in response to that compliment: *What a smart nigger!* And they joked, and they meant it as more praise. "Would your master sell you to us?"' He looked at Cale, eye to eye. 'And that flattery, too, hit its mark.'

'So, then we came to Ohyo, a free estate where there were no slaves, and crowds of coloured people gathered round us, telling us we were fools to think of going on and surrendering ourselves to a new owner: we could all be free, all be our own masters. The men and women under me were much excited and signs of insubordination began to show themselves. And I, too, began to feel my own resolution giving way. I'd always wanted to be free, but I had always thought of buying my freedom. I longed to walk into my master's house, lay ready money on the table and show him that we were done. He no longer had a hold on me of any kind. I'd never dreamed of running away.' He smiled. 'Dominic, I had a sentiment of honour on the subject.'

Cale knew enough about what used to happen to escaped slaves to understand the fear of attempting to escape. He had, after all, been forced to run away from the Sanctuary when, after slaughtering the Lord of Discipline, the consequences of staying suddenly exceeded the cost of running away and being caught. But now was not the time to express shock; now was the time to keep his mouth shut, if he wanted Joseph to finish his story.

'You must try to understand,' Hanson continued passionately, 'my Redeemist ministers always urged the duties of a slave to his master, that he had been set over the Negro by the Lord himself. And my pride demanded it. I had made a promise, and a man who breaks his promise is no true man. And all along the road I had heard myself praised by the kind of men who despise the Negro and find him an object of ridicule. So, I thought, what a feather in my cap it would be to carry off such an undertaking, and how much I would be respected and praised when I surrendered my charges to my master's brother, and then I would see a doubling of this gratitude and high regard from my master when he arrived.

'And so, using all my authority, I sternly reasserted all my command and ordered my people on to the boat that was to take them on the last leg of our journey. The free coloureds cursed me as we went aboard, but the slaves I oversaw, like me, were too ignorant of the notion of liberty and trusted me so they offered no resistance.'

Then silence.

'So, what do you think of me now, Dominic Savio?'

This is not a question even the most virtuous person should consider answering. Cale was, of course, very far from being that person. There were millions who regarded him as a destroyer of tyranny, but there were millions who regarded him as its very personification. But even for those who felt this characterization was rather one-sided and that he had many qualities, all things taken into consideration, that were in a number of circumstances, if not admirable exactly, could be construed as, possibly, under the circumstances, to be not necessarily abominable, shameful or sinister, there were occasions when his actions could often be regarded as dubious and precarious, morally speaking.

The issue for Cale was not therefore one of ethics here, but of comprehension. Had he heard this story before meeting Joseph Hanson, he would simply have lodged it in that place where he kept things he would be interested in understanding but did not understand. Or very possibly dismissed Hanson as a servile turncoat. But Hanson had prepared the ground for his admission well – better than well, because Cale could now manage some sense of the way they differed. Cale loathed and hated his oppressors without reservation. Hanson did not, because his oppressors had managed to work their way under his skin, mixing cruelty with applause. He could see what a nasty trick this was. The real question now that Hanson was asking was whether he had set up the revelation of his terrible act of betrayal of his fellow Negroes so skilfully in order to manipulate his listeners: an admission from the outset of wrongdoing; a tale of deprivation and ignorance from which his native intelligence had allowed him to emerge; a further admission of pride, but also another kind of pride in his ability to carry out such a wrong, based on a deep commitment to being a man of his word. Perhaps Cale's willingness to understand was simply a sign that Hanson was also capable of charm, one that he used to excuse his actions by presenting them apparently candidly but in fact carefully dressed up so that his actions seemed more understandable than they really were. Is his claim to have done something unforgiveable, thought Cale, not a sincere admission of the unpardonable but a device to trick Cale and, more importantly, himself into the forgiveness of the unforgiveable, which, of course, rendered it not unforgiveable in the first place?

If Cale's thoughts on this matter seem to you convoluted, it might be because, unlike Thomas Cale, you have not so many very questionable acts to justify to yourself. However, Cale had to respond to Hanson's question.

'I'm not a good enough man to judge you, Joseph.' This was certainly true, but it was very far from enough, given what was being asked of him. Possibly for the first time, Cale's religious upbringing came to his aid. 'If I remember rightly, the apostle Saul was a great persecutor of the followers of the Redeemers until he was made blind on the road to Emmaus.'

'It was Damascus, the road,' said Joseph, unable to stop himself.

'Right,' said Cale, lightly irritated. 'Damascus. But wherever it was, he was blind, but then he saw.'

'Yes.' Hanson did not seem entirely convinced.

That was as much in the way of a pardon as he was going to get from Cale.

'But that was not the moment the scales fell from my eyes,' said Hanson. 'If only it had been. The truth of the matter was that I delivered my poor cargo just as I had promised I would do.' He poured the last of the wine into Cale's glass.

'It was there in that place that the worst and the best of all things happened in the same week. The plantation in Kentuckee was a fine and prosperous one, unlike the ruin I'd removed them from. Here the slaves ate better, were housed better and had a more intelligent master, wise enough to look after his possessions with more care than his brother-in-law. And with this, and having kept their loved ones with them, I persuaded myself that I'd done well by them.'

The shadows around Hanson's eyes, it seemed to Cale, began to darken as he spoke.

'And then something happened to further take my mind away from what I'd done: that was when I first saw the woman who was to become my wife. Do you believe in love at first sight, Dominic?'

'Not really,' said Cale.

He could have been even more brusque than this, given his true feelings on the nature of that treacherous beast.

'Well, for me, I can say,' continued Hanson, 'that's how it felt when I saw her in her master's house when I went to a summons from him. She looked at me while she was carrying a hot smoothing iron from the kitchen as if I were of no more significance than a wooden stool. But me? My heart opened and it never shut.

'Her master called me in and told me to accompany his overseer on some overnight business in Cudiz, about thirty miles away – said that a smart nigger like me could do real well on his plantation if he had the right attitude. So, on my way out, there was Matilde, looking like Polly Perkins with her nose in the air, and I thought, just for a second, she was going to speak to me, and my heart skipped a beat – but then her master came out and told her to get on with her work. Any rate, when I came back two days later I discovered all the people I brought there' – a deep breath – 'he'd sold into a plantation in

Loosianna where the slaves lasted about three years before disease or ill treatment put them in the ground.'

He finished his wine. 'Turns out that had been the plan all along. The Kentuckee plantation was just a staging post, not our destination. My master knew I wouldn't have led them all the way to the Lower South, but he needed to keep me believing all the slaves would be better off and all kept together so I'd take them through the Free Estates and persuade them not to run away.'

Hanson looked at Cale, expecting to be harshly and fairly judged.

'How did I know all this? Matilde sneaked out of the house the night I came back and told me so. She'd tried to tell me what was planned a few days before. That's when she tried to speak to me. Turned out that my master had intended to sell me down South with the others, but his brother-in-law thought pretty highly of me for bringing so many through the Free Estates and, knowing my reputation as a man of business too, he thought to use me himself as a replacement for his white overseer, who was costly, and stupid with it.' He looked up at Cale and smiled with great bitterness. 'But who am I to look down at anyone for their stupidity?'

Another silence.

'So that was when at last the scales fell from my eyes. And it only cost the lives of twenty people to make me see things as they truly were. I felt a rage like nothing I'd ever known, and I went outside and picked up an axe and headed for the house to kill every white man there. "What you doin', fool?" Matilde shouted at me as I strode away with axe in hand. And she kept on shouting, "What you doin', fool?" for the next quarter of a mile, holding on to my waist and leg and hitting me on the head all the way. And I didn't notice no more than if the blows were a fly buzzing around my head. On I went, murder on my mind most foul, revenge for forty years of shame and belittlement and pain and brimful of it, I came to the house and through the window in the candlelight was my betrayer with his family, as happy and loving and full of the milk of domestic bliss as the Holy Family in the manger, and I in a red rage ready to wreak bloody revenge on all of them – man, woman and child.

'And I'd have done it too. But then Matilde finally stopped me in my bloody tracks. "What?" she whispered in my ear, because a raised voice would have alerted them and destroyed us both, "Commit murder! And you a Redeemist?"' He laughed. 'It was the voice of God speaking to me through her.'

Cale was not someone inclined to give much credit to the supernatural forces of good.

'Why God?' said Cale. 'Why not just give the credit to your wife?'

Hanson laughed loudly this time, and with more ease than at any time that evening. 'Matilde did not believe then – or now – overmuch in forgiveness. *Betray me once – shame on you, betray me twice – shame on me.* That's Matilde's philosophy.'

'Good for her. So, why did she stop you, then?'

'Because Matilde has her head screwed on and facing in the right direction, unlike the man she agreed to marry. She knew that if I murdered a white man of substance the whole estate would be looking for me inside the hour and I'd be hanging from a rope inside a day.' He looked at Cale's empty glass. 'We have no wine. Would a beer suit you?'

'It would,' said Cale. Hanson left the room and came back two minutes later with a large pitcher and two mugs. 'So,' said Cale as Hanson poured, 'Mrs Hanson was as much in love with you, for all her pretend airs?'

'Not in the slightest,' replied Hanson. 'Matilde had long been looking for a means to run away. But she'd lived on that plantation all her life and knew nothing of the world outside. Knowing she'd be sold down to the Low South if she was caught, she lay in wait most of her life for the right opportunity. She listened to every conversation about the outside world at her master's table, played the ignorant Negro, stole a little, often the small change her owners left lying around, until she had quite a pile of cash. And so she waited and she planned.'

'And you turned up – her knight in shining armour.'

Hanson laughed, a little woefully, thought Cale.

'Not that, for certain,' said Hanson. 'While she knew it was a feat of sorts bringing twenty slaves a thousand miles through the Free Estates, she also thought I was an idiot and a wicked Uncle Tom

Cobley for doing it. It was only when she heard that the intention had been to sell us all down South that it occurred to her I could be turned – and turned to her advantage. She reasoned that even I must have a limit to my gullibility.'

'And she was right.'

'Up to a point. What even my clever wife didn't realize was that when I snapped it was like a wire stretched tight across a ford that could cut a man in half.'

'How did she know that appealing to Redeemist forgiveness would work?'

'She didn't know. She'd barely heard of the Hanged Redeemer. But she knew I was a follower, and she's a most intelligent person, Dominic. And she was desperate.

'So, I stood there, while rage contended with the word of God. Have you ever struggled, Dominic, with that battle between savagery and the better angel of your nature?'

Cale considered this question for a moment. Then:

'No, Joseph, I can't say that I have.'

'You would have killed him?'

'In my view, he certainly would have deserved forty whacks with a hatchet. But no, I wouldn't have killed him.'

'You see . . . your better angel is more formidable than mine.'

Cale shrugged. 'I suppose I have the desire to do the odd good turn for people – as long as the cost to me isn't too great. Is that an angel? I can't say that I think it is. I wouldn't have killed him for the same reason given you by your wife – no chance of getting away with it.'

'I can't believe you, Dominic. Your heroism in saving the Spanish girl shows that the divine spark is strong in you.'

Cale laughed, delighted at the idea. 'Have you noticed that when people who consider themselves morally upright do something wicked they say that they acted out of character? I can accept that. So why can't the same be true of bad people who unexpectedly do something noble? But have it your own way.' Hanson smiled. 'This battle between Heaven and Hell for your soul – how did it end?'

'So' – a pause – 'I looked at the man who had sold my friends to suffering and an early death and helped to make me a foundation stone of their fate. The blade of my axe longed for his flesh. But then all at once the truth burst upon me that this was a crime. The Redeemer demands that we forgive our enemies, not our friends. If the words I preached were not to be hollow, my tongue a lying tongue, then I had to refuse to give in to rage. I was guilty, too. I, too, needed forgiveness, and what forgiveness for what I'd done could I expect from God if I offered none to other guilty men?'

'So, it was a bit of forgiveness and a bit of self-interest, then?'

Hanson laughed. 'I am human, all too human, Dominic. So, I dropped the axe and allowed Matilde to lead me away. And over the new few days we planned how best to make our escape to freedom.' He smiled. 'And that's what we did.'

'What?' said Cale. 'You can't stop there. I want to hear everything – the desperate flight, the barking of the hounds, the narrow escape from the evil master, astounding courage, wicked deeds, the dreadful crossing, certain failure, the final triumph.'

Hanson sighed. 'My apologies – there are many such stories. Throw a stone in Munt Town and you can't help but hit someone on the head whose flight from slavery would freeze up your blood and raise the hairs upon your neck like spines upon a fretful quillypig. But mostly our journey to the free estates was not much more difficult than a bad excursion to drink the waters in Saratoga Springs.'

'If you ever write your life story, it would be a good idea to discover something more gripping.'

'But that wasn't how it happened.'

'There is, Joseph,' said Cale, as if wisely, 'such a thing as a higher truth.'

'Did you tell Mr Savio not to go into my private garden?'

A careful pause from Gaines. Then:

'Yes.'

'Why?'

'It had something, I believe, to do with the word *private.* You've made it clear to me often enough how much value you set by solitude. Or was I mistaken?'

This was asked with a certain insolence not lost on Arbell, nor was it meant to be.

'Why didn't you discuss it with me first?'

'I was under the strong impression that your attitude was very clear. I ask again – was I mistaken?'

She gasped with irritation. 'I expect you to use your good judgement.'

'I did.'

'I enjoy Mr Savio's company.'

The pause from Gaines – eloquent. Then:

'Now I know.'

'I want important decisions to be discussed with me first.'

'I didn't think it *was* important, except in the sense that your privacy has always been so. I stand corrected. Shall I schedule more time for discussions concerning all the matters that previously I thought you wanted me to deal with without bothering you?' He looked thoughtful. 'About three hours a day should do it.'

Another gasp. 'Why is everyone so insolent?'

'Everyone?'

'I have to put up with Cariola's impudence on an hourly basis. Now it's spread to you.'

Gaines looked at his mistress with a temperature on the high side.

'I have never shown you *impudence*. And I'm not doing so now. I was under the impression that you employed me to advise you. Given that I'm clearly wrong on that score, perhaps *you* can advise *me*. How would you approach a great woman to tell her that her behaviour is unwise? The whole of Malfi is talking about you and Cariola drinking together last Sunday . . . in public, where you could be seen.'

If lightning could be generated in the eyes.

'All right! All right! Enough today. Can I order you to be shot for insubordination? Can I do that?'

'No.'

'But what would happen if I did?'

'Given who you are, and what I am, hardly anything at all.'

They glared at each other.

'While we're on the subject,' continued Gaines, 'there's gossip about you and another servant.'

'Who?'

'You don't know?'

'For God's sake, say it and then you can get out.'

'I'd prefer just to get out.'

Which is what he did.

Back in his room, Gaines was mouthing off to himself about his mistress and her deficiencies in a blur of complaints involving her recklessness, her ingratitude, her moodiness; she was thankless, inconsiderate, feckless . . . and of course to this chorus of wrongs spilled all the other resentments that Gaines must hide from himself and from others, the seething of someone who must, minute by minute, choke back the terrible urge to let himself be overwhelmed by rage against the world and everything in it. 'WHAT AM I DOING?' he shouted, so loudly that even the servants heard.

'Oh, Cariola, honey, could you help me with the drapes in the Blue Room?'

Cariola did not see helping with the drapes, or anything else that touched on servant's work, as being anything but beneath her. But she liked Edmoria Floud, and hesitated. 'Come on, sweetheart, it'll be fine, only take five minutes.'

Feeling virtuous, Cariola agreed. She started to regret her generosity even before the claimed five minutes was up and they were just entering the Blue Room, which, Cariola not knowing every place in the vast warren of Malfi, she'd assumed was at hand. They entered a room which was indeed blue: carpets, wallpaper, even a predominantly blue colour to the paintings.

'I'll just get the holdbacks,' said Edmoria, and she was gone. A minute later and, just as she was about to leave, the door opened again. But it was Nick Van Owen. He closed it and leaned back, smiling at Cariola amiably.

'I seem to have missed your note about when you were coming to dinner. But you're here now.'

'But it's time I wasn't, Mr Van Owen. My mistress was calling for me when your servant asked me to help.'

'I'm sure Arbell can manage without you for a few more minutes.'

'I must go, Mr Van Owen.'

If Cariola was being more circumspect than the last time they met, it was because, once she'd the time to think over her behaviour, she wished she'd been more careful. It was not wise for a black maid to defy someone as powerful as Nick Van Owen in such a brash way, even if he couldn't understand what she was saying. The Blue Room, she now realized, was unfamiliar to her because it was part of Malfi set aside for Nick by his brother. Normally, all the doors between his extensive apartments and the greater house were locked.

She made her way to the door, not looking at him. He didn't move.

'Excuse me, sir.'

'Come over here and sit with me,' he said, very gently taking hold of her arm. Equally gently, and still not looking at him, she tried to ease his grip, but didn't succeed.

Slowly, he increased the pull on her arm over to a large daybed. Now she pulled back harder.

'Let me go, sir.'

'Look, I'm telling you right now you must come and sit with me.' He laughed softly, as if at the implausibility of his causing her any harm. He started to pull her more firmly to the daybed.

'Please let me go, sir. My mistress is expecting me.'

'You said that the last time, but you know, Cariola, I've noticed how she indulges you, so I'm sure she won't mind if you're a little late.'

Now she pulled harder, too, but he was tall, more than six foot, and strong, and she was as delicate as a china doll. He dragged her to the daybed and sat her down, still holding tight to her forearm.

'I'm not going to do anything to you. But I do want you to do something for me.'

Afraid and angry, this might be a way out. Just agree – and then leave.

'What?'

'I used to have a rubber – pretty, like you. You know, Cariola, what a rubber is?'

'No.'

'A woman who eases the sore muscles in a man's body by friction, by effleurage and petrissage. You could do that for me.'

'No.' She tried to pull her arm away and almost succeeded, but now he grabbed her with both hands.

'Oh, the girls always say no. *No. No.*' He imitated a girl laughing. 'But then some champagne and they try the rubbing and they can't get enough. I'll even rub you if you behave and stop being silly. Try it for five minutes. You don't want to ruin your friendship with me for five minutes, do you?' Then he pulled her right hand into his lap. But the revolting hardness she could feel swamped the fear with rage and she tore her right arm free and scraped his face with her long nails with all her strength, the top of her little finger catching him in the eye. With a scream of pain he let her go and she was across the room, out of the door and running down the corridor as Van Owen, crying out in pain, staggered over to the mirror, half blind, to see the damage she'd inflicted.

51

There are no such things as stories. There is only one. And here it is: *I had it tough. Everyone was against me. No one knows the trouble I've seen. I was betrayed – by life, my parents, my wife, my husband. I was betrayed by the whole world. I triumphed in spite of everything. I did it my way.*

This is the universal arc, then: that those who endure to the end shall be saved. In the great war of life, those who have grit and purpose and a little luck (let's be realistic, let's accept there will be tragedies along the way) will still be standing when the smoke of battle dissipates.

Did I say that there's only one story? That's true up to a point, the point being that while the one true story starts like the one above, it's, give or take, more like the one below.

Gordon the Good, perhaps of royal estate, is found in the bushes as a babe, brought up in obscurity and inherits his mysterious father's rare abilities (in an unrefined sort of way that requires an aged mentor to hone them). He exasperates his parents (either dull or shits), is launched through an absurd coincidence into a conflict with some sort of Nogbad the Bad. He triumphs after much adversity and gets the moll (invariably beautiful and upper crust) and finally is recognized by all as number one, a stand-alone, special and unique. Familiar? Of course it is. Does it ever happen? Yes, it does. About as often as a week with two Thursdays. The special baby in the bush usually starves to death. Or if he is saved he turns out to be a dud; or he has an adoptive brother who in a ludicrous mix-up is mistaken for the brilliant child by those who arrive to reveal his special status and restore him to the throne. Left behind, the special one ends up staring at a horse's arse for twelve hours a day and dies of an infected finger. His dullard brother, on the other hand, ascends to the throne and all ends happily because he has an adviser, born into humble circumstances, who knows his stuff. Being of an easily manipulated nature and too stupid to disagree, he always takes the wise counsellor's advice and the country prospers because finally someone with brains is really in charge and not the latest in a long line of noble chumps. His royal wife cheats on him with the clever chancellor and so the kingly line dies out and no one knows the dynasty that subsequently competently ruled for centuries was founded by a shifty peasant and a treacherous cow. This is the story haunting every tale, the story behind every life and every battle in that life.

It was that greatest of all war generals, Arthur Wellesley, who pointed out that the business of war was exactly the same as the business of life – the endeavour to find out what you don't know by means of what you do. He called this 'guessing what was on the other side of the hill'. All human life, all knowledge and the vast lack of it, is summed up in that phrase. And so, dear Reader, standing as you do now along with Cale, Arbell and the Van Owen brothers, tell me what will happen next on the other side of the hill.

52

Those who have followed the wonderfully entertaining but often sordid and distasteful tale of Thomas Cale's upbringing, his adventures in violence, madness, troubles with girls, and so on, may remember the great storm over Brazil – probably the most violent storm in recorded history. But even this great chaotic powerhouse had to have an end, and this end, the very last puff of wind, took place months after the height of the storm on the other side of the world. There was just enough strength in this puff to unsettle a butterfly on a lavender bush growing out of a crack in a badly tended bridge and cause it to fly off. In doing so it startled its fellow gorging butterflies into thinking there was an attack. En masse, they took to the air and frightened a draught horse pulling a wagon bearing a granite corner stone weighing more than a ton. The horse swerved, the wagon overturned, pitching the stone into the water below. Not being worth the effort of dragging it out, it was left in the river below a large sycamore. Six months later, its roots undermined by the altered flow of water around the stone, the sycamore collapsed into the river and blocked the passage of boats. Stripped of its branches by order of the mayor, the enormous log that remained to be cut down to size was floated downstream by a winter flood. Ten months later, after many snags, blocks and entanglements, and swollen with water so that it barely touched the surface, it crashed into boats leading an attack across the icy Mississippi to destroy the ships by night built by the Redeemers to take them over the river to begin the most hideous massacre of innocents in the history of butchery. The leader of the attack, the lovely and eccentric Artemesia Halicarnassus, once adoring lover of Thomas Cale, drowned, and what might have been a wonderful salvation failed utterly. Within six months this most extraordinary of women was forgotten by almost everyone.

Our trivial puff of wind about to launch the events to come concerned a tea party being held in the rooms of a few of the golden youths whose fathers were paying for them to fritter away their time at Malfi in the hope that they might catch the eye of the wealthy and powerful who gathered there, and perhaps even the eye of that richest of widows, Arbell Van Owen herself. Who knows? Life is strange. One of the young men eating cucumber sandwiches there was Davide De Lascelles, a standard-issue chinless wonder often teased by his friends for his intense desire for Arbell, or rather Arbell's breasts. Not even his delusions about his importance in the world stretched to any real expectations about his actual chances of marriage to that cold beauty; but he played up to his reputation as a lustful idolater by going so far as to write seven poems – not very long, it's true; that would have involved too much effort – praising various attributes of her, admittedly magnificent, bosom.

Poem 1: In praise of their swelling pout

Poem 2: In celebration of their breasty gibbosity

And so on.

He had just finished reading his latest verse on the subject, in which he commended the blueness of the veiny filaments of her silken pillows, when the sister of one of his friends joked that he made it sound as if 'Arbell was pregnant'.

This last remark was half overheard by a servant bringing in a further tray of cucumber sandwiches and a large pot of Earl Grey. Needless to say, Little Miss Big Ears, while sceptical of the idea, as anyone who knew Her Majesty the Snow Queen's reputation would be, nevertheless passed it on as an afterthought that night while chatting with her friends during the interval of the servants' showing of the popular operetta *The Elixir of Love*.

At any rate, this nonsense began to spread. What of that? Outrageous gossip about the beautiful and rich is like a kind of opera for the poor – hardly anyone takes it seriously; it's just a bit of fun, comic or melodramatic, as the case might be.

'Ridiculous. Pregnant? Ridiculous.'

'Is it?' said Nick.

'You really believe this mazzardfat rodomondate?'

'It doesn't matter what I believe. It matters what other people believe.'

'If Arbell has a bad reputation, it's only for her coldness towards everyone in general and men in particular. Surely not?'

The tone of disbelief (it was too good to be true) was accompanied by a look of intense hope.

'Lots of people have a reputation for, say' – Nick pretended to think carefully – 'forthrightness and plain dealing who are in fact completely two-faced and treacherous.' He smiled. 'Like yourself, for example.'

Louis looked at his brother, amused and irritated.

'Well, no one could ever say that you weren't exactly what you appeared to be.'

Nick laughed.

'Still, this could certainly be damaging. But only if it were true,' continued Louis.

'I don't see what that's got to do with it. All it has to be is plausible – I grant not so easy, given we're talking about Lady Snow Wuss.'

'You're disgusting.' A pause as Louis hammered it out. 'But who could it possibly be? She's the observed of all observers.'

'Una puta libidinosa will find a way – some strong-thighed bargeman, perhaps. Or the spotty Herbert who carries the coal up to her bedroom.'

'I refer you to the first sentence of my previous observation.'

'What about Thomas Cale?'

A loud gawp of disbelief from Louis. 'Nogbad the Bad? Yes, I can see her going all gooey-eyed over the undertaker's friend.'

'What if . . . ?' A beat. A provocation from Nick.

'What now?' Louis eyed his brother distrustfully.

'Well, I always thought there was something creepy about her behaviour with that nauseating little brat Denmark.'

'I take it back – what I said about you being disgusting. There's no word for what you are.' There was no levity about this at all. Louis Van Owen was angry.

'Oh, for God's sake, keep your hair on, Governor. It was just a joke.'

'She has the Van Owen name. You start that kind of rumour and it could poison all of us, and for ever.'

'It was a joke.'

'Well, keep your mouth shut. If something like that was traced back to us and people believed we started a lie of that kind – we'd be the ones who'd get burned.'

'All right! My God. Lips sealed.'

There was an unpleasant silence.

'As to this pregnancy – we watch and see where it goes. Do nothing. And say nothing.'

At Malfi, just as the two brothers were squabbling, a stronger wind was blowing through the house.

A lackey had come banging on Cale's door and insolently demanded that he come to Arbell's assembly room, 'At once, in whatever state he was, at once.'

Tempted to give the man a bloody good hiding for his impudence, Cale confined himself to giving him a mouthful of abuse and shut the door with a loud bang. He changed – but quickly, it had to be said, as something unpleasant was surely up. He was out in five minutes and in the assembly room in three.

There were about a dozen men waiting, with Cariola hovering in the background. It was especially odd that there was an assortment of the most important bureaucrats and managers of the estate. All of them were outside Arbell's trusted circle and were rightly, in one way or another, considered to be in Nick Van Owen's pocket. The one person not present was Gaines.

But in all of this strangeness, the most strange was the appearance of Arbell – her hair unkempt, her eyes wild and her skin white in the way of someone after a terrible shock. At the back of the room Cariola leaned against the wall as if, without it, she'd collapse, her eyes wide as a frightened child's.

'Thank you for coming,' said Arbell, in a tone lacking any kind of gratitude. 'This afternoon I learned that I have been betrayed by a man who I'd come to trust above all others. But I must be quick – details will have to wait. To sum up, my steward Saul Gaines has been stealing from me, from this estate, for years. He has robbed us of millions and, realizing he was about to be caught, he's vanished and can't be found.'

The room was astonished – silent gasps, open mouths, widened eyes.

'Be silent!' Anger – more, rage. 'Please! He has gone and is being hunted as we speak. But there are claims – and that is all they are – that Gaines had accomplices and that some of them are in this room.'

Shock, denial, outrage, hubbub and hullabaloo.

'For God's sake!' she shouted, beside herself. 'You must bear with me here. You must understand that I accept that this may be a lie. But action must be taken now, and those of you who are innocent must bear with me. To mitigate our loss, each one of you will be escorted to your rooms and locked inside with two guards to watch over you. You will be treated well while investigations and searches are taking place to see if there is any truth in this. Understand that I have no choice if there is to be any chance of avoiding a disaster that may bring this house to ruin.'

Immediately, three guards appeared in the room. Cale could see that in the corridor outside there were at least a dozen more. Sullen and astonished, the occupants of the room were escorted out. Thinking that, given his place in the house, the lives saved, and so on, that this did not apply to him, Cale walked over to Arbell and was about to speak when she angrily interrupted.

'This includes you, Mr Savio. Leave now.' Two guards were already at his shoulder. It was not easy to surprise Cale, but she had done so twice in as many minutes. Angry, he allowed himself to be led away and back to his rooms. His key was demanded. The door was shut. The lock was turned. And that was that.

53

And most of all would I flee the cruel madness of love,
The honey of poison flowers and all the measureless ill.

– The White Devil,
Aria, Act V, Amore e morte

It was nearly two hours before he heard the lock turn again. When Arbell walked through the door he was not sure whether he'd been expecting her or whether her appearance was a surprise. Of course, what everyone has in common with Cale is that before an uncertainty is resolved we guess as many of the possible outcomes as are reasonable – and no doubt some that aren't. When this uncertainty is resolved, lo and behold, we can look back and proudly declare our wisdom in predicting the event. That we also considered every other possibility is forgotten. But Gaines? *Gaines?*

The problem was, you never knew what people were capable of. When the greatest and most trusted friend is charged with monstrous crimes, 'Impossible!' you cry; 'Completely out of character.' But always somewhere deep inside there's the weevil-sized nagging doubt.

That Gaines could have done this seemed ever so slightly more plausible the more he thought about it. After all, here was a black man in a world where most of the people around him thought he should be owned. So, Arbell had been wonderfully generous to him. Might you not hold a grudge for that kindness? Who are you to be kind, to admire yourself for giving me what, by right, is already mine? Slaves, after all, who'd risen up didn't just kill the vicious masters and his whip-wielding minions, they killed those who had been fair with them and even kind. Kind, clearly, was not enough. But still, *Gaines*? Not only was Cale's judgement of character at stake in this but also his vanity. How could he have been so wrong?

But now she was here, still wide-eyed and looking slightly mad. Now perhaps some answers. But now, perhaps, to find himself accused.

'I am so, *so* sorry,' she said. Well, that was a relief; *he* wasn't going to be accused, at any rate. And then she grasped him in her arms in a grip as tight as if in holding on to him she was holding on to everything that the future held for her. My God! The smell of her skin. She stood back, holding the astonished Cale, astonished by her and astonished by himself, and looked into his eyes.

'I talked to them, the others, in their rooms. They said that they were suspicious of him all along. They said they knew I was determined to hear no complaint against him and blamed themselves for not risking everything to tell me what I would be certain not to hear – that he was a cunning nigger of the most devious kind, that he was a paederast who was never seen with a woman – that he never loaned a penny to those in need.'

She stood back and walked over to the other side of the room, holding herself in her arms. She looked at him, desperate. 'What do you think?'

Hearing this was like a sort of smelling salts to bring him back from paradise.

'What I think is that these scum, only this morning, would have loved to offer their fat and sweaty faces so he could put his stirrups through their nostrils and they could carry him on their backs.'

'But . . .' Whatever she was about to say, Cale was having none of it.

'I don't believe it! You've been *fooled*.' It was not an accusation but a powerful urging that she should know her friends.

She looked at him as if astonished at his outburst. But in fact he was no less amazed himself. The years of rage against her had been transforming for many months and in a moment the shedding of anger and resentment had taken place, revealing nothing exactly beautiful – no butterfly, no ladybird, no dragonfly – but something extraordinary all the same: a peacock spider, perhaps, venomous still but rainbow-rumped; or the poison-darted frog of multicoloured dazzling blues and reds. Or better still, the purple crown of thorns, colour of power and the hidden mind. He tore away the leavings of his metamorphosis. Now he was for her. His grudges thawed.

'Look for your brothers-in-law in this. They're the puppet masters pulling the strings of those lice you've just been talking to. Poor Gaines.'

'Poor? He's stolen millions from me.'

'He was *too* honest – there was not one second in the hour that he failed to work for your prosperity. Never once did I see him use his power and his influence for any interest except those of you and yours. And yet in all of this he wouldn't take the steam off a parakeet's piss for himself.'

Arbell seemed somewhat startled by this striking metaphor, and not because she had no idea what a parakeet was.

'Don't worry,' continued Cale. 'I know what Gaines thought of me. But I'm too vain to dislike a man just because he doesn't quite understand my virtues. I never met a man more sure of himself but less arrogant, wiser but less self-important. While Gaines watched over you, no harm could come to you.'

It might be wondered why Cale was so extravagant in his praise of Saul Gaines. Partly it was the vanity he so impressively admitted to – *I am not the sort of weak-minded individual who dislikes others because they dislike me* – partly it was that, again rather admirably, it was pleasurable to be able to praise someone for once for being decent and hardworking. But this generosity was also fuelled by the intensity of his happiness. After all these years, all this time, a glad morning. Free at last. She stared at him, a kind of wonder in her eyes.

She blinked. And then blinked again.

'Everything about you, Dominic, delights and dazzles me.'

This, in its intensity, was a shock. What was being said? The beats his heart missed.

'Ever since the first day I really talked to you after you so daringly, so' – she laughed – 'so *manfully* rescued Mona Afuentes from drowning without a thought for your own life. In all my observations of your watchfulness, your private wisdom, the sheer strength of everything about you . . .'

She stopped on the verge of finally revealing something long withheld at the deepest and most private level of her heart. As for Cale, his own seemed almost to vibrate with joy, as if, astonishingly after everything, after so much suffering and pain, the sudden possibility of a second return to life at the hands of the beautiful woman in front of him was now at hand. Now that it was coming true he could at last stare straight at the reason he'd come to Malfi. What Thomas Cale wanted was simple, but it was clearly so impossible, so ridiculous and childish that he could never face it: he wanted Arbell Materazzi to love him again so that everything would be all right and he could be happy again.

She smiled at him, blushing deeply, ' . . . your strength, which frightened me a little, it seemed so stern – until I saw its power and its grace in defence of my beautiful boy' – she looked at him, face glowing with adoration – 'of me.' She shook her head as if with wonder at what had taken place. 'And of my so, so precious husband, Saul . . .'

54

'FUCKING, FUCKING, FUCK, FUCK, FUUUUCK!'

At the sight and sound of the newly apprenticed farrier screaming in agony at the damage caused to his middle finger by a badly aimed hammer blow, there was a little mild wincing from some of the people in the large stables, but mostly laughter. Besides the unsympathetic farriers, there were two visitors: Cale and Saul Gaines. It was not long after Cale had arrived at Malfi and neither of the two had met. But this was a carefully calculated chance meeting. Nick Van Owen had ears and eyes everywhere, except in Arbell's private rooms, and Gaines was a creature of habit, taking his rides three days a week, at the same time.

While he waited, Cale had been studying one of the horses – even the uninitiated would have been able to see it was something special. He seemed to be on the move even while he was standing still. For a moment, Cale was lost in admiration.

'He's the most perfect horse I've ever ridden,' said Gaines as he came up beside Cale. 'Sinews of wire and legs like a deer. He must weigh two hundred pounds more than any other thoroughbred in this stable.' He laughed. 'Even his eyebrows have muscles. Are you a man for horses?'

Cale laughed. *'Out of brave horsemanship arise the first sparks of growing resolution that raise the mind to noble action.'*

'That may be so,' said Gaines, smiling back. 'I'm not sure riding has made me noble, but it has given me more pleasure than almost anything else. You're Savio, yes?' Cale nodded. 'I'm Gaines, the steward here.'

'Yes, of course,' said Cale.

'So what do you make of us so far?'

'It's an extraordinary place.'

A pause.

'And how have you found the guards in the lower grounds?' Gaines tried to make this sound casual.

'Honestly?' Cale tried to play the straightforward man of work. 'I find it saves time.'

'Terrible. But the advantage of them being so bad is that the improvements are dramatic.'

'Glad to hear it.' They regarded each other pleasurably, and genuinely so, despite the deep roots of suspicion common to both men.

'Look,' said Gaines. 'Why don't you come to dinner tomorrow?'

'I'd be glad to.'

At that moment a beautifully dressed black woman appeared.

'At last,' she said. A surge of alarm from Cale. Noises of recognition always unnerved him. But she was actually looking at Gaines. 'My mistress wants to see you.'

'I'm about to go riding. I'll be there in an hour.'

She smiled agreeably.

'My mistress wants to see you *now*.'

They held each other's eyes for a moment, Gaines irked, the woman's eyes full of mischief. 'Whether she wants your advice about the new shade of red paint on her fingernails or she's worried about the end of the world – it's all the same to you, Mr Gaines.'

Gaines smiled, good-humoured. 'I stand corrected.'

When Gaines arrived at Arbell's formal sitting room to obey his summons he was only a little curious about why he'd been called for at such short notice, this having become something of a habit with her in recent months.

She was staring out of the window, quite still, and cool as the statue of her next to her husband's tomb in the chapel. She was startled out of her wool-gathering as he entered.

'Oh!'

'You sent for me?'

'Yes. I sent for you.'

A pause.

'Yes?'

'Sit down.'

He did so.

'What did I say?'

'That I should sit down,' he replied softly.

'Oh, yes.' She laughed. 'I'm getting old. These days I'd forget my . . .' She seemed to lose the word.

'Head?'

'Father, that's what we used to say in Memphis.'

'Ah.' Another pause, and a smile to fill it. 'Everyone always says how young you look.'

Anyone listening would have agreed with Gaines that this sounded not just lame but fawning. Inside, he winced. She looked pleased, however.

'It's all because of you.' This time, it was his turn to be startled. 'I mean,' she added, 'you've taken all my cares on yourself, so I've nothing to worry about.'

'Thank you.'

'I want to think about the future.'

'Should I fetch the accounts?'

'Oh no, I mean that I intend to make my will.'

'You have a will.'

'I mean a new one.'

'Shouldn't your lawyers . . .'

'Oh, yes, but first I'd like to set it all . . . my thoughts . . . down roughly . . . I mean, informally. And you know what Malfi's worth better than anyone.'

He took out his general account book and a pencil.

'I mean,' she said, 'another reason I didn't want to start with the lawyers is that I've been thinking about marriage.'

This shook him. She could see he was shocked. 'Oh, I don't mean marriage to anyone in particular, just marriage, you know . . . from a legal standpoint.'

Gaines realized his reaction was unfortunate and tried to recover.

'It would be odd if a woman as young as you did not consider marrying again.'

'I don't think,' she said, 'that I'm really fit for marriage any more.'

'I don't understand.'

'I've got set in my ways. I'm used to doing exactly as I please. Having someone to consult every time I want to spend a small fortune on something. I just don't think I can do as I'm told any more.'

'You're exaggerating, ma'am . . .'

'Only so you can reassure me.'

'Choose a husband who understands you.'

'Who do you suggest?'

He smiled. 'You're Arbell Van Owen. Anyone you want.'

'I don't think so. The law puts the husband in charge of me. A man can flutter his eyelashes at me and tell me he'll always be under my thumb and adore the humiliation and the shame of being dutiful and obedient. But once the contract's signed . . .'

'Could you be happy with such a weakling?'

'I might if he were young and handsome enough. You see how unnatural I am – I want my own way all the time.' She stood up and started to walk slowly around the room.

'That's true of most people, isn't it?'

'But I don't want to wheedle my way through life.'

'Then you must remain single or hope to find some sort of god.'

'You don't think such a man exists?'

'I know he doesn't.'

'I think you're wrong.' Her mouth opened in surprised alarm. 'Saul, your eye – it's bleeding.'

Gaines put his hand to his eye and stood up. 'Damn, I get them every few months.'

Arbell took off the ring on her finger. 'My old nurse used to say a gold ring would stop the bleeding.' Gently, she raised it to his right eye. Astonished, he let her do so.

'This is my wedding ring. And I swore never to part with it unless it was to the man I love.'

If Gaines did not faint or have a heart attack, it was because it was as if he had suddenly been magicked into the quiet eye of a storm whose ruinous winds were circling only a few hundred yards away.

'You've parted with the ring now.' He spoke so softly she could barely hear.

'I told you, Saul, to help your eyesight, so you can see things clearly.'

'You've made me stark blind.'

'How?'

'There's an ambitious devil with a pitchfork standing in this circle and he's about to strike.'

She smiled. 'Then remove him.'

She took his left hand and slowly, looking into his eyes, slipped the ring on to his fourth finger. Then she kissed him for the first time, starving-hungry in the way of a widow who has not kissed a man she deeply loves for many years.

Poor Gaines blinked as she finally stopped and leaned a little back, smiling as if he'd eaten the kind of sugar reserved only for God. He blinked again.

'I have loved you since three days after I saw you . . .'

'Not at once?' she said, laughing. He ignored her.

'. . . but he's a fool who'd thrust his hands into a fire to warm them. How can I marry you? Who am I?'

'A man like no man who breathes.' This kind of hyperbole is, of course, insufferable except between people in love. She moved him over to the full-sized mirror hanging nearby. 'Look at yourself as I do and you'll see . . .' She searched for words extravagant enough. 'I don't flatter you when I tell you that here is the image of a complete man. See him,' she ordered.

The ruinous winds began to shift.

'I see your disgrace . . . and me hanging from a tree.'

'I have the power to protect us both. We have time to talk and plan how this is to be done. And if we have to leave, we have to leave. If you choose me, then nothing shall stop me. I will make every hardship my footstep.' She turned him around. 'Look how shameless you've forced me to be – though my mother would have used another word.'

His response was almost to laugh. 'Give me a few minutes, or hours or centuries, to go and find my soul in Heaven and Hell and I'll show you how much I love you. Lightning moves slow to it and thunder is silent.'

She laughed. 'My goodness, you're very good at this – have you done this before?' She stopped laughing. 'Kiss me as if you couldn't stop yourself, and let everyone else go to hell.'

So he did, and with all the passion of a man in love suddenly in possession of the thing he knew he'd never have. After thirty seconds Arbell pushed him away, panting heavily.

'How dare you, sir. Unhand me,' she said, and pulled him back to her lips.

55

We are just fools misreading shadows in a wood
Where even misunderstandings are themselves misunderstood.

– Willum Shagspeer, *Aria: Essere o non essere*
from Thomas Cale, Part 1

Arbell had discovered only a week before the gossip began that she was about ten weeks pregnant. She and Gaines had been alarmed, of course, but only up to a point. They quickly decided that before she began to show they'd go abroad for a grand tour, when there'd be plenty of time to work out a long-term solution. It was a terrible shock when they discovered that it had become widely known in so short a time. That it was just a ridiculous coincidence never occurred to them. What did occur was that, given her pregnancy had been discovered so quickly and mysteriously, what if the revelation about the father followed soon after? This was infinitely more than scandal. This was a day of hideous reckoning.

Discovery would mean prison for Gaines – although his chances of living long enough to be locked up would have been nil – and a lunatic asylum for Arbell. Voluntary sexual congress with a Negro was regarded as clear evidence of insanity. And the insane could not hold property.

It would be too harsh a judgement to say that they panicked. They believed they had to act and act at once. Everything they had worked for in the United Estates was lost. Survival now was all.

56

Cale stares at her, mouth open like an idiot – a ridiculous man dying in front of her. His lips and tongue shrink as if he'd swallowed vinegar, the blood heaves in his chest and pulses in his ears, life drains from his face, paler than summer grass, the cold shivers under his skin and a chilling sweat pours over him.

The Janes believe that each soul is born with a set number of blows it can receive at the hands of life, different in quantity for each soul. When that figure is reached the soul dies, although the physical body may continue to move and speak for many years. If this is true, then perhaps it was at that moment that Cale finally received all the assaults it was possible for his spirit to endure.

Arbell took Cale's heart-shocked expression at the incredible news she had married a Negro for amazement. Not even the most tolerant person, not even the most extreme abolitionists who regarded the former slaves as very nearly saints, would have failed to be shocked into silence by what Arbell had said.

She had rehearsed his reaction in her mind a thousand times. She grabbed his hand. 'Don't be amazed.' She searched his face for reassurance. 'All right. *Do* be amazed, but we must act quickly. Come to my apartment in an hour. I have plans to make and must send you to my husband. And be quick.' She sighed and bit her lip. 'But first I must tell Denmark.'

She squeezed his hand, a little put out, if truth be told, that he did not burst into praise for her bravery and open-heartedness for choosing a man to love of such a kind as would cause the foundations of the world to shake. But the more sensible part of her accepted that she had better get used to astonished muteness. And, of course, a great deal worse.

'In an hour,' she said, and slipped away.

Like a man surrounded by a half-dozen enemies armed to the

back teeth, Cale hardly knew where to strike first. Horror, humiliation (of many and various kinds), anger (the same again), loss, disappointment (bitter as neem). And in the distance, returning from its recent evaporated banishment, the black rain of hatred, frenzy and insanity.

If an hour seems nothing much to control a gang like this, it's only because few people have experienced the training undergone by Cale: twelve years as a child, holding back through every daily beating, every lecture on his sinful heart, the starvation and the bitter cold, he had contained his rage behind a skin calloused like the pad of a working dog.

'What do you think of all this?' asked Denmark, looking for all the world as if he were a struck gong.

'I don't know what to say is what I want to say.'

Denmark looked at his mother. 'Savio puts it well.'

Great fear and the beginnings of the flush of resentment coloured her expression.

'What's done is done,' she said. 'He's my husband, like it or not.'

Poor Denmark (though poor Arbell as well). Poor Cale (a man standing above a cellarful of gunpowder).

Arbell, now the ice queen of reputation, swept out of the room. The two men looked at each other, and what a library of books could be written in that stare.

'I've disappointed her,' said Denmark. Cale did not respond, indeed he barely heard. 'Does she know what she's done. Do *I* know?' He looked at Cale. 'Do you?'

'What's she's done is to launch you with her off Carfax Tower without first arranging to grow the pair of you a set of wings.' Denmark looked stunned by his bitter tone. 'But as for Gaines, God help him, she's thrown him over the edge and told him that she'll join him on the rocks below once she's come up with a plan.'

'He's a grown man. He could have said no.'

Cale laughed – although it was more like a bark; not quite sane, at any rate. Denmark had other things on his mind. It was, to be fair, asking a good deal of anyone born into such privilege as Denmark to grasp that his new father was a coloured person, formerly a slave, in a country where many people, not obviously mad or stupid, seriously questioned whether he was a human being or not. A grunt from Denmark by way of a rebuke to himself.

'This is a long way to travel at the speed of lightning.' He took in a deep breath and blew it out heavily. 'It might be horribly unwise, but it's not wrong, what she's done. I will. I must do everything I can to help.'

'I wonder,' said Cale.

'What?' Denmark was puzzled at his tone.

'Whether something horribly unwise can ever not be wrong.'

It was once stated by Willum Slief (the philosopher who claimed that human nature was like a windmill) that as recently as three thousand years ago mankind had no words for *because* or *why*. For them, things just happened. They did not reflect or ask themselves questions about their inner lives, they just acted on instinct. It is now generally accepted that Slief was unique as a thinker in one chief respect: everything he ever said (except for the thing he may have said about windmills) was completely wrong. But in respect of Cale's mental state at that time, it could be said that it somewhat resembled this state of unreflective action. Whenever he was threatened with a crisis, his terrible upbringing, so devastating for his sanity and happiness in general, emerged to put him in a state of mind which, in the short term, had saved his life on many occasions. Although, of course, it should be pointed out it was the upbringing that was largely, if not solely, responsible for putting him in these situations in the first place. But given this, consider how useful a device it is to call on whenever there is a threat to one's survival – physically or mentally – to be able to banish fear and anger into a deep, dark hole for a time and merely act like a clockwork machine with awareness but no feelings.

An hour later Cale, all volcano capped with snow, listened as Arbell set out her plan in detail in the presence of Denmark and Cariola, who, it became clear, had been in her confidence about her feelings for Gaines for months before she proposed to him.

The plan was simple enough: to move as much of her wealth to

Mehxico as possible. Gaines was to rendezvous with her in Reedville before they journeyed on together to the Port of Corpus Christie and then to safety, along with their diamonds and rubies, to Vera Cruz. Cariola would proceed there also, but via Port Freeport, and she hoped that Cale would do the same by way of Galveston. Denmark, it turned out, had decided that whatever the future held for him, it would not be in Mehxico. The young man's feelings about his mother and what she'd done were many and various and took haphazard turns to move to the front of the queue: love, fear, exasperation, anger, loss, worry. But in all his concerns there was also the central concern of any young man: how do I become free? How do I become myself?

'I'm not going.'

'But . . .'

'I'm not going, Mother. There's nothing . . . I don't want to go to Mehxico. Why would I?'

She looked at Denmark, waves of sadness flowing through her and sorry that she had brought all this on him when he was still so young. There should have been time for this to have been done properly, to ask for forgiveness and understanding and to admit that her decision was, right or wrong, always likely to be ruinous. The question she faced properly for the first time was the extent of that ruin and who, if she fell, would fall with her.

'I'm sorry,' she said.

Denmark was almost in tears. 'Don't be.' It sounded as if he meant it and, mostly, he did. But he was not going to have his future decided by his mother, no matter how much he loved her.

'There's money. What will you do?' she said after a moment.

'New York, probably. Perhaps I'll take a look over the Four Quarters till this blows over. I imagine I can bribe Savio to be my guide when he gets back.'

She looked at Cale. Although he had no intention of going anywhere near the Four Quarters, he nodded.

There were hugs and a kiss on the cheek. Then she stepped back. 'But stay away from Memphis. Promise.'

'I promise.'

'I haven't slept for two days,' she said. 'I'm shattered.' Then she was gone, leaving the three of them together. Cariola presented Cale with a most carefully prepared itinerary of his journey and enough diamonds in a carefully designed waist pack to buy a place in Heaven. Having finished her briefing, Cariola was making to leave when Denmark called after her.

'What do you think of all this?'

It was not just curiosity. He was not best pleased that she'd been his mother's confidante through all this. While he often regarded his mother's love for him with exasperation and her obsession with his long-dead father as excessive (he would now have to revise this opinion – clearly, her widowhood had been over for some time), his nose was out of joint because of his exclusion – not least because her decision presented him with difficulties that became more daunting with every passing moment. It was not that he disliked Gaines – on the contrary – nor was it the case that he disapproved of the idea of his mother marrying him in principle. But he did not, nor did they, live in principle, they lived in the United Estates, where the marriage – even in the North – was not just illegal but seriously massively epically illegal and involved long prison sentences, along with the confiscation of all joint property. In Texas law, where assets on marriage became the possession of the husband, this meant the vast fortune of Malfi would pass to members of the family who could prove they had not been aware of the crime.

Cariola turned and, for once, there was nothing of the mocking smile.

'Whether she's a great woman or just a mad one I can't exactly say. I wish we'd never set eyes on Saul Gaines.'

And then she was gone, too.

There was a peculiar silence in the room.

'And you?' asked Cale.

'I don't know what to think. No, that's not it. I don't know what to feel.' Another pause. 'Good God.' He looked at Cale. 'You?'

A burst of poisonous rage in Cale was made flesh only in a dismissive shrug.

'The thing is, Dominic . . . the thing is, I'm starting to have some' – he tried to choose his words carefully – 'some ungenerous thoughts about my mother.'

A flicker of emotion from Cale. 'How so?'

'Maybe that's the wrong word. Maybe I thought I understood her – had her in a box. I suppose all sons love their mothers but, I don't know, look down on them in some way.'

'I don't know,' said Cale. 'Never had a mother.'

'I mean, I was a bit puzzled why she suddenly went mad about stopping slavery being reintroduced.'

'You doubt her sincerity?'

Denmark looked awkward. 'Not exactly. I doubt her straightforwardness.'

Cale, of course, had never had any doubts about her straightforwardness. She had made him feel adored then sold him into a terrifying death and managed to live with herself perfectly well. Finally, the long-dead Bosco had what he desired: everything human was now consumed by rage.

'I'm a brat,' said Denmark, smiling. 'I see that now. How dare someone – how dare my mother – drive a stick into my spokes. Malfi belongs to me – I went to all the trouble of being born to earn it.' A strange laugh.

Within two hours Cale was supposedly on his way to Nacogdoches for his first of two stops before arriving in Galveston.

In fact, he was at his destination within an hour and would have been earlier if he'd not stopped to deposit the pack of diamonds and cash in the bank of Palestine. From there it was only a twenty-minute ride to the lodge owned by the Van Owen brothers.

57

'God Almighty, it makes me puke to think of that bush pig filling her stinking axe-wound with nigger grease!'

'Control yourself.'

But Nick barely seemed to hear his brother.

'I can see her now, stuffing her fat box with purple jigger meat, her poosal belching with cunt butter and groid slurry.'

'Are you mad, Nick? Stop this or get out.'

Nick turned on his brother, amazed. 'Aren't you as torqued as much as me by the thought of this bitch? Our own brother gave our honour into her hands and now she's smearing that family honour with nigger slime, stuffing her cat-heads into his thick-lipped gob, sucking his pizz . . .'

'Enough! If you won't go, I will.' Louis walked to the door.

'All right. All right. I'm done.' A beat. Louis Van Owen walked back into the room. 'I don't understand why you're not angry.'

'I can be angry, Nick, without being unhinged. I've seen mad dogs foaming at the mouth more self-possessed than you.'

Nick stared at him. Then it was as if all the steam vented from him in one great, gasping sigh. But it was not, thought Cale, because of anything his brother had said. Something was up with Nick Van Owen. He turned and walked over to the window and stared out into the dark, his left hand clutching at his thigh.

Louis watched him, fearful and puzzled. After a moment he turned to Cale.

'I feel rather foolish asking you this, but the truth is that I'm so amazed by what you've told us I can't stop myself. If we move against her on this and it turns out to be wrong, we'll be finished. Politically . . . socially – complete death. You're sure of this?'

Cale not only declined to answer, he declined even to change his expression.

'Is she mad?' It was not a rhetorical device, an expression of disbelief, but a softly spoken question. Again, Cale's expression didn't change. 'I suppose,' continued Louis, 'I might have made something like this up myself in order to bring her down.' A pause. 'But I was wise. No one would have believed in an act so' – he searched for the right word – '. . . ridiculous.'

'Nasty,' said Nick. 'Repulsive. Vile.'

'Yes, Nick, I suppose. But she's handed back our fortune tied up in a ribbon.'

'What good is Malfi without honour?'

'Honour can be restored, in my experience. It just takes a sacrifice of some kind.' For some reason, Nick's eyes widened in genuine shock. If this gave Cale some sort of pause for thought, he didn't show it. Louis looked at his brother. 'Take however many men you need and arrest them in . . . ?'

'Reedville,' said Cale.

'Bring them back to Malfi.'

Cale looked at him. A beat. Then:

'I need to shave.'

'Shave?'

'I need a room and a barber before I leave.'

'There isn't t—'

'I need a room and a barber before I leave.'

'Very well.'

He called in a servant, gave him instructions, and then something occurred to him. 'Where was the girl going – the black girl – servant?'

'She didn't say.'

Louis looked at him. 'I wonder if you're telling the truth.' But again, no change of expression. 'She has a fortune belonging to us wrapped around her waist.'

'I can't tell you what I don't know.'

Louis turned to the servant. 'Take him to the Red Chamber. And when you've done that, send Feely to me.'

The two brothers stood silently in the room. Louis went to sit down, watched carefully by his brother.

'Did I hear you correctly?' asked Nick.

'About what?'

'You know very well.'

'I can assure you that I don't,' said Louis, pretending to read some papers. Nick looked at his brother as he carried on not reading the documents, weighing him up.

'I want to know if you meant what you said about the way to restore our honour. I only know of one way reputation can be restored after such a crime.'

Louis sighed and looked up. Another of those strange speaking looks that might say anything. 'People talk wildly sometimes when they're upset. Pay no attention. Just do what's required of you.'

A long wait as Nick thought about the room and what was going on.

'All right, Louis.' He moved to the door and turned back. 'I'll be here for about another ten minutes. So that's how long there is if you want to say anything to me.'

Louis went back to examining his papers with a fierce lack of concentration. 'Right. Fine,' he said, as if he'd barely heard his brother and his mind was now on something of more pressing significance.

'By the way,' said Nick, 'I'll deal with Cariola.' Louis looked at him, blank. 'Arbell's maid.'

'Oh.' Louis went back to scrutinizing the documents in his hand with intense concentration, and Nick left.

Once he'd gone, Louis looked up. Then he sat down. Then he stood up again. Within twenty minutes three groups of five men were on their way to Vera Cruz, Galveston and Freeport in search of Cariola.

Upstairs in the Red Chamber, Cale was having his hair cut off by Nick's barber. When he had finished all that the scissors could do he lathered his scalp and, taking out his razor, began to smooth away what was left. Once this was done, he commenced with Cale's beard. Finished, Cale looked at himself in the mirror. Then he bent down, opened his holdall and removed a carefully packed object wrapped in soft lint and then silk. It was the mask of the White Devil he'd stolen from the opera. He put it to his face and tied it, with a little difficulty at first, at the back. He looked at himself again and thought of something IdrisPukke was always saying: *the human face is the best picture of the human soul.*

Then he went downstairs. When he entered the room Louis started back in alarm, in the way that sinners are prone to do when confronted by a masked man.

'I'll send word when I have them,' said Cale. Then he left.

58

And so the dramatic chase. This must involve unforeseen delays, the nick-of-time arrival, the smashing down of the door, the astonished victim – safe but now caught; or the thwarted hunter – the birds have flown; or the heroic resistance and the daring escape; or the heroic resistance and the bitter surrender. But I am on oath to tell the truth, to render the events as life itself narrates. The truth was that a hireling knocked on the door of the best room in the hotel, the knock was answered by a trusted aide to Arbell, who realized at once that, faced with half a dozen men, there was no point in holding out. The occupants were calmly detained and calmly escorted out. Everything was very dull. Except for the fact that Gaines was nowhere to be seen.

Arbell was helped up into the carriage that had brought her from Malfi; waiting for her in the corner was a man wearing a white mask decorated to achieve the expression of a creature not quite of this world and with an enigmatic smile.

Even the courageous Arbell (Arbell the foolish or ridiculous might also be added to mad or great) was cowed by this shaven-headed apparition. It took five hours to return to Malfi and it seemed to Arbell the masked man did not move his gaze at any point from her face. This intuition was entirely correct.

An hour before her arrival, Louis Van Owen's men had taken complete control of Malfi – easily done in that most of the guards there were controlled by people either in his pay or obliged to him in one way or another.

59

All slavery is the same. All slavery is different. All slaves are identical. All slaves are unique.

Cariola had been owned for the first fifteen years of her life. All slaves are the same. But, owned by Aristotle Van Owen, she had always been indulged. All slaves are unique.

She was freed by the Emancipation Proclamation after the War of Independence from Spain. All slaves are the same. She was loved by one of the richest and most powerful women in the United States. All slaves are unique. Perhaps Cariola then could be forgiven that, like the King of Switzerland, she thought the outside world smelled of new paint. Her life might have been one of paradoxical privilege, but it was privileged none the less. And it was a privilege that had suppressed her understanding of the intense sensitivity in the matter of skin colour that lived and breathed outside the walls of Malfi.

In one of Malfi's carriages she was making her way to Caro, accompanied by two riders and a driver, when by bad luck the carriage was stopped at a roadblock set up in a search for a Negro who had cut the throat of his employer over a disagreement concerning unpaid wages. He had also cut the throats of his employer's wife and their three children, all of them under the age of four. The bailiff in charge of the roadblock did not expect to find the murderer in a coach, of course, but being a person of intelligence and intuition, there was something not quite right about the answers. What if this foul murderer was holding the occupant hostage?

'Gotta check inside the carriage,' said the bailiff.

'My mistress is ill.'

'And I'm sorry 'bout that but I'm a Southerner so I know how to be mannerly to a woman.'

He knocked on the carriage door. 'Excuse me, ma'am. I'm real sorry to disturb you, but I need to check you're not being held hostage.' The screen went up, the window slid down. The bailiff's eyes widened at the sight of Cariola, handkerchief pressed to her mouth.

'Look all you want, Bailiff, no one here but me.'

It was not every day – or ever – that the bailiff was presented with the sight of a beautiful Yellow dressed in silk and with the voice – carefully executed – of the most high-born Southern chatelaine in Texas. But whoever she was, she was rich and therefore powerful. Whatever she was, she was not a murderer on the run.

'Sorry to have bothered you, ma'am.'

Cariola nodded gracefully and shut the window and the blind. The bailiff waved the block away and watched thoughtfully as the carriage moved down the road.

The bailiff returned to his office an hour later to find an employee of the governors had left a note asking for help in locating a suspect in a case of terrorism against the Estate and giving the unmissable description of Cariola. The bailiff did his duty, and the next morning Cariola was stopped leaving the town where she'd spent the night and was taken to Marley Fruit Farm, whose owner flourished on the services of black convicts supplied by the estate of Texas and so did not question the request that was not a request to vacate his home within an hour and not return until he was told to do so.

Her four servants were locked up in a chicken shed. Cariola was taken to the main house to be watched over by two men, who she spent the first hour insulting in a variety of inventive ways. Six hours later there was the sound of an arrival and Nick Van Owen entered the room.

Fear makes even the spirited and the strong cautious if they have any brains, and she was careful to be just indignant rather than indignant and offensive.

'By what authority do you keep me here?'

Nick was unusually calm in his reply, polite even.

'The authority of the governor.'

'Even the governor can't just go around arresting people for nothing.'

'No' – calmer still, and even more polite – 'but you are not accused of nothing, you're accused of stealing jewellery belonging to your mistress.'

'That's ridiculous. I've done no such thing.'

'Then this is a terrible misunderstanding and you have nothing to worry about – we'll all laugh about it over a glass of champagne.' A pause, and a faint smile. 'You aren't carrying any jewellery on your person?'

'No.'

'I'm delighted to hear you say that, although I'll have to search you. Of course, I don't want to do that – it would be very difficult for both of us, I think.'

Cariola's mother had taught her that she must never tell a lie under any circumstances, unless she could get away with it.

'I have some of my mistress's jewels. But I have a letter, signed, giving me the right to carry them and to sell them on her behalf.'

'May I see it?'

Cariola reached into one of the five concealed pockets in her dress and produced a letter. Nick took it from her, opened the seal and read it. He looked at Cariola, and she looked straight back, afraid certainly, but she was a person of considerable courage, after all.

'You will now let me go on my way . . . please.' The word came with some difficulty.

An expression of puzzled curiosity from Nick.

'I'm surprised' – he paused, as if reconsidering – 'no, surprised is right – that you so little understand how things are. I hardly know how to break it to you.'

'What do you mean?' Uncertain, and so even more alarmed.

He looked as if he were at a loss to explain. Then he raised his eyebrows a little, as if he had thought now of a satisfactory way to show what he meant. He walked over to the fireplace, took out a box of Dos Demonias matches and, striking one, set fire to the letter and thoughtfully watched it burn. He turned to Cariola.

'You have long slept in a golden dream. You are waking up now, I think.'

'You can burn the letter, but Arbell will put a stop to this rubbish.'

Again, the gentle, thoughtful look.

'But still a long way from seeing how things really are for you.' A long pause as he studied her face. '*Je préfèrerais*,' he said, at last, '*avaler une tête de sèpan a sonèt d'abord tout en nourrissant un bébé à un makak affamé que de toucher un cheveu de votre tête de tout tripay*.' He looked at her as if sadly disappointed. '*One hair of your shitty head.* Really, Cariola – not very ladylike.'

It was word for word, accent for accent, stress for stress, the sentence she had spoken to him in Creole that day in the corridor. 'You are afraid more than you were, Cariola, I think, but, you know, I'm unconvinced that you yet see clearly what your world has become.'

'Now,' said Nick, very matter of fact. 'I'm going to go outside this room and you will undress, if that is what is required, and remove all the jewels from Malfi you've hidden under your clothes and put them on that table. I have every detail of those valubales.' This was not true. 'If you attempt to keep anything back, you'll be very sorry.' He smiled, not at all sinister. 'Then we'll go for a walk.'

It was one of those Texas furnace blasters as the two of them emerged from the house almost instantly into an apple orchard full of mixed varieties, six of Nick's men following a hundred yards away. Nick Van Owen accompanied Cariola as if he were the most gentlemanly of Southern cavaliers out for a promenade with the blondest of the blonde dollies so despised by Cariola. Overhead, the varieties of apple trees gave them shade: Sponger and Winesap, Horse Apple and Yellow Transparent. Then, Nick still the Southern gentleman, politely ushered Cariola through an ornamental gate. Then it was the avenues of plum trees: Red Chickasaw, Black African, Early Sweet. Then the peach orchard (the half-a-dozen men following at a respectful distance): Peento, Stump the World and Wonderful. Then, turning back a little towards the house, the orange grove.

Nick kept up the conversation from time to time as they walked; Cariola, bewildered and ill at ease, replying mostly with yes or no or I suppose. 'We should grow all of our fruit in the South, you know.'

'I suppose.'

'I'd like to organize an opera – something small, of course – in an orchard. You know, a concert performance just for friends – I thought *The Loves of the Three Peaches* would be amusing. Have you seen it?'

'No.'

And now they were in among the oranges, the largest orchard of all, with nothing but trees bearing fruit ready to be picked as far as the eye could see.

Then Nick stopped and waited, just looking thoughtfully around. 'This is a Homossassa, I believe,' he said, pointing at one of the taller trees. 'And this is Mediterranean Sweet.' He looked at Cariola, smiling in a most benevolent way. 'Which do you prefer?' She barely glanced at either. 'No preference? Then I shall choose. Let it be . . . Homossassa, then. That will do.'

'Do for what?' asked Cariola, growing fear intense but vague.

He looked over her shoulder and gestured towards one of his men, now only twenty yards away, to come forward. He was carrying a rope with a carefully structured noose on the end.

'I'm going, my dear, to hang you from this orange tree.'

The heart and soul understand long before the head. A horrible surge in her chest and bowels as she stared at the noose walking towards her. There was no approaching man, no outside world – just the loop of rope and the ring of horror that held only Cariola, Nick Van Owen, the rope and the orange tree. *This is not happening. I am not here.*

'You're just trying to frighten me.' How hopeful the cry.

'Yes,' said Nick, agreeable. 'But I'm also going to hang you.'

'No!'

'But saying no won't stop anything. Your words are no longer any good. Not here. Not now.'

He gestured to the noose-bearer to throw the rope over the thickest bough of the orange tree. He threw it up – somewhat shakily, it should be said – and it struck a smaller branch and fell back, hitting Cariola on the head.

She cried out, throwing it away as if it were burning hot.

Nick gasped in irritation and the man, clearly shaking now, picked it up and threw again, this time successful, requiring only a few shakes to allow it to drop to Cariola's height above the ground.

'No. No. No. Please. Please.' A low moan followed like the sound of a child grizzling after an outburst of crying. 'I'll do whatever you ask. Please. Please.'

'I haven't asked you anything,' he said, and then peevishly: 'There's no point in taking on so. (*Please. Please.*) Your own tongue has brought you to this.'

'I'm sorry. I'm sorry.'

'Too late.'

'I'm pregnant.'

'No you aren't.'

He grabbed hold of her arm and pulled her over to the noose. Terror made her weak, but he was far too strong in any case.

'I am. I am.'

'All right, you are.'

Still he pulled her. Now she started to struggle so he held her around the waist and carried her in one arm, grabbing the noose in the other and trying to loop it over her head.

'Help me! Help! Please.'

But there was no help. She moved her head from side to side, but the noose was over it and pulled tight.

'Hold her,' Nick said to the guard, who stood looking on as if he were sick at sea. Nick stared at him. The guard gave in and hooked Cariola in both arms, closing his eyes as she kicked and screamed.

'No! No! Don't. Please! Please!' she cried.

Then Nick gave the rope a hefty pull and up she went, voice going from words to a horrible choking sound in an instant. He pulled and the man let her go too early; she dropped with her feet dragging along the ground, kicking up the dry dust like a little fire just blown out. Then Nick got a proper hold and pulled hefty again. Up she went into the air, kicking and choking, her body demanding to live, bending and twisting at the insult inflicted on its right to breathe. And then the oranges began to fall. Not quite ready to be picked, Cariola's struggle loosened the almost ripe fruit, and one fell and then two. Cariola bucked and heaved as Nick held on to the rope, perfectly calm. And still the oranges fell. Three, four and five. Then six and seven and eight and nine. Then ten and eleven and twelve. There was a pause in the falling of oranges, symbols of marriage and hope of resurrection and the life to come. Another orange fell, but only one now, as her kicking became less and less.

Then the bucking became a twitching, then a shudder, then a twitch again and then a shudder and then a shiver. But not enough, the shivers, to cause another fruit to fall.

He held her in the air, Nick Van Owen, for fully five minutes, just staring out over the vast orchard, although what he saw, whatever it was, had nothing to do with things that grow. Now her body was almost still in the air, only a very slight turning this way and that caused by the twisting working its way out of the rope.

Finally, he looked over at the waxy-faced man who brought the rope.

'Hold this,' he said.

He did as he was told, but there was a clumsiness in the swap and, perhaps the sweat on the man's palms had something to do with it. The rope slipped and Cariola's body crashed to the ground. It was not the landing of a living thing, resistant to the breaking of a fall. It was a thud, dull and empty. Both men stared. One in horror; the other – well, it would be hard to say what the look was on Nick Van Owen's face.

'Oh, for goodness' sake,' he said mildly. 'Well, help me get her back up.' They pulled. Up went Cariola into the orange and the green, just like a feather in the air. 'Now hold on,' said Nick. 'I'm going to let go.' This time the man held firm. Nick took the loose rope and looped it around the trunk just below a pruned bough which gave enough of a lip so that when he knotted it the rope would stick. 'Slowly now,' he said to the man.

Carefully, he loosened his grip, and very gently Cariola's body dropped a little to take the slack. 'Come on,' he said, blowing out a gasp as if at the end of a long day's work, and started off down the orchard to the house, the man following.

Cariola hung in the breeze by the neck, face purple and black, tongue protruding, and slowly turned in the breeze. Ten minutes after Nick Van Owen had left, another orange fell to the ground with a soft thud.

60

To the last I grapple with thee;
From hell's heart I stab at thee;
For hate's sake I spit my last breath at thee!

– 'A Curse for the One I Love', aria from the
pantopera *Oswald the Assassin* by Herman Melville

Arbell had been taken to secure apartments in the oldest wing of the house, left over from the days when Malfi was more fortress than opulent mansion.

Later, in his rooms, Nick was pouring himself a drink. Cale was sitting on a sofa without his mask, bald-headed, bald-faced and looking like a God knows what that had escaped from a dungeon in the lowest pit of Hell. Nick was all smiles, but not in the surprisingly good-humoured way he sometimes exhibited. They were the kind of smiles you didn't want to see, or, having seen them, ever see them again. They made quite a pair, these two.

'Excellent job,' said Nick. 'Knew we could rely on you. Great things ahead.' He paused to add a seltzer tablet to a tumbler of gin and water – a drink that had become all the rage at Malfi over the summer. After a few seconds the smiling stopped and he became utterly transfixed by the fizzily dissolving tablet boiling away in the glass becoming louder and louder until it deafened him and his expression changed to fear and confusion. Then it stopped. Still he gazed on in fascination for nearly a minute as the foaming tablet slowly diminished, becoming smaller and smaller until it vanished into nothing. During all this, Cale sat quite still. Eventually, Nick looked up and smiled again as if nothing had happened.

'I have an apology to make,' he said. 'I thought there was

something not right in the head about you when you turned up with the mask and the baldy thing. But now I understand.' He looked at Cale with a kind of excited shrewdness. Cale said nothing.

'I know I'm not wise enough to advise a man with your experience, but it would be best . . . yes, I think so . . . to kill her in a way that could plausibly claim to be suicide.' The shrewdness faded to stillness. 'I . . . you needn't be finicky, of course. People will expect it. I mean, they'll naturally believe it when they find out what's been going on. What else would she do? So, all I'm saying is not to cause the event in a way that couldn't be suicide.' A pause while he waited for an answer. None was forthcoming. 'So, I'll leave it with you.' Cale turned and headed for the door. 'No. Wait. I've . . . I want to be there.'

Cale looked back at him. 'There can be no witnesses.'

'No one will know of your involvement.'

'You're right, because there won't be any witnesses.'

'No one in the South will think badly of us for doing this. Not that many in the North either.'

'No.'

A silence.

'Then let me come with you and talk to her. Then I'll leave.'

Another silence. Then:

'On one condition.'

It was late when Cale and Nick Van Owen approached the locked door of Arbell's secure rooms. The guards had been removed and because this part of the building was decrepit and damp, it was barely used and there was no one else on that floor, or above or below. Everything was quiet as Nick took out the key, opened the door and the two men entered.

Arbell was sitting down on a small bench. Her face, already pale, went a terrible white when she saw Nick and the masked man who followed him into the room. She began to shake.

'You've come to kill me.'

'That doesn't sound like a question, so I won't treat it like one, you miscegenating cunt. After all, I can't believe a woman of your intelligence didn't realize that this is how it would end. What in

God's name made you think you could get away with this? I'm baffled . . . mystified . . . *mystified*.'

'Where's my husband?'

'You're concerned about Gaines? I *am* surprised. If you were foolish enough to think you could survive this business, you couldn't possibly have believed that he would. He was a dead man the moment you let him put his hands on your disgusting cooch.'

She sighed, her breathing catching in her throat. 'Kill me now. Anything so that I can be out of your hearing.'

'There's no rush. Perhaps . . . possibly if you can explain in sufficient detail why you did this. I mean, what you saw in Gaines. It's quite extraordinary. You could not have disgraced yourself more . . . with more . . . *disgustingness* had we come into your rooms to discover you fucking a donkey. I'm all ears. Tell me. We could tell people you went mad. What else could you be but mad and vain. You really thought, you deluded bitch, you could get away with this?'

There was a slight movement of Cale's head, barely perceptible. Certainly, the other two did not notice.

Poor Arbell. Consider her shaking soul. The prospect of death. The offer, impossible to believe, of reprieve. Quite impossible. And yet, what if? This was, she knew, only a torment. But what if there was some quality of mercy left in Nick. There couldn't be. But what, her shivering spirit screamed, what if she could live, love and protect Saul, live and protect her son?

The masked man leaned forward and whispered in Nick's ear.

'Too late,' Nick said to her regretfully but cheerfully. 'He tells me he has something important to do somewhere else and we must get on.'

Cale noticed that she was forcing the long, sharp nails of her right hand into the fingertips of her left.

'Well then, I'll leave you in this man's capable hands. He tells me that if you don't struggle it will be quick.' He laughed, but it was not the sound of evil triumphant but skittish and ill at ease. Again, the drawn-in, trembly breath from Arbell. 'It's not my fault,' he said, whining now. 'You brought this on yourself. I'm not to blame. If you'd controlled your . . . *appetites*, then everything would have been absolutely fine. You should be ashamed of yourself.' He sounded like a schoolteacher scolding a child. What Cale thought about this sudden change, you could read in the stars. He leaned forward. Nick jumped as if someone had shouted in his ear.

'What? Oh yes. Well, I must be going. Goodbye.'

He turned around and walked somewhat unsteadily to the half-open door, slid through as if it were stuck fast then softly pulled it behind him.

Shaking, Arbell stared at the White Devil in front of her, standing perfectly still. Death was in the room – she could hear the beating of his wings *mygodmygodpleaseiwant iwantsaulsaul myboymyboysonohowo godhmysaulmysonfeatherinthemysonmygod*

Then Cale began to speak, almost inaudible at first, growing steadily louder.

'If the dead can come back to this earth and move unseen around those they once loved – then I shall always be near you, in the garish day or the darkest night. And if there be a soft breeze upon your cheek . . .'

He stopped for a moment and in a voice as full of something strange – anger and betrayal would not do – he slowly reached behind his head and began to undo the ribbons holding the mask in place.

'. . . it will be my breath, or if the cool air fans your throbbing temple, it shall be my spirit passing by.'

And with that, very slowly, without any fuss or flourish, he removed the mask from his face.

She knew the words, all right, knew them by heart, but had not spoken them aloud for nearly twenty years, to Thomas Cale, lying naked and astonished beyond belief next to her. How could she make any sense of this? The voice familiar, but not the shaven face or head. But the voice.

'Dominic?'

'Try again,' said Cale. Such seething, and so pleasurable the act of turning into himself in front of the woman he had . . . what? I do not have the words. It was like breathing out after years of holding his breath as her eyes began to widen, her mouth to gape (how ugly she is).

'No.' An impossible dawning of the terrible real. When the superstructure of the People's Hall fell to the quake at Brandenburg it collapsed in tads and shards – a corner here, an arch, and then the tower of martyrs lurched and crashed in seconds. The granite walls of the hall stood firm but the greatest dome on earth split and fell with a noise like the end of the world. This was the crash of Arbell's understanding of her life. Out of the filthy air of dust and smog the treason of twenty years before took shape and form in front of her.

'Thomas?' Such dread *mygodmygodpleaseiwant iwantsaulsaul myboymyboysonohowogodhmysaulmysonfeatherinthemysonmygod*

'Yes, Thomas.' A smile of delicious loathing. How pleasurable it was to overwhelm with shock and pain.

In each tiny movement of her lips and eyes and clenching forehead the terrible understanding of who was in front of her spread like a stain over that beautiful face. The legend that he'd written in his heart was that Arbell had never thought of him, never dreamed of him; there was no trace of guilt for what she'd done. And even, according to his parable, if for a moment she had thought of him, it was with contempt.

This must change. She must from now wear her betrayal like a thorny crown.

In the corner of the room the Tiny Ones were overjoyed. Having written this charade for over twenty years, an ending of a sort was coming on. But it was not to be wasted after so much care – there was still plenty of glee to be had at their expense.

How much he delighted in her pain, how overcome, heart-blown, verklempt, how shook she was by his presence now.

'What do you want?' *iamgoing to . . . please . . . goingtodie . . . howcanhe howcanhebehere. saul Iwant . . . Iwant . . . myson myson. Iamgoing . . .*

Sing, Thomas, sing – lift up your voice to make her feel the anger and the loss.

'I've saved your life three times in all, the life of your husband, the life of your son. How in God's name do you come to be gawping at me as if I were the savage in the room. How dare you think so well of yourself, you treacherous bitch!' *howbeautifulyouare . . . youhound . . . lovemeagain.*

'I did a terrible thing.' *thisisnothappening* 'It broke my heart. He said he'd kill my father. I did everything to change his mind.'

'I know exactly what you did, Mrs Van Owen. I was there behind a curtain with a gag in my mouth.'

'I don't . . . then why was he trying to get me to give you up?'

'He never had any intention of harming me. He knew I loved you more than my own life, and he wanted to show me what kind of creature you were. The Redeemers don't make deals with little girls. But you knew that. He wanted to show me how easily you'd give me up. To show me what you were worth and what I was worth to you.'

'It was my father.'

'It was me.'

'It broke my heart.'

'They would have burned me to ash. But tell me: did you get lost?'

'What?' *keeptalkingkeeptalking . . . myson . . . dontwanttodie . . . notinthisplace . . . saul*

'Lost on the way to lover's leap.' His voice was higher than he wanted and slightly shrill, almost ridiculous. 'They must have one in Memphis, no? Surely that must have been where you were headed. I mean, how could you live after sending me to burn to death, that stupid little boy who loved you so and saved your life so many times?'

How unfair life is in mocking us, always on the side of those tiny laughing hags. Just as we're desperate to sing a perfect aria to explain ourselves, to show how deep the sorrow and the pain, the voice cracks, the orchestra goes out of tune, the song that was meant to break a listener's heart can only make them wince at the false notes choking the real grief.

Her hands flutter at her face. The tears should have poured then, but they would not come – fear and confusion stopped that flow. 'I was afraid.' She stared at him longer than for any time since he'd come into the room. 'I'm afraid now.' Without realizing it, she'd been backing away from him. Now her heel caught on the edge of the hearth of the unlit fireplace and she stumbled back against the wall.

This pathetic fall, so human, so frail, triggered a kind of ecstasy through him, a shiver of horror at what he was doing here. He hated the woman he loved all right, but after twenty years of obsession she was not just in his heart, she was part of its flesh, part of the blood beating through that heart – and who, after all, is able to destroy his own heart? He felt sick. He'd had enough.

In his mind-rehearsals he'd relished bringing her to the brink of Hell (just what she deserved), rejoiced in making her feel upon her pulse that the contempt he felt for her was right. Once she was reduced to despair, he'd set her free, but do so with a curse, always to feel forever that she was a kind of *thing*: false, disloyal, shallow, without worth. How right that musical pantomime says everything about us that you need to know – the wailing, the villains, the grand passions, the hysteria and the pain, the pity and the folly of it all. Poor puppets, dummies, marionettes. We are all leaded in our thoughts and feelings by the Tiny Ones. We all are playing in a play, each with their role, and they are the only ones who know the script. They make us do our play and speak our text, and nobody else but them knows how it will end.

Cale stepped forward to raise her up. Alas for him, she'd failed to read her lines. Her guess about what was on the other side of the hill was about to change everything. Terrified *savehusbandbabysonsaveme* . . . thinking Cale was pulling her up to finish her, she took his outstretched right hand with her left and as she came up to her full height grabbed the handle of the knife hanging from his waist, pulled it free and raised it to strike. Seeing what she was trying to do but with his hand gripped tightly in hers, he tried to pull away.

'I'm not going to . . .' But terror made her deaf to what he was not going to do.

She struck out at his face, but he moved and the blade scraped him deeply from the top of his head, sliced down through the middle of his left ear and to the top of his cheek. The pain was agonizing. It was the action of a second to twist the knife from her hand and in a fraction, faster than thought, stab her in the neck, chest and heart.

The cry that followed did not come from Arbell. She only stared, mouth gaping. And then she fell backwards, fetching her head an ugly blow on the wooden table. On her knees, the pain in her head much worse than her wounds, she stared at the blood pouring on to the stone floor.

nothappeningsaulmysonmysaulmybabymysonsaulmockinbirdsaulfeather-inthemy godmygodsaulsaulsnothappeninglistentolistento . . . myson . . . dontwanttodie . . . my godmygodsaulsaulsnothappeninglistentolistento . . . nothappeningsaulmysonmysaulmybabymysonsaulmockinbirdsaulfeatherinthemy godmygodsaulsaulsnothappeninglistentolistento . . . To—To—

She was calling Cale's name. She was. Was she? Was she?

Cale dropped down beside her, hands flapping to each wound in turn as if they could be mended by the same power that had inflicted them. The wound in her neck, atomized by that great heart, sprayed a fine mist of blood over every inch of his face until he pushed a large flap of skin from her neck back into the wound so that now it leaked unstoppably between his fingers.

The noise in her throat, a sort of horrible snore, mingled with an animal whimper as Cale tried to work out how to turn back time.

She stared at Cale, or perhaps it was at something at his back that had come to take her into the dark – who knows? Perhaps there was one moment when she saw his face and understood how the buried past had emerged into the terrible here and now. Her hand reached out towards Cale. To protect herself? A sign that she had something yet to say? A whisper.

'T—' His name again?

But then the hand dropped to her side. They lost focus, her eyes, the light dimmed. And then the still and sightless stare.

For Arbell Materazzi, life was over.

Who better than Thomas Cale to know when one lived and one did not? He looked down at her for a while, a catastrophe boiling in his heart and brain. Then he was up off his knees with a jack-in-the-box suddenness. When those you love die suddenly in front of you, everything stops making sense.

But still he kept his eyes on her, unreal and real, for a full minute. Then he heard a slight sound and slowly turned his head towards the equally slowly opening door for all the world moving as if by the hands of a small child aware that they should have been asleep by now but, unsettled by a bad dream, needing company. Gradually, a head peeped into the chamber. It was Nick Van Owen. He straightened up, looking at the body in amazement, as if he could never have imagined such a thing.

'What have you done?' he said at last. Cale looked at him, although without any change of expression. 'Cover her face,' he demanded. Cale's expression remained the same. Nick started patting himself down as if anxiously looking for a lost key. Finally, he pulled out a handkerchief – lace, small – and going over to the body, placed it over her eyes. It was as if someone had put an inadequate shade over a blinding light – but it helped a little to reduce the glare. Why should Nick be suddenly appalled at Arbell's death, when he had hanged poor Cariola in the orange grove without a second thought? In books, the wicked share one thing: the bad are clear, certain, focused, sure. In life, the vile are muddled and confused, more even than the rest of us. Explain why Nick was horrified? Ask me to explain the sun or what had just happened in that room.

'Why didn't you pity her?' he demanded. No change from Cale. 'Why didn't you rescue her? Take her to some sanctuary until I came to my senses. Why couldn't you, with all your power, have stood between her and me? But you . . . you . . .' He could not find the words. 'This is unconscionable. No law doomed her to not being. No jury delivered a conviction in a court. By what authority did you deliver up this judgement, unless it was an authority from Hell? If I told you to put your hand in the fire, you wouldn't have done it. So why do this? You . . . you should be ashamed of yourself.'

It is entirely possible Cale did not hear a word. Disgusted now with Cale's atrocities, Nick, indignant, turned around and walked into the corridor.

'Help!' he shouted. 'Murder! Murder! *Help!*'

Perhaps it was the odd tone of Nick's words that caused Cale to make his way back into the land of the living. They were not horror-stricken calls but loud and stilted, wooden and utterly out of place.

His face still unmoving, Cale looked back at Arbell and blinked. Every few seconds they blinked again.

High up in the room, in a crack in the decayed plaster, the three sisters watched. They were not laughing now. This was a precious moment even for these disciples of human suffering, an agony that must be tasted in absolute silence.

61

There should have been storms. There should have been hurricanes. Winds should have cracked, the air burst. But as Cale walked towards the quarry it was by the delicate light of a harvest moon, a gentle breeze fanning his cheeks, the crickets thrumming happily, the nightingale singing with full-throated ease. Although the mist of Arbell's blood had quickly dried on his face, the ugly wound to his head and ears was bleeding on to his left shoulder and staining the earth behind him in large drops, black in the moonlight.

There are two types of people who carry opium with them: the addicted user and the experienced soldier expecting there to be pain. It was not long before Cale had swallowed half the skee in his purse. If anyone needed stupefaction, it was Thomas Cale. And it worked. For two hours he wandered aimlessly, numb, blood pouring out of his head wound.

It was something of a tribute to his capacity for keeping an idea in his head that he managed to make his way to the lip of the Malfi quarry despite being bloated by so much opium. He stood on the edge, where he'd stood so often with Denmark, and looked over, swaying as he did so, at the black-water oblivion a hundred feet below.

'And where do you think you're going?'

Cale turned around in a dazed pirouette. It was Vague Henri.

'Not real,' said Cale. 'Go away.'

'No.'

'Go away!'

'No.' Cale moved from side to side, a slender tree in a light wind.

'I asked you what you were doing.'

'I killed her,' said Cale.

'That's why I'm here.'

A contemptible whimper from Cale.

'Kill myself,' he said.

'So you should,' said Vague Henri. 'But not yet. Later.'

'Oh,' said Cale.

'Stop the Van Owen brothers from killing Denmark.'

'Denmark.'

'And while you're at it, Gaines as well.'

'Gaines as well.' A long pause, wobbling and shaking in the moonlight. Then Cale fell down and began to snore loudly.

62

Oh it's such a pity, oh it's so very sad,
The rain it pitter-patters on the good and on the bad.
The sun that rises in all its brightnuss
It scorchifies the villun an' it roasts the rightyus.
The worms don' wurry if yore vile or edifyin',
The maggots only care that yure corpse is putrefyin'.

– 'Mungo's Song' from Ghandi Jim's *Crow Opry*

When Cale woke up he was puzzled to see his left hand making a scissors motion in the air with two fingers on his right hand. He stopped. Then, of course, he wondered where he was. Then he wondered how old he was. There was no mirror in the room, so he started examining the back of his hands to see if they were liver-spotted and wrinkled. They were not. The room was furnished well, but with simplicity – a rug a little thin in the thread, one rocking chair and next to his bed a table with a cup and a plate with a quarter of a sandwich.

He sat up. Then the memory came back. He began to shake, and a terrible, pathetic whimper came out from deep in his throat. The door opened and the sound stopped. In walked a slim black woman in late middle age. It was Matilde Hanson. She smiled.

'How 'bout that. It lives.'

'How old am I?' asked Cale. 'I mean . . . where is this?'

'The boarding house. You were found by Enoch, friend of my boys.'

'And that was?'

'Top of the old quarry. You was twice lucky.'

'Yes?'

'Sure. You coulda fallen in. Or you coulda been found by the kinda nigger or cracker who'da taken that wallet you had strapped under your shirt and just rolled you over. Lotta temptation to put in a person's way.'

'Yes. I'll have to thank him . . .'

'Enoch? To be honest, Mr Savio, I'm thinking he be expecting something more considerable than appreciation.'

'How long have I been here?'

'A month.'

'What?'

'Lost a lot of blood. Thought you were gonna die. Never seen anyone with a fever like yours who lived.' She let this sink in. 'You had some real bad mares.' A careful pause. 'That business up at the house?'

'What have you heard?' His bad conscience looked like fear to Mrs Hanson.

'Wasn't more than an hour after Enoch brought you in when that po' bucker Moseby came asking round town 'bout you . . . we knew something questionable was up. They were sayin' you killed Arbell Van Owen. But we know you saved her life – and her son's. Not too probable you killed her, I'd say.' She laughed. 'We wasn't going to believe a gold-toothed rat like Moseby over you.' Her face fell. 'Terrible 'bout that poor girl.' The expression on his face, you can easily imagine. Mrs Hanson took it for ordinary sorrow. He put his hand to his left ear – it even felt like a mess. But it didn't hurt.

'Couldn't risk getting the doctor to you. He's in Moseby's back pocket. The horse doctor stitched you up good enuff – but you ain't gonna win a prize in no left-eared beauty contest.' She looked at him thoughtful like. 'Lucky you was found by someone who knew you came here to dinner a few weeks back . . . The Lord up there loves you, I reckon.'

In the corner of the room the Tiny Ones cackled away. It was true that the three of them loved Thomas Cale, but in the same way that the pig farmer loves the pig.

'Please tell me what you know about . . . what's been happening. Do you know . . . what about Denmark?'

'Strong rumour is that the Van Owens took him down some place they live in Rouge. Said they was protectin' him from you, where he was safe.'

Then the door opened and in walked Joseph.

'You're awake, thank God. Excellent. Are you well? You look paler than cotton.'

'He's just come to. Told him Moseby came looking for him tellin' lies and he's been out for a month.'

'Please,' said Cale. 'Tell me what's been happening.'

Hanson pulled up a chair and sat down.

'Well, at first Moseby and his people were mad for you, turned the town upside down. The Van Owens wanted you at any price. But by God it's true that when the mighty fall they fall hard.'

'What do you mean?' His tone made it clear that he'd no patience for rhetorical flourishes.

'You haven't been asleep for just any four weeks, Dominic. The folks of the United Estates are never going to forget this particular month.'

By the time Joseph had finished talking some ninety minutes later two things were clear. One of them was that the Van Owen brothers had been extraordinarily unlucky. IdrisPukke had once been asked at some dinner what was the one thing that always changed history: *Events, dear boy*, he said. *Events*.

A week after Cale had collapsed at the quarry, a meeting of the Congress of the United Estates had been called in a last-ditch effort to save the Union. As the congressmen were failing to find some common ground during a rowdy and bruising session, thirty-six barrels of gunpowder hidden in the cellars of that great seat of government were exploded by a person or persons unknown. It was a day in which fifty-nine congressmen out of one hundred and sixty-two died, a day, as the Chancellor of the United Estates said of this terrible event, that would live long in infamy. But it was a new Chancellor who said it, Burchard Hayes. There were only six unionists killed in the Gunpowder Plot. One of them was Abrahan Lincoln.

Although the Gunpowder Plot removed the chief obstacle to the success of the Van Owens' plans, what the unknown murderers gave them with one hand devastated them with the other. Because the cellar had been located on the right side of the building where members from the South were accustomed to sit, it was there that the force of the explosion was chiefly felt. Fifty-three of them died most instantly, the rest as a result of their terrible injuries. A considerable number of them were Van Owen supporters. Even more unluckily for the Van Owen brothers, of the Southern delegates who did survive many were the ones most nervous of secession. Their political opponents in the South who only the day before had been resigned to future domination by the brothers had only lightly been touched by the angel of death.

Who was responsible for this atrocity?

It was black extremists. Or it was white extremists trying to trick the public into thinking it was black extremists. Or it was white extremists too stupid to realize which side of the House was occupied by Unionists. It was the Nish. It was a lone madman. It was a government conspiracy to kill off the secessionists. If the view that to discover the origin of a plot one should first consider those who benefit most from its successful execution, then this last claim was the favourite. This doesn't, of course, mean it was true.

But the Van Owens' bad luck did not end with the slaughter of so many of their supporters. An unforeseen unforeseen had emerged of a kind that beggared belief. When they announced the details of Arbell's marriage, with entirely sincere horror and revulsion, they were astonished to discover that, despite the truth of their claim that Arbell had committed the appalling crime of marrying a black man, hardly anyone believed that such a revolting act could possibly be the case. Southern ladies did not have carnal knowledge of black men (not entirely correct), let alone marry them (this certainly was, however). Add to this Arbell's widespread reputation for being a cold fish when it came to men, and implausibility came to the aid of shocked disbelief and denial. Rather than confirming her guilt, as the Van Owens had hoped, the news of her death by suicide made their Northern and surviving Southern opponents question their story. With so much influence lost by the death of their powerful supporters, nobody believed the Van Owens when they told the truth, and nobody believed them when they told a lie either. There was also the matter of Denmark's disappearance. Without any evidence, it was widely believed he must have been taken prisoner by the brothers. It was a measure of how far the brothers' political power had collapsed that the only alternative generally rumoured to the claim that Denmark had been kidnapped by them was that he'd been murdered. As for Gaines, no one knew, or cared, what had happened to him. Lincoln's successor was not idle either. He moved quickly to offer reassurances, admittedly rather vague, to the surviving Southerner congressmen about the rights of individual estates, along with genuine offers of government subsidies to ease the economic difficulties of the plantation owners. In this way – a mixture of extraordinary fluke, never-to-be-delivered promises and large bribes – the horror of a civil war faded away in a surprisingly short period of time. What might have been the end of a great civilization, or its new beginnings forged in the burning heat of blood and conflict, faded to become a footnote, if a long one, in the history of the United Estates. Most galling of all to Louis Van Owen was that the new Chancellor had agreed that it was now time that all Federal troops and bureaucrats leave the South. Lincoln and John of Boston had refused to move them in order to ensure that Louis could not introduce his plan for a modified slavery. But in order to become the new leader of the United Estates, Hayes had promised the surviving Southern politicians whose votes he required to take power that direct Federal control would be removed in a spirit of reconciliation and partnership. Poor Louis. His great plan for a new South not that much different from the old was about to be born with someone else taking all the credit.

Within two weeks of the explosion at Congress, the Van Owen brothers realized that they were no longer safe from the new Chancellor, who needed to make sure the pair of them were in prison, where they could not threaten to rebuild their power base. They moved out of Malfi, now surrounded by enemies who only a few weeks before had been friends, and escaped down to an area of the South where they were prepared to die for the right to own people in law, and not just in practice.

It is a truth universally acknowledged that those who succeed are successes and those who fail are failures. This is sometimes true, but very often not. Genuinely cunning plans by gifted thinkers of experience and subtlety frequently fail and do so dismally. Those who have never attempted anything more complicated than organizing a large picnic scoff at the incompetence of those who must oversee the fate of civilizations. Sometimes the fumbling and ham-fisted succeed. The same lookers-on applaud their daring and their insight. Sometimes the genuinely crafty and the genuinely inept come to grips but damage each other so badly in the process that only the boneless wonder who hid behind the trees is left. They wander, amazed, on to the battlefield after it's all over to bayonet the wounded and are hailed as brilliant strategists who cunningly allowed their opponents to destroy each other. Be nice to spineless mediocrities is my advice; they usually end up running things.

Where did Louis Van Owen fail? Look in the stars for the answer. One clever plan of his worked out, however. He had decided to stay away from the fateful meeting in Congress. So intense were the feelings against the brothers for lying about Arbell being married to a black man, he knew it was impossible for them to show their faces in Washingtone. Luck destroyed them, but luck kept them alive.

As for Cale, his horrible past came to his rescue. In times of terrible crisis, and this was of all the terrible calamities that had threatened both his life and his sanity the most dreadful, the steel doors cast in his childhood to protect his sanity shut fast. But not even these thick gates could hold back the terrible powers for long. But all he needed was to hold them back for a week or two. For a time, he could depend, probably, on being numb.

Two days later, just enough time to recover his strength, he called in Joseph and Matilde and gave them the details of the bank account in Palestine. 'If Denmark comes back without me, give this to him. I've written him to provide you with half. That's around twenty thousand dollars.' The response was one of silent astonishment.

'And if he doesn't come back?'

'Then look for Gaines. If he's still alive, make the same deal.'

'And if he's dead?'

'It's yours. Do whatever good you can with it.'

Matilde looked at him.

Joseph almost protested, but the truth was that he was already spending the money on a school. As for Matilde, she had listened to many fractured dreams while she kept watch over Cale, trying to find a shape in fragments and the muttered shards of that strangest of all lives lived by that strangest of all persons. For all that she so liked Savio, she would be glad to see the back of him.

Of course, even in the time of the breaking (or pretty much accidental saving) of nations, those nations must be about other business. A matter that had once seemed so vital to the United Estates had with the passage of months become merely important, not the central focus of things. It was the death of one man, after all, whereas a civil war was about the deaths of – who knows? – perhaps tens or even hundreds of thousands. While Cale was unconscious a committee of the great and the good – for once deserving of the label – had come to a considered and careful judgement. It might have looked conspiratorial-like, releasing the report when the focus of things was elsewhere, but who can say? Perhaps not even those involved were sure.

The Phinersee Commission Report

Conclusion:

This commission was charged with one central and sacred duty: to satisfy itself that the truth of the assassination of John of Boston is known, as far as it can be discovered.

The shots which killed Chancellor John of Boston were fired by Oswald Hidell. The Commission has found no evidence that anyone assisted Hidell in planning or carrying out the assassination. The Commission has found no evidence to show that Hidell was a part of any conspiracy by persons within the confines of the United Estates or that he was an agent of any foreign government. On the basis of the evidence before the Commission it concludes that Hidell acted alone.

– Judge Vivian Phinersee, Chairman, Richard B. Russel,
Hale Boggs, Gerald R. Vado, Allen W. Esdulles,
John J. McCloy, Juan Sherman Cobre

PART V
Peachtree

Melville's last pantopera, *Cale in America*, transcends its trite scenario of epic villainy and betrayed love to offer a meditation on the terrible consequences of childhood suffering, the nature of the chaotic and arbitrary in human existence, and the unfathomable way in which good and evil, longing and confusion, cut through every human heart. For some people, all that matters, apparently, is that it has some good tunes.

– Victoria Garfield Dubinksi, *Pantopera: The First American Art*

63

Tragic Lover (to Raven)

'Prophet!' said I, 'thing of evil!—prophet still, if bird or devil!
By that Heaven that bends above us—by that God we both love well—
Tell this soul with sorrow laden if, within the distant Aidenn,
It shall clasp a sainted maiden whom the angels name Arbell—
Clasp a rare and radiant maiden
Struck down by one the Heavens abhor.'
Quoth the Raven 'Nevermore.'

– Allen Gerald Poe, *The Raven, A Pantopera (It is thought that A. G. Poe decided to make the Tragic Lover anonymous to escape the certain ban on performances if he had identified Arbell Van Owen's paramour as Saul Gaines, a person of colour)*

The light thickened and the crows made wing to the rooky wood. Cale had been hiding in the trees since dawn, occupying his mind by counting the blackbirds out and now counting them back again. While he watched and waited, Cale opened a tin of Veribest corned beef with a knife and began eating as if it tasted of nothing.

Just over two miles away the Van Owen brothers had taken refuge at Peachtree, one of two old houses owned by the family near Mobile, a part of the United Estates where they retained the support that had deserted them so quickly elsewhere.

Peachtree, despite its charming name, was by far the least comfortable of the two houses, but it was its ugliness that was now its greatest virtue. During the war against the Spanish it had been used to train the rebellious natives how to attack fortifications. As a result, it was surrounded by trenches, staked and barbed fences, gabions and lunettes. The problem for the brothers was that while there were bodyguards to man them, there were not enough. In addition, they were designed to keep out troops in masses, not a skilled murderer creeping about in the dark with frightfulness on his mind.

Louis Van Owen was sitting on one of the few comfortable chairs left in the house, restlessly moving between watching his brother and trying to distract himself by reading. Nick lay on the bed, half upright against the wall, white-faced and black-eyed and two stone lighter than only a month before. He had not made a sound for two hours, just stared at the wall opposite. Several times, Louis had spoken to his brother without the slightest sign he'd heard a word. Finally, he walked to the side of the bed and twice clicked his fingers in front of his face. Nick didn't even blink. He went back and sat down and watched over him for a few more minutes.

There was a knock at the door.

'Come in.'

It was Moseby.

'I've word from O'Connell at last. He'll be bringing in five hundred volunteers into Mobile Bay next week.' Nothing from his boss. 'Good news at last.'

'Yes. It is good news. Thank you.'

It was clear that this was all he was going to get, and a disappointed, not to say irritated, Moseby turned and left. Louis Van Owen looked back at his silent, motionless brother.

'It's a bad business, but he can't live . . . Denmark.' A silence. 'You shouldn't have killed her. I didn't want it. I really didn't. We could have put her on trial and people would have known it was true. Dead, she's innocent. But what's done is done, isn't that right, Nick?' If Louis Van Owen was feeling rancorous towards his brother, it was hard not to understand why. He knew very well that ordinary bad luck and coincidence had done most of the damage, but it wasn't as satisfying to bitch at a series of terrible flukes. He'd genuinely tried to see where he'd gone wrong, would have taken the blame if he'd found it. At least things, life itself, would have made sense, been worth calculating and thinking about (*Next time I'll do better*). Very softly he sung a line from one of his favourite operas:

And all our plans are foooooools
To light our waaaaay to dusty death.

'Now, dear brother, we have to take this all the way to the end. I never liked him, the boy, but I don't want his murder on my . . . my *conscience.*' He smiled at himself, very bitter like. 'But there it is, I've said the word now. It's the cemetery for you, Master Denmark.'

Nick still did not move. Louis was silent for another minute then, very softly, began to talk again.

'I was waiting by the fish pond yesterday, mind wandering, you know, when I saw a thing under the water armed with a rake that seemed to strike at me.' Then, low at first, Nick started to moan, raising the sound and altering the tone so that it became a long, mournful howl. Louis stared, tiny footsteps moving up and down the length of his spine.

'Stop it!' he said.

Slowly the sound died away. Nick looked at him.

'Can't help it.'

'Don't be ridiculous.'

'I can't.' A pause. 'Didn't I tell you I'm a wolf? I was sure I had.'

Louis felt his heart beating faster.

'You're not a wolf, Nick.'

'Yes, I am.'

'No, you're not.'

'Yes, I am.'

'If you're a wolf, where's your fur?'

'Ah,' said Nick, as if this was a misunderstanding easily cleared up. 'I *am* a wolf, but with one difference.'

'And what's that?'

'I'm hairy on the *inside.*' He laughed, pleased to have cleared this up and got one over on his brother. It made Nick seem madder to Louis than if he had screamed and started rolling around on the carpet trying to bite himself. Nick looked at him carefully and sighed. 'You don't believe me.'

'You're not well.'

'I can prove it. Bring me a knife and I'll cut my arm open and you'll see the hair growing inside me.' Another sigh. 'It itches so.' Casually, he reached over to the cabinet beside him, took hold of the pistol he'd put there a week before for his protection, pointed it at his head and pulled the trigger.

Louis screamed. His brother, the back of his head covering the wall behind him in blood, brains and bits of skull, slumped forward but upright, like a very penitent child too ashamed to face his angry father.

Inside ten seconds the room was full of armed men. Louis Van Owen did not move, or at least so it appeared to the astonished guards looking on at this hideous sight. In fact, Louis was shaking, but so slightly that even if you had placed a hand on his lower back you would hardly have felt it.

'Dig a grave in the pear garden. Wide. Very wide.'

'It's almost dark, Governor.'

'You have lights.'

At the same time Cale was also trying to get a light going, not easy in the damp evening air. But eventually his casement lamp took a flame and he tried it out a few times. It had been developed by the Spanish for fighting at night and had been adapted and improved by the rebeldes de los estados. It was closed on three sides and had a flap on the front which could be opened to cast a strong beam in one direction but which could also be closed in an instant so as not to give away the carrier's position. There were smaller openings in the side which could also be flicked open and shut quickly but cast only enough light to see by dimly.

He started off towards the house while it was still light enough to see. After half a mile, he stepped carefully into a small clearing just as two of the guards from Peachtree entered from the other side. The only reason the men were in the clearing at the same time as Cale was because they were new at Peachtree and had got lost.

At least two options crossed Cale's mind in the two or three seconds in which the men stared at each other in astonishment. One was to claim that he was a lost stranger and could they put him right for the road to Mobile. Another was himself to pretend to be one of the guards who had got lost (given how they'd come to be there,

there is every possibility this would have worked, but Cale was, of course, not party to this information). So he decided to kill them. He smiled and said, 'Thank goodness, I thought I was going to starve out here,' and extended his right hand while pulling a knife with his left. He stabbed the first man through the eye then, as he fell, lashed out at the second, who stepped backwards, stumbled on a branch and took the knife in his chest as he tried to recover. Unfortunately (for Cale that is; fortune had already done its worst for the two men), there was enough time for a terrible swirling cry of pain and terror. It was cut short, inevitably given who was killing him, but not short enough to prevent it being heard by someone else who was in the wood that evening.

Cale did not waste time cursing his bad luck. He moved on with no more agitation than any mechanical man. It took over an hour in the blackness to make his way to within a hundred yards of the end of the wood.

Then, as he entered another small clearing he spotted a minute light far up above him, as if the Tiny Ones had built a petite tunnel to their home in the sky.

Of course, it could not possibly be such a thing. In the true dark of a moonless night under a canopy of thick-leaved trees, the world of up and down is an altogether different one. He waited, but whoever was leaking light was waiting too. Then the light went out and the world completely vanished.

Except, that is, for the world of sound. In such a situation as this, there is only one course of action: not to move. Minutes may pass, but you should do nothing more energetic than shake with terror. The black of a thick wood on a moonless night is a deep, deep black in which the creatures of the dark outside come to snuffle and scrape and hunt and the creatures of the dark inside do something of the same. It is not good, even for a mechanical man, to think in the dark and in the silence.

After five minutes Cale heard bees, the angry sort of course, the kind that made honey that could kill. Louder and louder they raged around his head. And then they left and silence followed again. But now his breath, so loud in his ears, was determined to betray him to whoever stood in the dark a few feet away. *Over here!* it bellowed. *What's the matter? Are you deaf?*

Then suddenly his breath was gone. There was only silence now, complete and absolute. Then, as he drifted, not sure if up or down, he heard a voice in the great distance getting closer and closer. *It can't be. It isn't.* But it most certainly was. Arbell was singing in the woods and coming nearer all the time. And there was laughter in her voice. But not the kind of laughter anyone alive would want to hear. It was a tune from the *White Devil.*

Me and the wolf and the shark
Will be waiting for you in the dark
To feed you for measureless hours
The honey of poison flowers.

Then the voice was gone and he began to feel himself turning and turning in the void, while little glow worms made their way across the inside of his eyeballs.

Then a shaft of burning light and a man lunging at him and screaming out of the black. He dived to his right as he caught sight of a long knife flashing close to his head. And then the light went out. Soot black again but this time with squares and blocks of green and yellow playing with the glowing eye worms.

He must stop – dead still, no matter how close he was. No movement. Trying to control the clamour of his breath. He listened and listened. Could he hear the breath of someone else – or was it his own – trying to betray him to his death? Careful. Careful. He snapped open the lamp and, as if he were fighting his twin, the same from the other man. He lashed out broadly with his sword. A cry! The lights went out. To see meant to be seen.

Again, the heavy breathing – of a wounded man – or was it his own? He flicked the lamp. Ten feet away a man on his knees, staring and wild. He opened his own lamp instantly – both of them blinded. Then out and the dark again and the green and yellow flashes. Lights on. The long knife and the sword gleamed – crossed with a tinny scrape. Then black again. A beat. Then the lights and three times the blades scraped across each other. Then black. Both were breathing heavily again, hideous lovers lusting in the dark. The lamps flared. The two men burst into the world, glared at each other for a time, and one lamp went out and the other followed. But this time with a cry of pain. Cale stepped back three times. Had he been hurt? In the dark it was impossible to know for sure. A lack of pain meant nothing.

He turned on the light: the man was hunched and barely moved. Cale stabbed him directly in the chest and danced away to the terrible cry as his opponent fell to his knees. Now, with his lamp shining directly on his attacker, Cale was able to recognize the man dying on his knees in front of him.

It is not easy to make a clockwork device call out in pain, but it was Cale's cry of horror that was the last sound Saul Gaines heard before he died.

64

The man of system thinks he can
Arrange us all to fit his plan,
Like wooden pieces on a board,
Of human moves believes he's lord.
But hidden hands our ends do shape,
In truth he blunders like an ape,
So when he trips and falls on gold,
He thinks this fluke was one foretold,
By him alone.

– Adam Smith, *The Invisible Hand: A Pantopera*

The worst is not, so long as we can say, 'This is the worst.' Do you believe in luck and how it works in the human drama? By now of course you do. Do you believe in character? No doubt you do as well. The trouble with understanding what Thomas Cale was feeling as he knelt in front of the dead body of Saul Gaines is that character and luck are so tightly wound about each other it can be almost impossible for any one of us to make out which is which. This may be just as well for our collective peace of mind. Cale now discovered that, having believed a few minutes before he had brought himself to the lowest pit of Hell, it possessed a hidden door into another, even more horrible one just below.

In one of the cellars at Peachtree, Louis Van Owen was pacing down another of the many mansions of Hell, the mansion where hope had still not been abandoned, the Hell in which there was still a belief against all reason that Hell might yet be avoided. He stopped in front of a heavy door with a bolt on the outside. He told the guard who was with him to get back to his position at the top of the corridor. Satisfied he was well out of earshot, Louis opened the sliding wooden panel of Denmark's prison cell that allowed conversation without the interrogator entering the cell itself.

Already twitchy, Van Owen gasped to discover that Denmark was already at the panel and staring at his gaoler. Van Owen stepped back.

'Where's my mother, you treacherous sack of shit?'

'I have my best people looking for her, I can assure you. But if it is true that she has married Mr Gaines, it's not surprising she's unwilling to be found.' A beat or two. '*Is* it true?'

'Who she marries is her own business. What's it to you?'

'It would be easy to say that it's nothing to me. God may or may not exist, but the world unquestionably exists, and the fact of her marrying Mr Gaines will still be a matter of horror one hundred years from now. Less of a horror, I should think, but a horror still. What she's done is not possible. You know that as well as I do – it has nothing to do with good or bad, it is just impossible now. Nothing can change that.' This answer stalled Denmark a little. 'But this action of hers will not just tear her down, it will take my brother and me with her. And Mr Gaines. And you, Denmark. So, I suppose, after all, it has at least something to do with me.'

'Why am I a prisoner?'

'For protection.'

'You've locked me up in order to protect me?'

'I didn't say it was just for your protection.'

'If all you want to do is help, why do you need protecting from me?'

Now that he'd got Denmark talking, Van Owen could feel his frayed nerves becoming calmer, as if under the effect of a sedative – he was at last in control of something again.

'I have many enemies, and I don't think it is unfair to point out you have always disliked and distrusted me. You confirm, I think, that your mother has married Gaines and has tried, if she has any sense, to leave the country. People are blaming me for her disappearance and claiming I have made up the marriage for some black purpose of my own.' A pause. 'And even that I have had her killed. Much as you loathe me, do you really think I'm capable of something so . . .' He tried searching for a word to do full justice to such a thing. He failed. '. . . *terrible*?'

Denmark might have been young and, in so many ways, wet behind the ears, but he was not going to be persuaded of Louis Van Owen's sincerity just because much of what he was saying he knew to be true. But it did make sense. Louis Van Owen had a point.

'So, I'm afraid,' continued Louis, 'that for my safety first – I hope you realize how honest I'm being with you – and for your safety second, that until all this Opera Intenso works itself out it's better for both of us, especially me, that you stay where you are.' He sighed – and he had plenty to sigh about, after all – with all the weariness of a man continually misunderstood. 'Look, Denmark, I doubt very much if one day you and I will laugh about all this – but at least we'll both be alive to continue to dislike one another.' Denmark, thought Louis, although still dismissive, also looked a little reassured. But Louis believed what he'd told him was at least plausible. His mother might well have escaped. If so, then the boy might not believe he was in as much danger as he'd thought. Denmark could be pretending, of course. Louis's confidence in his own cunning had taken a blow in the light of recent events. 'Have they been treating you well?' asked Louis.

Denmark simply stared at him. Louis shrugged as if to show that at least one of them had remembered their manners, then carefully slid the little door back into place.

Poor old Denmark, thought Louis.

Out of the woods, Cale, his eyes dark-adapted, was able to use what little light there was inside the camp to make his way past the fences and stakes, the ditches and redoubts, and creep up to the kitchen door without anyone hearing. There were now four problems that this creature of clockwork agony had to solve: how to get either of the brothers on their own, how to find out where Denmark was being kept (if he was still alive), and how to kill the Van Owens without causing any fuss so that, trickiest of all, he could get Denmark away and free. Denmark's life had to come first: but whether the best way of achieving this was to wander around the house in the hope of stumbling across one or both of the brothers, interrogate them as to where Denmark was and perhaps use them as hostages, or to leave aside revenge and begin the search for the boy immediately was a difficulty requiring a cool and careful weighing of one thing against the other. But he wanted to act, not think; thinking was to risk feeling, and feeling was an impossibility if he was to stay sane long enough to save Denmark and wipe the brothers from the face of the earth.

Having entered in through the kitchen door, he was hiding in a grubby niche when a man came past carrying a tray of food. It was reasonable to assume that such service was either for one of the Van Owen brothers or even, if they were holding him here, for Denmark.

Perhaps this was ordinary luck or perhaps the Kindly Ones had ordered events to play out in a manner they found entertaining. The tray-bearer turned to his left after a dozen yards and headed down a stairs. Cale followed at a safe distance and after just two flights came into another corridor on the floor below the kitchen. A quick look, and he could see the man turning to the right. He hurried as silently as possible in case there was a door he might lock behind him. But there was nothing but another long corridor. This time he arrived to see him stopped still. There was a seat in a small alcove, but no one there. The man waited. Then he turned and headed back. Cale shifted out of sight and waited, listening attentively. Then he stepped out in front of the man, holding out a knife, and with his fingers to his lips Cale gestured him to put down the tray. He did so.

'Don't,' said Cale softly as he saw he was going to make some sort of move. 'Where is he?' said Cale. Whatever *he* was being referred to, clearly the man had someone in mind. He turned and started down the corridor, past one door, stopping at the second. Cale could see it was slightly ajar. This was disappointing. Prisoners were not kept in rooms slightly ajar. He motioned the man inside and moved to be able to look inside.

'Get over by the window.'

He did as he was told. Lying on the floor was a man with his face beaten in. Whoever had done this was capable of unusual levels of violence.

'The guard?'

The man nodded. Cale backed out of the room, checked the corridor, then came back in, leaving the door open so that he could hear anyone coming and have time to get back out to deal with them.

'This may not be his lucky day,' he said, gesturing at the dead man, 'but it might be yours.' Hope for a man certain he was about to die is a powerful aid to cooperation. 'Answer my questions quickly and you'll live. Otherwise . . . you'll still answer my questions.'

'Who was kept in this room?'

There was little hesitation.

'Denmark Materazzi.'

'Did you bring him his last meal?' As he said this Cale moved to the body.

'Yes. Two o'clock.'

He crouched down and felt the neck of the dead man. He was not cold, but he was not warm either. He'd been dead, he guessed, for somewhere between two and four hours.

Well done, that boy.

Cale stood up. The man looked at him, terrified.

'Don't kill me.'

Cale looked him over. 'I won't insult your intelligence,' he said. 'Clearly, the wise thing to do *is* to kill you. Too risky not to, really.' A beat. 'But I meant it when I said it was your lucky day. I've had enough of killing, see. And even though I haven't finished, I'm choosing to think that you're a decent man, all said and done. It might not be true, but that's what I've decided. So indulge me. I want to know where Nick and his brother sleep.'

'Nick Van Owen went loco – killed himself this afternoon.'

A pause.

'His brother?'

The man gave him, a little shakily, an account of how to get to his bedroom. Using the sheets of the bed cut into strips, Cale tied the man up tightly, so tightly that it helped to calm the man. If he was going to kill him, he reasoned, he wouldn't be so careful. Before he gagged him, Cale looked into his eyes.

'Do you want to change anything in your story?'

'No.'

'If you're lying, I'll be back.'

'I'm not.'

Cale stuffed the man's mouth with cotton and left, closing and bolting the door behind him.

65

Life . . . *Bom bom bom*,
Is a tale . . . *La di da*,
Full of sound . . . *diddley dee*,
Full of fury . . . *tiddley pom*,
Told by a lout . . . *Tum te tum*,
Saying nowt.

– Willyum Sahekspeer, Thomas Cale,
Part 1, An Opera

Louis Van Owen was asleep. His mouth was open, not widely, and he was snoring, but very lightly, hardly at all really. The oil lamp next to his bed was lit, although it was burning very dimly, the oil being nearly all used up. It shed a rather beautiful halo of light around Van Owen's bed, but only lit the room a foot or so away from it. At the very margin of the line between light and dark Thomas Cale stood watching the sleeping man. There was no hate-filled expression of vengefulness here, just a quiet watchfulness. Then he pulled out a knife, but turned away and took hold of five or six of the inch-long tassels that dangled from the lampshade and carefully and slowly cut them free. He put the knife back in its sheath, took one of the tassels, held it over the sleeping man's open mouth and dropped it in.

For a few seconds, nothing. Then a slight cough and a splutter, then a slightly stronger cough. Then he swallowed uncomfortably, but did not wake. A pause of a few seconds. Then Cale held another of the tassels a few inches over his mouth and again let it fall. Another few seconds and the spitting and coughing began again. This time Van Owen's head began to move from side to side as the coughing increased. Finally, a huge cough which spat the offending object out. But still he stayed asleep. Cale took a third tassel and let it drop. This time, his sleep having been disturbed enough to bring him closer to wakefulness, Van Owen started coughing violently. Then, with a sudden lurch, the trunk of his body shot upwards, coughing and spluttering and gasping for breath. He did not notice Cale immediately because just after Cale had dropped the last tassel in his mouth he'd turned from the bed and gone to sit down in a chair a few yards away so that he was not instantly in the governor's eyeline in the semi-shadows. Van Owen continued to cough and spit and, putting his hand to his mouth, pulled out the offending object. He stared at it, mystified. But the odd sense that most of us have when being watched overwhelmed him. He looked out into the room and saw Cale sitting in his bedroom chair, observing him with an intense expression of curiosity. Who would have been surprised if his heart had given out at such a terrible apparition? His heart was not so kind.

He stared at Cale as the singular awfulness of his situation engulfed him.

'Have you come to kill me?' he said, at last. Cale did not react in any way at all to this, maintaining the same look of intense curiosity. Then Van Owen gasped, as if at a joke that was hardly funny in any way at all. 'Forgive me,' he said, shaking. 'Fear makes you stupid, I suppose.'

'Understandably,' said Cale. A pause.

'Still,' said Van Owen, swallowing hard. 'I'd like an answer.'

'I'm not going to kill you.'

Ah, hope again! Wonderful hope!

'What do you want?'

Cale looked at him thoughtfully. 'I want to know if you can hear it?'

'Hear what?'

'A sort of rushing sound.'

Through many years of dealings and doings it had become second nature to the governor to ask himself what is the true nature, the feeling tone, of any conversation where something is at stake. His nature did not desert him now, not even in this most awful conversation. *The feeling tone is odd. He's playing. He wants to make me ill at ease in a peculiar way. Is it a position being struck? Is a deal coming? Please let a deal be coming. If he wants to play, play along.*

'I think, I'm not sure . . . I think I can hear something.' A pause. A helpful turn of the hand. 'Is it a voice?'

Cale laughed, surprised.

'I don't think so.' A pause from him. 'In fact, I don't at all see how it can be a voice.' Another thoughtful pause. 'You don't hear a rushing sound?'

Again, Van Owen pretended to listen. *Careful. Careful.*

'I . . . uh . . . I'm not sure whether . . .'

But then, the oddest thing. He *could* hear something, and it was something, yes, something, like a rushing sound, and almost familiar . . . what was it? Slowly, it grew louder, a rushing, yes, but a very fast fluttering and a shushing sort of noise. A bit . . . a bit like the sound of the sea in a seashell, but getting louder all the time. He looked over to the window for what the sound might be – afraid, hoping, terrified, wishing, the hair on his arms rising up. But then he began to feel and not just hear the sound – a fluttering and a throbbing in his chest and face.

'You *can* hear it, can't you?' said Cale softly. 'It's the sound of your heart.' Louis Van Owen stared. 'It's beating so very hard because it's trying to make up for the blood leaking out of the wound on your neck I made while you were asleep.'

Van Owen reached up to his neck and felt the very slight soreness of a small puncture. But when he looked at his hand it was covered in blood. He cried out and looked at the pillow to the left of where his head had been lying. It was soaked. His lips drooped as he stared with difficulty at his shoulder – it was drenched in a terrible sopping redness.

A very slight cry and he put both hands to the wound and pressed hard.

'A friend of mine died from a little wound like that,' said Cale, barely audible. 'And I couldn't save him.'

Even in the shadows Cale could see the colour in Van Owen's face fading away. 'You might as well lie back, Louis.' Louis pushed the bloody pillow on to the floor, grasped the one on the right side of the bed and put it in place, but stayed upright. The sound in his ears grew to a roar, as if he was going to be swept away. And then it quietly began to fade. He looked over at Cale. A look of the most terrible misery seeped into his face. His mouth opened and his eyes widened as if he could see something in the dark shadows.

'Let me be laid aside,' he said, 'and never thought of.'

With that he leaned back on the bed like a very old man and closed his eyes. He was quite still, but Cale could see he was not dead, as the black stain under his head kept slowly growing for another three or four minutes. Then Cale went over to the bed and looked down at the body of Governor Louis Van Owen, eyes almost but not quite staring up at the ceiling. He looked at him as if he were waiting for something to happen. If so, he was to be disappointed. After some time, he turned away and left the room as quietly as he'd entered.

In two hours Cale was back in the boarding house on the edge of Mobile he'd left what now seemed weeks before. It was a huge attic, capable of sleeping half-a-dozen in comfort, were it not for the fact that it was stuffed with every kind of knick-knack and crappy furniture. With Denmark free, if God knows where, and the two brothers dead, something terrible was on the move in Thomas Cale. The numbness that had protected him was already receding and guilt and grief were scratching their ragged way out of the depths. Time was short.

Being the attic in a house that might have been nearly two hundred years old, there were plenty of strong beams from which he could hang the noose he'd prepared before he left. It was not one with thirteen turns, nothing fancy; just a simple Ichabod would do the job. Because of the clutter, consisting of chairs and stands and presses piled higgledy-piggledy and intertwined with one another, it would have taken far too long to clear a way to tie the rope around one of the thick beams that held up the roof. Fortunately, a still-substantial beam had been added over the free space in order to buttress the ancient walls built on inadequate foundations. Noisily dragging a heavy old commode underneath the beam, he climbed on top and was just able to tie the loose end firmly around the make-shift beam. He placed the noose around his neck, pulled the rope tight with his right hand and launched himself from the commode into eternity.

At first there was a blow, as if someone had struck him heavily on the head, then gaudy sparks flashed in front of his eyes, a terrible but not exactly painful pressure began building up in his eyes and he felt as if his whole head was bursting with blood. His hands quivered on their own and his feet, very slightly, began to draw themselves up. He had a rattling in his ears and a hissing. At the edge of his vision, a darkness with a distinct edge began to close on his eyes.

But there was a problem. No one could have survived such awfulness as a child unless at some level, the very deepest level, they were miraculously tenacious of life. Now, at the very moment he was about to pass out of existence, life rebelled again. Instantly, he began to struggle and kick, swinging himself back and forth and desperately trying to use his feet to catch the ugly fitments carved into the commode. He scrabbled and scraped as the darkness closed in. The pressure in his head ready to burst his skull, the visible darkness and the sparks taking him out of the world. And then the crude and rough-edged carving of the bodgers who made this most repellent article of furniture eighty years before gave him a helping hand. His feet caught on a particularly roughly carved finial. With the inspiration to strength that only death can inspire he dragged the commode forward and, with the luck of the devil, one of the legs of the commode, whose weakness had caused it to be stored there in the first place, collapsed and threw the monstrosity forward so that with the last vestige of consciousness Cale was able to put his weight on the back and in degrees pull himself so that he could stand. With some difficulty, he managed to unsnarl the rope around his neck and pull in deep, lung-burning gulps of air. Then, on the uneven surface, he slipped and crashed to the floor. And then he wept and wept and could not stop.

66

Three months later, Sister Wray was sitting down in a most comfortable chair, Poll on one arm, and listening to a patient complaining, not for the first time, about her unhappy life. On previous occasions Poll had barked, 'Unhappy? Join the queue!' But now she was bored with the woman's dreary personal problems and was pretending to be asleep. Then, her eyesight being far better than that of a human being, this uncanniest of uncanny creatures caught sight of something even she thought odd: three tiny old women, cackling with laughter, creeping under the door and looking about the room for somewhere comfortable to sit. How dare anybody come into his room without permission! But immediately she was distracted by a violent knock at the door. Sister Wray sighed with irritation. The sign outside stated very clearly that under no circumstances was she to be interrupted while seeing a patient. The knocking started again, urgent, not to be denied. Taking Poll with her, she walked in combative mood to the door and opened it.

'Oh my God!' called out Poll, with withering and joyous contempt. 'Look what the cat dragged in.'

Sister Wray's face, as always, was entirely concealed. No one could have seen her response to the expression of horrible anguish in the white face and black-encircled eyes of the man in the doorway. But there was something in the stillness of her body that cried out her shock at the ruin in front of her.

'Thomas,' she said, her voice full of pity and terror. 'Thomas, what have you done?'

He Cannot Chuse But Hear

'The past is never dead. It's not even past.'

– William Faulkner

Because there's no space here to detail modernism and post-modernism (sighs of relief all round), I'm going to put down a definition of both which I will be happy to defend more fully elsewhere if anyone cares to be shocked enough. Modernism has its roots in an emerging artistic sensibility from early on in the twentieth century that the internal world of the (great) artist could stand for the external world. T. S. Eliot even made a joke to this effect. While others were claiming that *The Waste Land* shows us the decay of modern civilization lost in a spiritual and intellectual desert, he said it was really just a piece of 'rhythmical grumbling'. In the mid-1920s Virginia Woolf declared that human nature underwent a fundamental change 'on or about December 1910'. This is a joke only insofar as she is presenting a deeply held belief in a light-hearted way so as to draw the sting of it being such a ridiculous claim. Many of the assertions of modernism and post-modernism are made with a similar mixture of hyperbole and lack of evidence. The (religious) cult of the great artist was on the rise and what the shamans were saying was that things were falling apart: the centre cannot hold. When (disappointingly) the death of civilization failed to occur, modernism was followed by post-modernism. Post-modern writers are alleged, again in general terms, to 'tend to depict the world as having already undergone countless disasters and being beyond redemption or understanding'. What? Entirely? Literary criticism added obscurity. This from the British Library: *Waiting for Godot* enforces a wait for its own meaning. It's easy to mock this kind of opaque portentousness (which is why we should do so), but I've got nothing against the opaque because it describes much of the world as we experience it. Like Eliot, Harold Pinter was deeply suspicious of these overblown critical generalizations, wittily describing his own 'opaque', but often very funny, work as being about 'the weasel under the cocktail cabinet'.

But the trouble with the categories of modernism/post-modernism is they include so many writers who don't really have much in common so almost anyone could belong to them. *The White Devil* is, according to these definitions, a post-modern text because it employs pastiche, intertextuality, metafiction, temporal distortion, faction, as well as explicitly 'rejecting the boundaries between "high" and "low" forms of art and literature, as well as the distinctions between different genres and forms of writing and storytelling'. The trouble is that literature has always done this. The verse novel *The Ring and the Book* (1868; 250,000 copies sold) by Robert Browning, who was born in 1812, uses nearly all these techniques, including having the same story told by ten unreliable narrators. Indeed, a list of pre-1900 writers who practice post-modernism would be very long indeed. Edwin Abbott's *Flatland* (1884), a satire on class and misogyny, is set in an authoritarian world where geometric figures persecute a square who claims there is a third dimension. Johannes Kepler's *Somnium* (1608) is not only a radical science-fiction novel it also contains the first serious scientific treatise on lunar astronomy. I look forward to an equally serious work of 'demanding' literary fiction that similarly advances our understanding of quantum gravity. Two and a half thousand years ago, that greatest of all misery guts, the writer of *Ecclesiastes* complained bitterly that everything in the world was falling apart and that all human struggle is 'hevel', or futile. Think of him as Samuel Beckett but harsher. He also employs a metafictional narrator other than his own 'voice'. One of his most well-known sayings turns out to be correct: 'There is nothing new under the sun.'

It would be interesting to speculate about the reason why bourgeois culture takes the big claims of critics when discussing the near-religious importance of twentieth-century artists and writers with such gullible eagerness when the real triumph of Western civilization is the development of intelligent scepticism. But there's no space to do it here – except to observe, I suppose, that people like to worship. None of this means that Woolf or Beckett are not important writers, merely that their large claims about the world, or the large claims made for them, should be subject to the same comprehensive scrutiny as, say, the claims of Donald Trump or David Icke. Or Paul Hoffman.

But the one area where these literary astrologies agree is on the subject of story. Everyone (who matters) pretty much agrees that narrative is a culturally generated technique that has had its day and should have evaporated as a serious tool of fiction somewhere around 1899 (assertion by date is clearly habit-forming). Again, the evidence to support this almost universal agreement on its deadness is absent. But in order to move on, I'll just quote American fiction editor Teresa Nielsen Hayden, who identifies when it comes to narrative what philosopher Gilbert Ryle calls a category mistake: 'Plot is a device. Story is a force of nature.' This really rather simple misunderstanding has been perhaps the single source of the decay of good novel writing (I do not say *serious*, the word 'serious' in this context, along with 'difficult', 'demanding', and so on, has become a smoking gun for a work that is pompous, dreary and lacklustre). It makes my heart sink (no, plunge) to think how many writers who could been good novelists have wasted their talent – and our time – over the failure to understand Nielsen Hayden's distinction.

What's my evidence that narrative, that story, is as fundamental to human understanding of the world as eyesight? Look out into the world and simultaneously into your soul (if you have one. Modernists think the soul is dying. Post-modernists are pretty sniffy about whether it exists at all). Everywhere, and in all things, a story. Take the remote and flick through the unending list of twenty-four-hour channels all telling you a story. Your thumb will wear out before these narratives stop flooding over you. And now, with rolling news and social media, a terrifying set of soft machines for generating stories has amplified the world of the story to a new and increasingly terrifying dimension. Why terrifying? Because not only is story as natural and inevitable to us as eyesight, so is using them to lie. And what is lying, what is all delusion, in any case, but a narrative that shapes the world in line with our desire to see it, and have it be seen, as we want it to be seen rather than the way it is? But lying implies truth, and truth has been a tricky one, at least since Pilate asked Jesus Christ what it was but didn't wait around for a reply.

The world of universal hyperfictions is strikingly recent. I'd give it a rough date around 1990 (now I'm doing it), when satellite TV multi-channels really started to become widely available worldwide. From around 2000, we could add an increasingly universal Internet. In ten years, I went from having only four television channels to commanding a digital world where there is no adjective in the English language sufficiently obese to describe the supersaturated glut that now exists. And almost everything in this teeming universe is a story of one kind or another. Worldwide we have binged so long and hard on Netflix, rolling news and the Internet that the human imagination must now look like some five-bellied slob too corpulent to get off the mind-sofa while our creepy enablers ply us with yet another plate of streaming junk. This is why the peculiar decision made by many writers (including academics and critics) who think of themselves as serious to dismiss this palpable human obsession with often false narratives is not so much a tiresome affectation as a shameful dereliction.

So, what do I mean by truth-telling stories now, in 2021? Truth is still, of course, tricky. And I've always had a great deal of sympathy for poor old Pilate.

Years ago, I came across an observation which has become lodged in my mind like a thought earworm: *The spirit of the times moves through everyone.* No Google search has ever revealed where it came from. Very possibly the original writer meant something very specific by it that has nothing much to do with the significance it has for me now – although I'm still not sure what that significance is. Is it true, for one thing? One aspect of it has emerged only over a long period of time and it lies in the slow discovery that other people were thinking along the same lines – albeit in a very different form. Although I'd heard of Daniel Kahneman, it was only with the publication of *Thinking, Fast and Slow* that I found out anything specific about his work which challenged the prevailing wisdom in economics that markets were fundamentally rational, as if the general irrationality of human beings somehow vanished when it came to one of the most significant of all human activities, buying and selling. We are what we buy and we buy what we are. Explaining why he is so centred on human psychology, Kahneman has written of his experience as a Jewish teenager in Nazi-occupied Paris when he was out after curfew and stumbled into a member of the dreaded SS:

> . . . he beckoned me over, picked me up, and hugged me. I was terrified that he would notice the (yellow) star inside my sweater. He was speaking to me with great emotion, in German. When he put me down, he opened his wallet, showed me a picture of a boy, and gave me some money. I went home more certain than ever that my mother was right: people were endlessly complicated and interesting. (Kahneman, 2003, p. 417)

I'm of Russian Jewish descent on my father's side but both my parents were born Catholics in Dublin. After they married they moved to England, where I was born in 1953. They brought their oppressors with them. Unlike Jews or ethnic minorities, Catholics don't need outsiders to persecute them; they have the Catholic Church. My seven years in a working-class Catholic boarding school made me into a writer because the only place of escape was into my imagination – nothing at all sophisticated, let me be plain: heroic adventures, followed by a heroic death and a magnificent funeral attended by weeping multitudes of beautiful teenage girls.

But my Kahneman moment (by this I mean a moment when we begin to see how tricky the human story is) came over a longer period and involved the music teacher at the school, Father McCarr. The education we received at the school was terrible (at sixteen I found myself without any academic qualifications), but McCarr was the exception. He brought civilized values into this 'sterile cess-pit', as my older brother, Robert, called it. He created an orchestra so skilled that it regularly won prizes at music festivals, and among the boys – mostly working class, as well as being liberally sprinkled with the psychopathic and the criminal – he fostered a deep love of music. He was so gentle and kind that we used to mock his inability to hand out even the mildest punishment. He had only one fault: he was an increasingly determined paedophile. For years he preyed on every child he deemed good enough to take for private music tuition. He finally overreached himself when he attempted to rape two of my closest friends: one – a strikingly physically formidable fourteen-year-old (and part model for Thomas Cale) pulled a knife on him and threatened to cut his throat; the other (a model for Vague Henri) was even more courageous and reported his abuser to the headmaster. Unusually, he was believed, and McCarr was on the night-boat back to Ireland within the day. Setting aside that this was his only punishment and he was soon sent out to start abusing children all over again, I was, even then, fascinated by the deep systemic but blatant contradictions inside the belief system of Catholicism: it was a faith rooted in ideas of love and compassion that for me and my friends, and throughout its long history in general, was overwhelmingly hostile and often murderously violent towards any expression of individuality or dissent.

But what clarified this experience of McCarr in particular and the Catholic Church in general into a profound moment of understanding was through reading a story when I was seventeen: *Middlemarch* by George Eliot. (To be clear, I've developed plenty of reservations about Eliot in the fifty years since that revelation.) My epiphany took place during a scene where the malignant but also deeply pious banker, Bulstrode, is publicly disgraced when it becomes public knowledge that he swindled a fortune out of his second wife. He seems to be the classic evil villain getting his comeuppance – except that, with all his hideous faults, he's been working to bring to the town a hospital employing all the latest medical techniques. Eliot works not to milk the scene for the pleasure of reader revenge but to dramatize the fact that Bulstrode experiences his justified fall not as a cardboard villain but as a human being enduring a kind of crucifixion as he is exposed to the crowd with every layer of self-delusion about himself as morally superior to others being agonizingly stripped away. But my conclusion about this was absolutely different from Eliot's conclusion (never worship artists). She saw this insight as a path to her own kind of Atheistical-Christian forgiveness.

Almost literally, in one moment, I was able to see my own story of violence and oppression in a different light: other people see and feel the world from their own point of view. No matter how vile they were, they existed in the same way that I existed. For me, it was a realization that had nothing to do with compassion (in what way would compassion for McCarr or the Catholic Church be anything but disgraceful?). But it had everything to do with understanding. This is what reading stories became for me, the extraordinary pleasure of uncovering the world, even if in only a small way, a world as it is, not as I wanted it or believed it to be. If a writer has to dismantle everyday language or go bravely into their study each day to advance the form of the novel, then do so. But if you don't give this pleasure, reading you is a dreary waste of time (unless, I suppose, you advance our understanding of quantum gravity). In this sense, all fictional stories are a way into actual life stories. Fiction is useful. It also *has* to be pleasurable and evasive, but that's also for another time.

But although my life as a Catholic remains my most extreme encounter with human contradiction, as I made my young man's journey through the world I found this conflict wherever I went: everywhere, people lived their lives (their story) in a state of often profound inconsistency. And this also applied to me. This also fascinating discovery meant that while you were interrogating what others were truly like, you could look inside yourself for some of the answers. The question 'What's your story?' has constantly to refer back to the question 'What's *my* story?' But others were also asking this question in a useful way in many different spheres. While I was being beaten in an institution devoted to mercy and love, the psychologist Harry Stack Sullivan had come up with the notion of selective inattention to explain what was going on. He defined this as the unconscious ability to repress any idea or emotion likely to raise an individual's levels of anxiety. This is so powerful a drive that people rewrite the story of what's happening to them even as it's happening.

But I had already seen this operating not just as something done by individuals in their interior drama but by entire institutions. It began to occur to me – and something of the same obviously occurred to Kahneman – that the private world and the public world must be manifestations of one another. To put it very simply, his conclusion over many years of testing (ideas for which he won the Nobel Prize for Economics in 2008) was that the way individuals thought and felt about the world was largely driven by instant emotional reactions sometimes supported by apparently carefully reasoned post-rationalizations whose only real purpose was to support the initial instinctive reaction. In other words, in almost every human attempt to understand the world, thinking is the slave of feeling, and one of the manifestations of this relationship is that it's mostly feelings that write the stories of the world. So a storyteller who can interrupt this usually self-serving and delusional process would have a serious role to play in how we came to understand who and what we are. While Kahneman was working on the evidence for his important, evidence-based, correction in public human understanding, I was coming at the same problem in my first novel, *The Wisdom of Crocodiles* (1999). Here I tried to dramatize the idea that human greed, emotional thinking dressed up in fake reasoning and the fundamental love of illusion would not lead just to the usual individual dramas of robbery, murder, fraud and adultery but also to something global: the collapse of the world financial system. When people buy things they don't need with money they don't have (lent by people who know they can't pay it back), they're not buying goods and services in the witless way that classic economics defines it, they are buying dreams of power and status (a fast car), goddess-like beauty (red Chanel lipstick), freedom from chance (an insurance policy). You can even buy purity of soul and body (bottled water – on which American consumers with good municipal tap water spend, according to Bloomberg, $24 billion a year). Kahneman insists that global economics is rooted in human unreason and I insist that everything is rooted in human unreason, economic activity being just one of its manifestations. It's a strange world out there because it's a strange world in here. What's being forged in the foundry of lies that is the human soul is, I think, probably, always a story of some kind.

What has this got to do with the price of fish, as my father used to say? More precisely, what's it got to do with a trilogy entering its fourth part in *The White Devil*? The complicated stories that make up

The White Devil are dramatizations of the view relentlessly fleshed out in all my work that the political and the personal world are inextricably, and usually incoherently, bound up together. A few months after this manuscript was finished, the death of George Floyd ignited the world, not just America, in exactly this connected way. We were watching, in almost real time, the past being turned into the present. This act of wilful cruelty so bizarrely played out in broad, filmable daylight was not seen by anyone as just an individual act of interpersonal violence of a kind that takes place every day all over the world but one that also represented the tip of a vast sociological, political, economic and psychological pyramid going back to before the events echoed in *The White Devil*. Statues were toppled, flags burnt, accusations emerged instantly from left and right with their stories about to what extent blame should be apportioned to which group and what action taken.

The world of *The White Devil* represents a kind of origin story for all of this but one altered enough to allow a sense of distance and universality to apply. However, it's not an historical novel because history is best left to historians and their readers who, together, must interpret the facts of the matter insofar as they can be discovered. It is not, and was deliberately intended not to be, history. It is not a dramatized documentary – a genre I can't abide. But it is historical in the sense that the general past can, sometimes, be used to describe the general present and the general future. By putting an avatar of Lincoln in the same setting as an avatar of JFK along with Martin Luther King, along with (very loosely) an avatar of Machiavelli (Louis Van Owen), along with an avatar of Lee Harvey Oswald, and then blending it in with an imagined history where slavery has developed in a different way, and where the issue is resolved without a Civil War through the occurrence of a 'gunpowder plot', we have, in my view, a chance to escape the problem of 'serious' historical fiction, where you don't know what is a fact and what is made up. *The White Devil* avoids this problem so that it can treat history in one of the two truly useful ways that make it so central as a field of human knowledge. I take these two ways to be History 1: specific studies of the facts and valid interpretations of a series of specific events (the origins of the First World War; the origins and development of racism in America). I am quite explicitly *not* doing this.

History 2: what's left over after we've read or just heard many histories is what makes up the 'historical' memory both of individuals and cultures. This is often deeply distorted – the 'lost cause' of Southern Independence, for example; or the attempt to understand slavery while ignoring the fact that all the ten million Africans enslaved to the Americas were initially enslaved by fellow Africans. There are a million others, from the stories that define the Long War in Northern Ireland to those of the Arab-Israeli conflict. What I'm doing in *The White Devil* is replicating something that everyone does with history – including professional historians – which is to create a sense of history in a general sense. In other words – this is what histories in particular tell us about what we are in general. History in *The White Devil* is that aspect of history that represents our collective memory, our collective experience of great events cut and edited together (either well or badly, but always partially), as we try to grasp them in the light of our own understanding. We all have this general historical story in our heads and what I'm trying to do is present – within my own limitations – a way of making it a more truthful, more complex story. Hence why there are so many uncertain and hidden narratives here – I mean hidden from the characters –some of which unfold to a climax while others evaporate into the unknown: Cale learns his conflicted hopes concerning the love of his life are a shocking delusion; the world never knows that the assassination of John of Boston was a conspiracy; Louis Van Owen dies in disgrace having abandoned his great plan to avoid a ruinous Civil War by getting the South to realize they can have slavery in all but name – but not before he learns that his hideous compromise has been realized with the death of most of those who opposed it in the bombing of Congress. And, of course, no one knows who is responsible for this cross between 9/11 and the gunpowder plot of 1605.

Much of the time, the characters – good, bad, intelligent or foolish – don't know what's going on in their own hearts, the hearts of others, nor do they have a truly solid grasp of the times in which they live and which most of them are trying to manipulate in one way or another. *The White Devil* is a novel in which our existence is dominated by, in varying degrees, a false or highly limited understanding of who we are and how our world works.

My defence of the idea that the novel in the twenty-first century can do much more than anything outlined in modernism and postmodernism (and desperately needs to) is made by wicked but smart Louis Van Owen in his review of Mark Tweain's fictional pantopera, *A Girl of the Wild West*:

> ... *let us acknowledge that Tweain has shown us a new way of understanding the modern world in a form that combines all forms – his work is realistic, comic, absurd, serious, tragic, vulgar, high and low. It is a world of extremes. In other words, it presents life in a form that accurately reflects the true story of human existence as it has* <u>*always*</u> *been in a way that no other art form has done before. Let it be* the *Estates art form from now on! As we have shown the world the way ahead with our votocracy despite the Old World's cries of horror, let us do the same in our art.*

But there remains a bigger problem and, in my view, one that merely reflects a fundamental aspect of human reality itself. Watching the news recently, I came across an item quoting a press release by a charity calling for something to be done to help children as, post-Covid-19, they re-emerge 'into an eerie world, full of uncertainty'. But eeriness and uncertainty are simply measures of the way things are for us. We are all atephiles (from Ate, greek goddess of delusion): we love having our delusional stories confirmed; conversely, we are atephobes: we hate having them challenged. But even if the world can be converted to listening to evidence when it conflicts with what it profoundly wants to be true, even if it becomes a more thoughtful place where every idea about how it functions is accompanied by carefully arrived at arguments that accept the inevitability of the limitations of those arguments. Even then. Wrapped in wisdom and understanding, mulled over with insight and painful self-examination, much of what we think about the world outside and the world inside will always be mostly or partially mistaken, or just completely wrong. As Heorge Ellias writes in the line from the S*cientifyk Amerikane* that opens the book: *We ar going to haf to liv with thaet uncertainti.*

Acknowledgements

I have come to write these acknowledgements to the words and ideas of others at the end of every book I write with increasing wariness. This regret arises from reading an Amazon review a few years ago that stated the reviewer had admired the way one of my books had been written until they'd read the acknowledgements at the end. They now took the view that I had more or less cut and pasted the entire novel from a selection of better writers. Actually, this seems to me to be quite an interesting idea and I may follow it up one day.

Plagiarism in the age of Google search is, alas, a black art consigned to the dustbin of history. My view is that you're unlikely not to know that Shakespeare is a great writer who wrote a play called *Hamlet* or that *Paradise Lost* is by John Milton. In general, I take the view that writers should develop the same power as the villainous Princess Mombi in *Return to Oz*, who owns thirty different beautiful and clever heads which she can wear whenever the mood or the need takes her. I use my stolen heads all the time. Here are some of the ones I used in *The White Devil.*

Josiah Hanson

To call an African American an Uncle Tom is perhaps the worst personal insult it is possible to aim at a black man. Merriam-Webster defines the term as: *a black person who is overeager to win the approval of whites (as by obsequious behavior or uncritical acceptance of white values and goals).* But this academic definition barely gives the sting of profound contempt and loathing that the insult contains in everyday life. In her 2007 book *Uncle Tom's Cabin as Visual Culture,* Jo-Ann Morgan argues that Harriet Beecher Stowe's actual presentation of

Uncle Tom in *Uncle Tom's Cabin* (1852) was as 'a muscular and virile man who refused to obey when ordered to beat other slaves' who is beaten to death when he refuses to give up the whereabouts of two of the novel's escaping heroines. But in a world before the existence of copyright there were dozens of rip-off stage plays that transformed Uncle Tom from Beecher's heroic Christian character into a stock minstrel-show caricature, a decrepit, servile old man entirely fitting in with the 'prevailing racist norms' that were the complete opposite of those presented by Stowe. These 'minstrel shows' were still being performed until well into the twentieth century, and they, and not the original book, are the basis for the slur. Patricia Turner, folklorist and professor of African-American studies at the University of California expressed her frustration at this distortion in an interview on National Public Radio: 'In Fifth Grade . . . I wept when Uncle Tom died at the end, and I didn't see him as any kind of a sell-out, and so I've always found myself wanting to correct people who accuse someone of being an "Uncle Tom." African Americans who have read the novel can appreciate what kind of heroism that took for a black man to sign away his life to save two black women.' However, she goes on to say: 'I don't think the real Uncle Tom will ever be able to escape the shackles of the distorted Uncle Tom.'

The character Joseph Hanson in this book is based upon a real person, Josiah Henson, whose life story was used in great part by Harriet Beecher Stowe as the basis for the character of Uncle Tom. And even though a fair reading of her novel would support the views of both Turner and Morgan, a reading of his biography presents a much more complex (and interesting) figure than the noble Christian of *Uncle Tom's Cabin.* This is not necessarily a criticism of Stowe. Novelists use characters from the real world as fodder for their own version of what is true in the world all the time. I've clearly done so myself with the same historical person. It's hard to be critical of Stowe when she felt that what her campaign to bring an end to the horrors of slavery required was a completely blameless and saintly central character. She was much more radical in her creation of the black women in the book, who must be among the strongest women (black or white) in nineteenth-century literature.

Nevertheless, I think my interest in Josiah Henson's biography goes much further and reflects someone who certainly has moments of nobility and courage but who also commits a terrible act of betrayal by delivering his master's slaves (and himself) to another slave owner when the opportunity to set them free readily presented itself. But, centrally, this is not an insight of mine but of Henson himself. This is the reason why I changed his name only slightly to signal that while I certainly altered some elements of his autobiography so that it would fit with my novel, I tried to do so without touching the profound grasp he has – almost unique in terms of anything I've ever read – of his own moral responsibility for what happened. The Wikipedia and Smithsonian articles on Henson attempt to put right the unfairness of the Uncle Tom slur in the same terms as I've done above. But they do so without making any reference to his delivery of slaves from one slave state to another through a free state where they could just have walked away – but rather that Josiah persuaded and cajoled them to stay with him. What makes Henson such a towering figure intellectually and morally, what really sets him apart as a thinker about right and wrong, is that he's ready to see himself and his actions for what they are, and he admits this freely without trying to shirk his – partial – responsibility for this terrible error. He sees that he was born into a system which, inevitably, distorted his view of the world to such an extent that he did something terrible. I can think of no writer who sets out so clearly and in such a forensic way how he came to do something terribly wrong so that his actions are entirely graspable – but without either excusing himself or making a self-serving drama out of his guilt. He sees slavery systemically and psychologically, and not just as a matter of good and evil.

For those who wish to read his fascinating autobiography themselves (*An Autobiography of the Rev. Josiah Henson (Mrs Harriet Beecher Stowe's 'Uncle Tom'*), it's available for free by searching 'Josiah Henson Text' on Google.

John Webster and The Duchess of Malfi

Relentlessly teased in *The White Devil*, Shakespeare's greatness does have one disadvantage in that his shadow runs so deep and dark that it obscures his contemporaries. This has been particularly damaging to John Webster, described by one critic, correctly in my view, as 'second only to Shakespeare and not always then'. I had studied and much admired his great work, *The Duchess of Malfi*, as a student, but it was as a teacher that I was obliged to become completely immersed in the play. Other than an academic specialist, no one except an English teacher of A-level students is obliged to spend so much time with any particular text. I had four groups of A-level students, so for two to three months I taught the selected texts relentlessly. I can't think of a tougher test for a novelist or playwright or poet. If at the end of something so intensive you still find any given work even more fascinating than when you started, this is a pretty good test of greatness. Studying *The Duchess of Malfi* in this way began a lifelong fixation which led to an attempt to write a film based on the play in a producing partnership with Dorothy Berwin, who, like me, had seen an extraordinary theatre production of the play in the early eighties starring Helen Mirren and Bob Hoskins. At the time we began our partnership, Dorothy was also trying to get another project off the ground, *Carol*, based on the novel by Patricia Highsmith. She succeeded to great acclaim in the latter, but only after another fifteen years of back-breaking effort. After four years of film-development hell with *Malfi*, and having written three produced scripts rendered pointless by the producers and directors, I decided that in future I'd stick to writing novels. But by now the fixation with *Malfi* had become more of a viral infection, a part of the DNA of my imagination. As I came to think about a fourth part to *The Left Hand of God* 'trilogy', these two fixations came together, albeit in an odd way. In the film script, I'd moved the setting from sixteenth-century Italy to Dallas in 1963. The opening twenty minutes of the script were my invention and completely free of dialogue. This long sequence showed Bosola (a villain just as complex as

Macbeth) arriving in Dallas with Lee Harvey Oswald in order to assassinate Kennedy, with Bosola as the man on the infamous grassy knoll. As in this novel (and of course in real life), Oswald is murdered himself, and in my invented section of the script Bosola pre-empts the inevitable attempt on his own life by going to kill Louis Van Owen, the politician who is behind the conspiracy. He ends up striking a deal to hide out on the Malfi plantation owned by Louis's widowed sister-in-law in exchange for spying on her. Once Bosola arrives in the Southern town of Malfi, the film script then follows the original play closely except that, as here in *The White Devil*, Arbell (the Duchess) marries a black man rather than a white man of inferior birth. The Bosola of the first silent twenty minutes of the film script and the character of Thomas Cale began to merge over the years and led to *The White Devil.*

I'm afraid I don't help things by using Webster's other great work, *The White Devil*, as the title for this book, although it has no presence of any kind except for that title. So I hope all is now clear as mud, as my father used to say.

Lee Harvey Oswald

When it came to reading up on books about Oswald in creating his avatar, Oswald Hidell, I was faced with a vast library of options, and not your local library, more a Bodleian or a Congress. Most famous but not of much help was Norman Mailer's unjustly renowned and vast *Oswald's Tale: An American Mystery.* It pours detail into his narrative as if, like some wind tunnel full of word-smoke, detail alone will reveal the shape of the man. It doesn't. Thankfully, I quickly came upon a biography by Priscilla Johnson McMillan: *Marina and Lee.*

McMillan had been an acquaintance of Kennedy's while he was on the rise in politics, but her shock on hearing of his assassination was not confined to horror that a great man she knew personally had been murdered but was amplified by the fact that she also knew the murderer. A fluent Russian speaker, she'd interviewed Oswald after he had defected to Russia several years before. Befriending Oswald's wife, Marina, McMillan spent the next thirteen years on this book. It may have largely been forgotten, but it remains a magnificent piece of work as she carefully and slowly unpeels the skin of this strangest of human beings.

My interest in Oswald proceeded in part from an old irritation with Hannah Arendt's observation about Adolf Eichmann to the effect that he revealed evil as it really was: utterly banal. I've known – and indeed have slept in the same room as – some truly evil people, but I've never been happy with this way of understanding the morally diseased. Interestingly, the Israeli who captured Eichmann, and talked to him at length, completely dismissed the idea there was anything banal about him. Insane, perhaps, but not empty in any essential way.

What McMillan reveals about Oswald is a character who is certainly banal in some ways but also intelligent and capable of real insight, all of these qualities jostling for position along with the madness eating away at him. Searching elsewhere for information about Oswald, I came across some fascinating recordings of him being interviewed about his socialist views on Florida radio. Local radio journalists were obviously more distinguished in the early sixties because, along with two also highly intelligent guests on the show, Oswald was given a lengthy grilling of considerable intensity. But he was calmness itself and gave a performance very much intellectually superior to anything offered by politicians on the left today. This is not to rescue him in any way but to show that someone generally dismissed as a non-person, the potato-faced nonentity famously pictured posing with the rifle in his backyard, is in fact a recognizable human being: a mixture of resentments, paranoias, idealism, hypocrisy, vanity, insight and, perhaps most strongly of all, a terrible fear of insignificance. He is not entirely incomprehensible – mostly, but not entirely. Trying to capture him was like listening to pop songs on Radio Luxembourg when I was a boy in the sixties (behind the curve as always, the BBC thought pop music was an unimportant and vulgar fad). Even a short song required constant turning of the dial to keep the signal strong enough to catch the tune, much of which was lost in the ether. But that was all there was.

But I don't confine myself to entire heads in the matter of theft – eyes, ears, noses: all are used to beautify my writing. If this approach was good enough for Shakespeare, it's good enough for me. As in the following:

> Cale stares at her, mouth open like an idiot – a ridiculous man dying in front of her. His lips and tongue shrink as if he'd swallowed vinegar, the blood heaves in his chest and pulses in his ears, life drains from his face, paler than summer grass, the cold shivers under his skin and a chilling sweat pours over him.

The best bits of this are lifted from a poem by Sappho.

Bear signs – as in bear shit – were the original name for donuts, because that's what they looked like.

> 'To cut a long story short, Dominic, it was no summer progress. A cold going we had of it, in the very dead of winter, just the worst time to take such a journey – the ways deep, the weather sharp.'

Many of you will think that I've stolen this from T. S. Eliot's *Journey of the Magi* but, like Eliot, I lifted the lines from a 1622 sermon given by Lancelot Andrewes. The reason it flows so naturally into Josiah Henson's writing style is that, as a Christian minister, he was steeped in the Bible and Andrewes was one of the translators of the original King James Version.

The following lines are ascribed to the pantopera *The White Devil* but are in fact from Tennyson's 'Maud':

> And most of all would I flee the cruel madness of love,
> The honey of poison flowers and all the measureless ill.

> 'What do you want me to do?' [said Hetty.] Cale thought for a moment. 'I can't think of anything at the moment but, some day,

and that day may never come, I might call on you to do a service for me.'

This is taken from *The Godfather* (Francis Ford Coppola, 1972).

The letter written by Arbell's grandfather (and which appears for the fourth time in the series) is closely based on one written by Sullivan Ballou to his wife, Stella, two weeks before he was killed in the First Battle of Bull Run in 1861.

The expression of Arbell's bewilderment at the way people react to her beauty and fame is taken from memory of an interview with George Clooney.

Sometimes I can remember the source of a line or phrase or image, but often not. For years, one particular scene I had written always made me proud of my visual ingenuity, only to discover while watching a Disney film with my daughter that it came from the opening of *Dumbo.*

'Well it turns out that Drapetomania is a disease of the mind that causes slaves to run away.' 'Really?' said Gaines, as if this was a most fascinating idea. 'You mean a sort of morbid desire to be free?'

This is a joke stolen from the late Jonathan Miller.

'If you're lying, I'll be back.'

A great line from James Glickenhaus's moderately vile rape-and-revenge pot-boiler, *The Exterminator* (1980). In the film the hero's threat is delivered to a villain who indeed turns out to be telling fibs. The hero returns, as promised, and feeds him slowly into an industrial meat-grinder.

We are all leaded in our thoughts and feelings by the Tiny Ones. We all are playing in a play, each with their role, and they are the only ones who know the script. They make us do our play and speak our text, and nobody else but them knows how it will end.

This is taken from lines spoken by Traudl Junge, Hitler's personal secretary, about the way in which he controlled the lives and thoughts of the people around him.

> There will be no question of Hamlet and his Uncle's Ghost being shown in Hustone. If the vulgar herd want to listen to that disgusting little ditty about cucumbers, they'll have to be content to hear it in degenerate Malfi. But not for much longer – the fancies who flock to that place don't yet realize that the wind of change is blowing through the South. A cold wind for them.
>
> – Llorde Reith, Mayor of Hustone, Ordinance 417

This is closely based on a memo by moralizing hypocrite Lord John Reith (first Director-General of the BBC, from 1922 to 1938), thundering that music-hall artist George Formby's witty song about a voyeuristic window cleaner 'When I'm Cleaning Windows' would never be heard on the BBC.

Further to my war against bourgeois high-mindedness, I'd quite like to point out that the complaints in the book about the vulgarity of some of the action in the pantopera, *The White Devil* (a woman farting out of the window at a rejected lover; the 'stand-up' who arrives out of nowhere and makes jokes about pissing and the impotence caused by drunkenness) are from Chaucer's *The Canterbury Tales* and Shakespeare's *Macbeth.* The lyrics to 'Hamlet's Death' from *The Tragical Comedy of Hamlet and His Father's Ghost* are all my own work but are partly inspired by George Formby and partly (but much better than) Mozart's lyrics to a tune apparently written by his sister (*'Leck mir den Arsch fein recht schön sauber' – 'Lick me in the arse nice and clean'*).

If you're suspicious about something else, that snitch Google beckons.

Thanks

First, profound thanks to my editor, Jillian Taylor, the 'quick study' who carried on a meticulous, witty and shrewd conversation with the book throughout the long process of shaping it – and always with great charm. My wife, Alex, for reading all the versions and her sweet but sharp honesty. And my son, Thom, for putting his finger on problems I had overlooked. Jeremy O'Grady for his comments which were, to my considerable annoyance, impossible to ignore. My agent, Anthony Goff, for his unflagging support. Sarah Day, the Franz Beckenbauer of copy-editing, always there to head off my errors.

Nick Szczepanik for drawing the sketch of me from nearly fifty years ago which became the false Wanted poster of Thomas Cale. Nick Lowndes for his clever interpretation of the complicated layout and the refinement of assorted illustrations and mastheads – and adding the scar to the Wanted poster.

Zana Chaka for her determined chasing up of all the details – and also for having the coolest name in England.

Finally to Lorraine Hedger who in typing up my illegible handwriting so remarkably accurately always reads everything I write first.

For more information about the work of the author go to
www.paulhoffman.co.uk

Discover the acclaimed
The Left Hand of God trilogy

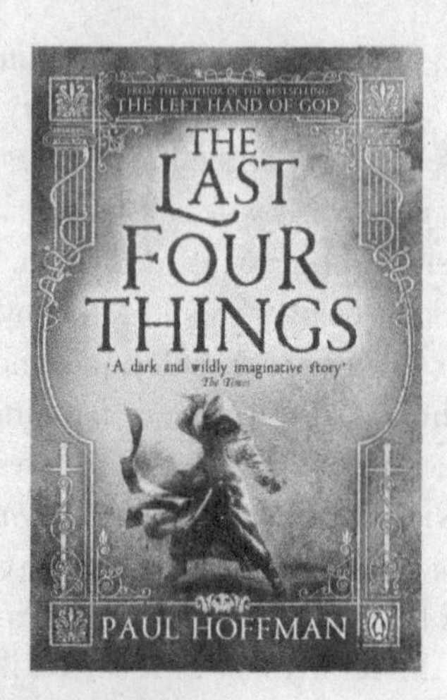

Available now